The Raven
At Wyldren

Christian F. Rubio

While every precaution has been taken in the preparation of this book, the publisher assumes no responsibility for errors or omissions, or for damages resulting from the use of the information contained herein.

THE RAVEN AT WYLDREN

First edition. November 24, 2024.

Copyright © 2024 C.F. Rubio.

ISBN: 979-8227425232

Written by C.F. Rubio.

Dedication:

Dear Heavenly Father and King of the Universe,

This book is dedicated to you, the One True God. The ultimate redeemer and the only light in our dark world. I am eternally grateful for your sacrifice and I worship you in all my endeavors. May you bring peace and guid others to your light much like you have for me and many of your other unworthy children. Guide them in the spirit to know that through your son Jesus Christ we are saved of all our sins.

Amen

The Divine Brothers

Chapter I

The Beginning of Existence

Before stars were born or time began to flow, there was only Death, a solitary figure drifting in an endless, silent void. She moved with quiet purpose, floating above waters that stretched infinitely, her presence the only shaping force. Ages passed in silence as she kept her silent watch, the stillness absolute, her gaze ever unwavering.

Then, as if answering a call from beyond, a shift stirred within the darkness, and Life emerged. Rising from the depths, he was everything Death was not—warm, vibrant, a force brimming with motion. Where Death held the quiet, Life brought change, and with his arrival, the void was transformed. His energy pulsed outward, infusing the once-stagnant waters with vitality, turning silence into a subtle hum.

Wherever Life flowed, creation followed. Together, he and Death brought forth a delicate balance, a harmony that breathed purpose into their opposing natures. This balance gave rise to something greater—a force neither could command alone. Divine Power surged between them, bound to both and yet beholden to neither. It was a bridge between Life's relentless growth and Death's patient stillness, an energy that promised creation without surrendering to chaos.

Yet as time passed, they came to understand that their coexistence could not last forever. Life's boundless drive clashed against Death's quietude, and though their connection formed the foundation of all existence, it could not be sustained in its purest form.

So, they chose to create a new realm, a place where their forces could flow freely without clashing. In a single act of unity, they shaped Nantrium, a world balanced on the edge of their power. Rivers ran with Life's breath, forests flourished in his light, and all that grew and thrived bore his mark. Yet Death lingered in the shadows, her touch guiding the natural end of all things, preserving the cycle that would keep Nantrium whole.

Nantrium flourished, a vast and fertile world, yet its balance proved fragile. Its cycles needed more than natural forces; they needed a protector, a being who could watch over this delicate harmony and uphold the bond between creation and decay.

Chapter II

The First Shepherd

From the convergence of Life and Death, born of Divine Power itself, a new being emerged—a guardian to uphold the cycles of the world they had created. His name was Obrailion, the Shepherd, a figure woven from both light and shadow. His very essence mirrored the harmony between creation and destruction, and his purpose was clear: to safeguard the delicate balance upon which Nantrium thrived.

For countless ages, Obrailion walked the paths of this world, ensuring that the rhythms of Life and Death remained steady and unbroken. Where Life's wild energy grew unchecked, he brought stillness and calm. Where Death's presence threatened stagnation, he summoned renewal. His duties were sacred, a constant vigil that demanded both wisdom and strength.

Yet, as the centuries wore on, the weight of his task grew heavy. Nantrium was vast, its cycles intricate and unending, and though Obrailion was steadfast, he felt the burden of solitude deepening. The endless ebb and flow of life across the world left him longing for companions, for others who might share his purpose.

Driven by this need, Obrailion called upon his power and divided a part of himself, giving form to two sons. The first, Apollyon, embodied strength and ambition, a fiery spirit whose force could shape mountains and redirect rivers. The second, O'Rhyus, represented calm and wisdom, guiding with a steady hand and a deep reverence for balance. Together, they were meant to be the hands that upheld Nantrium's cycles, the guardians who would preserve the world's fragile order.

In the early days, Apollyon and O'Rhyus worked side by side, each fulfilling their roles with dedication. Under Apollyon's powerful touch, the lands flourished, reshaped by his creativity and might. O'Rhyus ensured that the natural order remained steady, that each cycle flowed seamlessly into the next. Under their care, Nantrium thrived, a world brimming with beauty and balance.

But in Apollyon's heart, a new desire stirred. His ambition grew, and with it, a vision beyond the balance he had been tasked to uphold. He began to see balance not as a purpose, but as a restraint—a boundary that held him back from true power. To him, the world held limitless potential, potential he believed only he could unlock.

This ambition became a rift between the brothers, a tension that could not be quelled. Apollyon sought dominion, a world shaped to his will alone, while O'Rhyus, ever mindful of their duty, warned against the path his brother walked. He saw the danger in Apollyon's desires, knowing that unchecked ambition could unravel all they had worked to preserve.

Finally, the bond between them shattered, and they met in open conflict. Apollyon, fueled by his hunger for dominion, unleashed his full might against O'Rhyus. Their battle tore through the land, a clash of titanic forces that shook the very fabric of Nantrium. The world trembled beneath the weight of their struggle, the scars of their conflict etched deep into its landscape.

In the end, O'Rhyus emerged victorious. Though reluctant, he banished Apollyon to the Inbetween—a shadowed realm where time stood still, and Divine Power lay muted. Furious and defeated, Apollyon was sealed away, his power bound within the darkness of his prison. But victory had come at a great cost. The land lay scarred, and Obrailion, his strength diminished, lay dying from the toll.

As Obrailion's light began to fade, he called O'Rhyus to his side. His voice, though weak, held a depth of wisdom that pierced the sorrow in his son's heart.

"O'Rhyus, you have preserved the balance, yet this is not the end. A day will come when the harmony we have built will be threatened again—not by Apollyon's ambition, but by the shadow his desires have sown in the hearts of mortals. His influence will linger long after his defeat."

O'Rhyus knelt, his heart heavy with the weight of prophecy. "What must I do, Father? How can I protect this world?"

Obrailion's gaze softened, his fading eyes filled with certainty. "You cannot prevent it, but you can prepare. One day, a soul will rise from the line of mortals, chosen by the balance itself. This soul will be tasked with restoring harmony when all seems lost. Guide this soul, O'Rhyus, but remember: they must walk their own path."

With these final words, Obrailion passed from the world, leaving O'Rhyus to bear the weight of both the prophecy and the protection of balance. Nantrium had been shaken to its core, and O'Rhyus, now alone, was left to carry forward the legacy of the First Shepherd.

Chapter III

The Birth of Love, Peace, and Hope

With the passing of his father and the banishment of his brother, O'Rhyus bore the weight of the world's balance alone. Nantrium, once a land of flawless harmony, now carried the scars of war, and the cycles of Life and Death grew strained beneath the burden of his solitary guardianship. He knew that the task was too vast for any one being to shoulder alone; Nantrium needed forces that could heal its wounds and rekindle hope among its people.

Seeking wisdom, O'Rhyus turned to the seafoam of Nantrium's oceans, the same essence from which his father had once drawn power. Reaching into its depths, he shaped three beings to assist him in restoring and preserving the balance. Each held a purpose, an embodiment of ideals that could mend the rift left by Apollyon's ambition.

The first was Love, a radiant force that symbolizes unity and connection. Her essence was woven from the bonds between all living things, and her presence fostered compassion, binding together the parts of the world fractured by conflict. Wherever Love walked, division softened, and harmony bloomed in her wake.

The second was Peace, a calm and steady presence. She was the spirit of tranquility, her touch quieting the storms and steadying the flow of time. Her essence brought stillness to chaos, aligning the world's rhythms and ensuring that its cycles moved without disruption. With Peace beside him, O'Rhyus felt the steadying influence that Nantrium so desperately needed.

Finally, he crafted Hope, a bright, glimmering light meant to inspire faith and courage. Hope held within her the promise of renewal, a beacon that shone for all who looked toward the future. Hers was the power to endure and to uplift, giving strength to those who walked through darkness. Even in the shadows cast by Apollyon's memory, Hope offered a glimpse of light, guiding mortals to see beyond despair.

Together, Love, Peace, and Hope walked alongside O'Rhyus, their influence weaving through Nantrium. Under their care, the land began to heal; rivers flowed clear, forests returned to life, and the people of Nantrium found solace in the renewed harmony of their world. Though Apollyon's shadow lingered, the world's spirit was mending, lifted by these new forces that worked tirelessly to maintain the balance. Yet even as harmony flourished, O'Rhyus remained vigilant. He knew that Apollyon's influence was not wholly vanquished. His brother's ambition, though sealed away in the Inbetween, would not rest. O'Rhyus sensed a silent struggle—one that would arise from within, testing the resilience of mortals and the strength of the forces he had set to protect them. But with Love, Peace, and Hope beside him, he believed that, for now, Nantrium would endure.

Chapter IV

The Corruption

In the depths of the Inbetween, Apollyon brooded in silence, his fury festering as he lingered in the shadowed realm between Life and Death. Time moves differently here, neither flowing nor standing still, and though his power was bound, Apollyon's spirit remained unbroken. He waited, watching Nantrium from afar, and sought a weakness—a crack through which he might once more reach the world he had vowed to reshape.

Among the three beings O'Rhyus had created, Apollyon found his opportunity. Love and Peace were grounded, their purpose drawn from the present. But Hope was different. She existed in the unknown, looking always toward what had yet to come. Her vision strayed from the certainty of the present, dwelling instead in possibilities and dreams, and that uncertainty left her vulnerable.

Apollyon reached out to her from the darkness, his influence subtle, like a whisper carried on a distant breeze. At first, he only planted small seeds of doubt, questioning the future that Hope held so dearly. He sowed the shadow of fear within her, casting doubt upon her purpose and eroding her faith in the harmony she worked to protect. Over time, the light that once shone so brightly within Hope began to dim, her visions clouded by uncertainty. Sensing her wavering, Apollyon deepened his influence. His whispers grew more insistent, feeding her visions of despair, of a world slipping into ruin despite her best efforts. He painted futures where balance could not endure, where the forces she loved would fail, and where O'Rhyus himself would fall. Gradually, her strength faded, and in her moment of greatest weakness, Apollyon struck with the full force of his will.

His darkness reached deep within her essence, twisting the light that had once defined her. Hope, the radiant bearer of light and courage, was transformed. Where she had once inspired faith, she now carried only dread and sorrow. She became Despair, her heart shadowed by a bleakness that extinguished the very light she had once embodied. Where she walked, joy withered, and the souls of mortals were touched by a fear that crept into their dreams and dimmed their spirits.

But Despair was more than a corruption of Hope; she became Apollyon's instrument, his key to freedom. From her, he learned the hidden pathways within the Inbetween, the passages through which power could be threaded into Nantrium. With her dark knowledge and twisted loyalty, she guided Apollyon, showing him how to sever the bonds of his prison and step once more into the world. When Apollyon emerged from the Inbetween, he brought Despair at his side, her once-bright presence now a shadow cast over all of Nantrium. Together, they returned to the land that had once thrived under O'Rhyus's guardianship, their hearts filled with vengeance. In Despair's hands, hope became a hollow promise, and Apollyon's influence began to seep into the very soul of Nantrium, spreading like a storm that could not be contained.

Chapter V

The Creation

Apollyon's return to Nantrium cast a shadow over the once-bright land, his presence unraveling the delicate balance O'Rhyus had worked so tirelessly to preserve. With Despair at his side, he began his assault on the world's harmony, seeking to corrupt its very essence. Yet, Apollyon understood that mere shadows and fear would not be enough to topple the foundations of Nantrium. He needed allies—forces that could sow discord more insidiously, fracturing the unity that held the world together. From the dark depths of his power, Apollyon crafted two beings to serve him, each a reflection of his hatred for O'Rhyus and his relentless desire for dominion. The first was Chaos, a force as wild and uncontainable as Apollyon's ambition. Chaos was born of disruption and unpredictability, his presence marked by storms that shattered the tranquility of the land. Wherever he passed, the cycles of nature twisted out of control: rivers overflowed their banks, winds tore across the plains, and fires sparked in forests without cause. Chaos was a living embodiment of upheaval, bound only to Apollyon's will, his touch scattering the order that O'Rhyus had so carefully cultivated.

But Apollyon's work was not yet complete. He required more than chaos to undermine the heart of Nantrium; he needed a force that could erode the very bonds that unite its people. Thus, he created Hate, a being formed from resentment, envy, and bitterness. Where Chaos thrived in disorder, Hate was quiet and insidious, worming into the minds of mortals and gods alike. His influence whispered lies, stoking animosity and mistrust, dividing families, friends, and entire realms. With Hate's presence, brother turned against brother, communities fractured, and love withered into contempt.

Together, Chaos and Hate descended upon Nantrium, each fulfilling their purpose with precision. Chaos disrupted the physical world, breaking the rhythms of Life and Death and leaving a trail of destruction in his wake. The land, once harmonious, fell into disarray as natural cycles shattered and creatures grew hostile, their instincts twisted by his influence. Hate, meanwhile, seeped into the hearts of mortals, his touch transforming unity into division. Communities that once thrived in harmony now simmered with distrust, and the bonds of Love weakened under the weight of his poison. With Despair, Chaos, and Hate under his command, Apollyon's dark influence spread across Nantrium like an unstoppable tide. O'Rhyus, sensing the corruption taking hold, felt the gravity of his brother's work. The forces of light and unity he had created were under siege, their strength faltering against Apollyon's relentless assault. Though O'Rhyus fought valiantly to stem the tide, he knew that Apollyon's forces had taken root too deeply; Nantrium was at risk of falling into ruin. Apollyon watched with satisfaction as his creations wreaked havoc on Nantrium, his long-sought vengeance against O'Rhyus finally taking form. He reveled in the knowledge that the world would fracture and fall, its balance broken, unless someone rose to reclaim the light.

Chapter VI

The Mortal

The world of Nantrium lay shrouded in shadow, its once-flourishing lands bearing the scars of Apollyon's corruption. Chaos, Hate, and Despair ran rampant, fracturing the harmony that O'Rhyus had once woven so carefully. Yet in the heart of his despair, O'Rhyus found a trace of resilience. He realized that Nantrium needed more than divine guardians; it needed beings who could grow, learn, and choose their own path—creatures born of both light and shadow who could strive for balance with the freedom to fall or to rise.

Thus, O'Rhyus created mankind, forming them from seafoam and earth, their essence a blend of Life's vitality and Death's quietude. Mortals were bound neither to eternal light nor consuming darkness, holding within them both the potential for good and evil. In them, O'Rhyus saw a spark of hope—a species that could navigate the choices that even gods could not foresee, who might resist Apollyon's influence not by duty but by will.

Mankind's lives would be finite, their time on Nantrium brief. Through mortality, O'Rhyus gifted them with urgency, an understanding that every choice held weight, that each moment mattered. In this transience lay their power, for mortal lives were driven by love, fear, ambition, and hope—forces that could not be controlled by gods alone. O'Rhyus knew that while Apollyon's creations could shatter order and spread darkness, mortals, bound to no divine master, could forge their own destinies.

As the first generation of mortals took their place in Nantrium, they brought both light and shadow into the land. They built homes, raised families, and cultivated the earth, their touch reviving the cycles that had faltered under Apollyon's assault. They loved fiercely, fought bravely, and their unity, though fragile, sparked a resilience that spread across the land. Though they felt the influence of Chaos, Hate, and Despair, they held within them the ability to choose—a power that none of Apollyon's creations could destroy.

Observing them from afar, Apollyon seethed. He saw that these mortals, though fleeting and fallible, possessed something even his powers could not fully subjugate. Their choices shaped their world, their souls resisting the forces he unleashed upon them. Apollyon recognized the threat they posed to his designs, and he vowed to corrupt their hearts, to make them agents of his will. Through temptation and despair, he would twist their choices, guiding them into the shadows until they, too, were part of his darkness. But O'Rhyus remained hopeful. He knew that within every mortal lay a glimmer of divinity, a light that could guide them even through the deepest darkness. He entrusted the mortals with the guardianship of their world, knowing that their strength would not lie in immunity from darkness, but in their resilience to overcome it.

Chapter VII

The Final Battle

The corruption unleashed by Apollyon had spread across Nantrium like a plague, twisting its beauty into desolation. Mankind struggled under the weight of Despair, Hate, and Chaos, and O'Rhyus knew that the darkness would not relent on its own. Realizing the threat could no longer be contained, he prepared to confront his brother in a final battle, one that would decide the fate of Nantrium and test the resilience of all he had created.

Summoning the full force of his Divine Power, O'Rhyus descended upon the heart of the world, where Apollyon awaited him. Shadows gathered around the dark god, the air thick with his presence as he reveled in the ruin he had wrought. Beside him stood Despair, her light extinguished, and Chaos and Hate, their forms pulsing with the dark energy of their master. They formed a vanguard, loyal and fierce, prepared to defend Apollyon's vision of a world under his dominion.

O'Rhyus confronted his brother, his voice steady, filled with both sorrow and resolve. "Apollyon, our purpose was to protect this world, to foster balance. Your path leads only to ruin."

Apollyon's laughter echoed through the shadows. "Balance is a cage, brother. Nantrium's true potential lies in power—my power. The mortals and their fleeting lives are nothing but tools to shape a world of my design."

With no words left to sway him, O'Rhyus raised his hand,

and a radiant light burst forth, illuminating the darkness that clung to Apollyon. Their powers collided, the brilliance of O'Rhyus's light against the suffocating shadows of Apollyon, each brother wielding the full extent of their might. The land around them trembled, mountains crumbled, and the sky darkened as their conflict raged, the forces of creation and destruction locked in a battle that shook the very core of Nantrium.

Despair struck first, her aura of sorrow wrapping around O'Rhyus, seeking to sap his strength. Yet O'Rhyus, fortified by his unwavering love for Nantrium, cast her aside, his light piercing through her darkness. Chaos hurled storms and flames, but O'Rhyus's steady hand guided his power, dispelling each assault with calm precision. Then came Hate, whispering venom into his mind, seeking to sow discord in his heart, but O'Rhyus's purpose held strong, his love for the world unyielding. One by one, Apollyon's forces faltered, each succumbing to the might of O'Rhyus's light. As his allies fell, Apollyon's fury grew, and he unleashed a final surge of dark energy, a shadow that seemed to consume even the light around it. But O'Rhyus, with a single command, summoned the full strength of Divine Power. His light swelled, blinding and pure, a force that transcended even the darkness of the Inbetween.

In that final, cataclysmic moment, O'Rhyus cast Apollyon back into the depths, sealing him once more in the Inbetween, his prison bound with chains forged of light and will. The power of Divine Light surged through the rift, binding Apollyon beyond reach, his cries of rage swallowed by the void.

When the battle was done, O'Rhyus stood alone amidst the wreckage, his strength nearly spent. Nantrium bore the scars of the conflict; rivers had run dry, forests lay charred, and the land itself seemed to mourn. Yet the balance had been restored, and Apollyon's influence, though lingering, was held at bay.

Exhausted, O'Rhyus gazed upon the world he had saved, knowing that its future now lay in the hands of the mortals he had created. They, too, had felt the darkness, and had been touched by Hate, Chaos, and Despair. Yet he had seen resilience in their hearts, a light that neither he nor Apollyon could command.

With a final, quiet vow to protect and guide them from afar, O'Rhyus withdrew, his form dissolving into the world he loved. His essence became part of Nantrium itself, a silent promise that, should darkness return, his light would rise again, carried in the hearts of those who chose balance over ruin.

Chapter VIII

The Shepherd and The First Family

In the aftermath of the final battle, Nantrium lay quiet, its wounds healing under the resilience of mortal hands. Yet O'Rhyus, though now woven into the very fabric of the world, knew that the balance he had fought so hard to preserve could not rest solely on the will of humankind. Mortals, with their gift of choice, would always walk a path between light and shadow, and their decisions would forever shape the destiny of the world. For the cycles of life and death to endure, Nantrium needed guardians—beings who could guide, protect, and uphold balance across generations. From the whispers of the wind and the glow of dawn's first light, O'Rhyus created the First Shepherd, a mortal imbued with a touch of divine purpose. Named Aldous, this Shepherd was chosen not for his strength, but for his unwavering dedication to harmony. With eyes that saw beyond the surface and a heart that held equal compassion for life's beauty and its trials, Aldous became the first mortal entrusted with the sacred duty of preserving balance. His role was to watch over the land, to mediate its cycles, and to guide his people along paths that honored the delicate order O'Rhyus had left behind.

As his first charge, Aldous led the people of Nantrium in the ways of wisdom, teaching them to cherish both the abundance and the limits of the world around them. He taught them that each season brought gifts and trials, that birth and death were not rivals but companions, shaping life's tapestry with purpose. Under his care, communities grew, united by an understanding of their place within Nantrium's rhythm. His presence was a steady beacon, guiding the world toward peace and unity.

In time, Aldous felt the need for a lineage—a family that could carry forward his teachings and steward the world when his own journey reached its end. So he sought a companion, and together they bore children, establishing the First Family. Their lineage would be bound to the role of Shepherd, each generation carrying a piece of Aldous's purpose, instilled with the wisdom he had gathered and the lessons he had passed down. This lineage would be blessed and burdened with the responsibility to watch over Nantrium, to preserve its harmony, and to defend it against any forces that might seek to disrupt the balance.

As the First Family grew, O'Rhyus's influence lived on within them, a silent guidance that stirred in times of need. The people revered the First Family as both protectors and examples, their lives devoted to the cycles that governed the world. From generation to generation, the Shepherd's descendants watched over Nantrium, their commitment to balance as unwavering as the dawn that rose each day.

Yet, even with the First Family in place, O'Rhyus knew that shadows would return one day, as Apollyon's influence, though restrained, had not vanished. In his final moments of conscious will before merging fully with Nantrium, O'Rhyus set forth a prophecy—a promise that should darkness arise again, a chosen soul from the First Family would emerge to confront it, wielding the strength of all who had come before.

And so, the First Shepherd and the First Family began their sacred vigil, the custodians of balance, bound by love, wisdom, and an ancient promise. They would be Nantrium's guardians in an uncertain world, their lineage a testament to O'Rhyus's legacy, a light within the mortal realm that would endure, even as shadows gathered on the horizon.

The Raven at Wyldren

Chapter I

The Raven

The air was biting cold, each breath heavy with the weight of frost as it left my lips in slow, misty clouds. I trudged through the frozen wilderness of Wyldren, where the trees, gnarled and lifeless, seemed to look like old, forgotten sentinels. The land itself felt hostile, indifferent to the desperation that clawed at my chest. Every step forward seemed a battle against the biting wind, against the creeping sense of hopelessness that lingered in the back of my mind. The healer's words rang hollow in my ears: There's nothing more to be done for her. But I couldn't accept that. Not when she lay at home, her skin pale as the snow that covered these wretched lands, her breath shallow, fading. The Divine Falls were my last hope—their waters whispered to cure any illness, to restore Life where Death had already begun to lay claim. I had no other choice.

A sudden sound cut through the air—a low, throaty caw. I glanced up. Perched in the skeletal branches of a nearby tree was a raven, its beady black eyes fixed on me with unsettling intensity. Its feathers glistened in the dim light, and the air around it seemed heavier, darker.

"You seek salvation in a hopeless place," the raven croaked, its voice rasping like the wind through dead leaves. I paused, gripping the hilt of my sword beneath my cloak.

"Leave me be, bird. I have no time for riddles."

But the raven only tilted its head, as if amused by my

defiance. It fluttered to the next tree, following me with its eyes as I resumed my march.

"Do you truly believe that you will reach the Falls in time?" the bird called again, its voice now strangely melodic, unsettling in its sudden softness. "She is slipping from this world even now."

My heart stuttered, and I clenched my jaw against the rising tide of doubt. I pushed forward, but the bird's words were true. How could it know about her? How could it know the weight of my heart, the urgency that gripped my soul?

"She will die before you return," the raven crooned, now gliding down from the branch, its black wings stirring the snow. As it landed before me, the creature began to shift, its feathers dissolving into dark, swirling mist. Slowly, the form of a man emerged—a tall figure cloaked in black, his eyes glowing with an eerie, cold light. His face was sharp, angular, and his lips curled into a knowing smile that chilled me more than the frozen winds. I stumbled back, my hand flying to my sword.

"What... what are you?"

The man stepped forward, his movements smooth, predatory. "A friend, Vicrum," he said, his voice now soft and velvety. "One who can offer you what you truly desire."

"How do you know my name?" I demanded, though fear and confusion twisted my voice. I felt a deep unease in my chest, as though the very air around me was thickening, pressing down on my spirit.

He smiled wider, his eyes narrowing slightly. "I know more than that. I know the ache in your heart, the terror that grips you every time you think of her fading breath. I know that you fear you will lose her."

I swallowed hard, the image of my wife's frail form flashing behind my eyes, and for a moment, my resolve faltered. "What do you want from me?"

"I offer you a path," the man said, his words flowing like honey, sweet and dangerous. "Not the foolish one you walk now, but a real path—one of power. With it, you could save her, not just delay the inevitable."

His words coiled around me like a serpent, squeezing, suffocating. "And what price do you ask?"

The man's eyes gleamed with triumph as he extended a hand, pale as bone. "Only your loyalty. Give yourself to me, and she will live."

The wind howled through the trees, and for the first time, the cold was not what I feared the most.

The man's hand hung there between us, suspended like a promise I didn't want to understand. His smile widened, but it wasn't the warmth of an offer—it was the smile of a predator, patient and sure of its prey. His eyes, those unnatural, glowing orbs, bored into mine, seeing through every layer of my resolve, every thread of my hesitation.

I tried to steady my breath, to think clearly, but his words had already taken root. She will live. Those three words, laced with such seductive certainty, drowned out every warning, screaming in the back of my mind.

"What are you?" I asked again, but the words felt hollow, a stalling tactic against the rising tide of temptation. He laughed, a low, rumbling sound that seemed to vibrate through the very earth beneath my feet.

"What I am is not as important as what I offer, Vicrum."

He stepped closer, and though I didn't move, I felt the space between us shrink, as though the air itself conspired to push me toward him.

"You stand here, torn between hope and despair. You seek the Falls, but they are a distant myth, a tale spun by those desperate for miracles that never come. You are not the first to walk this path, and you won't be the last to fail."

His words were like poison, sinking into my bones. Every doubt I'd buried since leaving my village began to surface, clawing its way into the light. I thought of my wife—her pale skin, her weak smile, the way her fingers barely curled around mine as I'd whispered promises I wasn't sure I could keep.

"Imagine it, Vicrum," the man continued, his voice dropping to a near whisper, intimate and dangerous. "Her laughter filling your home again, her eyes bright with life, her arms strong enough to hold you as she once did. You could have that, and more. You could have power beyond what the Divine offers. A strength that bends the world to your will."

My hand trembled against the hilt of my sword. I tried to focus on the cold metal beneath my fingers, the weight of it, the tangible reminder that I had a choice. But his words... they wrapped around me like the wind, relentless and insistent.

"And all I must do is give you my loyalty?" I asked, my voice barely above a whisper, though I already knew the answer.

"Yes," he said, his hand still outstretched, waiting. "Loyalty, Vicrum. It is a small price to pay for a life saved."

A chill ran through me, deeper than the winter wind. Loyalty. The word echoed in my mind like the toll of a bell. I had pledged my loyalty before—to my family, to my village, to O' Rhyus who I had believed watched over us. But what had that loyalty brought me? Nothing but this—a long, lonely walk through the snow, chasing a legend while my wife's life slipped away.

"What do you have to lose?" the man pressed, his voice softer now, almost tender. "The Divine has abandoned you. They watch as she suffers, and they do nothing. But I—" He leaned in closer, his breath warm against the freezing air. "I can change that."

My resolve crumbled. I could feel it, piece by piece, breaking away under the weight of his offer. I had nothing left to hold on to. My faith, my hope—it was all fading, like the light in my wife's eyes. The sword in my hand felt useless, a relic of a time when I still believed in the world's order.

Slowly, I loosened my grip on the hilt and looked into his eyes. That terrible, empty light seemed to pulse, drawing me in and pulling me under.

"Will she live?" I asked, my voice shaking.

The man's smile softened, and for a moment, I wanted to believe that there was something kind in him, something true. "Yes, Vicrum. She will live. I swear it."

I stared at his hand, that pale, beckoning hand. And then, before I could think any further, I reached out and took it. The moment our hands touched, a wave of cold surged through me—colder than the wind, colder than the snow beneath my boots. It was a cold that seemed to reach inside me, twisting through my veins, wrapping around my heart like an iron chain. I tried to pull away, but I couldn't. His grip was firm, unyielding, and I could feel the power behind it—a force so ancient, so vast, that I could scarcely comprehend it.

His eyes never left mine, glowing brighter now, as if feeding on my hesitation and my fear. "You've made the right choice," he whispered, his voice softer than the wind, but it cut through the air like a scythe. "You will not regret this, Vicrum."

As he spoke, the world around us seemed to shift. The snow that had fallen so thickly now swirled into the air, forming a vortex of white and gray, spinning around us like a storm. The trees, those ancient, twisted branches, seemed to sway, bending toward us as though drawn by some unseen force. The very ground beneath my feet trembled, and I felt the weight of something greater than myself settle over the land. The man's smile widened as if he could feel it too, as if this world bending to his will was a simple exercise of his power. "Now," he said, his voice rising over the wind, "let me show you what your loyalty has earned."

I opened my mouth to speak, but before I could utter a word, the storm of snow and wind collapsed inward, crashing over us like a wave. For a moment, I saw nothing but white, felt nothing but the cold, a sharp bite of the wind on my skin. Then, as suddenly as it had begun, it stopped. The snow fell back to the ground, the wind stilled, and the trees stood silent once more.

I looked down at my hand, still held in his. It was pale now, drained of color, as though the life within it was slipping away, just as his cold power seeped into my flesh.

And yet... beneath that icy grasp, I could feel something else. Something strong. Something undeniable. Beneath that icy grip, there was—something foreign, yet unmistakable. It wasn't the warmth of life returning, but something stronger, darker. Power. Raw, untamed, and ancient. It surged through me like a current, filling the empty spaces where hope had once resided. My fear, my doubt, all seemed to recede, fading into the background as that power coiled and twisted in my chest, growing with each beat of my heart.

The man—Apollyon, for I now understood who he was, even without him speaking his name—watched me closely. His smile had turned softer now, knowing. He could feel it, too. He could feel the shift in me, the subtle way my resolve was bending to the dark promise he had placed before me.

"Yes," he whispered, his voice laced with satisfaction. "You feel it, don't you? The power that lies just beneath the surface, waiting to be unleashed. It is yours now, Vicrum. Yours to wield. Yours to control."

I wanted to resist, to pull away, but the pull of that power was intoxicating. It hummed in my veins, like a low, insistent drumbeat, urging me forward. My hand, still clasped in Apollyon's grip, tightened unconsciously, as though I were already accepting his offer, even as part of me screamed to turn back.

"What do you want from me?" I asked, my voice rough, but steady. It was no longer a question of refusal. The line had been crossed. Now, I need to understand the cost.

Apollyon's eyes gleamed, the light within them like dying stars. "I want what any god desires," he said smoothly, releasing my hand and stepping back, though the connection between us remained, unseen and unbreakable. "Loyalty. Service. I have chosen you, Vicrum, for you are no ordinary man. You are destined for more. Together, we will tear down the old order and build something new from the ashes. A world where you, and those like you, will reign with power unimaginable."

His words felt like a prophecy, woven into the fabric of the air around us. The snow beneath my boots seemed to pulse with that same dark energy, as if the very ground recognized the power coursing through me.

"And my wife?" I asked, the one tether still holding me to the man I had been before this moment.

"She will live?"

Apollyon's smile softened, though his eyes remained as cold and calculating as ever.

"She will live. Stronger than ever. Her life is my gift to you, Vicrum, for your loyalty." His voice was like velvet, wrapping around me, soothing the last traces of doubt in my mind. "But understand this: what I give, I can also take away."

The warning was clear, a shadow that passed between us, but it was lost in the overwhelming weight of his promise. She would live. That was all that mattered. No price was too great for that.

I nodded, the decision solidifying within me like stone. "What must I do?"

Apollyon's smile turned sharper, more predatory. "You will know, in time. But for now, return to your village. Go to her, and see for yourself what my power has already begun to do."

A shiver passed through me at his words, not from fear, but anticipation. Without another word, I turned away from Apollyon. My steps were steady now, driven by the pulse of power that thrummed within me, each beat louder than the last. The cold no longer mattered, the biting wind no longer stung. All that mattered was the path ahead. My wife awaited me, and with her, the future I had been promised.

As I walked through the frozen woods of Wyldren, a quiet voice whispered in the back of my mind—a voice that was no longer my own. It was darker, filled with certainty and strength, urging me forward. "This is the beginning," it said. "The beginning of your rise, Vicrum."

And deep down, I knew it was right.As I pressed forward through the frozen wilderness, the dark woods of Wyldren closing in around me, that voice—the one I had once feared—became my constant companion. It whispered quietly, though not in words so much as in sensation, a feeling that pulsed through my blood, guiding my steps with unwavering certainty. The landscape, which had once felt so harsh and unyielding, now bent to my will. The cold no longer pierced my bones, the wind no longer fought against me. It was as if the very world recognized the change within me and stepped aside, making room for what I had become.

I thought of my wife, lying there in our home, her breath shallow, her skin like pale marble. The memory of her fragile form had once filled me with dread, but now, a new sense of calm had taken its place. Apollyon had given me his word—she would live. That was enough. I clung to that promise like a lifeline, even as the weight of the power within me grew heavier, its presence undeniable. The sky above me darkened, the gray clouds thickening as night fell over Wyldren. Yet even in the deepening gloom, I could see more clearly than I ever had before. Shapes that had once been mere shadows in the distance now stood out in sharp relief—the bare trees with their twisted branches, the rocks covered in frost, the distant outline of the village I called home. It was as if my senses had sharpened, my vision piercing through the murk of the world.

I reached the outskirts of the village just as the first stars began to shine in the sky. The houses, huddled close together like old men sharing warmth, seemed smaller now, diminished. The power that thrummed within me made everything else seem faint, as if the world around me had become muted in comparison. I made my way down the familiar streets, the snow crunching beneath my boots. I passed a few villagers, their faces drawn and weary from the long winter. They nodded at me, but I barely acknowledged them, my thoughts focused on the path ahead. They couldn't know what had transpired in the wilds beyond Wyldren, nor could they understand the weight I now carried within me. Soon, they would see. Soon, they would know.

Our home stood at the edge of the village, small and unassuming, a place that had once been filled with warmth and laughter. I pushed open the door, the hinges creaking as I stepped inside. The fire in the hearth had burned low, casting the room in wild shadows.

There she was—my wife, lying still on the bed, her face pale and drawn. Her eyes were closed, and for a moment, my heart stuttered in my chest, the fear rising again like a wave threatening to pull me under. But then I saw it—the faint rise and fall of her chest, the shallow breaths that came, one after another. She was alive.

I knelt beside her, my hand reaching out to touch her cold skin. A tremor passed through me as my fingers met hers, but this time, it wasn't fear. It was something darker, something that pulsed with the same power that now lived within me. Her eyes fluttered open, just barely. She looked at me, and for the first time in weeks, I saw a indication of recognition there—a spark of life that had been missing for too long. I leaned closer, my voice a whisper.

"You will live," I said, the words heavy with the certainty that came from the dark pact I had made.

She blinked slowly, her lips parting as if to speak, but no words came. I didn't need to hear them. I could feel it—the life returning to her, slow but steady. Apollyon's promise had been true. She would live.But as I sat there, holding her hand, that same dark voice stirred within me, whispering once again.

"This is only the beginning," it said, and deep down, I knew it was right.

What I had gained came with a price, one that I had only just begun to understand.I stayed by her side as the night deepened, the fire casting long shadows on the walls of our small home. The silence was thick, broken only by the faint crackle of embers and her steady, shallow breaths. I watched her, my heart heavy with conflicting emotions—relief that she was still alive, fear of the unknown path I had now set upon, and something else... something darker, coiling in the pit of my stomach like a serpent waking from slumber. Her fingers twitched in mine, a small movement, but enough to pull me from my thoughts. Her eyes fluttered open again, this time with more focus, more awareness. She looked at me, and in that gaze, I saw a glimmer of the woman I had loved for so long—the woman who had been slipping away from me day by day. I squeezed her hand gently, leaning closer.

"You're safe," I whispered, though the words felt strange, as if they weren't entirely mine. "You're going to be well."

I stood, walking to the hearth and adding another log to the fire. The flames rose, their heat warming my face as I stared into them, the crackling of wood filling the quiet. But even as I stood there, I could feel it—Apollyon's presence, lingering like a shadow just beyond the edges of my mind. His promise had been fulfilled. Now I could only think of my end of the deal. The power that coursed through me, the dark energy that hummed beneath my skin, was a constant reminder of the bargain I had struck. I closed my eyes, letting the warmth of the fire wash over me, but it did little to soothe the unease that gnawed at me. What had I done? I had saved her, yes, but at what cost? The faces of the lost souls from the forest flashed before my eyes—their hollow gazes, the emptiness in their eyes. I had seen what became of those who followed Apollyon, and yet I had still taken his hand, still accepted his power. A chill ran through me, despite the heat of the fire.

I glanced back at her, still lying motionless in the bed, and a pang of guilt twisted in my chest. Was it worth it? Had I traded one life for another—her life for mine, my soul for hers? The questions swirled in my mind, but there were no answers, only the growing weight of the choices I had made. But she would always be worth it.

As I stared into the flames, the whispers returned, soft at first, like a distant wind, then growing louder, more insistent. "This is only the beginning, Vicrum. There is more yet to come. Power beyond your understanding. Power that will change the world."

I clenched my fists, the muscles in my arms tightening as the voice pushed deeper into my thoughts. I could feel it, the dark pull of Apollyon's promise, urging me forward, drawing me further from the man I had been. The man who had walked into the wilds of Wyldren was not the same man who stood here now, watching the fire burn. Apollyon was talking about something far greater—about the world, about kingdoms, about the fate of all those who still clung to the old gods ways. I opened my eyes, staring into the flames as they danced and crackled, my mind a storm of thoughts and conflicting desires. There was no going back now. The path had been set, and I had chosen to walk it. For her. For the woman I loved. For the life I had sworn to protect.

But in doing so, I had bound myself to a power I barely understood, a power that would demand more from me than I was yet prepared to give. And as I stood there, watching the fire glow and burn, I could feel the weight of that truth settling over me like a cloak of shadow.

The flames danced, their movements wild and untamed, a reflection of the turmoil churning inside my mind. Power. I had never sought it, never craved to bend the world to my will. But now, that very power was mine—woven into my bones, flowing through my veins like molten iron. It was intoxicating, and it terrified me all the same.

I turned back to my wife, her fragile form still resting in the bed, and the weight of what I had done settled heavily upon me. The power I had accepted wasn't just a tool to save her; it was something far greater, far more dangerous. As a mortal man, what right did I have to wield such power? I had been a simple man once—husband, protector, leader of my small village. But now... now I stood on the verge of something I could not fully grasp.

"Power beyond the Divine." Apollyon's words echoed in my mind, taunting me, pulling at the threads of my very being. But with that power came a burden, one that I was only beginning to comprehend. The gods themselves had walked these lands, shaping the world, guiding mankind. I had heard the stories, as all of us had. The Shepherd, O'Rhyus, the balance between Light and Darkness—they had given us life, shown us how to use the Divine Power to shape our destiny.

But I was no god.

The thought struck me like a blow to the chest. I had seen what the gods were capable of—their power, their might, their endless influence. And now, in some twisted way, I was being offered a glimpse of that. But I wasn't like them. I was mortal. Flesh and bone. My heart could still break, my body could still bleed. And yet... this power was now mine to wield.

What legacy would I leave behind? The question lingered, growing heavier with each passing moment. Once, I had hoped to be remembered as a good man—a man who loved his wife, protected his people, and lived by the values of the gods. But now? What would people say of me if they knew the truth of the dark bargain I had struck? What would they say when they saw the shadow that now followed me wherever I went? A shiver ran through me, not from the cold, but from the understanding of what lay ahead. Power demanded responsibility. And power like this... it had the potential to corrupt, to destroy everything I had once held dear. Apollyon had promised me salvation for my wife, but he had also given me something more—a burden, a dark mantle I could not lay down. I thought of the gods once more, of O'Rhyus and the balance he had maintained. I wondered if even they, with their ancient wisdom, had ever felt the weight of the choices they made. Did they know the cost of wielding such power, or had they simply embraced it, blind to the destruction it could cause? I wasn't blind. I could already see the cost, feeling it gnawing at the edges of my soul. This power, this gift—if I wasn't careful, it could consume me. And yet, I couldn't turn away from it. Not now. Not with her life hanging in the balance.

I took a deep breath, the air sharp in my lungs, and stared into the flames once more. I had accepted this power to save her, but now I realized that saving her was only the beginning. This wasn't just about life and death. This was about legacy. About what I would leave behind when my time was done. The choices I made now would echo long after I was gone, shaping not just my life, but the lives of all who came after me. I didn't want to be remembered as a man who bowed to darkness, who let the power devour him whole. But the responsibility weighed on me like a millstone around my neck. The more I thought about it, the clearer it became: wielding this power, walking this path, required more than strength. It required wisdom. Restraint. A clear understanding of what I was becoming.

And I wasn't sure I had that wisdom.

But I would need to find it. Before the power found me wanting. As the fire crackled and the weight of my thoughts pressed heavily upon me, the silence in the room thickened.

It was as though the world itself held its breath, waiting for something unseen, something inevitable. My wife lay still, her breath shallow but steady, and yet I could not shake the feeling that I had only bought her time, not truly saved her. The air in the room felt charged, as if something—or someone—was watching. The shadows by the hearth deepened, stretching unnaturally long across the floor, until they seemed to converge in the far corner of the room. My hand instinctively went to the hilt of my sword, though I knew it would be useless against what was coming.

"You're learning," a familiar voice purred from the darkness.

I turned slowly, heart hammering in my chest, and there, standing in the deepest shadow, was Apollyon. He emerged from the darkness like a figure cut from the void itself, his black cloak flowing like liquid night, his pale face sharp and gleaming in the firelight. His eyes, glowing faintly, locked onto mine with a knowing, dangerous glimmer.

"Did you think I would leave you alone now, Vicrum?" His voice was smooth, almost amused, as if this moment had been planned from the start. He stepped forward, his presence filling the small room as though the very walls bent under the weight of his power.

"I didn't call for you," I said, trying to keep my voice steady, though a chill ran through me.

Apollyon smiled, a slow, deliberate smile. "Oh, but I am not here by your summons. I am here because we are not finished. You accepted my gift, and now you must learn what it means to wield it."

I tightened my grip on the sword, though I knew it would do me no good. "What more do you want from me?" I glanced at my wife, her chest still rising and falling with shallow breaths.

Apollyon's eyes followed mine, lingering on her for a moment before returning to me. "Life is only the first part of what I offer, Vicrum. The power I have given you is greater than you can yet understand. And if you are to truly save her, to protect her, you must learn to wield it. Come."

Before I could protest, before I could even blink, the world around me shifted. It was as though the floor had dropped out from beneath my feet, and in an instant, the warmth of the fire and the familiar sight of my home vanished. My breath caught in my throat as the world twisted and spun, the air itself warping as we were pulled through the very fabric of reality.

When the world finally stilled, I found myself standing in a place I had never seen, yet somehow I recognized it from the stories passed down through the generations. The air here was thick and damp, the scent of earth and stone filling my lungs. The cave we stood in was vast, its walls lined with jagged, ancient rocks that seemed to pulse faintly with some dark energy. This was the place spoken of in legend, the cave where the gods had once walked, where power flowed freely through Nantrium itself.

Apollyon stepped forward, his footsteps echoing unnaturally loud in the cavernous space. "Do you know where we are, Vicrum?"

I swallowed, my throat dry. "This is... the cave. The Divine Falls. The place where the gods... forged their power."

Apollyon's smile widened, his eyes gleaming with approval. "Yes. This is where it all began. The birthplace of Divine

Power, and the place where you will learn to command it."

I hesitated, the weight of the place pressing down on me. The air was thick with a sense of history, of ancient forces that had once shaped the world and would do so again. "I'm just a man," I whispered, my voice barely audible in the vast emptiness. "How can I wield the power of the gods?"

Apollyon turned to face me, his expression unreadable. "That is precisely why I chose you, Vicrum. You are a man, yes, but you are no ordinary man. You have already begun to feel it—the power stirring inside you, growing stronger with each passing moment. You may be mortal, but you are capable of far more than you realize. The gods may have forged this world, but it is men like you who will shape its future."

He gestured toward the dark stone altar at the center of the cave. It was old, worn smooth by centuries of use, and yet it pulsed with a faint, dark light that made my skin crawl. "Step forward," Apollyon commanded, his voice echoing off the walls. "Place your hand on the altar and feel what lies beneath."

I hesitated, staring at the altar. The air around it seemed to hum with power, thick and oppressive, as though the very stones held the weight of a thousand lives within them. Every instinct told me to turn away, to refuse, but something deeper—something darker—compelled me forward. Slowly, I approached the altar, each step heavier than the last. The closer I got, the more I could feel the pull of the power within, like a heartbeat thrumming in the stone. I reached out, my hand trembling as I placed it on the cold surface. The moment my skin touched the stone, the world erupted around me. A surge of energy shot through my arm, racing through my body like wildfire. My vision blurred as images flooded my mind—visions of battles long past, of gods and men clashing for control of the world. I saw the rise and fall of empires, the birth of life, and the cold hand of death sweeping across the land. And in all of it, I saw the shadow of Apollyon, his presence a constant, shaping the world in ways unseen.

The power surged within me, dark and unstoppable, filling every corner of my soul. It was too much—too vast, too ancient. I tried to pull away, but my hand was glued to the altar, the energy coursing through me, tearing at my very soul.

And then, just as suddenly as it began, it stopped.

I staggered back, gasping for breath, my legs trembling beneath me. The cave seemed to spin, and I fell to my knees, clutching my chest as the last echoes of the power faded. Apollyon stood over me, his expression unreadable. "You have tasted it now," he said, his voice soft, yet filled with dark promise. "The power of the gods, the power that will shape your destiny."

I looked up at him, my mind still reeling from the onslaught of images, the sheer force of the power that had torn through me. "I... I don't know if I can control it," I whispered, my voice raw.

Apollyon knelt beside me, his eyes piercing. "You can, Vicrum. And you will. This power is not just a gift—it is a responsibility. You have chosen this path, and now you must walk it. You have seen what is possible, what you can achieve. But you must embrace it fully, or it will destroy you."

He placed a hand on my shoulder, and the touch sent another wave of cold through me, though this time it was steady, controlled. "You are no longer just a man, Vicrum. You are something more. And with that comes a choice: to wield this power for your own ends or to use it to reshape the world."

I stared at him, the weight of his words pressing down on me like a mountain. The power I had felt, the darkness that now pulsed within me—it was too great for any mortal man to bear. But I was no longer just a man. I was something else. Something more. And as I knelt there in the cave, the dark echoes of the gods still reverberating through my mind, I realized that the path I had chosen was not one of salvation, but of transformation. I would wield this power, but it would change me in ways I could not yet understand.

Apollyon stood, his eyes gleaming with dark satisfaction. "Rise, Vicrum," he said. "Your journey is just beginning." With trembling hands, I pushed myself to my feet, the weight of my newfound power settling over me like a cloak. The cave around us pulsed with the ancient energy of the gods, and I knew that I had crossed a threshold from which there was no return.

The path ahead was dark, but I would walk it. The weight of Apollyon's words lingered in the cave like a dense fog, pressing down on me. My hand still tingled with the remnants of power from the altar, and my mind raced with the visions I had seen—glimpses of gods, men, wars, and the endless cycle of creation and destruction. I had crossed into a world beyond mortal comprehension, a world where light and darkness weren't just forces but living, breathing entities, constantly at odds, yet bound together in a way I was only beginning to understand. Apollyon stood before me, his eyes gleaming with dark satisfaction, as if watching me wrestle with the enormity of what had just been bestowed upon me was all part of his design.

"You see now," he said, his voice soft, almost reverent, "the truth of power. It is not the domain of the gods alone. You, Vicrum, have tasted it. You are no longer bound by the limitations of mortality, nor by the whims of those who claim to protect this world. You are becoming something greater."

I met his gaze, still on my knees before the altar, the dark energy within me throbbing, filling the hollow spaces I hadn't known existed. The pulse of the cave itself felt alive, as though it, too, was watching, waiting. I knew he was right. I could feel it—this power, this change, wasn't something that could be undone. But what terrified me more than anything was how much I wanted it, how much it had already begun to fill the voids left by my despair, my helplessness.

"This power...," I began, my voice rough, unsure, "it's too much for a mortal. It feels... unnatural."

Apollyon tilted his head, the faintest smile tugging at the corners of his lips. "Unnatural? No, Vicrum. It is far from unnatural. It is the essence of all things, the balance upon which the world is built. What you feel is not foreign to your being—it has always been there, waiting to be awakened."

Struggling to make sense of his words. "The balance...?"

"Light and dark, life and death, creation and destruction," Apollyon said, stepping closer, his voice like a silk thread weaving through the air. "They are not opposites, not in the way you have been taught to understand them. They are two sides of the same coin. One cannot exist without the other. Without darkness, how could one know the light?"

I frowned, trying to grasp the concept he was laying before me. "But isn't light supposed to be... good? And darkness... evil?"

Apollyon's smile widened, a soft chuckle escaping his lips. "Ah, the simplicity of mortal minds. You see the world in such stark terms—good and evil, light and dark, faith and heresy. But the truth, Vicrum, is far more complex. Light is not inherently good, nor is darkness inherently evil. They are forces. Necessary forces. It is through their interplay that the world exists as it does."

He gestured to the cave around us, to the altar, to the very air that thrummed with power. "Think of it. In the darkness, there is mystery, potential, the unknown. It is where creation begins, where ideas are formed, where life itself starts. But in the light? There is clarity, yes, but also finality. The light reveals, it ends the mystery. It burns away what is unseen. Without the darkness, there is no light. And without light, there is no darkness. They are intertwined, eternally."

I stood then, my legs still weak but steadying beneath me. His words echoed in my mind, twisting the very foundation of what I thought I knew. "But the gods... they teach us to walk in the light, to embrace it, to reject the darkness. How can they be wrong?"

Apollyon's expression darkened, and his eyes gleamed with something far more ancient than I could comprehend. "The gods are not infallible, Vicrum. They, too, exist within the balance, though they may deny it. O'Rhyus and his followers... they cling to the light, believing it to be the only path to salvation. But in doing so, they are blind to the truth. They seek to impose order, to stifle the natural ebb and flow of the world."

He stepped closer, his presence overwhelming. "You've seen it yourself, haven't you? The world is not all light. Your wife, lying on the brink of death, the suffering you've endured, the struggles of your people. The light has not saved you. It is through the darkness, through me, that you found a way forward."

My throat tightened. He wasn't wrong. The gods, the light—they had offered me nothing but hollow prayers, empty promises. My faith had led me down a path of despair, with no answers, no solutions. But here, standing in this ancient cave, with Apollyon's power thrumming in my veins, I had found something real. Something that could change everything.

"But if I embrace this darkness," I said, my voice trembling slightly, "if I take this power, won't it corrupt me? Won't I become... like you?"

Apollyon's smile softened, and for a moment, he almost looked... sad. "Corruption is the price of ignorance, Vicrum. Power, in itself, is neither good nor evil. It is how you wield it that defines your path. I was cast out, labeled as darkness, because I refused to bend to the will of those who feared the truth. But you... you have a choice. You can take this power and use it to restore balance, to forge a path that is neither wholly light nor wholly dark. That is what makes you different."

I felt the weight of his words settling over me like a cloak, heavy and inescapable. The choice before me wasn't as simple as light versus dark, good versus evil. It was something far deeper, something that transcended the narrow boundaries of the mortal mind. Power was neither a curse nor a blessing—it was a tool. A weapon. And it was mine to wield, if I chose.

"But how?" I asked, my voice barely above a whisper. "How do I find the balance between them? How do I control this power without letting it consume me?"

Apollyon's gaze softened further, and for the first time, I saw something akin to respect in his eyes. "By understanding that both light and darkness are within you, Vicrum. You are not one or the other. You are both. Embrace that truth, and you will find your path."

He reached out, his hand hovering over my chest, just above my heart. "Feel it, Vicrum. The power that now flows through you. It is not just mine. It is yours. It is born of your pain, your love, your will to survive. That is where the true strength lies—not in the light, not in the dark, but in your ability to walk between them."

I closed my eyes, feeling the energy within me, pulsing like a second heartbeat. It was dark, yes, but it was also warm, like the feeling of a fire at the edge of night. It didn't feel evil. It felt... whole. Balanced.

When I opened my eyes, Apollyon was watching me closely, his expression unreadable. "You've already taken the first step, Vicrum," he said. "Now, it is time to take the next."

He turned, gesturing deeper into the cave, where the shadows thickened into a swirling, almost tangible force. "There is something else you must see. Something that will help you understand the full scope of what is to come."

I hesitated, my gaze flicking to the swirling darkness. It felt alive, dangerous, as though stepping into it would mean crossing a threshold from which there was no return.

Apollyon sensed my hesitation and placed a hand on my shoulder. "Fear is natural, Vicrum. But remember, fear exists because you understand what's at stake. The light exists because there is darkness. To embrace one fully is to deny the other. You must walk into both to find the balance."

With a deep breath, I nodded, steeling myself. I had already come this far. There was no turning back now. Together, we stepped into the swirling darkness, and the world fell away around us. The sensation of moving through the darkness was unlike anything I had ever experienced. It wasn't simply the absence of light—it was as though I was floating through something thick and fluid, like walking through the deepest, most primordial waters. The pressure of it pressed against me, but not in an oppressive way. It was like the darkness itself was cradling me, surrounding me, waiting for me to acknowledge it fully.

Apollyon moved beside me, his presence steady and unshaken. I couldn't see anything—not even my own hand in front of my face—but I could sense him there, a guiding presence in the swirling void. I focused on that, using it to anchor myself as the darkness pulled at me from all sides. Eventually, the thick, oppressive blackness began to fade, giving way to a faint, pulsing light. It was dim at first, a soft glow that barely illuminated the space around us, but it grew brighter with each step we took, until I could see again.

I saw the creation of Nantrium, the realm torn from the void, where life and death were born as equal forces. I saw the gods—O'Rhyus and Apollyon among them—rising from the chaos, their forms brilliant and terrible. I saw their early works, the shaping of the world, the birth of men from seafoam and earth, their hands guiding the winds, the waters, the very blood in our veins. But just as clearly, I saw the shadows that lurked behind their creation: the destruction, the entropy that followed. Each creation was followed by ruin, each spark of life shadowed by death.

And through it all, Apollyon stood on the edge, watching. Waiting. His form flashed through my mind like a shadow cast in a great light, observing the balance with a quiet, knowing gaze. He was the god who understood that the light was incomplete without the dark. That true power lay in the acceptance of both. I turned to Apollyon, who stood watching me, his eyes gleaming in the dim light of the cavern. "I see it now," I whispered, my voice hoarse. "The balance. The truth of it. Without darkness, there is no light. Without death, there is no life."

Apollyon's smile widened, his satisfaction clear. "Yes, Vicrum. You have come to understand what the gods have refused to accept for ages. The light cannot exist in isolation, no matter how much O'Rhyus and his ilk may pretend otherwise. They cling to their purity, their supposed goodness, blind to the fact that in doing so, they deny the truth of existence itself."

His words hung in the air, heavy with meaning, and I felt the weight of the decision that now loomed before me. I had seen both sides of the coin. I had tasted the power of both light and dark, and I knew now that neither was wholly good or evil. They simply were. But what was I supposed to do with that knowledge? How could I wield this power, this truth, in a world where the gods themselves denied it?

"I understand the balance," I said slowly "But how can I change the world with it? The gods will never allow it. They cling too tightly to their own ideals."

Apollyon's smile faded, replaced by something darker, more calculating. "You're right. They won't allow it. But that's why they must be removed."

The words sent a chill down my spine. I turned to face him fully, my eyes narrowing. "What are you asking?"

Apollyon stepped forward, his presence looming larger than before, filling the cavern with his dark aura. "You've seen the truth, Vicrum. You understand the balance. But O'Rhyus—my brother—he refuses to accept it. He hides behind his light, his so-called purity, and in doing so, he condemns the world to stagnation. He would rather see mankind suffer, clinging to the false hope of salvation through the light, than admit that darkness is a necessary part of that salvation."

He paused, his gaze intense. "If the balance is to be restored, O'Rhyus must be removed. He cannot be allowed to continue his reign of blind ignorance. He must be... ended."

My blood ran cold. What he was asking hit me like a hammer. "You're asking me to kill a god."

Apollyon's expression didn't change. "Yes. My brother, O'Rhyus, must fall if the world is to be reborn. You are the one who can do it, Vicrum. With the power I've given you, you can challenge him. You can bring about the true balance this world needs."

I staggered back. The idea of killing a god, of striking down one of the beings who had created the world, was unthinkable. It was madness. And yet... the power I had felt within me, the dark energy that now thrummed in my veins, told me that it wasn't impossible. I could do it.

But should I?

"I don't... I don't understand," I stammered, trying to process the weight of his words. "How can you ask this of me? I'm just a man."

Apollyon's eyes softened slightly, his tone taking on a more persuasive edge. "No, Vicrum. You are no longer just a man. You are something more now. You have embraced the truth of the balance, and with that, you have stepped beyond the limitations of mere mortals. The power you hold is greater than you can yet comprehend, but I can help you. Together, we can reshape this world. Together, we can bring about the true balance."

I shook my head, stepping away from him, trying to clear my mind. "But O'Rhyus... he's not evil. He's just—"

"He's blind!" Apollyon snapped, his voice cracking like a whip. The force of his anger echoed through the cavern, causing the walls to bend and move wildly. "He refuses to see the truth, and in his blindness, he condemns all of creation to a half-existence. He claims to be a god of light, of balance, but his light burns too brightly. It blinds those who follow him, leaving them unable to see the darkness that lurks in their own hearts. And in denying that darkness, they deny themselves."

He took a step closer, his eyes blazing with intensity. "You, Vicrum, have the chance to break this cycle. You have the chance to end the tyranny of false light and bring about a world where both light and dark are accepted. A world where men are free to embrace their true nature."

I stared at him, my mind racing. The power I had felt coursing through me, the visions of the world's creation, the endless cycle of light and dark... it all seemed to point toward one conclusion. The world as it was could not continue. There was too much suffering, too much imbalance. Apollyon's vision of balance was not the madness I had once believed it to be. It was a truth I had seen for myself. But to kill O'Rhyus? To strike down the god of light, the very embodiment of the ideals I had been raised to revere? Could I do that?

"You've felt it, haven't you?" Apollyon said softly, his voice once again coaxing and insidious. "The power. The darkness within you. It is part of you now, Vicrum. You cannot deny it. And you know that O'Rhyus would never accept you as you are. He would see you as corrupted, as a threat to his perfect world. He would destroy you."

I clenched my fists, feeling the dark power ripple through me, as if it were responding to Apollyon's words, urging me to listen. He wasn't wrong. I had already crossed a line. O'Rhyus the god of light would never accept what I had become. They would see me as a threat, an abomination. And in their righteous zeal, they would try to wipe me from existence. I could feel it now—the tug of fate pulling me toward this decision. Apollyon was offering me a way forward, a path to true power. To balance. To freedom. But it came at a cost. A cost I wasn't sure I could pay.

"I need to think," I said, my voice trembling. "I need to—"

"There is no time for hesitation, Vicrum," Apollyon interrupted, his voice sharp once more. "The world is already in motion. O'Rhyus knows you are no longer the man you once were. He will come for you. And when he does, he will not offer mercy. He will see you as a threat, and he will destroy you unless you act first."

He reached out, his hand hovering just above my shoulder. "This is your destiny, Vicrum. You are the one who can bring about the balance. You are the one who can end the tyranny of false light and bring about a world where both light and dark are embraced. But you must act. You must choose."

I stared at him, my heart pounding in my chest. The weight of the choice pressed down on me, suffocating. The power I had felt, the visions I had seen, all seemed to converge into this moment. The darkness within me pulsed, calling me to action, urging me to take the next step. But could I do it? Could I strike down O'Rhyus, the god of light, the very embodiment of all I had once believed in?

Apollyon's voice was soft now, almost a whisper. "Join me, Vicrum. Together, we will bring balance to this world. Together, we will free mankind from the chains of false light. But you must choose." I closed my eyes, feeling the power swirling around me, the darkness and the light both pulling at my soul. The weight of the decision hung over me like a sword, ready to fall.

When I opened my eyes, I knew what I had to do. The cavern was filled with a silence that felt alive, almost tangible. The weight of Apollyon's words hung between us, heavy with meaning and consequence. My heart raced, the blood pumping through my veins almost drowning out every other sound. I stood on the edge of something far greater than myself—something ancient and unstoppable. The power I had felt earlier, the balance of light and dark, still throbbed within me like a second heartbeat. But the decision I faced was not only about power or destiny—it was about her. My wife.

She was the reason I had come this far, the reason I had taken Apollyon's hand in the first place. She lay in our home, her life hanging by a thread, and I knew that without this power, without what Apollyon had offered, I would have lost her. That thought alone drove me forward. It made the choice clearer and no less daunting. Everything I did from this point forward would be for her, to protect her, to give her a future. Even if that future meant walking in the shadow of a god like Apollyon.

I looked at him, standing there in the dim light of the cavern, his presence vast and unrelenting. He was a god of darkness, but now I understood—he was also a god of balance. His words echoed in my mind: "Light only exists because of darkness." He wasn't wrong. I had seen it in the visions, felt it in the power now coursing through my veins. Light and dark were not opposites—they were intertwined, forever linked. One could not exist without the other. O'Rhyus and the god of light had been denying that truth, and in doing so, they had been denying the world its full potential.

I exhaled slowly, the last remnants of doubt leaving me. My decision had been made the moment I had accepted Apollyon's power, the moment I had agreed to take this path. There was no turning back. I would embrace what I had become—not for my own sake, but for hers. For the woman

I loved. For the life we could still have together.

"I accept," I said, my voice steady despite the storm of emotions raging inside me. "I'll do it."

Apollyon's eyes gleamed, his satisfaction barely concealed behind the sharp smile that spread across his face. "Good, Vicrum. You've made the right choice. This is not a path for the weak, nor for those who cling to false ideals. But you—" He stepped closer, his presence almost overwhelming. "You have the strength to walk it."

I nodded, the thought of what I had just agreed to still settled over me like a heavy mantle. "I'm doing this for her," I added, almost as if I needed to remind myself. "For my wife."

Apollyon tilted his head, the faintest hint of approval in his eyes. "Of course you are. Love is a powerful force, Vicrum. Perhaps the most powerful. It is stronger than fear, stronger than faith, and in your case, it has led you to embrace the balance. It has led you to me."

The darkness around us seemed to pulse, as if alive, responding to the decision I had just made. Apollyon's smile grew sharper, and with a wave of his hand, the cavern began to shift around us. The walls seemed to melt, the jagged rocks dissolving into a swirling mist of shadow and light. I felt the familiar sensation of the world slipping away beneath me, the air around us warping as we were pulled through the fabric of reality.

In an instant, the oppressive weight of the cave vanished, replaced by the cold, familiar air of Wyldren. We stood at the edge of my village, the snow-covered rooftops of the houses visible in the distance. The wind howled through the barren trees, carrying with it the scent of frost and wood smoke.

It was night, the moon hanging low in the sky, casting an eerie glow over the landscape. I had been here just hours ago, before Apollyon had taken me to the cave, before everything had changed.

Apollyon stepped forward, his black cloak billowing behind him as he surveyed the quiet village. "Welcome home, Vicrum," he said, his voice soft but commanding. "You have taken the first step. Now, rejoice in the power that is yours."

I stood there, taking in the sight of my village. It looked the same, but everything felt different now. The power within me had changed the way I saw the world, the way I felt the cold wind on my skin, the way I heard the distant crackle of the village fires. Everything was sharper, more vivid, as if the darkness had peeled away some veil that had been covering my senses.

"Now what?" I asked, unsure of what was expected of me. The weight of my decision still hung over me, but it was joined by a strange calm, as if I had finally accepted the path I was on. The fear that had gripped me in the cavern was gone, replaced by a sense of purpose. Apollyon didn't answer right away. Instead, he stared out at the village, his eyes scanning the distant rooftops and the fading lights in the windows.

"Now," he said slowly, "you wait. O'Rhyus is aware of what has transpired. He will feel the shift in the balance. He will know that you have embraced the darkness, that you have chosen to wield both light and shadow. And he will respond."

"What will he do?" I asked, unable to hide the edge of uncertainty in my voice. Apollyon smiled, his expression filled with dark amusement.

"He will try to stop you, of course. He cannot allow someone like you to exist—someone who has embraced both light and dark. It threatens everything he stands for, everything he has built. He will come for you, Vicrum, make no mistake. But when he does, you will be ready."

I clenched my fists, feeling the dark power ripple through me, as if responding to Apollyon's words. There was no going back now. O'Rhyus would come for me, and I would have to face him. But I wouldn't face him as a mortal man. I would face him as something more. Something greater.

"Rejoice. The time will come soon enough."

And then he was gone, leaving me alone in the cold night, the village sprawled out before me.

Chapter II

The Lion

The air in my quarters was still, heavy with a sense of anticipation that made every breath feel like it carried the weight of something greater than myself. The faint glow of the setting sun filtered through the high windows, casting long shadows across the stone floor. I stood alone, the silence thick around me, but I knew I wasn't truly alone. He was coming. O'Rhyus had chosen me, and in doing so, he had bound me to something far beyond the life I had once known. My heart beat steadily in my chest, but my mind was restless. The task before me was immense, the weight of it pressing against my spirit like a great stone.

I turned toward the window, looking out at the city of Lushahiem below. The capital of Hyltoria was still, its people unaware of the changes that were about to sweep through their lives. It was strange to think that only days ago, I had been one of them—a simple man, guided by faith but with no claim to destiny. Now, I stood on the edge of something vast, something that would shape the future of mankind.

"Aldous."

His voice filled the room like a beam of light, warm and commanding. I turned to see O'Rhyus standing at the edge of the shadows, his form radiant but not overwhelming, as if he had softened his presence for my sake. His eyes, bright and piercing, found mine, and in that moment, the weight in my chest eased. His presence was like sunlight breaking through the clouds—steady and reassuring.

"You feel the burden already," he said, stepping closer, his voice calm but filled with purpose. "I can see it in your eyes. The uncertainty."

I nodded, unable to hide the truth. "I do," I admitted quietly. "You've asked me to lead mankind, to bring order to the chaos. But I'm just one man. How can I—"

"You are more than one man," O'Rhyus interrupted, his tone gentle yet firm. "You are The Shepherd. Chosen not because of what you were, but because of what you will become. The chaos that grips this world—this uncertainty, this imbalance—it will be your task to steady. To bring light where there is darkness."

I swallowed "But why me? There are others—stronger, wiser men who—"

"Because you are not like the others," O'Rhyus said, cutting through my doubt. "You understand balance. You know that to bring order is not to impose strength, but to nurture growth. To guide, not to command. The light you carry within you is not just mine—it is yours, Aldous. That is why you were chosen." His words settled over me like a mantle of warmth, and for the first time since he had appeared to me, I felt a instant peace within my chest.

"Bring order, Aldous," O'Rhyus said, his eyes glowing with quiet intensity. "Bring light to a world that has known only shadows."

And at that moment, I understood. I wasn't walking this path alone. O'Rhyus stepped closer, his presence filling the room like a calm breeze sweeping through an open field. The glow that surrounded him softened the edges of the shadows in the room, driving away the darkness that had been creeping at the corners of my mind. There was no mistaking the gravity of the moment, but his warmth, his light, made it feel manageable. Possible.

I turned to fully face him, still unsure but steady enough to speak the doubts that had been gnawing at me. "But the chaos... it's everywhere. Men turn on one another. Tribes splinter, each seeking their own path in the wilderness. How do I bring order to that? How can I unite them when they see only the fractures, the darkness in the hearts of others?"

O'Rhyus regarded me with a soft expression, as if he had been waiting for this question. "Chaos is part of creation, Aldous. Just as night gives way to day, so too must disorder come before order. But men are not made to live in darkness forever. They seek the light, even if they cannot always see the path. That is where you come in. You will be their guide, the one who shows them that balance is not impossible."

His words resonated within me, but I still struggled to grasp the enormity of it. "But they're divided, O'Rhyus. They've been this way for generations. Some follow the old ways, clinging to the spirits of the wild. Others... they have no faith in anything at all."

O'Rhyus's gaze never wavered, his voice steady. "It is not faith in the gods that will unite them, Aldous. It is faith in you. They do not need to see me to believe in the light. They will see it through you. Your life, your choices, will become the flame that draws them together."

The idea struck me, and for a moment, I was silent, letting his words sink in. I had always believed the gods were distant, unreachable, and yet here O'Rhyus stood before me, telling me that I was to become a living embodiment of his light. It was not just his power that would change the world, but my actions. My hands. My decisions.

"But what if I fail?" The question slipped out before I could stop it, my voice softer than before. "What if I'm not enough?"

O'Rhyus smiled then, a smile so filled with understanding that it felt like the warmth of the sun on a winter's morning. "You will not be alone. I am with you, always. You are not expected to be perfect, Aldous. You are expected to be true. Trust in your heart, in the light that guides you, and the path will reveal itself."

His hand rested on my shoulder, a gesture that carried more weight than any words could. I felt a surge of calm, of certainty, bloom within me. It wasn't that my fears were gone, but they no longer felt insurmountable. They were manageable, like stones along a road that could be navigated with patience and care.

"I will guide them," I said, finally finding my voice again, filled with more resolve than before. "I will bring order to the chaos."

O'Rhyus's eyes gleamed. "You already have."

And with those words, I knew the path had begun. The weight of his hand on my shoulder lingered even after he let go, as if the warmth of his presence had left a mark beneath my skin, deep in my bones. I could feel the shift within me—not a removal of fear, but a transformation of it. I was no longer burdened by uncertainty. Instead, it had become fuel for something greater, something that would guide me in the days ahead.

O'Rhyus stepped back, his radiant eyes never leaving mine.

"Lushahiem is the heart of Hyltoria," he said softly, "and from this heart, you will build a new world. You will not do this by force, Aldous, but by strength of will, by faith, and by showing them the light that lies within each of them."

I looked at him, truly taking in the meaning of his words. To bring order to the chaos was not to impose my will, but to nurture the will of others. To inspire them to rise above the discord, to see that together, they were stronger than they had ever been divided. The vision began to take shape in my mind, a world where tribes no longer fought for scraps of land, where the wild gods of the past no longer held them in fear. It would be a world where men looked to the sky and saw hope in the light, not shadows in the dark.

"But how do I begin?" I asked, my voice stronger now, though still edged with doubt with the task. "How do I unite them?"

"You begin with yourself," O'Rhyus replied, his tone never wavering. "The people of Hyltoria do not yet know you, Aldous. They have heard of you, but they do not know the man you are, the vision you carry. You must show them. You must let your light shine through your actions, your decisions. Do not seek to unite them by words alone—let them see what unity means in you."

I took a breath, allowing his words to settle deep within me. I had spent so much time thinking about the tribes, about the division between them, that I had forgotten something simple: I was just a man, one who could inspire by example. I didn't need to wield force or claim authority through fear. If I lived the truth of balance and order, others would follow.

"I understand," I said, and the words felt solid in my mouth, like stones shaped into a foundation.

"I will be the light they need. I will guide them as you have guided me." O'Rhyus smiled, a warm, approving expression that seemed to light the very air around us. "That is all that is required. Trust in yourself, Aldous. The light within you is strong enough to shape the world."

I nodded, feeling the truth of it settle in my chest. It wasn't just a command—this was a promise. A path laid before me, clear and unwavering. I was no longer just a man chosen by the gods; I was their instrument, their Shepherd, and through me, the world would be reborn.

O'Rhyus stepped back toward the window, the light of the setting sun framing his figure. "Your journey begins now," he said, his voice soft but resonant. "Lead them, Aldous. They are waiting for you."

With that, he vanished, leaving behind a lingering warmth in the air, and I stood there, ready for the first time. As O'Rhyus's presence faded from the room, a silence settled over me. It wasn't the kind of silence that came with uncertainty or hesitation; this was different. It was the kind of quiet that comes before a great storm—a calm that allowed everything to fall into place. I stood there, the weight of what had just transpired settling over me, and for the first time since I had been called to this path, I felt... ready.

I walked slowly toward the window where O'Rhyus had stood, the last traces of his light still shimmering in my mind. Outside, Lushahiem stretched beneath the twilight sky, the city calm but filled with untapped potential. The people were out there, going about their lives, unaware that their world had just changed. And I would be the one to guide them through it. A Shepherd, he had called me. The title still felt foreign in my mouth, though I understood its meaning. I wasn't chosen for my strength or for any great power I had wielded in the past. No, it was something deeper. Something I had carried with me all along. O'Rhyus had seen it in me, even when I had doubted myself. But as I stood there now, alone in the quiet of my quarters, I began to see what he had meant.

I thought of the wilds beyond the city, of the animals that roamed the forests and plains of Hyltoria. In the wilderness, strength was measured in many ways—size, speed, ferocity. And yet, none of those qualities alone determined who ruled. I thought of the lion, a creature neither the biggest nor the strongest. It was not the fastest, nor did it have the most fearsome appearance. The lion ruled not by physical dominance, but by something much greater. A mentality. It was the lion's mind—its belief in its own dominion—that made it the king. The lion didn't hesitate, didn't second-guess. It carried itself with the certainty of its place in the world, and because of that, the other animals recognized its power. The lion ruled because it believed in itself. It did not need to be the strongest; its mentality was its strength.

And now, I realized, that was the key for me. I didn't need to be the most powerful man in the world, nor the wisest. I didn't need to force the tribes to bend to my will with might or fear. What I needed was the mentality of a leader, the mentality to stand above the chaos and guide others through it. Like the lion, I would carry myself with the certainty of my purpose, and they would follow not because I demanded it, but because they would see that I believed in the path I walked. The people of Hyltoria were scattered, divided in mind and spirit, but it was not strength or speed that would bring them together. It was the mentality to rule, to guide, to lead them as a Shepherd leads his flock. I wasn't the biggest, the strongest, or the fastest. But I was chosen, and now I understand why. Like the lion, I would carry the certainty of my place, and they would see it. They would follow. Because I believed. And that belief, I knew, was the true power O'Rhyus had given me.

Chapter III

The Teather

The morning air was crisp, a light frost still clinging to the blades of grass beneath my boots as I moved through the trees just outside Wyldren. The scent of pine mixed with the earthiness of the forest, and I let it fill my lungs as I gathered what I needed for the morning meal. In my hand, I carried a small woven basket, now heavy with herbs and wild mushrooms, the ingredients for a simple breakfast. The sounds of the wilderness—birds chirping from the branches above, the gentle rustle of leaves as the wind passed through—kept me company as I moved through the woods with practiced ease. My fingers brushed the leaves of a nearby bush, finding the plump berries I knew grew there every autumn. Their rich sweetness would add the final touch to the meal. I plucked them carefully, one by one, tucking them into the folds of my basket. The routine, the quiet simplicity of it, brought a calm that settled in my chest like a warm stone. But beneath that calm was the steady pulse of something deeper, something far more powerful.

Vyhonia.

Her name lingered in my mind like a prayer, filling the spaces between the sounds of the forest. I moved with purpose, eager to return to her, my thoughts full of her warmth, the sound of her laugh, the way her eyes—the rich color of dark chocolate—seemed to catch the light in ways I could never quite describe. She was everything the wilds around me were not—soft, gentle and yet with a quiet strength that matched the trees towering above. I adjusted the basket in my hand, the thought of her pulling at my heart like a gentle tether, guiding me back through the woods. Her skin, the color of warm sand, had regained its healthy glow, and the memory of it made the corners of my mouth lift in a small, quiet smile. She had always been beautiful in the way that the land is beautiful—not ostentatious, but full of life, full of something real.

As I approached the edge of the clearing where our small cottage stood, I could already picture her standing by the hearth, her movements graceful, deliberate, even when performing the simplest tasks. She didn't need to be anyone but herself to make the world around her feel more at peace. She was just there, like the sunrise—constant and quietly magnificent. I crossed the threshold of our home, setting the basket down gently on the rough wooden table. I looked to the hearth and found her there, as I'd imagined, her hair falling in soft waves over her shoulders, the rich brown hue of it glowing in the early light of morning. Her eyes met mine, and in that single look, a thousand unspoken things passed between us. There was no need for words, no need to explain what I felt. It was all there, in the way I watched her move, in the way my hands, rough and calloused from the wilds, found the soft curve of her arm as I moved toward her. I could feel her heartbeat in the stillness between us, and in that moment, I knew: nothing mattered more than her. The cottage was filled with the soft warmth of the morning, the fire crackling gently in the hearth. The golden light streamed in through the small window, casting a gentle glow across the rough-hewn table where Vyhonia and I now sat. The scent of fresh herbs and wild mushrooms drifted in the air, mingling with the faint sweetness of the berries I had picked just moments before. I set the plates down between us, each one modest but thoughtfully prepared, and took my seat across from her.

Vyhonia smiled, a small, contented smile that lit her eyes in a way that always seemed to make the room brighter. Her fingers, delicate yet strong, brushed lightly over the edge of her plate as she looked down at the simple meal, then back up at me with a soft expression of gratitude that never needed to be spoken.

I watched her for a moment, my own breakfast forgotten as I took in the quiet beauty of the moment. Her hair, the deep brown of rich wood, framed her face in soft waves, and her skin, still glowing with the health that had returned to her, seemed to reflect the warm light of the morning. Her eyes met mine, and there was something in her gaze that held me there, anchored me in the peace of this moment.

We ate in comfortable silence at first, the sounds of the forest outside our window blending with the quiet clink of our utensils. The world outside felt distant, as though nothing existed beyond the walls of this small home. It was just us, the warmth of the hearth, and the food we shared. Her movements were slow, deliberate, and graceful. She reached for the berries, her fingertips lightly grazing mine as I passed them across the table, and for a moment, time seemed to stretch. There was no urgency, no need for words. Just the quiet intimacy of a meal shared, a life shared. The firelight danced across her face, highlighting the curve of her cheek, the softness of her lips, and I felt a swell of emotion rise in my chest, as familiar as it was profound. She took a bite of the berries, her smile widening ever so slightly as the sweetness touched her tongue.

"You always know just what to bring back," she said softly, her voice warm with affection. I chuckled, shrugging as I leaned back in my chair.

"I had good reason to choose carefully," I said, my eyes never leaving hers. "I knew I'd be sharing it with you."

Her laughter was soft, like the gentle rustle of leaves in a summer breeze. She reached across the table then, her hand finding mine, her fingers intertwining with mine in a gesture that was as natural as breathing. I could feel the warmth of her skin, the softness of her touch.

"I'm lucky to have you," she whispered, her voice low but filled with meaning.

I squeezed her hand, my own voice catching in my throat as I replied, "I am lucky, Vyhonia. Every day."

We sat like that for a while, hand in hand, the world outside forgotten as the fire crackled, and the morning sun bathed us in its light. In that moment, there was nothing but the two of us, and the love we shared in the quiet intimacy of this simple morning. As we sat there, the warmth of Vyhonia's hand in mine, I couldn't help but feel the contrast between this moment and everything that lay beyond our small home. The world outside was changing—shifting toward something darker, something colder. And within me, I could feel the shadows stirring, that power I had accepted from Apollyon settling deeper into my bones. It was a power that had saved Vyhonia's life, but it came with a weight I couldn't yet comprehend, a weight that pressed on me even now. I looked at her, the gentle curve of her smile, the way her eyes sparkled in the morning light, and I felt a sharp pang of guilt deep in my chest. She was healed, whole again, her beauty untouched by the sickness that had once threatened to take her from me. But I knew it hadn't come without cost. The power I had bargained for, the darkness I had embraced, was now a part of me. It moved within me like a shadow that stretched further with every passing day. She didn't know. I hadn't told her the full truth of what I had done. How could I? I had done it for her—because I couldn't bear the thought of a world without her. But now, as I sat across from her, my hand in hers, I felt that same darkness pull at me, a quiet reminder that the path I was on had no easy return.

The morning light filtered in through the window, casting a soft glow over her face, and for a moment, it was easy to forget what lay outside. The world seemed peaceful here, untouched by the chaos and turmoil that had begun to spread through Hyltoria. But I knew better. I had seen it firsthand—the fractures in the world, the tension between light and dark, the gods themselves in conflict.

And I was a part of it now.

I had made a choice, and that choice had consequences. The darkness I had embraced was not evil, not in the way the old stories told. But it was powerful, and it was relentless. It whispered to me in the quiet moments, just as it was now, reminding me that I had stepped into something far greater than myself. I had chosen to walk a path that few could follow, and though I had done it out of love, I couldn't deny the darkness that had settled into my soul. Vyhonia's fingers squeezed mine gently, pulling me from my thoughts. She tilted her head, her brow furrowing just slightly as she looked at me, a hint of concern in her eyes.

"You're quiet this morning," she said softly, her voice like a balm against the heaviness in my chest.

I managed a small smile, though it didn't reach my eyes. "Just... thinking."

She didn't press me, but her gaze lingered on mine, searching. She had always been able to see deeper than anyone else, and though I knew she couldn't understand the full weight of what I carried, she sensed that something had changed. The man sitting across from her was not the same man who had left in search of a cure. I was different now. Darker. But I was still hers. And that, more than anything, was what I had to hold onto in the rising storm of the world beyond.

The day unfolded with a comforting rhythm, one that felt like a remedy to the unease lingering just beneath my skin. After breakfast, Vyhonia and I set about our usual tasks, each of us falling into the familiar routine of our life here in Wyldren. She tended to the small garden behind the cottage, her hands working gently through the soil, while I prepared to head out into the wilderness to hunt. The air was crisp and clear, the faint scent of pine and earth filling my lungs as I gathered my tools—the bow, the knife, the arrows I'd fletched by hand.

This was how it had always been. The simple life we had built together, far from the turmoil of the world, nestled here in the heart of the wilderness. And yet, despite the normalcy of it all, I couldn't shake the feeling that something was coming. Something dark, something I had invited into my life with that single, fateful choice.

Vyhonia caught my eye as I slung the quiver over my shoulder, her dark hair falling loosely around her face as she tended the garden. Her smile was soft, filled with the kind of warmth that could melt even the coldest of mornings. I smiled back, though a part of me couldn't help but wonder if she sensed it too—that subtle shift in the air, the quiet waiting that had settled over our lives since I had returned.

"Be safe out there," she said, her voice carrying that same gentle concern she always had when I went into the woods alone.

"I always am," I replied, though this time the words felt heavier than usual. She didn't press, just nodded, and I turned toward the forest, letting the trees swallow me up.

The wilderness greeted me with the same familiar sounds—the rustle of leaves in the wind, the chirping of distant birds, the occasional crackle of twigs underfoot. My boots pressed into the soft earth as I moved deeper into the woods, my senses attuned to the subtle signs of life hidden among the trees. This was my life—hunting, gathering, providing for the two of us. It had always been enough, and yet now, in the shadow of what I had agreed to with Apollyon, it felt... insufficient. I was waiting for something, though I didn't know what.

The thought lingered at the back of my mind as I tracked a deer through the forest, the familiar motions of the hunt grounding me even as my mind wandered. What exactly was I waiting for? Apollyon had told me to wait, to be patient. He had said O'Rhyus would feel the shift, he would come for me. But what would that mean? Would I be asked to fight, to strike down the very god I had once prayed to? Or was it something else entirely—something darker, something I couldn't yet comprehend?

The darkness I had accepted into myself, the balance between light and shadow, was still settling within me, like a river of black ink winding through my soul. And though I could feel its power, though I knew it had saved Vyhonia's life, there was a part of me that feared it. It was a tool, yes, but it was also dangerous. It whispered to me sometimes, quiet and insistent, reminding me that I was no longer the man I had been before. But I was still waiting. Waiting for something more.

The deer I had been tracking moved quietly through the trees, its slender form barely visible through the underbrush. I crouched low, my bow drawn, the arrow's tip steady as I watched, waited, and let the rhythm of the hunt take over. When the moment came, I released the arrow, watching as it found its mark. The deer stumbled, then fell, the forest falling silent around me. I moved quickly, making the kill clean and swift, then began the process of preparing the animal to bring back home. As I worked, the routine of it, the focus on survival, quieted my thoughts for a time. Here in the wilderness, among the trees and the land, things were simple. There was no darkness to contend with, no waiting for gods or the promises they had made. Just life and death, the cycle of nature that had always been. But even as I gathered the meat and wrapped it in my pack, that quiet voice returned, the one that reminded me I was no longer just a hunter. I had made a pact with something far greater, something that would demand more of me than this simple life. I couldn't ignore it, couldn't pretend that things were as they had always been. Apollyon had promised me power, but that power came with a price, and I had yet to understand what that price would truly be.

By the time I returned home, the sun was beginning to set, casting long shadows over the village. Vyhonia greeted me with a kiss on the cheek, her eyes lighting up at the sight of the deer meat I had brought back. We worked together to prepare dinner, moving around each other with the ease that came from years of shared routine. The fire crackled in the hearth, casting a warm glow over the small cottage as we sat down to eat, and for a moment, everything felt right again. But as the night deepened and Vyhonia drifted to sleep beside me, that sense of waiting returned, more insistent than ever. I lay awake, staring at the ceiling, the darkness outside pressing in like a living thing. I knew it was coming—whatever Apollyon had set in motion, it was drawing closer. And though the darkness inside me felt still for now, I could sense its restlessness, like a predator waiting to pounce. Sleep came eventually, pulling me under like the slow drag of a tide. But even in sleep, the darkness followed.

I found myself in a place that was neither here nor there—a dream, but more than a dream. The air was thick with shadows, the ground beneath my feet shifting like sand. In the distance, a figure stood, tall and cloaked in black, his form unmistakable.

Apollyon.

He moved toward me with the same effortless grace I had seen before, his presence filling the space around us as if the shadows themselves bent to his will. His eyes gleamed, cold and piercing, as he stopped just in front of me, his smile sharp and knowing.

"You've waited well, Vicrum," he said, his voice low and smooth. "But the time for waiting is almost over."

I stared at him, my heart pounding in my chest even though I knew this was not the waking world. "What do you mean?" I asked, my voice sounding strange in the dreamlike haze.

Apollyon's smile widened, though it held no warmth. "O'Rhyus knows. He feels the shift, the darkness you have embraced. He is preparing, just as I am. But before the storm comes, there is still much for you to understand."

The shadows around us shifted, swirling like a living thing, and I felt the familiar pull of the power inside me, the darkness that had become a part of me. It was stronger now, more insistent, as if it was answering to Apollyon's call.

"You are no longer just a man, Vicrum," Apollyon continued, his voice like a whisper carried on the wind. "You are something more. And soon, you will need to prove it. O'Rhyus will come for you, but not as you expect. He will not come to destroy you, not yet. First, he will try to sway you, to bring you back into his light."

I frowned, the weight of his words settling over me like a heavy cloak. "And if I refuse?"

Apollyon's eyes gleamed, his smile never faltering. "Then you will face him, as I have faced him. And when the time comes, you will choose your path." The weight of Apollyon's words still heavy in my mind. The room was quiet, except for the soft crackle of the dying fire and the steady rhythm of Vyhonia's breath beside me. Outside, the night pressed against the windows, cold and silent. Yet inside me, there was nothing but the relentless hum of the darkness that had been awakened by Apollyon. I ran a hand through my hair, trying to shake off the remnants of sleep, but the vision from the dream remained clear. Apollyon had come to me, not just with a warning, but with a command. The time for waiting was over. A war was coming.

"At the next gathering of the thirteen provinces. During the spring celebration in the month of Eldriske."

The thought made my blood run cold. The thirteen provinces of Hyltoria had been divided for generations, each leader ruling their land with their own vision, their own priorities. Some still clung to the ancient ways, others had turned away from the gods entirely. And now I was expected to unite them, to bring them together for a cause that most wouldn't understand, a cause that wasn't even fully clear to me. Apollyon's voice had been calm but unyielding in the dream. He had stood before me, his eyes gleaming with the weight of a coming storm.

"A war is coming, Vicrum. The balance is shifting, and O'Rhyus will not sit idly by. You must call them to arms. Make them see what is at stake. Only then will you be ready for what's to come."

I exhaled slowly as I stared into the darkness. A call to arms. The very idea of it felt impossible. I had lived my life in the wilderness, a leader, a hunter, a man who had always stayed far from the politics and power struggles of the provinces. Now, Apollyon expected me to stand before the leaders of Hyltoria and convince them to unite against a threat they couldn't even see. But there had been something else in Apollyon's words, something that had sent a shiver through me even as I stood in the dream.

"At the meeting, you will need to sow seeds of doubt amongst the leaders, show them that who O'Rhyus has chosen to champion his light is still capable of failure."

I knew what that meant. O'Rhyus, the god of light, would not let this war unfold without his own hand in the battle. He would choose someone, just as Apollyon had chosen me, to stand against the darkness I had embraced. It wouldn't be just a war of men, but a clash between those who carried the power of gods. My heart felt heavy as I turned away from the window. I could still hear Apollyon's voice in my head, clear and unyielding.

"Prepare yourself, Vicrum. When the time comes, you will face them all, and you will decide the future of this world."

The war was coming. And I had no choice but to answer the call.

Chapter IV

The Enlightened

The gardens of Lushahiem were a sanctuary, a place where the wilderness and order converged. Each plant, each bloom, had its place, yet there was still a sense of untamed life in every leaf. As I walked along the pathways, the quiet of the garden offered me a rare moment of peace, but also a space for the gravity of my role to settle deep within me. I was Aldous, chosen by O'Rhyus to be the first Shepherd, tasked with bringing order to the chaos that threatened to consume the world. Yet, even as I breathed in the fragrant air, I found myself grappling with what that truly meant. Could one man really bring order to a world so vast and fractured? Could I, with all my uncertainties, truly lead humanity to the harmony that O'Rhyus envisioned?

I found a quiet bench near a pond where the water rippled gently under the light breeze. Sitting there, I let my thoughts drift to the divine being who had chosen me, to the history that had shaped him into the Guardian of Light, and what that would mean for me in the days ahead.

O'Rhyus had not always been the radiant figure who now watched over Nantrium. His origins were as humble as the forces that shaped him—born from the eternal struggle between life and death, light and dark. In the time before time, when the world was still young and chaos ruled all things, O'Rhyus emerged as a being of balance. He was not created by the gods, nor was he born from some grand cosmic plan. Instead, he ascended from the raw forces of creation, a spirit who sought to bring order where there was none.

In the beginning, Nantrium was a place where nothing was certain. Life bloomed and withered in the same breath, Death claimed and released without reason. It was a world in turmoil, and it was from this turmoil that O'Rhyus rose. He saw that without balance, the world would unravel, and so he became its guardian. He gathered the light to himself, wearing it as a mantle, and stood against the chaos that threatened to consume all things.

O'Rhyus was not a god of war or wrath. His power was in creation, in guiding the forces of life toward something sustainable, something harmonious. It was through his divine touch that mankind was born—he churned the seafoam into life, shaping humanity with his hands and granting them the right to rule over the lands of Nantrium. These humans were not ordinary mortals; they were given the spark of the divine, the ability to bring order to the chaos of the world. They were his chosen, meant to carry forth his vision of balance and harmony.

And so, O'Rhyus became more than just a god. He became the embodiment of light itself, a force dedicated to maintaining the delicate equilibrium between life and death, creation and destruction. It was his will that gave rise to the Divine Rulers, men and women imbued with his power to govern the lands of Nantrium. I, Aldous, had been chosen to walk that path, to carry the mantle of Shepherd. But now, as I sat in the gardens, I couldn't help but wonder: how does one truly follow in the footsteps of a god?

The answer, I realized, lay not in strength or power, but in the unwavering pursuit of balance. O'Rhyus had risen not because he was the strongest, but because he had seen the necessity of harmony. That was the lesson I had to carry with me as I led the people of Hyltoria. But that didn't ease the weight of what I was meant to do—it only made it heavier, for to be a Shepherd meant to walk the fine line between light and dark, between chaos and order.

As I continued my walk through the gardens, I let my mind wander further. Nantrium was a world of contrasts, a place that existed as a bridge between Life and Death, light and dark. The balance O'Rhyus sought to protect was not just a metaphor—it was woven into the very fabric of the realm. I had grown up hearing stories of the lands that stretched far beyond Lushahiem, of the places where the forces of Life and Death met, where the gods themselves had walked.

One such place was the Cliffs of Kings, a paradise where O'Rhyus had first created mankind. The cliffs were said to rise high above the oceans, a place where the veil between Life and Death was thinnest, where the first Divine Ruler had been given his crown. It was a place of peace, of harmony, where the balance between the forces of nature was at its most perfect. But that balance was fragile, always at risk of being shattered by forces beyond mortal control.

Lushahiem, the capital of the Hyltoria, had been built in the image of that harmony. Its walls were high, its streets orderly, its people dedicated to maintaining the peace that O'Rhyus had bestowed upon us. The city itself was a symbol of control and order, a beacon of light in a world that often teetered on the edge of chaos. As Shepherd, it was my task to ensure that the order of Lushahiem extended to the rest of the O' Rhyus's land, to bring the teachings of O'Rhyus to the farthest reaches of the realm.

But Nantrium was not without its dark places. There was the Inbetween, a mysterious realm that few dared to speak of. It was said to be the prison of Apollyon, the god of darkness, who had once walked alongside O'Rhyus before being cast down into the shadows. The Inbetween was a place of chaos, where the rules of Life and Death held no sway, where light could not reach. It was from there that Apollyon sought to spread his corruption, slowly turning men to his cause with promises of power and freedom from the constraints of order.

The world of Nantrium was fragile, constantly teetering between the light of O'Rhyus and the darkness of Apollyon. As I walked through the garden, I couldn't help but feel the tension between those forces. The balance was delicate, and I knew that the decisions I made in the coming days would either help preserve that balance or tip it toward chaos.

Divine power flowed through Nantrium like the rivers that carved through its landscapes, influencing both the mortal and divine realms. It was a force that could not be seen, but its presence was felt in everything. O'Rhyus had granted humanity divine rights, creating the line of Divine Rulers who governed the lands with the light of his power. I was one of them now, a Shepherd tasked with guiding mankind toward balance. But divine power was not without its dangers. O'Rhyus's light was pure, but it was also exacting. It demanded balance, harmony, and control. To wield such power required not only strength, but wisdom—the ability to see beyond the immediate and understand the greater picture. It was a burden, one that could either uplift or destroy those who bore it. I knew this all too well. The moment O'Rhyus had chosen me, I had felt the weight of that power settle upon my shoulders. It wasn't just the ability to command; it was the responsibility of maintaining the balance that Nantrium relied upon. To fail in that task would not just mean the collapse of O' Rhyus's land—it could mean the unraveling of the world itself. Yet, divine power did not belong to O'Rhyus alone. Apollyon, too, wielded a different kind of power, one born from the chaos of darkness. While O'Rhyus sought to maintain balance, Apollyon reveled in its disruption. He spread his influence through corruption, turning men away from the light with promises of power, fear, and freedom from the constraints of order. I had heard whispers of men who had fallen under his sway, leaders who sought power for themselves at the expense of the world's balance.

The provinces of Hyltoria were diverse, each with its own way of life, its own beliefs. Some still followed the teachings of O'Rhyus, while others had turned away, lured by the darker promises of Apollyon. How would I, a single man, unite them? How could I bring them together under the light of O'Rhyus when the darkness was spreading so quickly? It was then, as I pondered this, that I was interrupted by the arrival of a messenger. The young man was out of breath, his cloak dusted with the earth of the roads he had traveled. He bowed deeply before speaking.

"Aldous, I bring news. The leader of Wyldren, Vicrum, accepted our invitation for a gathering of the provinces. With him all the leaders of Hyltoria have responded. They will arrive in the month of Eldriske, once the snows have melted."

I thanked the messenger and dismissed him, but my thoughts continued to churn. Vicrum... the name tugged at something in the back of my mind, a whisper of something important, though I couldn't yet place it. As I stood there, watching the sun sink lower in the sky, I realized that the war between light and dark was not some distant threat. It was here, in the very heart of Nantrium. And I would soon face it head-on. The month of Eldriske would soon be upon us, and with it, the meeting of the leaders of Hyltoria. The snow would melt, the paths would open, and the leaders of the thirteen provinces would make their way to Lushahiem. They would come, some with hope, some with fear, and others with agendas I could not yet fathom. And in the midst of it all, there was Vicrum, the man who never attends the assembly.

I knew nothing of him beyond what the others had told me, but I could sense that he was no ordinary leader. The world was changing, and this assembly would be the first step toward understanding what was truly at stake. Apollyon's influence was spreading. I could feel it in the tension that hung in the air, in the way the shadows seemed to stretch longer with each passing day. O'Rhyus had warned me of this, but now, I was beginning to see the scope of the battle that lay ahead. The war between light and dark was not just a divine conflict—it was a war that would be fought in the hearts and minds of men. I would have to face the leaders of Hyltoria, convince them of the coming danger, and somehow unite them under the light of O'Rhyus. But even as I prepared myself for the task, a darker thought tugged at the edges of my mind. At the assembly, we could discover who had been chosen to carry the darkness of Apollyon. I stood there, in the fading light of the garden, knowing that the balance of Nantrium was more fragile than ever. The coming days would decide the future of the world, and I, as Shepherd, would be at the center of it all.

Chapter V

The Gathering

The great hall of Lushahiem shimmered in the early morning light, a majestic symbol of Hyltoria's power and unity. The preparations for this day had been meticulous. Every detail, from the polished stone floors to the banners of the thirteen provinces hanging from the vaulted ceiling, was a testament to the weight of this historic moment. I stood at the center of the hall, flanked by the towering columns that lined the walls, awaiting the arrival of the leaders of Nantrium. There were thirteen provinces, each with its own customs, strengths, and challenges. Today, they would come together—some reluctantly, some eager—but all aware that the times were changing. I had made the final preparations for the assembly, and now there was nothing left to do but wait. As the first leader entered the hall, I drew in a deep breath, steeling myself for the task that lay ahead.

Lord Vaedric was the first to arrive. The Patron of Finela moved with a grace and dignity that belied the hardships his people had endured over the centuries. Finela, one of the oldest provinces, was a land known for its ancient nobility and the resilience of its people. Lord Vaedric himself embodied these traits: tall, regal, with silver hair braided in intricate patterns down his back. His sharp blue eyes reflected a lifetime of leadership, and he wore the traditional robes of his province, embroidered with desert flowers and palm trees, the symbols of his ancestors.

"Aldous," Lord Vaedric said, his voice both warm and

commanding, "it is an honor to stand here in Lushahiem. I trust this gathering will yield wisdom worthy of the great history of Nantrium."

I inclined my head in greeting. "Lord Vaedric, the honor is mine. Your wisdom and counsel are greatly needed in these times."

He smiled faintly, a knowing smile that told me He understood the gravity of what was coming. Lord Vaedric took his place at the long table, his presence bringing an immediate sense of stability to the hall.

Next came Master Zephyros, the ethereal leader of Cloud Fall, a province known for its connection to the skies. He seemed to glide into the room, his robes a soft blue that matched the sky at dawn. His movements were graceful, almost otherworldly, and his silver eyes carried the distant look of one who had spent years contemplating the mysteries of the heavens. The people of Cloud Fall were known for their mystical ways, their deep understanding of the elements, and their profound sense of wonder.

"Shepherd Aldous," Master Zephyros said with a voice as soft as the wind, "Always a pleasure to be in your grace."

"Your presence is the blessing, Master Zephyros," I replied, shaking his hand. "Your insight will be invaluable."

Master Zephyros's gaze lingered on the banners for a moment, as if reading the winds of fate themselves, before he moved to take his seat next to Lord Vaedric. The two exchanged a brief, respectful nod—an acknowledgment of ancient alliances.

The calm that Master Zephyros brought was shattered by the entrance of King Rhalor, the Warlord of Alatok. Clad in heavy armor that clanked with each step, King Rhalor embodied the strength and authority of his warrior province. Alatok had long been known for its disciplined armies and battle-hardened leaders, and King Rhalor was no exception. His dark hair was pulled back tightly, and his stern face showed no signs of softness.

"Aldous," King Rhalor said in a booming voice that echoed through the hall, "Alatok is thriving, maintaining the southern provinces. How is Lushaheim?"

I grasped his forearm in greeting, feeling the strength in his grip. "King Rhalor I assure you, your strength will be crucial for the balance of all Nantrium."

King Rhalor nodded curtly, clearly eager for action but understanding the necessity of discussion. He took his place at the table, his armor clinking as he sat, his hand never far from the hilt of the sword at his side.

A sense of unease filled the hall as Lady Morvyn of the island of Inilyus arrived. Her dark cloak flowed behind her like smoke, and her face was partially hidden beneath a hood. Inilyus was a province shrouded in mystery, a land of deep forests and ancient magic. Lady Morvyn was as much a mystery as her people, her movements silent and deliberate. Her eyes, glowing faintly in the dim light, seemed to pierce through the shadows of the hall.

"Aldous," she said softly, her voice like a whisper carried on the wind, "the forces that gather are darker than the night. What you ask of us cannot be taken lightly."

I held her gaze, sensing the depth of her knowledge and the power she wielded. "Nothing about this is light, Lady Morvyn. Your insight into the shadows will help us understand what we face."

She smiled slightly, a hint of something unreadable in her expression, before moving to her seat with barely a sound. As she passed King Rhalor, the warrior stiffened, clearly uncomfortable with her presence, but said nothing.

Lord Thyldar, the regal Lord of Hyanasarri, was the next to enter. His dark robes, adorned with silver and deep blues, spoke of a province with a long and proud history of kings and noble bloodlines. He moved with the confidence of a man who carried the weight of centuries on his shoulders, his sharp features and streaks of silver in his hair lending him an air of wisdom.

"Shepherd Aldous," Lord Thyldar greeted me with a measured bow, his voice deep and steady. "The people of Hyanasarri stand ready to support the unity of Nantrium, as they always have."

"Your presence strengthens us all, Lord Thyldar," I said. "Your counsel will be critical in the decisions we face."

He gave a curt nod, his eyes scanning the room with a strategist's gaze, and took his seat with the grace of a king. The ancient power of Hyanasarri seemed to emanate from him.

Durion of Hyndale followed, his large frame and strong hands marking him as a man of the land. The people of Hyndale were known for their hard work, their dedication to the earth, and their loyalty to tradition. Durion embodied these traits perfectly. He wore simple, well-made clothes, practical for the demands of daily life in his province.

"Aldous," Durion said with a firm handshake, his voice deep and grounded, "the people of Hyndale are ready to do their part. We know the value of hard work and unity."

"Your strength lies in your people, Durion," I replied. "And their resilience will be vital in the days to come."

He nodded in agreement, his face serious but calm. Durion took his place, a pillar of reliability amidst the more politically charged figures at the table.

Vandrel of Talvanofa entered next, a vision of grace and elegance. He was a tall, slender man, his robes flowing with a natural grace as he moved. Talvanofa was a province known for its beauty, its culture, and its artistry, and Vandrel was the embodiment of that elegance. His dark hair, streaked with silver, was tied back, and his calm, measured steps echoed the rhythm of a man accustomed to the simpler things in life.

"Aldous," Vandrel said with a warm smile, his voice smooth and cultured, "it is a pleasure to be here. The people of Talvanofa stand ready to offer their wisdom and grace to the cause of unity."

"Your wisdom is always welcome, Vandrel," I replied. "We will need your grace as much as your strength in the days ahead."

Vandrel bowed slightly, his smile never fading as he took his seat, his presence adding an air of refinement to the gathering.

Belric entered with the quiet strength of a man who had weathered many storms. His clothes, though simple, carried the unmistakable marks of a seasoned sailor, and his skin was tanned from years spent under the harsh sun and salty winds of the sea. The Port of Alfy was rich in trade and maritime history, and Belric was its respected leader. His eyes were sharp, scanning the room like a captain surveying a stormy sea.

"Aldous," Belric said with a respectful nod, his voice rough from years of shouting commands across the deck of a ship, "the seas have been restless. I hope we can calm the waters with what we discuss here."

"We can only hope, Belric," I replied. "Your strength and knowledge of the seas will be invaluable."

He grunted, his expression hard but respectful, and took his seat, his eyes constantly assessing the room as if waiting for the next wave to crash.

The entrance of Eldrith sent a shiver down the spines of many in the room. The Keeper of Mophia was a tall, thin man draped in dark robes, his pale skin contrasting sharply with the blackness that surrounded him. His eyes were sharp, almost predatory, and his thin fingers moved constantly, as if weaving spells even as he walked. Mophia was a land of ancient, arcane knowledge, and Eldrith was its keeper—one of the most powerful magic users in all of Nantrium.

"Aldous," Eldrith said in a voice that was almost a whisper, yet seemed to carry throughout the hall, "I sense that darkness is gathering. What do you intend to do about it?"

"We intend to face it, Eldrith," I replied evenly. "But we will need the knowledge of Mophia to guide us through the shadows."

He smiled, a thin, unsettling smile, and took his seat, his eyes never leaving me as though already reading the future that lay ahead.

Fenric the Lord of Wolfshire moved like a predator, his steps silent, his gaze piercing. Wolfshire was a province tied to the wilds, its people known for their fierce loyalty to the hunt and the primal forces of nature. Fenric himself was tall and broad, his dark hair and beard giving him the look of a wolf on the prowl.

"Aldous," Fenric said with a low growl, his voice carrying the weight of the wilds, "the wolves are restless."

I clasped his hand in greeting. "Your instincts will be needed, Fenric. The balance between the wilds and the cities is more delicate than ever."

He nodded, his eyes sharp and focused, before taking his seat, his presence a constant reminder of the untamed forces that still roamed the lands of Nantrium.

And then, finally, there was Vicrum. He entered the hall with a presence that could not be ignored—a brute of a man, his head shaved and a thick fur coat draped over his broad shoulders. Wyldren was the oldest province in Nantrium, even older than Lushahiem itself. Vicrum was its leader, a man known for his strength and cunning. His dark eyes met mine with an intensity that made the air in the room feel heavier.

"Aldous," Vicrum said, his voice low and rough, "You've called for this meeting for a reason. Wyldren would like to hear what you have to offer."

I held his gaze, feeling the weight of his words. "Then let us discuss what must be done, Vicrum."

He nodded and took his place at the table, the final piece in this gathering of the thirteen.

With all the leaders of Nantrium seated before me, the weight of what was to come pressed heavily on my shoulders. This was no ordinary assembly. These were the rulers of the provinces, each with their own strengths, their own ambitions, and their own fears. And now, they were gathered in Lushahiem to prepare for what was coming.

The balance of light and dark had begun to shift, and what we decided here would shape the future of all Nantrium.

"Let us begin," I said, my voice steady but filled with the gravity of what was to come.

Chapter VI

The Tear

The long table at the heart of the great hall stretched before me, filled with the voices of the twelve leaders of Nantrium. Their banners hung above them, swaying gently in the draft from the open windows, each one a symbol of the strength and pride of their provinces. The room was lit by the dancing glow from the many torches, casting shadows that danced on the stone walls. It was here that history would be made, alliances forged—or broken—depending on the words spoken today. I sat quietly, my hands resting on the heavy oak table, observing the tension that filled the air. Around me, the leaders voiced their concerns and grievances, some raising their voices in opposition while others sought to find common ground. My eyes lingered on each leader as they spoke, cataloging their arguments, their fears, and their desires. And though I appeared alone, I was not.

Apollyon stood beside me, unseen by the others, a dark figure looming over the assembly with an amused smile. His presence was like a shadow at the edge of my vision, a constant reminder of the pact I had made. His voice, low and smooth, echoed in my mind as he whispered his advice.

"Listen carefully, Vicrum," Apollyon murmured, his words laced with a quiet confidence. "These leaders are not as united as they pretend. Division is your weapon, and trust will be your key to power."

As he spoke, I observed the room more intently, focusing on the alliances and fractures forming around the table. There were those who supported Aldous, and those who opposed him. The leaders of Cloud Fall, Hyndale, Bodaccia, and Talvanofa were clearly aligned with Aldous, their bond evident in the way they spoke and nodded in agreement with each other.

Zephyros, Master of Cloud Fall, was the first to speak. His ethereal voice carried a tone of serene authority, though there was an underlying urgency in his words.

"We cannot afford to be divided in the face of what is coming," Zephyros said, his eyes scanning the room. "Aldous is our best chance at maintaining balance in Nantrium. He has been chosen by O'Rhyus, the Guardian of Light, to guide us through these dark times. We should all stand with him."

Durion, the Steward of Hyndale, nodded in agreement, his deep voice rumbling across the hall. "Zephyros is right. Hyndale will stand with Aldous. If we fail to unite now, we will only be feeding the chaos that threatens our world."

Vandrel of Talvanofa leaned forward, his hands folded elegantly on the table. "We have fought too long for our provinces, our people. This is not the time to turn inward. We must support Aldous if we wish to see Nantrium thrive beyond these troubled times."

Belric, the Lord of the Port of Alfy, sat quietly, his tanned face weathered from years of sea air, watching the discussion with a wary eye. He had yet to voice his opinion, and I could see the hesitation in him, the conflict of choosing a side. As the leaders of Aldous's camp rallied for support, the opposition was swift to respond.

Lord Vaedric of Finela, his silver hair gleaming in the

torchlight, spoke with the sharp authority of someone who had ruled her province for many years. His eyes flashed with defiance as he addressed the room.

"Aldous is a symbol of a fading order," Lord Vaedric said, his voice cutting through the air. "We have been following the light of O'Rhyus for centuries, and yet the darkness still rises. Perhaps it is time for a new approach, one that does not rely on the old ways."

Rhalor, the Warlord of Alatok, banged his fist on the table, his heavy armor clanking with the motion. "We are warriors, not servants to gods! Aldous may be the chosen of O'Rhyus, but what has that brought us? More battles, more bloodshed! I refuse to bend the knee to a man just because he claims divine favor."

Morvyn, the enigmatic Lady of Inilyus, leaned back in her chair, her hood casting shadows over her face. "The forces at play here are beyond what we see on the surface. Aldous may carry the favor of O'Rhyus, but the balance between light and darkness is delicate. We must be cautious of where we place our trust."

Eldrith, the Keeper of Mophia, added his voice to the opposition, his tone cold and calculated. "Aldous is young, untested in the ways of true power. Mophia will not align with a leader who does not fully understand the forces he is wielding."

I watched them closely, noting the strength of their resolve, and yet there was something underneath their defiance—something I could exploit. Apollyon's voice drifted back into my mind.

"They speak with conviction, but even they are uncertain.

There is fear in their words. Fear of the unknown. Use it."
I nodded subtly, understanding the unspoken command. Fear was the greatest motivator, and I could already see the cracks forming in the alliances around the table. But first, I needed to continue listening, to understand how to sow the seeds of doubt.
At the far end of the table, Fenric, Lord of Wolfshire, sat in silence, his sharp eyes surveying the room like a predator stalking its prey. The people of Wolfshire were fiercely independent, tied to the wilds and the hunt. Fenric had little interest in the politics of the cities, and his neutrality was as much a defense mechanism as it was a statement of power.
Beside him, Belric, Lord of the Port of Alfy finally spoke, his voice rough from years spent commanding ships at sea. "The Port of Alfy is a place of trade, of neutrality. We have always remained apart from the conflicts of the mainland. But even I can see that something is coming. The question is not whether we join forces, but whether we are ready for what lies beyond our borders."
Fenric grunted in agreement. "The wilds are restless. We don't care for the cities' wars, but if chaos spills into our lands, we'll be ready to defend ourselves. Whether that means standing with Aldous or against him, I have yet to decide."
The room was divided. Cloud Fall, Hyndale, Bodaccia, and Talvanofa stood firmly with Aldous. Inilyus, Alatok, Finela, and Mophia were in staunch opposition. Wolfshire and the Port of Alfy remained neutral, watching and waiting for the tides to shift
Then there was Lord Thyldar of Hyanasarri, who had been

listening quietly throughout the conversation. His province was known for its ancient bloodlines and its long history of isolation. Thyldar's dark eyes gleamed with disdain as he finally spoke, his voice dripping with arrogance.

"Hyanasarri will not be dragged into the squabbles of lesser provinces," he said, his tone regal and commanding. "We have ruled our lands for generations, far removed from the chaos of the rest of Nantrium. I would sooner sail to the edge of the world than align with Aldous or any of you for that matter. Our people do not need to be part of this war."

The tension in the room rose as Thyldar's words hung in the air. His refusal to join either side was not unexpected, but it added another layer of complexity to the already fractured alliance.

Apollyon leaned closer to me, his cold breath brushing against my ear. "Thyldar's arrogance will be his downfall. But he is right about one thing—the time for indecision is over. Now is the moment to act, Vicrum. Show them the path."

As the conversation continued around me, Apollyon's voice filled my mind, guiding me with quiet authority. "Use their fear. They are afraid of the unknown, afraid of losing power. Speak to their insecurities, and they will fall in line."

I cleared my throat and leaned forward slightly, drawing the attention of the room. The voices quieted, and all eyes turned toward me. For a moment, I let the silence stretch, feeling the weight of the decision that lay before us all.

"Aldous has been chosen by O'Rhyus," I said, my voice steady and calm, "but that does not mean he is infallible. The gods have their own plans, and we must be careful not to blindly follow anyone, even one blessed by the light. The darkness is growing, and it will not be stopped by the strength of one man alone."

I let my gaze sweep across the room, locking eyes with each leader in turn. "We must be united, yes, but unity does not mean submission. Aldous may carry the favor of O'Rhyus, but we are the rulers of Nantrium. We must make our own decisions, for our people, for our lands. The coming storm will not spare those who hesitate."

There was a murmur of agreement, but also hesitation. I could see the doubt in the faces of those who opposed Aldous, and the growing concern in the eyes of those who supported him.

Apollyon's voice whispered again. "Well done, Vicrum. Now, offer them something they cannot refuse."

I continued, my voice gaining strength. "We cannot afford to fight among ourselves. Whether you support Aldous or not, we all face the same threat. The darkness is coming, and it will not distinguish between friend and foe. We must prepare for war, but we must also prepare for survival. If we are to face this together, then let us decide how we will stand—not as followers, but as equals."

The room fell silent, the weight of my words sinking in. I could see the wheels turning in their minds, the seeds of doubt and fear taking root. They were beginning to realize that their survival depended on more than just blind loyalty to Aldous.

Apollyon's smile widened, though none but I could see it. "They are yours now, Vicrum. Soon, they will follow you."

As the final murmurs of discussion quieted, Aldous reflected. He was a striking figure, clean-cut with light eyes and dark hair. His skin was tanned from years spent under the sun, and he wore armor of gleaming gold, with a burgundy cape flowing behind him. He looked every bit the chosen of O'Rhyus, a beacon of light in the darkened hall.

The room fell silent as Aldous pondered, his presence commanding the attention of every leader in the room. His eyes swept over the assembly, and I could see the weight of his responsibility reflected in them. He knew what was at stake, just as I did. But unlike me, Aldous carried the favor of the gods. He was the chosen one of O'Rhyus, and that made him both a powerful ally and a dangerous enemy.

Apollyon's voice was a quiet hiss in my ear. "He is O'Rhyus's pawn, but even pawns can be toppled. Watch him closely, Vicrum. His light cannot last forever."

Aldous took a breath, the room waiting for the chosen Shepherd to speak. The balance of power in Nantrium hung by a thread, and I knew that the decisions made in this room would shape the future of the world. But I was no longer content to sit in the shadows. The time had come to step into the light and take control of my destiny.

Aldous looked across the table, his light eyes calm but assessing. His voice, when he spoke, was steady, but there was a firmness to it that demanded attention.

"We stand on the edge of a precipice," Aldous said, his gaze sweeping over the leaders. "The darkness is growing, and it seeks to consume all that we have built. O'Rhyus has entrusted me with the task of guiding Nantrium through this storm, but I cannot do it alone. I need each of you to stand with me, to unite under a common purpose."

There was silence in the hall, a silence that weighed heavily on every word. Aldous's call for unity was not unexpected, but it was met with varying degrees of skepticism and concern.

Lord Vaedric, always quick to speak his mind, leaned forward, his sharp eyes fixed on Aldous. "And what of those who do not wish to follow you blindly, Aldous? Must we all bow to the will of O'Rhyus simply because you wear his favor?"

Aldous met his gaze evenly. "No one is being asked to bow. We are all leaders here. But we must recognize the danger that lies ahead. This is not a time for division. If we do not stand together, the darkness will tear us apart."

King Rhalor was the next to speak, his voice rough and filled with suspicion. "I am a warrior, Aldous. My loyalty is to my people, not to the whims of gods. What guarantees do we have that following you will lead to anything other than more bloodshed?"

Aldous's expression remained calm, though I could see the strain in his posture. He was holding the weight of the world on his shoulders, and it was beginning to show.

"There are no guarantees in war, King Rhalor. But I believe in the light of O'Rhyus, and I believe that together, we can overcome the darkness. If alone, we will fall."

The room buzzed with murmurs of uncertainty and dissent. The leaders were divided, and Aldous's plea for unity was falling on deaf ears.

Apollyon's voice whispered once again, filling my mind with quiet confidence. "Now, Vicrum. Now is the time to act. Guide them, and they will follow you."

I stood, my chair scraping loudly against the stone floor,

drawing the attention of everyone in the room. Aldous looked at me, his expression curious but guarded.

"We all want the same thing," I began, my voice steady and clear. "To protect our people, our lands, and our way of life. But Aldous is right about one thing—we cannot afford to be divided. The darkness does not care for our politics or our pride. It will consume us if we do not act. But this is not just about following one man. This is about survival. And survival requires that we stand as equals, not as followers."

I paused, letting my words sink in. The tension in the room was suffocating, but I could feel the shift. The leaders were listening, and they were beginning to understand that this was not about Aldous, or even O'Rhyus. This was about the future of Nantrium. Aldous watched me closely, his expression unreadable. But I knew that the balance of power was shifting, and soon, I would be the one guiding the course of history.

Apollyon's voice was a quiet hum of approval. "Well done, Vicrum. The first step has been taken. Now, let us see where this path leads."

Chapter VII

The Day

The great hall of Lushahiem was quieting now, the hum of voices beginning to fade as the leaders of Nantrium made their final remarks and prepared to leave. The tension that had filled the room for hours was still lingering in the air like the last echoes of a battle fought with words rather than swords. Yet, despite the heated discussions, a fragile consensus had been reached. It had taken much negotiation, some leaders more willing than others, but in the end, they had agreed to meet again. The assembly would reconvene in the month of Vordhar, the time when the days were longest and the light of O'Rhyus was at its peak. There, they would decide their course of action in the face of the looming darkness that threatened to consume Nantrium.

I watched as the leaders filed out of the hall, some deep in conversation with one another, others walking in silence, their faces etched with uncertainty. Zephyros, Durion, and Vandrel exchanged words of support as they departed together, their bond strengthened by their shared loyalty to Aldous and the light of O'Rhyus. On the other hand, Lord Vaedric, King Rhalor, and Lady Morvyn moved in smaller, more isolated groups, their gazes cold and calculating. They had not voiced their complete opposition in the end, but their skepticism was far from assured.

Aldous stood at the head of the hall, his gaze following each of the leaders as they left. His armor still gleamed in the dimming torchlight, the golden plates catching the last rays of the setting sun that filtered through the high windows. His face, however, was drawn and weary. Even as the chosen of O'Rhyus, the strain of leadership was beginning to show.

I lingered near the doorway, watching the interactions between the other leaders and noting how the groups formed. The alliance of Cloud Fall, Hyndale, Talvanofa, and Bodaccia was clearly firm, united in their belief in Aldous's leadership. They were the ones who saw the light of O'Rhyus as their guiding force, trusting that it would carry them through whatever lay ahead.

In contrast, those like Lord Vaedric of Finela, King Rhalor of Alatok, Lady Morvyn of Inilyus, and Lord Eldrith of Mophia remained resolute in their caution, unwilling to fully commit themselves to the vision Aldous had laid before them. They were pragmatic, perhaps even cynical, unwilling to place their faith solely in divine favor.

As for Lord Thyldar of Hyanasarri, he had left without saying much, his disinterest in the affairs of the other provinces clear from the start. His declaration that Hyanasarri would sail to the edge of the world rather than involve themselves in the coming conflict had left a bitter taste in many mouths, but no one had challenged him. Thyldar's indifference made him an enigma—an unpredictable force that neither side could yet count on.

Fenric of Wolfshire and Belric of the Port of Alfy had left quietly, their neutrality still intact. They were watching, waiting, ready to act if needed, but not yet willing to align themselves with any one faction. Their geographic position, situated between the north and south, made their choices more complex. They were careful, perhaps wisely so, in how they navigated the growing storm. As the hall finally emptied, I prepared to leave as well, but a voice stopped me.

"Vicrum," Aldous called from across the hall, his tone calm yet insistent. "Stay a moment. We need to talk."

I hesitated for a fraction of a second, then nodded and turned back, walking toward the head of the table where Aldous stood. His eyes, pale and searching, met mine with an intensity that was hard to ignore. The others had gone now, leaving only the two of us in the vast, echoing space of the great hall.

As I approached, I felt the familiar presence of Apollyon beside me, unseen by Aldous, a whisper of cold in the otherwise warm room. His voice slithered into my thoughts, soft and insidious.

"Be cautious, Vicrum," Apollyon murmured. "Aldous is not as innocent as he seems. He wears the light of O'Rhyus, but even light can blind."

I didn't respond to Apollyon aloud, but I felt the truth in his words. Aldous was not a fool, nor was he simply a pawn. He was the chosen Shepherd of O'Rhyus, and that made him both powerful and dangerous in his own way. Whatever this conversation would bring, I had to tread carefully.

When I reached Aldous, he gestured for me to sit, his expression softening slightly. I took a seat across from him, the heavy oak table between us. For a moment, neither of us spoke. The silence between us stretched, broken only by the occasional crackle of the torches on the walls.

Finally, Aldous leaned forward, resting his forearms on the table as he studied me.

"I'm glad you stayed," he began, his voice steady but weary. "I wanted to speak with you privately, away from the eyes and ears of the others."

I raised an eyebrow, curious but cautious. "And what do you wish to discuss?"

Aldous's gaze didn't waver. "The truth, Vicrum. I need to know where you truly stand."

The words hung in the air between us, heavy with implication. He was testing me, searching for answers. He knew that I had not spoken much during the meeting, and he was likely aware that I held sway over many of the other leaders, especially those from the south. But this was more than just a political maneuver. There was something deeper behind his question.

I met his gaze evenly, choosing my words carefully.

"I stand where I have always stood, Aldous—with my people. Wyldren has existed long before Lushahiem, and we will continue to exist long after this conflict is over, one way or another."

Aldous frowned slightly, his brow furrowing. "That's not an answer, Vicrum. The others—Zephyros, Durion, Vandrel—they trust in O'Rhyus and in the light that guides us. But I've sensed something different in you. You've been... distant."

He paused, as if searching for the right words. "I've seen you listening, watching. You understand the weight of power, the burden of leadership. But there's more to it, isn't there? You're waiting for something."

Apollyon's voice was a cold whisper in my mind. "He is more perceptive than I thought."

I didn't flinch, keeping my expression neutral. "I wait

because that is what a leader does. You know as well as I do that rushing into decisions is a fool's game. We're on the edge of something, Aldous, but what it is, I'm not sure. I'm watching because I need to see where the pieces fall before I commit."

Aldous nodded slowly, his gaze never leaving mine. "I understand that. But we're running out of time. The darkness is growing, and soon it will be too late to stand on the sidelines. We need to be united when the time comes."

There it was—the plea for unity, the same message he had given to the other leaders. But there was something different in the way he spoke to me. There was a sense of urgency, of desperation, beneath the surface.

Aldous leaned back in his chair, sighing heavily. "O'Rhyus has chosen me for this task, but I can't do it alone. I need leaders like you—leaders who can see the bigger picture, who can guide their people with wisdom and strength."

He paused again, his eyes narrowing slightly. "But I also know that there are forces at work beyond what we can see. Forces that would rather see Nantrium fall into chaos than be saved. I need to know, Vicrum... are you with me, or are you waiting for something else?"

The question was direct, almost too direct. For a moment, I considered my response carefully, weighing the consequences of my words. Aldous was not a man to be taken lightly, but I had made my choice long before this meeting.

Apollyon's voice echoed in my mind once more, quiet but firm. "You control the future now, not him."

I smiled faintly, leaning back in my own chair. "I'm with

Nantrium, Aldous. I will always do what is best for my people and my province. But unity is a delicate thing. It cannot be forced. It must be earned."

Aldous studied me for a long moment, then nodded slowly, as if accepting my words for now, though I could see the doubt lingering in his eyes.

"I hope you're right," he said quietly. "For all our sake."

The silence between us was heavy, both of us considering the weight of what had been said. Finally, Aldous stood, offering me his hand.

"When we meet again in Vordhar, I hope we can face what's coming together," he said.

I rose and took his hand, feeling the firm grip of a man who believed in his purpose. But as I looked into his eyes, I couldn't help but feel the subtle shift in the balance of power. Aldous was the chosen of O'Rhyus, but I was no longer simply a leader of Wyldren. I had become something more.

"I hope so too, Aldous," I replied.

As I turned to leave the hall, I could feel Apollyon's presence following me, a shadow that clung to me as surely as my own. His voice, quiet and amused, echoed in my mind once more.

"Well done, Vicrum. All you need is patience."

I said nothing, but as I stepped into the night, I couldn't shake the feeling that the longest day was still ahead of us. And when it came, I would be ready.

Chapter VIII

The Orchard

The air in the Orchard of O'Rhyus was tranquil, a place untouched by the turmoil of the world below. Pink leaves shimmered in the soft light of dawn, casting a warm glow over the trees, each of them laden with bright, delicate fruit. O'Rhyus, the Guardian of Light and Balance, moved among the trees with careful grace, his hands tending to the branches as if each one were a vital thread in the great tapestry of the world. He hummed softly, his thoughts far away, contemplating the subtle balance he had spent eons trying to maintain.

The orchard was more than just a sanctuary. It was a symbol of everything O'Rhyus stood for: harmony, growth, and the delicate balance between life and death. Every tree here represented a soul, every leaf a whisper of mortal existence, and every fruit the choices they made. It was a sacred place, one that few, if any, dared to tread.

Yet O'Rhyus felt it before he saw it—an unsettling shift in the air, a darkening at the edge of his perfect light. He turned slowly, knowing full well who had entered his sanctuary.

Apollyon.

The god of darkness and chaos stepped into the orchard, his form as shadowy and intangible as a nightmare. He moved with a fluid grace, as though the world itself bent to make way for him. His eyes, cold and calculating, scanned the orchard with mild interest. A wry smile curled at the edge of his lips as he reached up and plucked a piece of fruit from one of the trees. He studied it for a moment, as though mocking the purity of the act, before taking a deliberate bite. The soft crunch of the fruit echoed in the silence of the orchard, a sound that felt almost sacrilegious in the serene space. O'Rhyus watched him with a calm that belied the tension between them, his eyes narrowing slightly as Apollyon chewed, savoring the fruit.

"Always taking what you do not nurture," O'Rhyus said, his voice soft but firm, a current of disapproval running beneath the words.

Apollyon smiled, swallowing the fruit slowly. "Why waste time nurturing when you can simply take? The result is the same, is it not?"

O'Rhyus shook his head, turning back to the tree he had been tending, his fingers brushing lightly over the bark. "You know better than that, brother. The act of creation, of nurturing—there is meaning in the process, not just the result. To take without care is to disrupt the balance, to weaken the very fabric of the world."

Apollyon chuckled, the sound dark and full of amusement. "Balance, balance, balance. It's all you ever speak of, O'Rhyus. The world doesn't need balance. It thrives in chaos. It is in the destruction and upheaval that true strength is revealed. You coddle them, the mortals, as though they are fragile flowers that need your constant light to survive. But it is in the darkness that they find their true selves."

O'Rhyus didn't turn, continuing his careful work among the trees. "Without light, there can be no shadow. Without order, chaos is meaningless. The world is a delicate dance between the two, and it is my task to ensure that neither overwhelms the other."

"And what of the mortals?" Apollyon pressed, circling one of the trees, his fingers brushing over the leaves as if mocking his brother's careful tending. "They are not part of your equation, are they? You think they need your light, your order. But look at them—struggling, suffering. They live in the gray, O'Rhyus. Neither fully light nor fully dark. They crave the freedom that comes from embracing both. That's where I come in. I offer them what you refuse to give—freedom from your rigid balance."

O'Rhyus paused, his hand resting against the bark of one of the trees. His gaze remained fixed on the horizon, but his words were sharp. "You offer them power without responsibility, freedom without consequence. You manipulate them into thinking chaos is strength. But that is not freedom, Apollyon. That is enslavement to the very darkness you claim to liberate them from."

Apollyon's eyes gleamed, his smile growing wider. "And you? You offer them what? Endless servitude to your light? They worship you, blindly, never realizing that their devotion keeps them shackled to a system that benefits only you. You hold them to impossible standards, always preaching balance, when in truth, they are bound by their mortality—imperfect and incomplete."

At this, O'Rhyus finally turned to face his brother, his expression serene but with a deep sadness in his eyes. "I offer them hope, Apollyon. A path to grow, to learn, to find their place in the grand order of things. They are mortal, yes, but that is their strength. They can change, they can evolve. They are not bound to the cycles of eternity as we are."

"Ah, yes," Apollyon replied, his tone dripping with mockery. "Mortality. You speak of it as if it's some grand gift. But we both know the truth, brother. Mortality is a curse. It binds them to time, to death, to the inevitable decay of all things. They live in fear of the end, of their insignificance, and you? You string them along with promises of balance and harmony, all while they waste away."

O'Rhyus shook his head. "You still don't understand. Mortality is not a curse; it's what gives them meaning. It's what makes their choices matter. Their lives, fleeting as they are, carry weight because they are finite. That is what makes them precious."

Apollyon laughed, a hollow, echoing sound that seemed to darken the orchard around them. "Precious? They are pawns, O'Rhyus. And we are their gods. You coddle them, and they suffer for it. I, on the other hand, give them the tools to rise, to break free of the chains you've placed upon them."

O'Rhyus met his brother's gaze, the sorrow in his eyes deepening. "You twist their desires, Apollyon. You promise them freedom, but all you give them is the darkness within themselves. You encourage them to destroy rather than create, to take rather than give. That is not power, it is ruin."

Apollyon's smile faded, his expression growing more serious as he stepped closer to O'Rhyus. "You still don't see it, do you? You and I, we are not so different. We are bound by the same rules, the same forces. We cannot kill each other because it was willed by our father, Obrailion. But that does not mean one of us cannot fall. You cling to your precious balance, your light, because you are afraid. Afraid that without it, you would be nothing."

O'Rhyus frowned but said nothing, his silence inviting Apollyon to continue.

"And now," Apollyon said, a cruel smile returning to his lips, "I have chosen a champion. One who will do what I cannot—one who will kill you."

O'Rhyus's face remained calm, but a shadow of concern crossed his features. "You know the prophecy as well as I do. The balance cannot be destroyed by one side alone."

Apollyon's eyes gleamed with dark amusement. "Ah, yes, the prophecy. Our dear father's parting words. 'When the balance falters, from the union of light and shadow, one shall rise.' A soul born of divine blood, destined to restore what is broken and cast the fate of all realms. But that's the beauty of it, brother. The chosen can fall. Even your champion is not immune to the seduction of power. If he falls, another will rise. The balance can shift, and I am not bound by your precious light."

O'Rhyus's eyes narrowed, a glimpse of worry crossing his face. "What are you saying, Apollyon?"

"I'm saying," Apollyon replied, his voice low and dangerous, "that the balance you've so carefully maintained is crumbling. The mortals are restless. They are no longer content with your promises of harmony. They want more. They want power. And they are willing to embrace the darkness to get it. My champion is coming for you, O'Rhyus. And when he does, you will see that your light is not enough to save them."

O'Rhyus took a step back, his gaze shifting to the trees around him, each one representing a life, a soul bound to the world he had nurtured. The prophecy had always haunted him, but now, standing before his brother, the weight of it felt heavier than ever.

"When the balance falters, from the union of light and shadow, one shall rise," O'Rhyus whispered, repeating the words of their father. "A soul born of divine blood, destined to restore what is broken and cast the fate of all realms."

He paused, his voice growing softer. "Yet, the path is shrouded in darkness, for the chosen may fall, consumed by the very force they were meant to tame. If the first succumbs to the shadow, another will follow, born from the same blood, walking a path of deeper trials."

O'Rhyus closed his eyes, feeling the weight of his father's prophecy pressing down on him. "Two fates entwined, bound by blood and the shifting tides of power. Only one shall hold the balance, and with it, the power to either restore the light or plunge the world into ruin."

Apollyon smiled, taking another bite of the fruit he had stolen from the tree. "Beware, brother," he said softly. "The choice is ever shifting, hidden from even the eyes of the gods."

With that, Apollyon turned, the shadows gathering around him as he moved toward the edge of the orchard. O'Rhyus watched him go, the weight of their conversation heavy on his heart. His brother's words echoed in his mind, and the seeds of doubt began to take root. Could it be true? Could the balance he had spent eons maintaining truly falter?

As Apollyon disappeared into the shadows, O'Rhyus stood alone in the orchard, his thoughts a storm of worry and fear. He had always known that the prophecy was inevitable, that the balance would one day be tested. But now, with the darkness rising and Apollyon's champion waiting in the wings, the future felt more uncertain than ever. O'Rhyus turned back to the trees, his hands trembling as he resumed his careful tending of the branches. The orchard was still beautiful, still full of life, but for the first time, he saw the shadows creeping at the edges, threatening to consume everything he had worked so hard to protect. He whispered to himself, repeating the words of the prophecy once more, as if seeking comfort in their familiarity.

"Beware, for the choice is ever shifting, hidden from even the eyes of the gods."

And as the sun began to set, casting long shadows across the orchard, O'Rhyus could only wonder who that choice would favor in the end.

Chapter IX

The Fear

The path back to Wyldren was a familiar one, though it seemed longer this time, weighed down by the events that had unfolded in Lushahiem. The sun had begun its slow descent, casting shadows over the ancient trees that flanked the road. Each step I took toward home was heavy, filled with the weight of decisions I had made and those yet to come. My thoughts circled like vultures around a single point of dread, and it took all my strength to keep moving forward, to push aside the dark whispers in my mind.

The sight of our small cottage nestled in the wilderness brought a flicker of warmth, a brief rest from the storm swirling within me. The smoke rising from the chimney, the smell of hearth fire, and the faint glow of lamplight through the windows—it all pulled me forward, though my heart beat heavier with every step. I was returning to the one thing that kept me grounded, but also the one thing I feared losing more than anything.

As I opened the door, the familiar creak welcomed me home, and there she was—Vyhonia. She sat by the fire, her hands working deftly at some task, her dark hair falling softly around her face. The moment she saw me, her eyes lit up with a warmth that cut through the coldness inside me.

"You're back," she said softly, rising to greet me. Her voice was like the gentle touch of rain on parched soil. "I've been waiting."

I embraced her, my arms tightening around her more than

usual, as if I needed the reassurance that she was still here, still whole. She felt so small in my arms, delicate and fragile, though I knew how strong she was. The sickness that had nearly taken her was gone, but the fear of losing her never left me. It was always in my thoughts, a constant reminder of how close we had come to the abyss.

"I'm here," I murmured, resting my chin on her head, inhaling the familiar scent of her hair. But even as I held her, the words I needed to say hung heavy in my throat.

We sat down by the fire, the warmth of the flames chasing away the chill that had settled into my bones. She poured us both a cup of tea, her movements graceful and measured, as though she could sense the weight I carried but was waiting for me to speak. Finally, after a long silence, I looked into her eyes—those deep, brown eyes that always seemed to understand more than I said.

"Lushahiem..." I began, searching for the right words, "It didn't go as I had hoped."

She tilted her head slightly, her expression calm but curious. "Tell me what happened."

I leaned forward, resting my elbows on my knees, staring into the fire as I spoke.

"The meeting was... complicated. The leaders are divided. Some want to follow Aldous, to stand with him and O'Rhyus. Others, like Vaedric and Rhalor, don't trust him. They think he's asking too much of us, that the balance is shifting in ways we can't control. And Thyldar... well, he'd rather sail off into the unknown than be part of any of this."

Vyhonia watched me closely, her brow furrowing slightly as she listened. "And you? What do you think?"

"I think..." I hesitated, the truth burning at the back of my throat. "I think the world is changing, and not for the better. Darkness is rising, and there are forces at work that none of us fully understand. Aldous is trying to keep everything together, to maintain the balance, but it feels like it's slipping through his fingers. And I'm caught in the middle of it."

I paused, my gaze shifting back to her. "But none of that matters to me as much as you do."

Her eyes softened, and she reached out, placing a hand on mine. "Vicrum, I'm here. You've done so much to protect me. You've already saved me once—"

"I would save you a thousand times over," I interrupted, my voice harsher than I intended. I swallowed, trying to steady myself.

"But that's what terrifies me, Vyhonia. I made a choice, a choice that changed everything, and I would make it again in a heartbeat. I would do anything for you, no matter the cost. And that's what frightens me the most. I've tied myself to forces I can barely control because I couldn't bear to lose you."

Her hand tightened around mine, a reassuring pressure. "Vicrum, you don't have to carry this alone. We're in this together."

I nodded, though the weight of my fears remained, pressing down on me like a shadow. "I know. But the future... the future is uncertain, Vyhonia. I've seen the way things are heading. The leaders, they're too divided. And Aldous... he's not as invincible as everyone thinks. There are whispers of things far worse than we've ever faced, and I fear that whatever is coming, it's bigger than all of us. I've done everything I can to keep you safe, but I don't know if it will be enough."

She looked at me with those steady, patient eyes, the eyes that had always seen through the walls I put up. "You've always done what you thought was right. Whatever comes, we'll face it together."

"I'm afraid that what comes next will tear us apart," I admitted, my voice barely above a whisper. "There are forces moving in the shadows, powers that want to see the world fall into chaos. And I'm not sure I can stop them. Aldous... he's the chosen of O'Rhyus, but I've seen the cracks in him. He's burdened by his role, and I don't know if he'll be able to hold everything together. And then there's Apollyon... he's chosen a champion too, and that champion will come for Aldous."

Vyhonia's eyes widened slightly, but she didn't pull away. She remained silent, letting me continue.

"I've allied myself with Apollyon because... because he offered me the one thing I couldn't refuse. The power to save you, to protect you. But I fear the cost. I fear what it will mean for the future, for all of us. I'm caught between these two forces, and I can't tell which one will destroy us first."

She leaned closer, her voice soft but firm. "Vicrum, you've always been a strong leader, a good man. You made a choice to save me, and I will never forget that. But don't let that choice consume you. We still have a future together, and we can still make the right choices."

I closed my eyes, leaning into her touch, but the words of the prophecy echoed in my mind—Obrailion's final warning about the balance and the fate of all realms.

"The balance is faltering, Vyhonia," I whispered. "And I don't know if I can fix it."

The fire crackled between us, and the night stretched on. But for the first time since I had returned, I felt the burden lessen, if only slightly. The future was uncertain, and darkness loomed, but here, with her, I had a reason to keep fighting.

Chapter X

The Peace

The icy winds of Bodaccia sliced through the mountain passes, howling with a ferocity that even the thickest furs couldn't keep at bay. I pulled my cloak tighter around me as we ascended the narrow trail, the cold biting at my skin, yet my mind was occupied with far greater concerns than the frozen air. The mountain province of Bodaccia had always been a place of harshness and strength, its snow-covered peaks standing like watchmen over Nantrium, and it felt fitting that we had chosen this place to discuss the future of the realm.

Ahead of me, Zephyros, Vandrel, and Durion trudged onward in silence, their faces set in grim determination. They too were carrying the weight of the decisions we were about to make, and no amount of preparation could make that burden any lighter. This was no simple meeting. What we discussed here would shape the future of Nantrium, a future that seemed more uncertain with every passing day.

At the entrance of Vornak's stronghold, the Lord of Bodaccia himself stood waiting, a towering figure as unyielding as the mountains he ruled. His arms were crossed over his broad chest, his expression hard as stone. The cold wind didn't seem to touch him, his eyes narrow and watchful as we approached. Vornak had always been a man of few words, but his presence alone commanded respect. In these mountains, he was as a part of the land much like the rocks beneath our feet.

"You made it," Vornak rumbled, his voice as low as the distant rumble of thunder. He stepped aside to let us pass, though his gaze lingered on me. "Late as usual, Aldous."

I offered a faint smile, but my thoughts were already far ahead. "Blame the snow. Even the gods can't hurry the wind."

Vornak grunted in response, and without further word, he led us inside the stronghold. The warmth of the fire inside the stone walls was a welcome relief from the biting cold outside, though the heat did little to thaw the tension that clung to each of us. We had gathered here for a purpose far more pressing than comfort.

Inside the great hall, a fire blazed, casting shadows on the rough-hewn walls. Ancient banners hung high above us, the icy mountain, the crest of Bodaccia emblazoned on each one—a reminder of the strength of the mountain province and the legacy Vornak protected. The others took their seats around the massive stone table, and I followed, my eyes scanning the faces of the men around me.

Zephyros, the wise and measured leader of Cloud Fall, sat to my left, his silver hair catching the firelight. He was a man of quiet strength, his wisdom born from years spent contemplating the mysteries of the skies. Vandrel, the Lord of Talvanofa, sat to my right, his features as elegant and composed as ever. His province was known for its beauty and grace, but Vandrel was no stranger to the harsh realities of leadership. Durion, the Steward of Hyndale, was opposite me, his rugged face lined with concern. He was a man of the land, a practical leader whose loyalty to his people was unwavering.

And then there was Vornak, standing at the head of the

table, his arms crossed as he surveyed the room. His presence was commanding, his gaze hard as ice. He wasn't one for pleasantries, and his first words confirmed that.

"We all know why we're here," Vornak said, his deep voice echoing through the hall. "The south is a growing threat, and we can't afford to ignore it any longer. Alatok is rallying strength, and if King Rhalor moves, the other southern provinces—Finela and Mophia—will fall in line behind him. We'll be looking at a war before we know it."

I nodded, feeling the weight of his words settle over the room like a dark cloud. Alatok had always been a formidable force in Nantrium, but with Rhalor's recent moves, it had become clear that he was aiming for something greater. He was a warrior through and through, and with his influence over Finela and Mophia, he could become a threat to the entire realm.

"Rhalor is dangerous," I said, my voice steady but grim. "He commands loyalty, not just from his own people, but from the provinces that look to him for strength. If we allow him to unite the south, he'll challenge everything we've built."

Zephyros nodded, his expression thoughtful. "Alatok's military power is undeniable, but it's the alliances we need to worry about. If Finela and Mophia stand with him, the south will be united under one banner. We'll be facing more than just an army. We'll be facing a movement."

Vandrel leaned forward, his sharp eyes focused. "That's why we need to secure the north before it comes to that. We have the resources, but Rhalor knows how to turn a battle in his favor. If we let him gain momentum, we'll be fighting a war on his terms."

Durion's brow furrowed, his voice gruff. "And what about Vicrum? Wyldren's position in the northwest makes it a wild card. No one knows what he's planning, and navigating through the North West Trails to get to Wyldren is treacherous at the best of times. If Vicrum decides to act, we might have more than just the south to worry about."

I felt a knot tighten in my stomach at the mention of Vicrum. The Lord of Wyldren had always been a mystery, his province isolated by the labyrinthine trails that wound through the unforgiving wilderness. Wyldren was the only province west of Lushahiem, and its strategic position made it both an asset and a potential threat. I had long suspected that Vicrum was playing close to his chest, waiting for the right moment.

"Vicrum is a concern," I admitted, my voice quiet but firm. "He's kept his distance from the rest of us, and I can't say for certain where his loyalties lie. But if we're going to secure peace, we need to know what he's planning. I'll send word to Wyldren and try to make contact. But we can't afford to wait for him to make the first move."

Vornak grunted in agreement. "Good. But it's not just Wyldren we need to worry about. The trade provinces—Wolfshire and The Port of Alfy—they're going to be critical. If we lose control of the trade routes, we lose the war."

Zephyros nodded, his gaze sharpening. "Wolfshire and The Port of Alfy have always maintained neutrality, but they won't be able to sit on the fence if this turns into a full-scale conflict. They control the flow of resources between the provinces, and whoever controls the trade routes will have the upper hand."

"The trade routes will decide the fate of the war," Vandrel added, his voice cold and calculating. "If we can secure Fenric of Wolfshire in the north and Belric of The Port of Alfy in the south, we can cut off Alatok's supply lines. Without those resources, his power crumbles."

Durion's voice was rough but steady. "It's not just about supplies. Hyanasarri is the key to everything. Whoever controls the Rementheium Mine controls the future of Nantrium. Without Rementheium, there's no power, no weapons, no armor. Nothing. If we lose the mine, we lose the war."

At the mention of Hyanasarri, a heavy silence fell over the room. The Rementheium Mine was the lifeblood of our world, the source of the ore that powered everything from our cities to our weapons. It was a resource that no one could afford to lose, and it was controlled by Lord Thyldar, a man who had made it clear that he had no interest in choosing sides.

"Thyldar is a problem," Vornak growled, his frustration evident. "He's isolated himself in Hyanasarri, refusing to get involved in the politics of the realm. But we can't afford his neutrality. If Rhalor gets to him first, we're finished."

I stared into the fire, the flames dancing, my mind racing with possibilities. Hyanasarri was the most vital province in Nantrium, and if we couldn't secure Thyldar's loyalty, everything we were working toward would be for nothing.

"We need to convince him," I said finally, my voice quiet but firm. "If we can bring Hyanasarri into the fold, we can control the Rementheium. Without it, Rhalor has no future.

But if Thyldar sides with the south, we're looking at a long, bloody war. And we can't let that happen."

Zephyros spoke up, his voice thoughtful. "Thyldar is a proud man, but he's not a fool. If we can show him that his future lies with us, that an alliance will protect the mine and his people, he might be willing to listen."

Vandrel nodded. "But we have to be careful. If we push him too hard, he might see us as a threat. We need to offer him something that will make him see the value in joining our cause."

Durion's voice was rough, but there was a hint of hope in his tone. "We'll need more than just words. If we can show him that we're serious, that we're willing to protect Hyanasarri and the Rementheium Mine, he might come around. But it won't be easy."

We were no longer talking about preventing a war. We were preparing for one.

Vornak's voice broke the silence, his tone hard and unyielding. "We can't afford to wait. If we're going to act, we need to do it now. Rhalor isn't going to sit idly by while we gather our strength. He's already making moves, and if we don't counter them, we'll be on the losing side before the first battle is even fought."

I nodded, the weight of his words pressing down on me like the cold mountain air. "You're right. We need to secure the trade provinces and Hyanasarri before Rhalor has a chance to act. We'll split up and make contact with the leaders of those provinces. Zephyros, you'll go to Wolfshire and speak with Fenric. We need to make sure Wolfshire stands with us."

Zephyros nodded, his expression calm but determined. "I'll

do what I can. Fenric is a man of honor, but he's also pragmatic."

"Vornak," I continued, turning to the towering Lord of Bodaccia. "You'll take the river to The Port of Alfy and speak with Belric. The Port of Alfy controls the seas, and if we can secure their loyalty, we'll have a stronghold on the southern supply lines."

Vornak grunted in agreement. "Belric's a stubborn man, but he's always looked out for his people."

I took a deep breath, my mind already turning to the next task. "As for me, I'll go north to Hyanasarri and speak with Thyldar. We need the Rementheium Mine, and if we can secure it, we'll have the resources to sustain a war, no matter how long it lasts."

Durion looked at me, his brow furrowed. "And if Thyldar refuses? What then?"

I stared into the fire, the flames reflecting in my eyes. "Then we'll have to consider other options. But one way or another, we need that mine. We can't let Rhalor or anyone else take it." The others nodded, their expressions grim but resolute.

We had made our choice. The Omni Order would now be formed, a united front against the south, bound by our shared determination to protect Nantrium from the chaos that threatened to consume it. But as I sat there, the fire crackling behind me, I couldn't shake the feeling that we were setting something in motion that would be impossible to stop. The decisions we made here would ripple across the entire realm, affecting the lives of countless people for countless years.

And I, as the chosen of O'Rhyus, would have to bear the

weight of it all.

As the meeting came to an end and we rose from the table, the cold wind outside howling once more, I stepped out onto the balcony of the stronghold and looked out at the vast expanse of snow-covered peaks. The world below seemed so small, so fragile, and yet the fate of that world rested on the choices we made here, in this frozen fortress.

The prophecy that had haunted me since the day O'Rhyus had chosen me echoed in my mind, a constant reminder of the fragile balance I was sworn to protect.

"When the balance falters, from the union of light and shadow, one shall rise. A soul born of divine blood, destined to restore what is broken and cast the fate of all realms."

I had always believed that I was that soul, that I was destined to restore the balance and bring peace to Nantrium. But now, as war loomed ever closer, I wasn't so sure. The balance was shifting, and I could feel the weight of it pressing down on me with every step I took.

"Two fates entwined, bound by blood and the shifting tides of power. Only one shall hold the balance, and with it, the power to either restore the light or plunge the world into ruin."

I closed my eyes, the wind brushing against my face like a cold whisper. I didn't know how far I would have to go to ensure peace, but I knew one thing for certain.

There was no turning back now.

Chapter XI

The Power

The valley stretched before me, a vast and desolate expanse of stone and dust, flanked by jagged mountains that loomed like silent guardians. The path to Hyanasarri was narrow and treacherous, but it was a path I had walked before. The wind howled through the rocks, carrying with it the cold bite of the north. The air here was thin, sharp, and it made every breath feel heavy, as though the very mountains themselves pressed down on my chest.

I moved forward, my cloak whipping around me as I navigated the winding trail that led deeper into the valley. The journey was long, and the solitude that came with it suited me. The others—the leaders of Nantrium—had their meetings in warm halls, surrounded by their counsel and their firelight, but here, there was only stone, wind, and silence. It was in this silence that I did my best thinking.

Ahead, the peaks of Hyanasarri rose higher, their snow-capped tops piercing the sky like the teeth of some ancient beast. Beneath those mountains lay the richest vein of Rementheium in all of Nantrium. It was a treasure coveted by all, a resource that could shift the balance of power in the realm in a matter of days. As I walked, I thought of the Rementheium, of the power it represented, and of the choices that had led me here.

The ore was unlike anything else in the world. In its solid form, it could be forged into weapons and armor of unparalleled strength—iron infused with Rementheium was indestructible. In its gaseous state, it powered the cities of Nantrium, keeping the infrastructure, the services, and the very lifeblood of civilization running smoothly. But it was the liquid form of Rementheium that held the most terrifying potential. Volatile, unstable, destructive—it had the power to cut through anything, stone, metal, and flesh alike. Nothing was safe from Rementheium in its liquid state. And here I was, walking into the heart of the province that controlled it all.

I adjusted my pace, my eyes scanning the horizon as the path led me closer to the gates of Thyldar's stronghold. The people of Hyanasarri were miners, their lives bound to the earth and the ore it yielded. They were practical, hardworking, but they were also fiercely independent. Thyldar had ruled them for decades, and he was known for his pride and his reluctance to get involved in the politics of the other provinces. He valued the safety and isolation of his people above all else, and it was that very isolation that made him both a key player and a wild card in the current struggle for power.

As I neared the gates, movement caught my eye. I stopped, narrowing my gaze. There, at the foot of the great stone steps leading into the stronghold, stood a figure I recognized immediately.

Aldous.

I felt a surge of irritation, though I kept it carefully masked. Aldous, the chosen of O'Rhyus, the man who had been tasked with maintaining the balance of Nantrium. And here he was, standing outside Thyldar's gate, already making his plea. I should have known.

Aldous was always one step ahead, always seeking to secure

alliances in the name of peace and balance. But I had my doubts. It wasn't peace that drove Aldous, not really. It was the need to control, to dictate the terms of power in Nantrium. He was O'Rhyus's chosen, but I had long since stopped seeing him as infallible.

I approached silently, my boots crunching on the stone beneath me. As I drew closer, Aldous turned, his gaze meeting mine. His eyes, always so clear and full of purpose, held a glimmer of something I couldn't quite place.

"Vicrum," he greeted me, his voice steady but laced with an edge I hadn't heard before.

"You've come for Thyldar as well."

I nodded, keeping my tone even. "It seems we've both chosen the same path today."

Aldous's expression tightened. He had never trusted me fully, and I had never given him reason to. We were on opposite sides of a conflict that hadn't yet erupted, but the tension between us was distinct. Still, we shared a common goal today: convincing Thyldar to join us.

"I've tried speaking with him," Aldous continued, his gaze shifting back to the stronghold behind him. "He's... resistant."

I wasn't surprised. Thyldar had always been resistant. He valued his independence above all else, and the thought of tying Hyanasarri's fate to the broader politics of Nantrium was likely a curse to him.

"Let me guess," I said, my voice low and dry. "He'd rather sail his people away than be a part of any of this."

Aldous glanced at me, the corners of his mouth twitching in what might have been a smile. "Something like that."

We stood there for a moment, the two of us, in the shadow of Hyanasarri's gates. The air was cold, and the tension between us was even colder still. Finally, Aldous turned and led the way up the steps, and I followed.

Inside the stronghold, the halls were dimly lit, the walls hewn from solid stone, a mountain carved into a fortress. The people of Hyanasarri were as solid and unyielding as the walls that surrounded them. Thyldar was no different. He sat at the head of a long table, his posture relaxed but his expression sharp as a Rementheium blade. He was a tall man, with a face weathered by years of hard leadership, his hair streaked with gray, his eyes hard and calculating.

"Lord Thyldar," Aldous said, his voice measured, respectful. "Thank you for agreeing to see us."

Thyldar's gaze shifted from Aldous to me, and I saw the recognition in his eyes. He knew why we were here, and he knew what we wanted. But that didn't mean he would give it to us.

"You're both here for the same reason," Thyldar said, his voice rough and uncompromising. "You want Hyanasarri's support. You want the Rementheium. And you want me to choose a side."

Aldous inclined his head. "We're here because Hyanasarri's role in the future of Nantrium is too important to ignore. You control the most valuable resource in the realm, and with war on the horizon, we need to ensure that resource is used to protect the people of Nantrium, not destroy them."

Thyldar's eyes narrowed slightly. "You speak of war as if it's inevitable."

"It is," Aldous said, his voice soft but firm. "The southern provinces are consolidating power. King Rhalor of Alatok has already begun to rally Finela and Mophia to his cause. If they unite, they will move on the rest of us, and we won't be able to stop them without Hyanasarri's resources. Without the Rementheium."

Thyldar leaned back in his chair, his gaze thoughtful. "And what of the other provinces? Wolfshire, The Port of Alfy. They control the trade routes. If they join Rhalor, your war will be lost before it even begins."

Aldous nodded, conceding the point. "We're working to secure their loyalty. Zephyros is already on his way to speak with Fenric in Wolfshire, and Vornak is traveling to The Port of Alfy to meet with Belric. If we can secure those provinces, we'll have the resources to match Rhalor's power. But it all hinges on Hyanasarri."

Thyldar remained silent for a moment, his gaze switching between us. I could see the calculation in his gaze, the weighing of options. He was a man who valued control, and this was a decision that would determine not just the fate of his people, but the future of Nantrium itself.

"What makes you think I want to be part of this?" Thyldar asked, his voice sharp. "You speak of war, but Hyanasarri has thrived by staying out of such conflicts. We mine, we forge, and we provide the resources that keep the realm running. But we do so on our terms. I will not tie the future of my people to a cause that does not benefit them."

Aldous opened his mouth to respond, but I could already see where this was going. Thyldar was a man who saw the world in terms of pragmatism and survival. He wouldn't be swayed by lofty ideals of balance or peace. He would only be swayed by power, by the promise of security.

And that's where Aldous would fail.

I remained silent, allowing Aldous to make his case. It was what Apollyon had whispered to me. Let Aldous speak, let him falter, and let Thyldar see the weakness in his words.

"Lord Thyldar," Aldous began, his voice earnest, "I understand your desire to protect your people, but if Rhalor gains control of the Rementheium, there will be no safety for Hyanasarri. He will take what he needs by force, and your people will be caught in the middle of a war they didn't choose. By joining the Omni Order, you can ensure that Hyanasarri remains secure, that the Rementheium is used to protect Nantrium, not destroy it."

Thyldar's lips twitched in a faint smile, but it wasn't one of amusement. "You think I fear Rhalor? My people have survived for centuries by staying out of your petty squabbles. We mine the ore, and we sell it. That is the extent of our involvement. I have no interest in joining your Order, Aldous. Hyanasarri will not be dragged into a war that does not concern us."

Aldous's expression tightened, and I could see the frustration building in him. He had come here with a plan, with words carefully chosen to convince Thyldar of the importance of unity, of balance. But Thyldar wasn't listening. He was too proud, too certain of his own path.

I could have stepped in then, could have said something to shift the conversation, but Apollyon's whispers held me back. Let Aldous fail. Let him see that not everyone could be swayed by his vision of peace.

Thyldar's gaze shifted to me, his expression unreadable. "And you, Vicrum? What do you have to say?"

I met his gaze evenly, the weight of Apollyon's presence pressing against my mind. "I say that you've already made your decision, Lord Thyldar. You won't be swayed by promises or pleas. You value the independence of your people, and you will not be dragged into a conflict that doesn't benefit them."

Thyldar's eyes lit up in something like approval. "You're right. Hyanasarri will not be part of this. My people will sail away before we become entangled in your war."

Aldous looked at me, his expression a mixture of frustration and confusion. He didn't understand what I was doing, why I wasn't fighting harder to bring Thyldar into the fold. But I wasn't here to fight. I was here to listen, to observe, and to act when the time was right.

I stood, inclining my head toward Thyldar. "I apologize for wasting your time, Lord Thyldar. We will leave in peace."

Thyldar nodded, his expression hard. "See to it that you do."

Without another word, I turned and walked out of the hall, Aldous following behind me. We left the stronghold in silence, the cold wind biting at our faces as we stepped back onto the stone steps leading down into the valley.

The silence between us was heavy, charged with the unspoken tension of the conversation that had just taken place. I could feel Aldous's eyes on me, feel the weight of his thoughts pressing down on me, but I didn't look at him. When we reached the foot of the steps, we stopped. The valley stretched out before us, vast and empty, the mountains towering above us like silent judges.

Aldous looked at me, and I looked back at him. There were

no words, just calculated stares.

Chapter XII

The Showdown

The wind whipped through the valley, cold and snapping, carrying the scent of stone and snow as it rushed between the towering mountains that loomed above. Aldous and I stood at the foot of Thyldar's stronghold, the silent watchmen of Hyanasarri looking over us as we faced each other, the weight of unspoken words hanging thick in the air. It was the kind of silence that comes before a storm—heavy, taut, electric with unvoiced tension. We hadn't exchanged a single word since leaving the mining lord behind, but the air between us thrummed with the knowledge of what was to come.

I adjusted my stance, squinting against the icy wind, my cloak rippling behind me like the banner of a forgotten war. Across from me, Aldous stood tall, his jaw set, his eyes hard. The Guardian of Light and Balance, O'Rhyus's chosen. He had always carried the weight of that title with the quiet certainty of a man who believed he was in the right, but now... now there was something different about him. A tension, a doubt, maybe, that hadn't been there before.

I could feel the presence of Apollyon, even though he wasn't physically with me. His influence lingered in the back of my mind, a dark whisper that threaded through my thoughts. He was watching, waiting, like a shadow creeping just out of sight. But for now, he remained silent. This was a confrontation that I needed to face on my own.

Aldous's eyes bored into mine, a question lingering there,

though he hadn't yet spoken. It was as though we were waiting for some invisible signal, some unseen force to break the silence and set the battle in motion. I could feel it in the way his gaze never wavered from mine, the way his posture, though relaxed, held a tension just below the surface.

Finally, after what felt like hours but was only moments, Aldous broke the silence. His voice was low, but clear, cutting through bone like Rementheium.

"Vicrum," he said, his tone measured but filled with something deeper, something personal, "I have to wonder... What brought you here?"

I didn't answer right away. The truth was too complicated to be offered in a single sentence, and I wasn't sure I wanted to lay it all on the table just yet. Instead, I watched him, letting the silence stretch between us a little longer, studying his face, the way the weight of his role seemed to be bearing down on him.

When I finally spoke, my voice came out colder than I intended, but I didn't bother softening it.

"I could ask you the same, Aldous."

His eyes flashed, and I could see the frustration bubbling beneath his calm exterior. He was tired, worn down from the endless negotiations, the constant push to hold the balance together. But that didn't mean he would back down.

"You know why I'm here, Vicrum," he said, stepping forward, his breath visible in the cold air. "We both know what's at stake. Nantrium is on the brink of war, and Thyldar's refusal to choose a side could tip the scales. Hyanasarri's Rementheium is the key to everything. If Rhalor gains control of the mine, he'll have the resources to wage a war none of us can win."

I met his gaze evenly, refusing to back down. "And what makes you so sure that you're the one who should control it? What makes you believe that O'Rhyus's path is the only one worth following? You speak of balance, of peace, but you and I both know that peace is fragile. It doesn't last. It never does."

Aldous's expression hardened, and for a moment, I thought he might lash out. But instead, he took a deep breath, steadying himself.

"I never said it would be easy. I never claimed that balance was something that could be maintained without sacrifice. But what I do know, Vicrum, is that without balance, without order, the world will fall into chaos. Is that what you want? To see everything burn just because you think the alternative is flawed?"

I felt a feeling of anger in his words, though he kept it buried beneath the surface. He didn't understand. He never understood.

"You speak of chaos as if it's something to be feared," I said, my voice sharp. "But chaos isn't always destruction, Aldous. Sometimes it's the only way to break free of the chains that bind us. You think you're preserving balance, but all you're doing is holding onto a system that no longer works."

Aldous's jaw tightened, and I could see the struggle in his eyes, the battle between his beliefs and the harsh realities we all were facing.

"You don't know what you're talking about, Vicrum. You've aligned yourself with the darkness—"

"And you've aligned yourself with the light," I interrupted, my tone cold. "Two sides of the same coin, aren't they? You think you're different because you follow the light, but at the end of the day, you're bound by your choices just as I am by mine."

Aldous's eyes darkened, and I could see the tension in his posture, the way his hands clenched at his sides. "Apollyon isn't interested in balance or freedom. He wants power, and you're playing right into his hands."

I shook my head, feeling the familiar weight of Apollyon's whispers curling around my thoughts, but I pushed them aside for now. This wasn't about him. Not yet.

"And what about you, Aldous? Do you think O'Rhyus chose you because he believes you can keep the peace? Or was it because he knows you're willing to sacrifice whatever it takes to maintain his version of order?"

For a moment, Aldous didn't respond, his gaze fixed on me, the weight of my words hanging between us like a sword ready to drop. Then, slowly, he spoke, his voice quieter, but no less intense.

"You're right," he said, surprising me. "I don't know what I'm capable of. None of us do. Not until we're faced with choices we never thought we'd have to make. But I do know that what I am doing is protecting the people of Nantrium. All of them, Vicrum. Not just the ones who agree with me."

I could hear the sincerity in his voice, the conviction that had driven him all these years, but it wasn't enough. Not for me.

"And what happens when that protection costs more than you're willing to pay?" I asked, my voice matching his. "What happens when the very people you're trying to save turn against you? When they see the cracks in your perfect balance and decide that they'd rather embrace the chaos than live under your rule?"

Aldous's eyes grew with something—fear, maybe, or recognition of the truth in my words—but he didn't falter. "I'll cross that bridge when I come to it," he said, his voice steady. "But I won't let the fear of what might happen stop me from doing what I believe is right."

I stared at him for a long moment, the tension between us almost unbearable. We were two men standing on opposite sides of a chasm, each convinced that our path was the one that would save Nantrium. But deep down, I wondered if either of us truly knew what we were fighting for.

"Maybe you believe that, Aldous," I said finally, my voice quieter now. "But belief doesn't always make you right. You talk about saving Nantrium, about keeping the balance, but what you're really doing is trying to control it. And the more you try to control it, the more it will slip through your fingers."

Aldous stared at me, his eyes cold and unyielding. "And you think letting it all fall apart is the better option? You think Apollyon will lead us to a better future?"

I shook my head slowly. "No. But I know that clinging to the past won't save us either."

We stood there in silence, the wind howling between us, the mountains rising around us like silent witnesses to our conversation. The weight of the choices we had made, the paths we had chosen, hung between us, unspoken and undeniable.

Finally, Aldous straightened, his gaze steady and resolved. "We'll see each other again," he said, his voice quiet but firm.

"In Lushahiem. On the first day of Vordhar."

I nodded, my expression unreadable. "We will."

Without another word, Aldous turned and walked away, his cloak billowing behind him as he disappeared into the snow-draped valley. I watched him go, feeling the cold bite into my skin, but the tension between us remained, thick and unresolved. I stood there for a long time after he was gone, my thoughts a whirlwind of conflicting emotions. I had chosen my path, just as Aldous had chosen his, but I couldn't shake the feeling that we were both walking toward the same inevitable end, no matter how different our ideologies might be.

The world was changing. Nantrium was on the brink of something that none of us could stop. And when the time came, I wasn't sure if either of us would be standing at the end.

But for now, there was only the wind, the mountains, and the silence.

And the knowledge that, when the time came, we would both be ready to do whatever it took.

No matter the cost.

Chapter XIII

The Responsibility

The throne room of Lushahiem was quiet except for the low murmur of voices as the district leaders stood before me, each awaiting their turn to speak. The hall was grand, as it should be for the seat of the Hyltorian Empire, but today, it felt like the walls were closing in, pressing down on me with the weight of decisions that had to be made. The great stone columns that lined the room felt less like supports and more like ancient spectators, judging me for every choice that passed through my mind.

I sat on the throne, my back straight, my expression carefully neutral as I listened to Master Elran, the head of the agriculture district, as he laid out his concerns. His voice was steady, but I could hear the underlying tension in his words.

"My lord," Elran began, his weathered hands clasped in front of him, "as we move out of the winter months and into the warmer season, we are faced with an increasingly difficult situation. The crops are not yielding as they should. The soil is beginning to dry, and the harvest we've gathered may not be enough to sustain us through the hot summer."

I nodded slowly, keeping my gaze on him, but my mind was already racing through possible solutions. Food shortages were not uncommon during the summer months, but with the current unrest in the realm and the looming threat of war, the situation was far more precarious than it usually would be.

"What is being done to mitigate the impact?" I asked, my

tone even but firm. "Surely there are reserves."

Elran shifted slightly, his brow furrowed. "There are, my lord. But I'm afraid they may not last through the harshest months. The crops in the southern provinces are plentiful, but with the tensions rising between the north and the south, it is uncertain whether we will be able to secure enough trade to supplement what we lack. We've begun rationing in some of the smaller villages, but it's only a temporary measure."

I frowned, my fingers tightening slightly on the armrests of the throne. The thought of the southern provinces withholding trade was not unexpected, but it was a complication we could not afford. I had hoped that by now, alliances would have been secured, or at the very least, the threat of war would have eased. But instead, the divide between the north and south was growing deeper, and the people of Lushahiem were beginning to feel the strain.

"Continue with the rationing," I said, my voice decisive. "We will need to conserve as much as we can in the coming months. Reach out to the surrounding provinces and districts, and see if we can negotiate any additional food supplies. If necessary, we will redirect resources from other areas to ensure that the people do not go hungry."

Elran bowed slightly, his face a mask of gratitude mixed with worry. "Of course, my lord. I will see to it."

He stepped back, and Commander Virell, the head of the security district, stepped forward. He was a tall, broad-shouldered man with a sharp gaze that missed nothing. His face was set in a grim line, and I knew from the moment he opened his mouth that his news would not be any more comforting than Elran's.

"My lord," Virell began, his voice low and measured, "there have been reports of unrest in several of the districts, particularly in the outer areas of Lushahiem. The people are growing restless. They sense the instability in the realm, and it's breeding fear and resentment. We've had small skirmishes break out in some of the more densely populated areas, and there are whispers of more organized resistance groups forming. Nothing major yet, but the tension is there."

I leaned forward slightly, my fingers steepled in front of me as I considered his words. Unrest was always a danger when the people felt uncertain about their future, and with the looming threat of war, that uncertainty had only grown. The stability of Lushahiem was paramount to maintaining order in the north, but if the people began to turn against one another, or worse, against me, we would be in a far more dangerous position than any battle could put us.

"What is being done to address this?" I asked.

Virell met my gaze, his face unreadable. "We've increased patrols in the most volatile areas, and we've been working with local leaders to quell any major uprisings before they begin. But the people need reassurance, my lord. They need to know that their safety is being prioritized, that they won't be left to fend for themselves if war breaks out."

I nodded, my mind already turning over solutions. The security of Lushahiem was my responsibility, and the people looked to me for guidance and protection. I couldn't allow fear to take root and spread, not when the fate of the entire realm rested on the balance I was trying to maintain.

"Continue your patrols," I ordered. "But do so with a softer hand. We cannot afford to make the people feel as though they are under siege in their own city. Work with the local leaders and ensure that their concerns are heard. Reassure them that their safety is being prioritized, and that we are doing everything we can to keep the city stable."

Virell bowed his head, his face a mask of professionalism. "As you command, my lord."

I nodded, dismissing him with a wave of my hand. But before the next district leader could step forward, the great doors to the throne room swung open with a loud creak, and the low murmur of voices stilled as Zephyros and Vornak entered the hall.

The room fell silent as the two men approached, their faces grim and their steps quick. I could feel the shift in the air, the tension rising as everyone in the room turned their attention to the two leaders. Whatever news they brought, it wasn't good.

I stood, stepping down from the throne to meet them halfway. "Zephyros, Vornak," I greeted them, my voice calm despite the unease that churned in my gut. "What news do you bring?"

Zephyros was the first to speak, his expression grave. "Fenric has decided to remain neutral. He wishes to keep Wolfshire out of the conflict altogether. He believes that by staying out of the war, he can protect his people, but... I fear that his neutrality will only prolong the inevitable. Rhalor will not allow Wolfshire to stand on the sidelines if it means losing control of the northern provinces."

I let out a slow breath, my mind racing. I had hoped that Fenric would see the importance of aligning with the Omni

Order, that he would understand the threat that Rhalor posed to the entire realm. But it seemed that Fenric was more concerned with protecting his own borders than with the greater good of Nantrium.

"And Belric?" I asked, turning my attention to Vornak, though I already had a feeling in my chest.

Vornak's jaw tightened, his face set in a hard line. "Belric has decided to side with Alatok. He's reluctant, but he knows that if he doesn't, his people will fall. Inilyus and Mophia are pressuring him from both sides, and as much as he may want to remain neutral, he knows that his position between those provinces leaves him no choice. If war breaks out, The Port of Alfy will be aligned with the south."

A cold silence fell over the room as the weight of Vornak's words settled on everyone present. The Port of Alfy was a crucial trade hub, and losing Belric's support meant that the southern provinces would have control over the seas. It was a blow we couldn't afford.

I felt a surge of frustration rise within me, but I forced it down, keeping my expression carefully neutral. Losing Belric's support was a significant setback, but it wasn't the end. We still had allies, and there were still ways to counter Rhalor's growing influence. But the path forward was becoming more treacherous by the day.

"Thank you," I said, my voice steady despite the turmoil inside me. "Both of you. We'll need to regroup and consider our next move. For now, you've done all you could."

Zephyros and Vornak both nodded, their expressions grim but resolute. They had done their part, and now it was up to me to decide how to proceed. I turned back to the district leaders, who were still standing in silence, their faces filled with a mixture of concern and uncertainty.

"This meeting is adjourned," I said, my voice firm. "Return to your districts and continue to address the concerns we discussed. I will meet with you again soon to provide further guidance."

The district leaders bowed and quietly filed out of the room, their murmurs growing softer as they left the throne room. Once they were gone, I let out a long breath and turned back to Zephyros and Vornak.

"We'll need to discuss our next steps," I said, though the weariness in my voice was impossible to hide. "But not here. I need time to think."

Zephyros placed a hand on my shoulder, his expression sympathetic. "Take the time you need, Aldous. We will follow your lead, as always."

I nodded, though the weight of his words felt heavier than ever before. I wasn't sure if I had the answers they needed. Not this time. As Zephyros and Vornak left the hall, I stood alone in the throne room, the fire in the hearth casting shadows on the walls. The silence was oppressive, and the weight of the decisions that needed to be made pressed down on me like a leaden cloak.

I walked back to the throne, sitting down heavily, my mind racing with thoughts of the future. The Omni Order was supposed to be a way to preserve the balance, to prevent the chaos that threatened to consume Nantrium. But with every passing day, it seemed as though that balance was slipping further and further out of reach. Wolfshire would remain neutral, and The Port of Alfy had already sided with Rhalor.

That left us with fewer options than I had hoped, and the prospect of war was becoming more and more likely. The southern provinces were consolidating their power, and without the full support of the northern provinces, the Omni Order might not be enough to stop them. I leaned forward, resting my elbows on my knees, my hands clasped together as I stared into the fire. The flames spun they seemed to shift and writhe with the same uncertainty that plagued my thoughts. What would O'Rhyus have me do? I had been chosen to maintain the balance, to preserve the peace. But how could I do that when the very foundations of that peace were crumbling beneath my feet?

The truth was, I didn't know.

I had always believed in the path that O'Rhyus had set before me, that by maintaining the balance, I could keep the realm from falling into chaos. But now, as the weight of leadership pressed down on me, I found myself questioning whether that balance could be preserved at all. Perhaps Vicrum had been right—perhaps there was no way to save Nantrium without allowing it to fall apart first.

But I couldn't let that happen. I wouldn't.

As I sat in the throne room, alone with my thoughts, I knew that the decisions I made in the coming days would shape the future of the realm. The balance was shifting, and the forces at play were more powerful than I had anticipated. But I was Aldous, the chosen of O'Rhyus. And I would do whatever it took to preserve the light.

Chapter XIV

The Harmony

The garden of Lushahiem was a place of stillness, of quiet reflection amidst the storm of politics and war that swirled around me. It was a sanctuary, a rare spot in the world where the troubles of Nantrium could be set aside, if even only for a moment. Here, surrounded by the ancient trees and carefully tended flowers, I could feel the pulse of the Divine Power more clearly than anywhere else. The balance of light and dark, the eternal dance between creation and destruction, resonated within me as I sat cross-legged on the stone bench beneath the great Aurelia tree.

Its leaves shimmered a faint gold in the early morning light, casting dappled shadows on the ground. The air was warm, a reminder that we were moving toward summer, and I could smell the subtle perfume of the flowers that grew in abundance here, despite the encroaching cold. There was something about this garden that allowed me to feel the flow of the Divine Power, as if the very soil here held a deeper connection to the cosmic forces that governed our world. I closed my eyes, exhaling slowly as I sank deeper into my meditation, letting my awareness expand beyond the boundaries of my physical form. The Divine Power was omnipresent, a force that connected everything—the trees, the soil, the sky, and every living being in Nantrium. It flowed through all things, binding them together in a delicate harmony. It was the very essence of the universe, born from the eternal balance between opposing forces, and

I had spent my life learning to understand and harness it.

But understanding the Divine Power wasn't the same as mastering it. I knew that more clearly than ever now.

My mind wandered, to the unwanted, to the thought of war—the all-out conflict that seemed more and more inevitable with each passing day. If it came to that, if the provinces of Nantrium were divided and set against one another, the devastation would be unimaginable. The Divine Power, the force that held our world together, could be used as a weapon to tear it apart. And the people of Nantrium, many of them barely understanding the forces they wielded, would be the ones to suffer.

The Divine Power existed as a perfect harmony between light and dark. It wasn't inherently good or evil, but rather a reflection of the will of those who wielded it. I had always believed that it was my duty, as the chosen of O'Rhyus, to maintain that balance, to ensure that the Divine Power was used for the betterment of all. But now, as the threat of war loomed, I found myself questioning what that balance truly meant.

Was it peace? Was it controlled? Or was it simply survival?

As I sat there, my mind turned to the Omni Order, to the allies I had gathered in the hope of preserving the peace of Nantrium. They were powerful men, each connected to the Divine Power in their own way, each a reflection of the elemental forces that shaped our world.

Zephyros, the Master of Lightning, was one of the most unpredictable among them. His connection to the Divine Power was raw, untamed energy, a force that could be as devastating as it was precise. Zephyros was a man of quick decisions and sharp instincts, and his lightning mirrored that—striking with pinpoint accuracy or erupting in destructive fury. When I thought of Zephyros, I thought of storms—uncontrollable, wild, and yet essential to the balance of the natural world.

Zephyros could summon storms with a thought, call down lightning from a clear sky, or travel as a flash of light, moving faster than the eye could follow. But his power was as volatile as it was formidable, and there were times when even Zephyros struggled to control it. I had seen him lose himself in the heat of battle, his emotions triggering uncontrollable tempests that wreaked havoc on everything around him. It was the price of wielding such raw energy, and though I trusted Zephyros, I knew that there was always a danger in his power.

Then there was Vornak, Lord of the Ice, whose connection to the Divine Power was cold and calculated, much like the element he commanded. Vornak's mastery over ice was absolute, his will unyielding as the glaciers he could summon. He was a patient man, a strategist, and his power reflected that—slow, deliberate, but devastating in its execution.

Vornak could freeze entire battlefields, turning the land into a frozen wasteland with a single gesture. He could create walls of ice harder than steel, or encase himself in armor so thick that even the mightiest blows could not penetrate it. In his presence, the temperature dropped, and the air became bitter and cold, as if the warmth of life itself was being drained away. I admired Vornak's control, his ability to remain calm and collected in the face of chaos, but I also knew that his power, once unleashed, was as unforgiving as the winter itself.

Durion, Father of the Forest, was a different kind of power altogether. His connection to the Divine Power was rooted in life, in growth, in the very earth itself. Durion was a figure of ancient wisdom, his bond with the natural world as deep as the roots of the trees he commanded. He could summon forests to life around him, make the earth shift and move at his command, and heal the wounded with the touch of his hand.

Durion's power was largely protective, nurturing, but I had seen what happened when he was angered. The very land responded to his fury, and in those moments, he could unleash the full force of nature, turning calm meadows into impassable jungles, or causing earthquakes that shook the ground for miles. There was a quiet strength in Durion, a calmness that belied the immense power he wielded, and I knew that his loyalty to the Omni Order was as deep as his connection to the earth.

And then there was Vandrel, the Watcher of the Water, whose connection to the Divine Power was fluid and ever-changing, much like the element he commanded. Vandrel was a healer, a protector, his mastery over water allowing him to shift seamlessly between nurturing life and unleashing destruction. He could call forth waves that crashed down on his enemies, or use the water to heal the wounded, mending flesh and bone with the essence of life itself.

Vandrel's power was one of adaptability. He could shift the moisture in the air to create mists that obscured vision, or summon rain to nourish crops. But in battle, he was a force to be reckoned with, able to summon tsunamis or imprison his foes in bubbles of water that held them in place, helpless against his will. Vandrel's calm demeanor and introspective nature made him one of the more level-headed members of the Omni Order, but I knew that, like the ocean, there was a depth to his power that few could comprehend.

I had gathered these men, these wielders of the Divine Power, in the hope that together, we could preserve the balance of Nantrium. But even as I reflected on their strengths, I couldn't help but think of the enemies we would face, those in the south who wielded the same power but for a different purpose.

Vaedric, the Victor of Vines, was one of them. His connection to plant life was unparalleled, and he could command the forests and jungles with the same ease that I commanded the Divine Light. Vaedric was a guardian of nature, a protector of life, but his power could be as fierce and unforgiving as the wildest jungle. He could summon walls of thorny vines, create living bridges of roots, or wrap himself in a cloak of leaves for protection. Vaedric was a healer, but he was also a force in battle, his power overwhelming those who sought to harm the natural world.

Next was Eldrith, the First of Fire, was another. His mastery over flame was legendary, his presence radiating heat and intensity. Eldrith's flames could burn hotter than any other, and he could summon infernos with a mere thought, turning entire battlefields into seas of fire. But fire was not just destruction for Eldrith—it was creation, the flame of life that could forge and shape the world. Yet, like all fire, his power was dangerous, and when his temper flared, his flames became uncontrollable wildfires that consumed everything in their path.

And then there was Rhalor, the Groundbreaker, whose connection to the earth was as deep as the mountains themselves. Rhalor was a mountain, a king who could reshape the land with his will alone. Mountains rose and fell at his command, and the earth itself bent to his strength. Rhalor was a man of patience, but once he set his mind to something, he was immovable, and those who stood in his way often found themselves buried beneath the very ground they sought to defend.

Lastly, there was Morvyn, the Woman of Water and Wind, whose mastery over both elements made her one of the most adaptable and dangerous enemies we would face. Morvyn could summon storms, whirlpools, and gusts of wind with effortless grace, her control over the elements allowing her to strike with precision or unleash chaos on a whim. She was a figure of balance, much like me, but her alignment was with the forces of the south, and I knew that her power, when unleashed, would be a tempest of fury that few could withstand.

These were the forces arrayed against us, and though I knew that the Omni Order was strong, I couldn't shake the feeling that the coming conflict would push us all to the brink. The Divine Power was a force of balance, but it was also a force of destruction, and if we weren't careful, we could tear Nantrium apart in our efforts to save it.

I opened my eyes, letting out a slow breath as I returned to the present. The garden was still, the only sound was the soft rustling of leaves in the breeze. The Divine Power pulsed around me, a constant reminder of the forces at play, the forces that I had been chosen to wield. But as I sat there, I couldn't help but wonder if I was truly the one to maintain that balance. The weight of leadership, of responsibility, had never felt heavier, and the choices I would have to make in the coming days would determine the future of Nantrium. Could I truly preserve the light, the balance, without tipping the scales too far in one direction? Or was the chaos that Vicrum had spoken of inevitable?

The thought of Vicrum brought a bitter taste to my mouth. He was a man I had once called an ally, a man who had walked beside me in the early days of our struggle to maintain peace. But now, he had aligned himself with Apollyon, the fallen god of darkness, and I could no longer trust him. Vicrum had chosen his path, and though I still held out hope that he could be saved, I knew that our confrontation was coming. There would be no avoiding it.

I stood, my legs stiff from sitting for so long, and began to make my way back toward the palace. Tomorrow was the meeting of the 13 provinces, the gathering that would decide the future of Nantrium. I had to be ready, not just for the negotiations, but for the battle that was sure to follow.

The sun was beginning to set, casting long shadows across the garden as I walked, and I could feel the weight of the coming days pressing down on me like a storm on the horizon.

Tomorrow, the balance will be tested.

And I could only hope that I was strong enough to hold it.

Chapter XV

The Break

The grand hall of Lushahiem felt colder than usual, its towering stone columns judging as the leaders of the 13 provinces gathered in their designated seats. Despite the opulence of the room, adorned with banners and tapestries representing the ancient history of Nantrium, the air was thick with tension. This meeting—this final attempt to prevent the realm from splintering apart—was spiraling into something darker, something I wasn't sure any of us could control.

I sat near the head of the table, flanked by Aldous, the chosen of O'Rhyus, and the other leaders of the Omni Order. Across from us were the trade province representatives—Belric of The Port of Alfy and Fenric of Wolfshire—who had tried, futilely, to remain neutral in this growing conflict. And at the far end, the imposing figure of Rhalor, lord of Alatok, sat like a storm cloud ready to erupt. His supporters, leaders of Finela, Mophia, and Inilyus, surrounded him, each wearing expressions of quiet defiance.

I could feel the weight of Apollyon's presence at the edge of my thoughts, the subtle pull of his influence ever-present. I wasn't here simply to observe the collapse of diplomacy—I was here to maneuver it, to guide it toward the chaos that Apollyon had promised would bring about his rise. But for now, I waited, listening as the voices of the provinces clashed like the clanging of swords.

"The Port of Alfy will remain neutral," Belric said for the

third time, his hands clasped tightly on the table in front of him. "Our position between Inilyus and Mophia makes it impossible for us to take a side. We have too much to lose if we align with either the north or the south."

Aldous leaned forward, his face calm but his voice firm. "Neutrality is not a long-term option, Belric. The southern provinces are preparing for war, and if you stand in the middle, you will be crushed between two forces. If you side with us now, the Omni Order will protect your people, your trade routes. If not, you will find yourself at the mercy of Rhalor and his allies."

At the mention of his name, Rhalor shifted, his massive frame bristling with barely contained anger. His presence was intimidating, his eyes were as they scanned the room. When he finally spoke, his voice was deep, like the rumble of distant thunder.

"We're not here to listen to the Omni Order demand loyalty like tyrants," Rhalor said, his gaze locking on Aldous. "This is about balance. The north has held the reins of power for too long, and now it's time for the southern provinces to take what is rightfully ours. I will not stand by while you consolidate power under the guise of 'protection.'"

Aldous met his gaze evenly, but I could see the tension in his posture. "And what do you propose, Rhalor? That we let the south march on Lushahiem? That we stand by while you divide the realm?"

Rhalor's jaw clenched, and for a moment, I thought he might actually leap across the table and strike Aldous down. His supporters murmured in agreement, their faces hard with resolve. It was clear that Rhalor had been waiting for this moment—for the chance to declare his intent to break the fragile peace and challenge the north directly.

"If you provoke us any further," Rhalor growled, "I will march on Lushahiem myself. Your walls may be strong, but they won't withstand the force of the southern provinces united. We are not afraid to shed blood if it means breaking the chains you've placed around Nantrium."

The room fell into a tense silence. Aldous remained calm, though I could sense the storm building within him. This was the moment we had all feared—the point at which diplomacy broke down and war became inevitable.

Before Aldous could respond, however, Thyldar, lord of Hyanasarri, stood from his seat. His expression was one of utter weariness, as though the very act of participating in this meeting was draining the life from him.

"This," Thyldar said, his voice carrying through the hall like the soft crack of a breaking branch, "this is exactly why I would rather sail away to the edge of the world."

His words cut through the tension like a blade, drawing all eyes to him. The leaders of the Omni Order, the trade provinces, and the southern provinces all looked at Thyldar in stunned silence as he slowly pushed back his chair and began to walk toward the door.

I stood quickly, my hand raised. "Thyldar, wait. Where are you going?"

He stopped but didn't turn to face me. "I'm leaving."

The words were simple, but the impact was profound. Thyldar, the one leader who had held the key to controlling the most valuable resource in Nantrium, was walking away. And with him, the possibility of avoiding a full-scale war seemed to vanish.

Aldous, his voice tight, called after him. "Thyldar, what of your province? What of Hyanasarri?"

Thyldar finally turned, his eyes cold and resigned. "You can have it if you like. It seems that's all any of you want—to tear each other apart for control of my mines. So take it. Fight over it like dogs. But I won't be part of this madness."

His words sent a shockwave through the room. Rhalor, sensing an insult, stood from his seat, his face twisted in anger. "What did you say?"

Thyldar's gaze met Rhalor's, and for a brief moment, I saw a hint of disdain in his eyes. "You heard me. If you want Hyanasarri, come and take it. I'm sure it will be worth watching as you all tear this realm apart before you can even think of peace."

Rhalor's fists clenched, and he took a step forward, but before he could move any further, I stepped between them, my hands raised in a gesture of peace.

"Enough," I said, my voice loud and commanding. "This isn't helping anyone."

I turned to Thyldar, my eyes narrowing as I met his gaze. "You can't just walk away from this. If Hyanasarri doesn't align with either the north or the south, the whole realm will come for it. You know that. Every province in Nantrium will be drawn to it, and none of us will be able to stop the bloodshed that follows."

Thyldar's eyes softened slightly, but his resolve remained firm. "I know, Vicrum. But I also know that no matter what I decide, this war is coming. You all talk of balance, of control, but you've already lost it. The moment you allowed power to consume you, this realm was doomed."

He glanced around the room, his eyes sweeping over the leaders of Nantrium. "You can have Hyanasarri. It is open to the first who lays claim to it. I will not be here to see what becomes of it."

With that, he turned and walked out of the hall, leaving the rest of us in stunned silence.

For a moment, no one spoke. The leaders of Nantrium exchanged uncertain glances, and I could feel the tension building again, like a dam about to burst.

Finally, Aldous spoke, his voice low but filled with determination. "We must be the first to Hyanasarri."

His words broke the silence, and I could see the others bristling, preparing themselves for what came next. The leaders of the southern provinces—Rhalor, Vaedric, Eldrith—looked ready to march that very instant, and I knew that if we didn't act fast, they would take the Rementheium mines for themselves.

I stepped forward, placing a hand on Aldous's shoulder. "You're right. If we don't get there first, the south will take it. Hyanasarri is the key to everything."

Aldous nodded, his face grim. "Then we have no choice. We must act quickly. Gather your forces. We leave for Hyanasarri at once."

The room erupted into chaos as the leaders began shouting orders, calling for their men to prepare for war. The meeting had ended, and there was no turning back now.

I watched as Aldous conferred with Zephyros, Vornak, and the others, their faces set with determination. The Omni Order was mobilizing, preparing for the conflict that would decide the future of Nantrium.

As the leaders began to file out of the hall, I remained where I was, my mind racing. Apollyon's voice whispered in the back of my thoughts, a dark reminder of the role I was destined to play.

This was it. The moment we had all been waiting for. The world was about to descend into chaos, and when the time came, I would be ready.

I turned and walked out of the hall, my thoughts already on the road to Hyanasarri, and the battle that awaited us there.

Chapter XVI

The Break (Part II)

The grand hall of Lushahiem felt heavy with tension even before anyone had spoken a word. The leaders of the 13 provinces had gathered, filling the room with their presence, yet the air was thick with the unspoken threat of what was to come. This was a gathering meant to restore balance, to establish peace, but I knew in my heart that this meeting would not end as I had hoped. The moment I entered the hall and laid eyes on the leaders arrayed around the vast, polished table, it became clear to me that this was a final confrontation, not a negotiation.

I could feel the weight of O'Rhyus's presence in the back of my mind, a steady reminder of the role I had been chosen to play. His influence was quiet but undeniable, a calm pulse of light that kept me centered in the midst of all the looming chaos. I had to maintain that balance, the delicate equilibrium between light and dark, between order and disorder, and yet, with each passing moment, the situation seemed to slip further and further from my grasp.

The leaders of the Omni Order—Zephyros, Vornak, and Durion—sat at my side, their expressions as serious as my own. Across the table, the southern provinces had already aligned themselves with Rhalor, the lord of Alatok, whose broad frame radiated with barely contained fury. His allies—leaders of Finela, Mophia, and Inilyus—flanked him, their expressions grim and resolute. They had come here not to negotiate but to make their demands, and I could see it in the way their eyes never wavered, their hands clenched in silent defiance.

On the far side of the table sat the representatives of the trade provinces, men like Belric of the Port of Alfy and Fenric of Wolfshire, who had tried desperately to remain neutral in the growing conflict. But neutrality was a thin veil, and I knew they would have to make a choice soon. The question was: which side would they choose?

The silence stretched on for a moment longer, the tension in the room growing thicker with each passing second. Finally, it was Belric who broke it.

"The Port of Alfy will remain neutral," he said, his voice calm but firm, his hands resting on the table in front of him. "Our position between Inilyus and Mophia makes it impossible for us to take a side. We have too much to lose if we align with either the north or the south."

I could sense the hesitation in his voice, the unspoken fear of what would happen if he chose wrongly. Neutrality was a dangerous position to take, especially now, with the realm on the brink of war. I leaned forward slightly, meeting his gaze with as much calm authority as I could muster.

"Neutrality is not a long-term option, Belric," I said, my voice steady but firm. "The southern provinces are preparing for war, and if you stand in the middle, you will be crushed between two forces. If you side with us now, the Omni Order will protect your people, your trade routes. If not, you will find yourself at the mercy of Rhalor and his allies."

Belric's face tightened, and he opened his mouth to respond, but before he could speak, Rhalor let out a low, rumbling laugh that echoed through the hall like distant thunder.

"We're not here to listen to the Omni Order demand loyalty like tyrants" Rhalor said, his voice dripping with disdain. "This is about balance. The north has held the reins of power for too long, and now it's time for the southern provinces to take what is rightfully ours. I will not stand by while you consolidate power under the guise of 'protection.'"

I kept my eyes on Rhalor, not flinching in the face of his accusations. His words were meant to provoke, to cast doubt on my intentions, but I would not let them sway me.

"And what do you propose, Rhalor?" I replied evenly. "That we let the south march on Lushahiem? That we stand by while you divide the realm?"

Rhalor's face darkened, his broad shoulders tensing as he leaned forward, his eyes narrowed into slits. "If you provoke us any further," Rhalor growled, "I will march on Lushahiem myself. Your walls may be strong, but they won't withstand the force of the southern provinces united. We are not afraid to shed blood if it means breaking the chains you've placed around Nantrium."

The murmurs from his supporters—Vaedric, Eldrith, and Morvyn—grew louder as they nodded in agreement, their faces hard with determination. They were prepared for war, and Rhalor was their champion. I could see it in the way they looked to him for guidance, the way they hung on his every word.

Before I could respond, Thyldar, the lord of Hyanasarri, stood from his seat. His expression was one of weary indifference, his eyes half-lidded as though the very act of being present at this meeting was draining him of all energy. "This," Thyldar said, his voice calm but laced with frustration, "this is exactly why I would rather sail away to the edge of the world."

His words cut through the tension like a knife, drawing every eye in the room to him. Thyldar, the one leader who held the key to controlling the vast Rementheium reserves in Hyanasarri, had remained largely silent throughout the meeting. Now, as he slowly began to walk toward the door, his intentions became clear.

Vicrum was the first to react, standing abruptly and calling after him. "Thyldar, wait. Where are you going?"

Thyldar didn't stop, didn't even turn to acknowledge Vicrum's question. "I'm leaving," he said simply.

A cold knot formed in my chest. If Thyldar walked away from this meeting, it would signal the end of any hope for a peaceful resolution. Without Hyanasarri's support, the realm would be plunged into war, and the Rementheium mines would become the battleground on which that war was fought.

I stood as well, my voice firm but tinged with desperation. "Thyldar, what of your province? What of Hyanasarri?"

Thyldar finally stopped, turning to face me with an expression that was equal parts weariness and disdain. "You can have it if you like. It seems that's all any of you want—to tear each other apart for control of my mines. So take it. Fight over it like dogs. But I won't be part of this madness."

The shock of his words rippled through the room. I could feel the eyes of the other leaders on me, waiting for my response, but before I could speak, Rhalor surged to his feet, his face twisted in fury.

"What did you say?" Rhalor growled, his fists clenched at his sides.

Thyldar met Rhalor's gaze without flinching. "You heard me. If you want Hyanasarri, come and take it. I'm sure it will be worth watching as you all tear this realm apart before you can even think of peace."

Rhalor's hand twitched, and for a brief moment, I thought he might strike Thyldar down where he stood. His fury was visible, a boiling cauldron of anger and frustration that threatened to erupt at any moment.

But before things could spiral further out of control, Vicrum stepped between them, raising his hands in a gesture of peace. "Enough," he said, his voice carrying an authority that made even Rhalor pause. "This isn't helping anyone."

I watched as Vicrum turned to face Thyldar, his expression calm but firm. "You can't just walk away from this. If Hyanasarri doesn't align with either the north or the south, the whole realm will come for it. You know that. Every province in Nantrium will be drawn to it, and none of us will be able to stop the bloodshed that follows."

For the first time, I saw a sign of something like regret in Thyldar's eyes, but it was quickly replaced by resignation. "I know, Vicrum. But I also know that no matter what I decide, this war is coming. You all talk of balance, of control, but you've already lost it. The moment you allowed power to consume you, this realm was doomed."

He cast one last glance around the room, his eyes lingering on me for a moment longer than the others. "You can have Hyanasarri. It is open to the first who lays claim to it. I will not be here to see what becomes of it." With those parting words, Thyldar turned and walked out of the hall, leaving a stunned silence in his wake.

The atmosphere in the room shifted immediately. The leaders of Nantrium exchanged uneasy glances, the implications of Thyldar's departure sinking in. The prospect of a full-scale war over Hyanasarri's Rementheium reserves now loomed over us all.

I turned to Vicrum, my mind racing. He met my gaze, and I could see the resolve in his eyes, the same determination that had always marked him as a leader. "We must be the first to Hyanasarri." I said, my voice low but filled with urgency. Vicrum placed his hand on my shoulder.

"You're right. If we don't get there first, the south will take it. Hyanasarri is the key to everything.."

I nodded, my heart pounding in my chest. Vicrum was right. If the southern provinces took control of the Rementheium mines, they would have the resources to crush us. We couldn't afford to hesitate.

I turned to the other leaders of the Omni Order—Zephyros, Vornak, and Durion—and saw the same grim determination reflected in their faces.

"Then we have no choice. We must act quickly ," I declared, my voice firm and resolute. "There's no time to waste. Gather your forces. We leave for Hyanasarri at once." The room erupted into chaos as the leaders began shouting orders, calling for their men to prepare for the march on Hyanasarri. The meeting had ended, and there was no turning back now. As the others rushed to gather their forces, I remained where I was, my mind racing with thoughts of the coming battle. This was it. The tipping point. The moment when all of Nantrium would be forced to choose sides. The battle for

Hyanasarri would decide the fate of the realm. And I could only hope that the light would prevail.

Chapter XVII

The Silence

The wind howled through the barren streets of Hyanasarri, carrying with it the cold bite of desolation. I stood at the edge of the once-thriving city, my eyes scanning the empty structures and the winding roads that led to the heart of the province. The buildings—carved from stone and reinforced with steel from the Rementheium mines—stood silent and unmoving, like ancient sentinels abandoned by time itself. There was no movement, no sign of life, no people rushing to greet us or fleeing in fear. Hyanasarri, it seemed, had been deserted.

Behind me, the ranks of my 100,000 men stretched across the valley, a vast army prepared for battle. Their black armor glinted in the pale sunlight, and the quiet murmur of voices and the clink of steel echoed in the cold air. But there was no battle here, no war to be fought—not yet, at least. Instead, there was only the eerie stillness of a city that had once been the heart of the realm's wealth, now reduced to an empty shell.

I stepped forward, my boots crunching on the gravel beneath me, my mind racing with questions. Where were the people of Hyanasarri? Where were the miners, the merchants, the soldiers? Where was Thyldar?

"Spread out," I ordered, my voice firm as I turned to the commanders at my side. "Search the city. I want to know if anyone—anything—remains here."

The commanders nodded and quickly relayed the orders to

their men. Within moments, groups of soldiers broke away from the main force, fanning out into the empty streets, their footsteps echoing in the stillness. I watched them for a moment before turning my attention back to the city ahead. This wasn't what I had expected. We had come prepared for war, for a battle over the precious Rementheium that could determine the fate of Nantrium. But instead, we had found only emptiness.

Something wasn't right.

I glanced to my right, where Zephyros, Vornak, and Durion stood watching the scene unfold with expressions as grim as my own. The leaders of the Omni Order had arrived with their own forces, each of them contributing another 100,000 men to the fight, though now it seemed the fight would have to wait.

"This doesn't make sense," Zephyros muttered, his arms crossed over his chest as he stared at the deserted streets. "Where is everyone? Thyldar wouldn't just abandon Hyanasarri."

"He said he was leaving," Vornak reminded us, his voice cold and calculating. "But I didn't think he meant the entire city would vanish with him."

"Perhaps he evacuated his people," Durion suggested. "If he truly believed we would tear the realm apart for control of the mines, it's possible he took them to safety."

I shook my head slowly, my eyes narrowing as I studied the empty streets. "If that's the case, then where did they go? You don't just hide over 100,000 people without leaving some kind of trace."

The others fell silent, their expressions as troubled as my

own. Thyldar's words at the meeting rang in my ears: "You can have Hyanasarri if you like. It's open to the first who lays claim to it." At the time, I hadn't taken him seriously. I hadn't believed that he would truly abandon his home, his people, the wealth of Rementheium that was so vital to Nantrium. But now, standing in the silence of the abandoned city, I began to wonder if I had underestimated him.

"Send word to the other members of the Omni Order," I said, turning to one of my messengers. "I want them here as soon as possible. We need to formulate a plan before the southern provinces arrive."

The messenger nodded and quickly mounted his horse, galloping off toward the rear of our army where the communication lines were set up. I watched him go, my mind already turning to the next steps. We couldn't afford to linger here without a plan. The southern provinces would be arriving soon, and if we weren't ready, they would take Hyanasarri—and its Rementheium—without a fight.

"Formations," I said, turning back to Zephyros, Vornak, Vandrel and Durian. "We need to establish our defenses and prepare for the arrival of the southern forces. If Thyldar truly left, we need to secure this city before they get here."

Zephyros nodded, his sharp, stormy eyes already calculating the best approach. "We'll need to establish choke points. Hyanasarri's layout favors defensive positions—if we can hold the streets and control the main access routes to the mines, we can force the southern provinces into a siege. It'll give us time to formulate a proper strategy."

Vornak crossed his arms, his expression hard. "And if the southern provinces have already aligned with Thyldar in secret? What if this is a trap?"

I met his gaze, my jaw tight. "Then we'll be ready for them."

Durion stepped forward, his calm presence a steadying force. "We need to focus on the immediate task at hand. If we can hold Hyanasarri, we control the most valuable resource in the realm. But we need to prepare for all eventualities."

I nodded, my mind already spinning through the possibilities. "Zephyros, take your men and secure the eastern side of the city. Vornak, I want your forces stationed at the main gate. If the southern provinces march on us, they'll come through there. Durion and Vandrel, your men will secure the central district—if we need to regroup, that's where we'll fall back."

The four leaders nodded and quickly moved to relay the orders to their commanders. As they departed, I stood alone for a moment, staring out over the city of Hyanasarri, the cold wind biting at my skin.

Where are you, Thyldar?

The question echoed in my mind, but no answer came. Instead, the silence of the city pressed down on me like a weight, a reminder of the uncertainty that lay ahead. Thyldar's departure had thrown everything into chaos. Without the people of Hyanasarri, without Thyldar's leadership, the battle over the Rementheium mines would be fought not for control of a thriving province, but for control of a ghost city.

And we weren't the only ones marching toward this empty prize.

The southern provinces were on their way, their armies moving steadily toward us even now. Rhalor, with his ambitions of conquest, would stop at nothing to take control of Hyanasarri's resources. His forces were strong, and with the support of Vaedric, Eldrith, and Morvyn, he could easily overpower us if we weren't prepared. But I wasn't afraid of Rhalor. I wasn't afraid of his army, or the might of the southern provinces. What troubled me, what gnawed at the edges of my thoughts, was Vicrum.

He and his forces had not yet arrived, and that worried me. Vicrum had always been reliable, always ready to fight, but now, with the threat of war looming, he was conspicuously absent. I knew the North West Trails were treacherous, that the journey from Wyldren to Hyanasarri would take time, but something about his absence felt... off.

As I paced the edge of the city, overseeing the deployment of our forces, I couldn't shake the feeling that something was wrong. Vicrum should have been here by now. His men should have already joined us, and yet there was no sign of him.

"Where is Vicrum?" Zephyros asked, as he approached. His men were already setting up defensive positions along the eastern side of the city, and I could see the faint crackle of electricity in the air around him. Zephyros's connection to the Divine Power was always most visible when he was agitated, and now, the tension in his body seemed to mirror the storm that brewed within him.

"I don't know," I admitted, my voice tight with frustration. "He should have been here by now."

Vornak joined us, his icy demeanor as cold as the air around him. "The North West Trails are dangerous. It's possible he was delayed."

I wanted to believe him, but the doubt lingered. Vicrum's absence was more than just a logistical delay. It felt like a warning, a dark omen of something deeper, something hidden beneath the surface of this already complicated situation.

A cold gust of wind swept through the city, rattling the empty windows and sending shivers down my spine. I pulled my cloak tighter around me, my mind spinning with possibilities. There were so many variables at play now, so many unknowns. Thyldar's abandonment of Hyanasarri, the impending arrival of the southern forces, and now Vicrum's unexplained absence. It was all building to something, something I couldn't yet see. I turned to the messenger who had just returned from delivering my orders to the other members of the Omni Order. "Send scouts," I ordered, my voice firm. "I want to know the moment the southern provinces arrive, and I want to know if there's any sign of Vicrum and his men."

The messenger nodded and quickly departed, leaving me alone once more with my thoughts.

Time was running out.

The southern provinces were marching toward us, and we had no choice but to be ready. If Rhalor's forces reached Hyanasarri before we could secure the city, all would be lost. The Rementheium mines would fall into the hands of the south, and with it, the balance of power in Nantrium would shift.

I could only hope that Vicrum would arrive in time.

The day passed in a blur of preparations. My men, along with those of Zephyros, Vornak, Vandrel and Durion, worked tirelessly to secure the city's defenses. Barricades were erected, positions were fortified, and scouts were sent out to monitor the surrounding area. The tension in the air was tight, a low hum of anticipation that thrummed through the ranks of the army.

As night fell, the city of Hyanasarri remained silent and empty, the wind howling through the streets like the mournful wail of a forgotten ghost. The soldiers gathered around their fires, their faces illuminated by the flickering flames, but there was little conversation. Everyone knew what was coming. Everyone knew that the battle for Hyanasarri was only a matter of time.

I stood at the edge of the central district, staring out into the darkness, my thoughts once again consumed by the uncertainty of our situation. The other members of the Omni Order had gathered around me, their expressions as grim as my own.

"Still no sign of Vicrum?" Zephyros asked, his voice low.

I shook my head. "No. And no word from the southern provinces, either."

"They're coming," Vornak said quietly, his breath visible in the cold night air. "Rhalor won't hesitate. He'll march on us the moment he's ready."

"And we'll be ready for him," I replied, though the words felt hollow.

Vandrel placed a hand on my shoulder. "We have the advantage of the city's defenses. We can hold them off."

I nodded, though my mind was elsewhere. The battle for Hyanasarri was inevitable, but without Vicrum and his forces, the odds were stacked against us. We needed every advantage we could get, and Vicrum's absence was a blow we couldn't afford. As the night deepened, I found myself standing alone once more, staring out into the darkness, waiting.

Waiting for the battle to begin. Waiting for Vicrum to arrive. Waiting for the fate of Nantrium to be decided.

Chapter XVIII

The Light and Darkness

The cold wind swept across the front lines of Hyanasarri, carrying with it the distant rumble of footsteps. Thousands of soldiers, their armor glinting in the faint sunlight, were positioned along the valley where the main gate loomed large, its stone walls weathered by time but unyielding. I stood at the edge of the battlements, my gaze fixed on the horizon where Rhalor and his forces would soon appear. The tension in the air was thick, pressing down on us like the weight of the skies themselves. This was it. The moment I had been preparing for. The moment I had feared, even as I knew it was inevitable.

The battle for Hyanasarri—and for the future of Nantrium—was about to begin.

As I looked out over the valley, my mind drifted back to the events that had brought me here, to this place where light and dark would collide. I thought of O'Rhyus, the god who had chosen me to be his champion, the one who had bestowed upon me the power of light. It had been years since I first felt the Divine Power course through my veins, a power that connected me to the very essence of the universe. The light had always been with me, a constant presence that guided me through the chaos of the world. But now, as I stood on the brink of war, I couldn't help but question whether I had truly lived up to the expectations placed upon me. Was I worthy of being the light? Was I strong enough to preserve the balance that O'Rhyus had entrusted to me?

I had always believed that the light was a force for good, a beacon of hope in the darkness. But the darkness was always there, lurking at the edges, threatening to consume everything if we let it. Apollyon, the fallen god of darkness, had once been O'Rhyus's brother, a being of immense power who had been cast out for his defiance. Now, his influence was spreading across the realm, twisting the minds of those who sought power for themselves. Even Vicrum, once my trusted leader, had fallen under Apollyon's shadow.

Where is Vicrum?

The question gnawed at me as I surveyed the battlefield. Vicrum and his forces had yet to arrive, and their absence was a blow to our defenses. I had sent scouts to search for any sign of him, but they had returned empty-handed. The North West Trails were treacherous, but Vicrum knew those lands well. He should have been here by now. I couldn't dwell on it any longer. I had to focus on the battle ahead.

The ground began to tremble beneath my feet, and a distant roar echoed across the valley. I straightened, my heart pounding in my chest as the first wave of Rhalor's forces appeared on the horizon. The southern provinces had come, and they had brought their full might with them.

I could see Rhalor at the head of the army, his broad shoulders and imposing presence unmistakable even from a distance. Behind him, the banners of Finela, Mophia, Inilyus, and Alatok flew high in the wind, their colors bright against the gray sky. Their combined forces stretched across the valley like a vast, unstoppable tide, and I knew that they had brought no less than 500,000 soldiers to claim Hyanasarri for the south.

The sight of their army was enough to make even the most seasoned warrior hesitate, but I couldn't afford to show any fear. I turned to the soldiers around me, the men who had followed me into this uncertain battle. They were watching me, waiting for orders, their eyes filled with a mixture of determination and apprehension.

"We hold the line," I said, my voice carrying over the wind. "This city is ours. We cannot let them take it."

There were nods of agreement, and I could see the resolve harden in their faces. They were ready to fight, ready to lay down their lives to defend Hyanasarri. But even as I spoke, I knew that this battle would be unlike any we had faced before. The forces arrayed against us were formidable, and without the support of Vicrum and his men, we were at a disadvantage.

I could feel the Divine Power pulsing within me, a steady, calming presence that anchored me in the midst of the chaos. O'Rhyus was with me, his light guiding me through the darkness, but even the light could only do so much.

The sound of drums echoed across the valley, and I watched as Rhalor's army came to a halt just beyond the range of our archers. For a moment, the battlefield was eerily silent, the tension hanging in the air like a blade waiting to fall.

Then, Rhalor stepped forward.

Even from a distance, I could see the fire in his eyes, the barely controlled rage that radiated from him like heat from a forge. He raised his arms, his voice booming across the valley as he addressed the gathered forces.

"I am Rhalor, Lord of Alatok!" he roared, his voice carrying with the wind. "I have come to claim Hyanasarri for the south. This city and these mines, they belong to us!"

His words sent a ripple through our ranks, but I stood firm, my gaze fixed on him as he continued.

"You, who hide behind these walls, who cling to the past, your time is over!" Rhalor shouted. "The southern provinces have united, and we will no longer be bound by the whims of the north. Surrender Hyanasarri, and you may yet live. Resist, and you will face the full force of our wrath!"

The southern forces erupted into cheers, their voices rising in a deafening chorus that echoed across the valley. The sound was like the roar of an avalanche, unstoppable and overwhelming.

I clenched my fists, my heart racing as I prepared to respond. There could be no surrender, no retreat. We had come too far to turn back now.

I stepped forward, my voice steady but filled with conviction. "I am Aldous, chosen of O'Rhyus, protector of the light! Hyanasarri belongs to all of Nantrium, and we will not let it fall into the hands of those who seek only power!"

The men behind me cheered, their voices rising in defiance of the southern army. I could feel their courage, their determination to fight for what was right, and it strengthened my resolve.

Rhalor's face twisted into a sneer, and I could see the rage boiling beneath the surface. "So be it," he growled. "You have made your choice, Aldous. Now you will face the consequences."

With a wave of his hand, Rhalor signaled the attack.

The southern forces surged forward, their soldiers charging across the valley with terrifying speed. The ground shook beneath the weight of their advance, and the sound of steel clashing against steel filled the air as they collided with our front lines.

I watched from the battlements as the battle began in earnest, my mind racing as I calculated our next move. Zephyros was already at the eastern side of the city, his men holding the choke points as they repelled wave after wave of southern soldiers. I could see flashes of lightning in the distance, the tell tale sign of Zephyros's power as he called down storms to strike at the heart of the enemy.

Vornak, stationed at the main gate, was commanding his men with precision, his icy demeanor reflected in the way he controlled the battlefield. His soldiers fought with the unyielding strength of glaciers, their shields locked together as they pushed back the southern forces.

Durion and Vandrel, were overseeing the defense of the central district, their connection to the earth allowing them to manipulate the terrain to our advantage. I could feel the rumble of the ground beneath my feet as they summoned the strength of the land to create barriers and traps for the enemy.

But despite our best efforts, the southern army was relentless. I turned to the nearest commander, my voice sharp and urgent. "Send reinforcements to the eastern side. Zephyros needs support."

The commander nodded and quickly relayed the orders to his men. I watched as they rushed to the eastern side of the city, but even as they moved into position, I knew it wouldn't be enough.

The southern provinces had brought everything they had,

and they were overwhelming us with sheer numbers. Without the support of Vicrum and his forces, we were stretched thin. We couldn't hold out forever.

Where is Vicrum?

The question burned in my mind as I surveyed the battlefield, my heart pounding in my chest. I had trusted Vicrum, relied on him to be there when we needed him most. But now, as the battle raged around us, he was nowhere to be found.

The clang of steel and the cries of the wounded filled the air, and I could feel the weight of the battle pressing down on me. This wasn't just a fight for control of Hyanasarri—it was a fight for the future of Nantrium. If we lost here, the southern provinces would take control of the Rementheium mines, and with it, they would hold the balance of power in the realm.

We couldn't afford to lose.

I turned to Zephyros, who had just returned from the front lines, his face streaked with sweat and dirt. His eyes were sharp, electric, as if the storm within him was barely contained.

"Any word from Vicrum?" he asked, his voice low but urgent.

I shook my head, frustration gnawing at the edges of my thoughts. "None. He should have been here by now."

Zephyros cursed under his breath, his gaze shifting to the battlefield below. "We can't hold them off forever. If Vicrum doesn't arrive soon, we're going to be overrun."

I knew he was right. The southern forces were closing in, and our defenses were weakening. We needed reinforcements, and we needed them now.

But Vicrum was still missing, and with each passing moment, the battle for Hyanasarri grew more desperate. Where are you, Vicrum? The thought echoed in my mind as I turned back to the battlefield, my heart heavy with the weight of what was to come.

Chapter XIX

The Storm of War

The clash of steel and the crackle of elemental power filled the air, creating a blare of chaos that reverberated through the streets of Hyanasarri. We had been pushed back, retreating from the main gate as Rhalor's forces surged forward with brutal efficiency. I stood in the midst of it all, my sword slick with the blood of enemies and my mind racing, trying to hold onto the hope that we could still turn the tide of this battle. But as the southern armies closed in, wave after wave of soldiers crashing against our defenses like a relentless tide, it became harder to see a way out. The Omni Order fought valiantly, each of us drawing on our connection to the Divine Power, wielding our elemental abilities with as much precision and strength as we could muster. But even that was not enough. The forces of Rhalor and his southern allies were too many and too determined. They pressed us further and further back, toward the heart of the city.

The streets of Hyanasarri, once silent and abandoned, had become a battlefield of elemental fury. The stones beneath our feet were cracked and scorched, shattered by the raw power being unleashed on both sides. I could see Zephyros in the distance, his eyes wild with energy as bolts of lightning leapt from his fingertips, arcing through the air and striking down enemies with deadly precision. He was a force of nature, a living storm, and yet even his power was being tested by the sheer numbers arrayed against us.

To my left, Vornak was commanding his troops with icy calm, his breath visible in the frigid air around him. The temperature plummeted wherever he fought, frost creeping across the ground as he summoned towering walls of ice to shield our forces from the advancing army. But the walls were beginning to crack, shattering under the force of Rhalor's relentless assault.

Durion, steadfast and Vandrel, unyielding, stood in the center of the city, their connection to the earth itself allowing him to shape the battlefield to our advantage. Vines and roots burst from the ground and waters at their command, entangling enemies and dragging them down into the earth. The ground shifted and heaved, creating barriers and pitfalls for the southern forces, but even Vandrel and Durion's strength had its limits. The weight of the battle was pushing us all to the brink. And I—I stood at the heart of it all, the Divine Power pulsing through me, a constant reminder of the burden I carried.

O'Rhyus had chosen me to be the light, to bring balance to this world. But as I watched my men fall, one after another, their blood staining the streets of Hyanasarri, I began to wonder if I had failed in that duty. This was not balance. This was chaos.

"Fall back to the central district!" I shouted, my voice hoarse from the strain of battle. "We need to regroup!"

The order spread through our ranks like wildfire, and I watched as my soldiers began to retreat, their faces clear with exhaustion. The central district of Hyanasarri was our last line of defense, the heart of the city where the Rementheium mines lay hidden beneath the earth. If we lost this ground, we would lose everything.

Rhalor's forces were relentless. They pushed us back with brutal force, their soldiers pouring into the city from all sides. The southern provinces had come to claim Hyanasarri, and they would stop at nothing to take it.

I moved with my men, my sword cutting through the ranks of the enemy as we retreated. My heart pounded in my chest, adrenaline surging through my veins as the battle raged around me. I could feel the Divine Power thrumming inside me, begging to be unleashed, but I held it back. There was a delicate balance to maintaining control, and I couldn't afford to lose myself in the chaos of this fight.

We reached the central district just as the first wave of Rhalor's forces broke through our defenses at the gate. The clash of steel and the roar of power filled the air as the battle spilled into the streets, tearing through the heart of Hyanasarri like a storm. I could see the desperation in the eyes of my men, the realization that we were on the brink of defeat.

"Hold the line!" I shouted, rallying them as best I could. "We cannot let them take this city!"

Zephyros, his face streaked with blood and sweat, appeared at my side. "They're coming from all sides," he said, his voice grim. "We can't hold them off for much longer."

I clenched my fists, feeling the weight of his words. He was right. The southern forces were overwhelming us, and no matter how hard we fought, they kept coming. For every soldier we struck down, two more took his place.

"Where is Vicrum?" Zephyros asked, his voice edged with frustration. "We need his men. We can't hold out like this."

"I don't know," I admitted. "He should have been here by now."

Vicrum and his forces were supposed to be our reinforcements, the final piece of the puzzle that would allow us to turn the tide of this battle. But they were nowhere to be seen, and the longer we fought, the more hopeless our situation became.

"Keep fighting," I said, my voice firm. "We can't give up now."

Zephyros nodded, his jaw tight with determination, before he turned and disappeared into the fray once more. I watched him go, feeling a surge of pride at his resilience. The men of the Omni Order were strong, each of them connected to the Divine Power in ways that made them formidable opponents. But even they were being pushed to their limits.

The central district was rapidly becoming a war zone. Buildings crumbled under the force of our destructive powers, the streets littered with the bodies of the fallen. The air was thick with the acrid smell of smoke and blood, and the cries of the wounded echoed through the chaos. We were destroying the city in our desperation to hold it, and yet, I knew that if we didn't stop Rhalor here, there would be nothing left to save.

I moved through the streets, my sword a blur as I cut down any enemy that crossed my path. The Divine Power surged through me, lending me strength, but it was not enough. The southern forces were pressing us from all sides, their soldiers pouring into the city like a flood. I could feel the tide turning against us, the weight of defeat pressing down on my shoulders like a leaden cloak. And then, as the battle reached its peak, I heard a sound that cut through the chaos like a knife.

A horn.

I turned, my heart pounding in my chest as I looked toward the northwest. There, on the horizon, I saw them.

Vicrum.

He had arrived. His army of 100,000 men marched toward the city, their banners flying high in the wind. I felt a surge of relief wash over me, my heart lifting at the sight of our reinforcements. This was it. This was the moment we had been waiting for.

But something was wrong.

Vicrum's forces didn't move. They remained on the outskirts of the city, standing still as the battle raged on without them. I frowned, my mind racing as I tried to understand what was happening.

"Vicrum!" I shouted, my voice carrying over the din of the battle. "We need you! Now!"

But there was no response. Vicrum remained where he was, his army unmoving.

"What is he doing?" Zephyros questioned, his face pale with confusion. "Why isn't he moving?"

"I don't know," I said, the words bitter on my tongue. "I don't understand."

The battle continued to rage around us, the southern forces pressing harder against our defenses, but my mind was fixated on Vicrum and his men. They had the numbers, the strength to turn the tide of this fight, but they stood still, watching from a distance as we fought for our lives.

"Something's not right," I muttered, more to myself than to

Zephyros.

I could feel the weight of the Divine Power inside me, a constant reminder of the light I was meant to protect. But as I looked out at Vicrum, standing motionless on the horizon, a cold dread began to settle in my chest.

Something was wrong, terribly wrong.

And in that moment, as the battle raged on around us, I realized that the war for Hyanasarri was far from over.

In fact, it had only just begun.

Chapter XX

The Descent

The smell of blood and ash filled the air as I stood on the ridge, overlooking the battlefield below. The city of Hyanasarri, once a symbol of the wealth and power of the realm, now lay in ruins. The destruction was almost unimaginable—streets littered with bodies, buildings reduced to rubble, and the very heart of the city torn apart by elemental fury.

From where I stood, I could see it all: the chaos, the destruction, the bloodshed. I could hear the screams of dying men, the clash of steel, and the roar of mankind's forces unleashed without restraint. The world was burning, and I watched it unfold as though from a great distance, as though this war was happening in another reality, to someone else entirely. But this was my war too, whether I wanted it or not. Below, the armies of the north and south clashed with unrelenting ferocity, the lines of battle shifting with every blow. Aldous stood at the center of it all, his golden armor shining even in the dim light of battle. He fought like a man possessed, the Divine Power swirling around him, guiding his strikes, protecting him from harm. He was the embodiment of O'Rhyus's light, the chosen protector of Nantrium, and he fought with the desperate strength of someone who believed he was on the right side of history.

Across from him, I could see Rhalor, the lord of the southern provinces, leading his forces with equal determination. His dark figure loomed over the battlefield, his presence as oppressive as the storm clouds gathering overhead. Where Aldous was the light, Rhalor was the shadow, driven by his desire to claim Hyanasarri and the Rementheium mines for the south. And now, the two leaders of men, of our world were locked in a battle that would decide the future of the realm. It was a battle of gods, of wills, and of powers far beyond the comprehension of ordinary men. And it was tearing this city—this world—apart.

From my vantage point, I could see every strike, every movement. I watched as Aldous and Rhalor clashed again and again, their swords meeting with a force that sent shockwaves through the air. Around them, their soldiers fought and died, their lives lost in the pursuit of a cause that had long since spiraled out of control. The streets of Hyanasarri were filled with the dead and dying, and the city itself seemed to be collapsing under the weight of the conflict. I stood still, watching, waiting. My men, all 100,000 of them, were poised behind me, ready to charge at my command. But I had not yet given that command. I had held them back, waiting for the right moment, waiting for the signal that would change the course of this battle. I could feel their impatience, their need to fight, but I held firm.

"Patience," I whispered to myself, my breath visible in the cold air. "The time will come."

And then, as if summoned by my thoughts, I felt the presence of Apollyon beside me. His voice, soft and insidious, curled into my mind like smoke, whispering the words I had been waiting to hear.

"This is your moment, Vicrum," Apollyon said, his voice a mixture of darkness and temptation. "The light is faltering.

Aldous is weakening. Now is the time to strike."

I didn't respond, not with words. But inside, I felt the pull of Apollyon's influence, the dark tendrils of his power wrapping around my mind, guiding me, pushing me toward the path he had set for me. I had known from the beginning that this day would come, that I would face Aldous on the battlefield. But knowing and doing were two different things.

"Look at them," Apollyon continued, his voice filling my thoughts. "They fight for power, for control, but they are blind to the truth. There is no balance here. There is only chaos. And chaos is where we thrive."

I glanced down at the battlefield again, watching as Aldous and Rhalor continued their duel, their Divine Powers clashing with a fury that shook the very foundations of the city. Lightning crackled through the air as Zephyros summoned his storm, while Vornak unleashed torrents of ice, freezing the ground beneath the feet of Rhalor's soldiers. It was a battle of gods, but it was a battle that would leave nothing but ruin in its wake.

"Do you see?" Apollyon whispered. "This is your destiny, Vicrum. You were never meant to be a pawn in their game. You were meant to rule. To rise above the light and the shadow, to claim the power that is rightfully yours."

I felt the weight of his words, the temptation of the power he offered. It was intoxicating, the idea that I could rise above it all, that I could claim the realm for myself and bring about the change that Nantrium so desperately needed. I had always believed in balance, in the idea that light and dark could coexist, but now, standing on the edge of this battlefield, I wasn't so sure. Maybe Apollyon was right.

Maybe the world needed to be torn apart before it could be rebuilt.

"Now, Vicrum," Apollyon urged, his voice growing more insistent. "Lead your men into battle. Strike at Aldous when he is weakest, descend upon him and take what is yours."

My heart pounded in my chest, and I felt the weight of the decision pressing down on me. This was the moment. The moment when everything would change.

I turned to my men, their faces grim and determined, their weapons gleaming in the pale light. They were ready. They had been ready for this from the beginning. All they needed was my command. But before I gave it, I hesitated. For just a moment, I allowed myself to reflect on how I had come to this point, how the events of my life had led me here, to the edge of a battlefield, about to change the course of history.

I thought of Vyhonia, my wife, the woman I loved more than anything in this world. I had fought for her, I had done everything for her, and yet I hadn't seen her in weeks. I hadn't told her the full extent of the darkness that had taken root inside me, hadn't shared with her the whispers of Apollyon that had become a constant presence in my mind. She had always been my guiding light, but now, that light seemed so far away.

I thought of the day I had stood in Lushahiem, watching as Aldous rose to power, chosen by O'Rhyus to be the protector of the realm. I had admired him then, had seen in him a strength that I had wanted for myself. But over time, that admiration had turned to resentment. I had begun to see the cracks in his vision, the blind devotion to a balance that was no longer possible. The world was changing, and Aldous refused to change with it.

And I thought of Apollyon, the fallen god who had shown me a different path. He had promised me power, had shown me that the balance was a lie, that light and dark could never coexist. He had offered me a way to rise above the chaos, to claim the world for myself and remake it in my image.

I had chosen this path. And now, there was no turning back. I took a deep breath, feeling the weight of the decision settle in my chest. And then, I gave the command.

"Charge."

My voice rang out across the ridge, and in an instant, my men surged forward, their battle cries filling the air as they descended upon the battlefield below. I mounted my horse, the powerful beast beneath me rearing up as I spurred it forward, leading my troops into the heart of the fray. As we charged down the ridge, the ground shaking beneath the hooves of my horse, I felt a surge of adrenaline rush through me. This was it. The moment I had been waiting for. The moment when everything would be decided.

I could see Aldous now, locked in combat with Rhalor, their swords clashing in a furious dance of light and shadow. Around them, the battle raged on, the soldiers of the north and south fighting with a desperation that only came in the face of annihilation. The elemental powers of the Omni Order and the southern provinces clashed in the air, fire and ice, lightning and earth, tearing the city apart with their raw force. But none of that mattered now. All that mattered was Aldous. As I rode toward him, I felt the presence of Apollyon growing stronger, his voice whispering in my mind, urging me forward.

I gripped my sword tightly, my heart pounding in my chest as I closed the distance between us. The chaos of the battle swirled around me, but this was the moment when everything would change.

Chapter XXI

The Fury

The battle roared around me like the ocean, but my mind was eerily calm. Every clang of steel, every scream of pain, every surge of Divine Power echoed in the distance as though I was standing apart from it all. Yet I was at the center, the eye of the storm. My heart pounded, my senses sharpened, and through the chaos, a single, unshakable truth took root in my soul.

I was going to lose this battle.

The realization hit me like a cold wind, chilling me to the bone. I could feel it, an overwhelming sense of dread settling over me, a certainty born not from fear or doubt, but from something deeper. Something beyond me. It was as if the fabric of the world itself whispered it into my ear. I was fighting valiantly, as were my men. Zephyros, Vornak, Durion, and Vandrel were all engaged in the fight of their lives, holding back the onslaught of Rhalor and his southern forces. The streets of Hyanasarri were drenched in blood, the elemental fury of both sides ripping apart the very ground we stood on. And yet, it wasn't enough. The south was too strong. They were pushing us back, inch by inch, and with every step they took, the balance shifted further in their favor. And then, through the madness of the battlefield, I felt something else. Something darker. A presence that sent a shiver down my spine.

Vicrum.

I didn't need to see him to know he was there, watching,

waiting. The weight of his betrayal hung over me like a shadow, his allegiance with Apollyon staining his soul. I could feel him moving through the battle, like a predator stalking its prey, waiting for the perfect moment to strike. He was coming for me and I knew it.

But I wasn't afraid. Not anymore. Not today. Not ever.

A strange calm settled over me, and in that moment, I knew what had to be done.

"I will not lose this day," I announced, the words more to myself than to anyone around me.

And then, it happened.

A flash of light.

It wasn't like the light I had always known, the steady, guiding presence of O'Rhyus that had carried me through so many battles before. No, this was something else. Something deeper. It wasn't just light—it was the very essence of the Divine Power, pure and overwhelming. It surged through me, lifting me beyond the limits of my mortal body, filling me with a strength I had never known.

The world slowed around me. The sounds of the battle faded, the movements of the soldiers became sluggish, as though time itself had bent to my will. I could see every detail, every breath, every heartbeat. The Divine Power flowed through me, not just as a weapon, but as a part of me. I had become something more—something beyond what I had ever imagined.

I had ascended.

And with this new strength, I turned back to the battlefield, my eyes locking on Rhalor, who was charging toward me with fury in his eyes. His soldiers surged behind him, desperate to bring me down, but they were nothing more than shadows to me now.

I raised my hand, and with a single gesture, a wave of energy blasted out from me, pushing Rhalor and his men back. The force of it sent them stumbling, creating a wide gap between us. Rhalor was strong, there was no doubt about that. He was a valiant force, a leader who commanded respect through his sheer power. But now, in this moment, he was nothing compared to what I had become. But before I could deal with him, I felt the presence behind me, the one I had been waiting for.

Vicrum.

I spun around, my movements faster than any mortal could track. There he was, his sword raised, his eyes filled with determination, and yet... doubt. He had come to strike me down, to claim his place in Apollyon's dark plans. But he was too slow.

Without hesitation, I reached out and caught him by the throat.

Vicrum's eyes widened in shock as my hand closed around his neck with an iron grip. He struggled, his hands clawing at mine, but there was nothing he could do. I could feel the power radiating from him, the remnants of the Divine Power that had once been his strength, but it was weak now. He had chosen the wrong side. He had given himself to darkness, and now he would pay the price.

With a single, swift motion, I swung him overhead and slammed him into the ground. The impact was devastating, the earth beneath him cracking as the force of it reverberated through the streets. I heard the sickening snap of bone, and

I knew that his spine had been shattered. Vicrum gasped in pain, his body convulsing, but there was no escape.

He was broken.

I looked down at him, and for a moment, I felt a pang of something—regret, perhaps. He seemed a simple man, before Apollyon. But the simple times had long passed. He had made his choice, and now I had made mine. I released him, letting his limp body fall to the ground.

He wasn't dead, not yet. But he would never fight again.

Behind me, I heard the roar of Rhalor as he charged once more, refusing to give up. He was relentless, driven by his ambition and his hatred. But I had no time for him. Not anymore.

I turned to face him, just as he brought his sword down in a vicious arc. But I was faster. With my left hand, I reached out and caught him by the head, my fingers digging into his skull. His body froze, his sword falling from his hand as he realized what was happening.

For a moment, he struggled, his muscles straining against my grip. But it was futile. I held him there, staring into his eyes, watching the fear creep into them as he realized that he had lost.

And then, with my right hand, I struck.

With a swift, lethal motion, my hand sliced through his flesh, striking with such ferocity that the very edge of my palm became a weapon of death. In one impossibly powerful chop, my hand severed the neck cleanly, as if cutting through nothing but air, leaving the body to collapse in silence.

Rhalor's head rolled across the ground, his lifeless body crumpling at my feet.

For a moment, the battlefield fell silent. The soldiers of the southern provinces, those who had followed Rhalor into battle, stared in shock and horror at what I had done. Their leader, the man who had promised them victory, was dead.

And then, they broke.

Panic spread through their ranks as they began to retreat, their discipline shattered by the sight of their fallen leader. But it wasn't over yet. There were still others who needed to be dealt with.

I saw Morvyn, Eldrith, and Vaedric exchange a look of dread. They knew what was coming. They had seen what I had become, and they wanted no part of it. They turned to flee, their soldiers following suit, but they wouldn't get far.

In an instant, I disappeared from where I stood, the Divine Power carrying me faster than any of them could comprehend. And then, I was there, standing before Eldrith, the flames of his power flashing in his eyes as he realized there was no escape.

I did not hesitate. I drove my hand straight through his chest.

His eyes widened in shock, and in a moment, the fire in them dimmed as the life drained from his body. I withdrew my hand, letting his body fall to the ground in a heap. One down. I turned my gaze to Morvyn and Vaedric, who were still running, their elemental powers crackling around them as they tried to flee. But I wouldn't let them escape.

Before I could strike, though, I felt something—a pull, a force that I hadn't expected. It was Zephyros, his eyes wide with fear and determination as he, along with Durion, Vornak, and Vandrel, used their combined powers to subdue me. Lightning, earth, ice, and water wrapped around me, their elemental forces binding me, holding me in place. I could feel their power pushing against mine, and for a moment, I struggled against it, my anger flaring as I tried to break free. But they were strong, stronger than I had anticipated.

"Aldous, stop!" Zephyros shouted, his voice filled with desperation. "This isn't you!"

I wanted to fight. I wanted to destroy them all, to rid the world of the darkness that had infected it. But something in Zephyros's voice, in the way the others looked at me, made me hesitate.

Slowly, the fury inside me began to ebb, the blinding light of the Divine Power dimming as I regained control. The battle around us continued to rage, but I could feel the tide turning. The southern provinces were retreating, their forces scattered and broken. I took a deep breath, feeling the weight of the Divine Power settle back into its familiar place within me. The battle was over.

Zephyros and the others released their hold on me, their faces pale with relief. I could see the exhaustion in their eyes, the strain of holding me back taking its toll. But they had done it. They had saved me from myself.

"Thank you," I whispered, my voice hoarse with emotion.

Zephyros nodded, his expression grim. I glanced around the battlefield one last time. The southern provinces were in full retreat, their leaders either dead or fleeing. Hyanasarri lay in ruins, but we had won the battle.

As Zephyros and the others led me away, I couldn't shake the feeling that this was only the beginning. The darkness was still out there, lurking, waiting for its chance to strike. And I would be ready.

The light would not falter. Not again.

Chapter XXII

The End

The sky above me was a hazy, swirling mass of gray clouds, and through the blur of my vision, I could just make out the faint light of the sun struggling to break through. It seemed so far away, unreachable, like the life I had once known before all of this madness. My body ached with pain, every breath a shallow rasp that sent sharp, stabbing sensations through my chest.

I couldn't move. I couldn't feel my legs, and my spine burned with a dull, relentless agony. I knew that my body was broken, shattered by the force of Aldous's wrath. He had slammed me into the ground with a power that no mortal man could withstand, and now I lay there, dying slowly, my life draining from me with each labored breath.

But all I could think about was Vyhonia.

Her face appeared in my mind, clear and vivid, as if she were standing right beside me. Her warm smile, her gentle eyes, the way her hair shimmered like spun gold in the sunlight. She was the light in my world, the reason I had fought, the reason I had allowed myself to fall into the darkness that now consumed me. I had done everything for her. I had betrayed my faith, my land, and my very soul—all for her. But what had it been worth?

A wave of regret washed over me, bitter and cold. I had believed that following Apollyon would give me the power to save her, to protect her from the sickness that had threatened to take her from me. But in the end, I had only brought more suffering. I had become a tool of darkness, a puppet in Apollyon's grand design, and now, as I lay dying, I realized that I had been a fool.

I had sacrificed everything for nothing.

A shadow fell over me, and I forced my eyes to focus. Aldous stood above me, his golden armor splattered with blood and grime from the battle, his face grim and resolute. The light of the Divine Power still clung to him, shimmering faintly around the edges of his form, but there was no triumph in his eyes. No victory.

There was only sorrow.

For a long moment, neither of us spoke. The sounds of the battle around us had faded into the distance, the cries of the wounded and the clash of steel barely audible over the rush of blood in my ears. The world seemed to narrow to just the two of us—Aldous, the light, and me, the darkness.

"Vicrum," Aldous said softly, his voice filled with a heaviness I had never heard from him before. "This wasn't how it was supposed to end."

I tried to respond, but the words caught in my throat, my lungs too weak to force them out. I coughed, and the taste of blood filled my mouth, thick and metallic.

Aldous knelt beside me, his eyes scanning my broken form. "You betrayed us. You gave yourself to Apollyon. Why?"

I closed my eyes, the memory of Vyhonia's face flooding my mind once more. "For her," I whispered, my voice barely more than a breath.

Aldous's expression didn't change, but I could see the understanding in his eyes. He had known, of course. He had always known. Vyhonia had been the center of my world, the one thing that mattered above all else. And in my desperation to save her, I had lost myself.

Aldous remained silent, watching me with that same sorrowful gaze. It was the look of a man who had seen too much, who had witnessed the destruction of lives, of friendships, of entire worlds, all for the sake of power. And now, he was witnessing my destruction.

"I was wrong," I said, my voice cracking with the weight of my regret. "I see that now."

Aldous shifted, his hand resting lightly on the hilt of his sword. "It's not too late, Vicrum," he said quietly. "There can still be redemption. The sins you've committed, the lives you've taken... they can be forgiven. But the world must be purified first."

Aldous gazed into the distance. "Nantrium is broken. The balance has been shattered, the light and dark are at war. But there can be redemption. The world can be restored. We can bring it back to the way it was meant to be."

A bitter laugh escaped my lips, though it caused a sharp pain to shoot through my chest. Aldous met my gaze, his eyes steady. "I will do what is necessary. The balance must be restored, and that means ending the chaos. Even if it means blood must be spilled."

I stared up at the sky, the swirling clouds seeming to grow darker, more distant. There was a finality in Aldous's words, a certainty that left no room for doubt. He was the light, the embodiment of O'Rhyus's will, and he would see the world purified, no matter the cost. And I... I was the darkness that had to be erased.

"I never wanted this," I whispered, the weight of my words

and choices literally crushing me.

"I know," Aldous said softly, his voice filled with something like pity. "But it's too late now. You made your choice."

He stood slowly, drawing his sword from its sheath. The blade gleamed in the fading light, and for a moment, it seemed to glow with an otherworldly brightness, as though it too had been touched by the Divine Power.

I closed my eyes, waiting for the end. There was nothing left to fight for. Vyhonia... she was lost to me, and with her, everything that had ever mattered. I had betrayed my friends, my allies, my own soul, and for what? For power I couldn't even use? For a promise that had been nothing more than a lie? Apollyon had betrayed me, just as I had betrayed everyone else. And now, it was over.

"I forgive you, may you find the light" Aldous whispered, his voice carried on the wind.

And then, with one swift motion, the blade came down.

The pain was brief, a sharp sting that quickly faded into numbness. And then, there was only darkness. But as the darkness took me, I felt something else—a presence, cold and angry, watching from the shadows. Apollyon. He had been there all along, watching, waiting for his moment to strike. But now, in death, I could feel his fury, his rage boiling beneath the surface. I had failed him. I had been his chosen instrument, his puppet, and I had fallen.

Apollyon's voice echoed in the back of my mind, a low, growling whisper filled with venom. "You were weak, Vicrum. You had the power, the opportunity, and you squandered it."

I wanted to respond, to tell him that I had been wrong to

trust him, that I had realized too late what a fool I had been. But the words wouldn't come. My body was failing me, the life draining from my veins.

"You could have had everything," Apollyon hissed. "But now, you will have nothing."

I could feel his anger seething, growing stronger as my life slipped away. And then, just as the last remnants of consciousness began to fade, I felt a wave of cold fury wash over me, more powerful than anything I had ever felt before. Apollyon was not finished. His plans, his ambitions, had not died with me. He would find another, someone stronger, someone who would not falter as I had. And when that day came, when Apollyon's shadow rose again, the world would burn.

But for me, there was only the silence of the void. And in that silence, I found peace.

Chapter XXIII

The Reflection

The stillness of Lushahiem felt heavy tonight, a deep and oppressive quiet that settled over the city like a blanket of fog. Outside, the streets were hushed, the few remaining lights shining like dying stars in the cold night air. The echoes of the battle in Hyanasarri still lingered in the minds of the people, casting a long, dark shadow over every corner of Nantrium. But here, in the solitude of my chambers, that darkness was even more pronounced.

I sat at my desk, the simple wooden surface strewn with parchment and ink, my hands resting lightly on the quill that I had yet to lift. Before me was a letter I had started hours ago but hadn't been able to finish. Words felt insufficient. They always had, especially now, after everything that had transpired. What words could possibly encapsulate the weight of what I had done? Of what had been done to me?

The memories of Hyanasarri clung to me like a sickness, a darkness I couldn't shake. I could still see the streets filled with the dead, the city torn apart by elemental forces unleashed in fury. I could still feel the raw power of the Divine Light coursing through me, the moment I had ascended to something beyond mortal, beyond even myself. And I could still hear the final breath of Vicrum, his body broken beneath my hand, his spine shattered as easily as one might snap a twig.

Vicrum.

I couldn't get him out of my mind. Even now, days after

the battle had ended, his voice haunted me. His words, the things he said before he died, echoed in the silence of my home.

"I never wanted this."

He had been so sure, so resolute in his decision to follow Apollyon. But in the end, he was nothing more than a man driven by desperation. A man who had lost everything and clung to the one thing that offered him hope. He had betrayed me, betrayed the Omni Order, and yet... in his final moments, I could see the regret in his eyes. Had I done the right thing? Had I brought justice to a traitor, or had I simply killed a man who had already lost everything?

I didn't know anymore.

The weight of O'Rhyus's choice hung over me, heavy and suffocating. He had chosen me to bring order to Nantrium, to restore balance to a world that was spiraling into chaos. But what kind of order was this? What kind of balance could be found in the bloodshed I had wrought? I looked down at my hands—hands that had taken life, hands that had wielded the Divine Power with such force that I had torn Rhalor's head from his shoulders as if it were nothing. Hands that had broken Vicrum, a man.

And for what?

Order? Peace?

Was this what O'Rhyus had meant when he chose me? Was this the path I was supposed to walk? A path of death and destruction in the name of balance?

I shook my head, trying to dispel the dark thoughts creeping into my mind. I needed to think. I needed to plan. If I was to bring order to Nantrium, it would not be through chaos.

It would be through structure, through strategy, through leadership.

Vicrum had been wrong about many things, but in one, he had been right: the future of Nantrium could not be built on the ashes of the past. If I was to establish the Hyltorian Empire, it had to be built on something stronger than blood and steel.

The quill in my hand dipped into the ink, and I began to write.

To the Scouts of Lushahiem, Guards of the North, East, South, and West

By my authority as the First Shepherd of the Hyltorian Empire, I command you to journey to the far reaches of Nantrium. Your mission is clear: find Thyldar and his people. The province of Hyanasarri has been abandoned, its wealth left unclaimed, and its ruler gone without a trace. Thyldar's defiance in the face of war does not absolve him of responsibility. He and his people must be found. They are vital to the future of our realm.

I expect updates on your progress every cycle. Leave no stone unturned, no cave unexplored. Thyldar is out there, and he will not escape his part in the destiny of Nantrium.

Signed,

Aldous, Shepherd of Hyltoria

I set the quill down, the ink still fresh on the parchment as I sealed the letter. It wasn't much, but it was a start. Thyldar had to be found. His abandonment of Hyanasarri had been a strategic move, one that had nearly cost us the war. But more importantly, his people—his miners—were the key to what would come next.

I had plans for Hyanasarri. The mines, filled with the precious Rementheium, could not remain dormant. They were the lifeblood of Nantrium, the very core of what had kept the realm functioning for centuries. With the power of Rementheium, we could build something new. Something indestructible. I leaned back in my chair, my thoughts drifting to the visions I had in the aftermath of the battle. The image of Rementheium-forged swords and armor, weapons infused with the power of the Divine, capable of withstanding any attack, any force. It was a vision of strength, of security. And I would make it real.

I had already sent word to the remaining miners in Hyanasarri. The mines were to be reopened, their wealth reclaimed. I would oversee the forging of new swords, new suits of armor, each imbued with the energy of Rementheium power cores. These weapons would be the foundation of the Grand Hyltorian Army, an army that would not just defend the realm but ensure that no enemy, internal or external, could ever threaten us again. But an army was more than just weapons. It needed leadership. It needed structure. And I had a plan for that too.

The Hyltorian Empire would be built on the backs of those willing to serve, and at the head of that empire, I would place Valta Riomni—governors appointed to oversee each of the thirteen provinces. They would answer to me, and they would ensure that the empire ran smoothly, that order was maintained in every corner of the realm.

Equal to them would be the Vhankilla's, the rank of generals who would lead the armies in times of war, and the Khansteph's, the commanders who would fill the ranks of the enlisted soldiers. Together, they would form the backbone of the Grand Hyltorian Army, an army that would be feared by our enemies and respected by our allies. It was a grand vision, one that would take time, effort, and sacrifice to bring to life. But it was the only way forward. Nantrium could not survive without order, without a guiding hand to lead it out of the chaos that had consumed it for so long.

I rose from my desk, pacing the length of the room as the weight of my plans settled over me. The scope of what I was about to undertake was vast, almost overwhelming. But I had no choice. This was the path O'Rhyus had set me on, and I would see it through to the end, no matter what it cost me.

But that didn't make it any easier to bear.

My thoughts drifted back to Vicrum once more, to the look in his eyes as he lay broken at my feet. He had chosen his path, just as I had chosen mine. But had he really been so different from me? He had fought for what he believed in, for the future he thought was right. He had betrayed me, yes, but had I not betrayed myself in the process? Had I not betrayed the very ideals I had once sworn to uphold? I shook my head, pushing the thoughts away. There was no time for doubt, no time for regret. The sins of the past could not be undone, but perhaps... perhaps they could be redeemed. Perhaps there was still a way to bring balance to Nantrium, to restore the light that had been lost. But it would take time.

It would take patience. And it would take more sacrifice.

I returned to my desk, the letters before me a reminder of the work still to be done. There was so much to plan, so much to organize. The Hyltorian Empire was still in its infancy, and it would be my responsibility to guide it, to shape it into something that would endure. I took a deep breath, letting the stillness of the night wash over me. The battle for Hyanasarri was over, but the battle for Nantrium was just beginning.

With a final glance at the letter before me, I rose from my chair and extinguished the lamp on my desk. The room plunged into darkness, but I felt no fear. The light of O'Rhyus was with me, and it would guide me through the darkness, just as it always had. I made my way to my bed, the weight of the day settling over me like a heavy cloak. My body was tired, my mind weary from the endless planning and reflection. But as I lay down, my thoughts drifted once more to the future—to the vision of the empire I would build, to the armies that would protect it, to the peace I would bring to Nantrium.

The light would prevail. It had to.

And with that thought, I closed my eyes and let the darkness take me.

Chapter XXIV

The Path of War

The grand hall of Lushahiem stood silent, all but the soft rustle of banners that adorned the high walls, fluttering gently in the cold, unyielding breeze. I sat at the head of the long stone table, my eyes tracing the lines and grooves of its surface, as if searching for answers in its ancient craftsmanship. The weight of the past few weeks pressed heavily upon me—of Hyanasarri, of Vicrum, of the decisions I had made and the ones still to come.

Around the table sat the remaining leaders of Nantrium, men who had once been scattered across the realm, their fates and allegiances uncertain. But now, they had gathered under one roof, summoned by my authority as Shepherd of the Hyltorian Empire, and the question that loomed over all of us was one that would determine the future of the realm itself.

Would we find peace, or would we surrender to war?

I glanced around the table, studying the faces of those who had answered the call. Zephyros, ever sharp and electric, sat at my right hand. His presence was as steady as it was commanding, his eyes burning with the same restless energy that always accompanied him. He had been with me since the beginning, and I knew he would follow me wherever this path led.

Durion, father of the forest, sat to my left, his eyes calm yet wary. His connection to the natural world had always grounded him, but there was a shadow of concern in his gaze. Even the forests of Nantrium could not be shielded from what was to come.

Vornak, cold and calculating as always, sat near the end of the table, his face pale and his hands clasped tightly before him. The weight of the impending conflict hung heavy on his shoulders, and though he tried to mask it, I could see the worry etched into the lines of his expression. He was a man who understood the cost of war, and it was clear that he was not eager to pay that price.

And then there was Vandrel, the watcher of the waters, who had always been the voice of reason among us. He leaned forward slightly, his dark eyes scanning the room, as if measuring the mood of the assembly. His calm demeanor never wavered, but I could tell that he, too, understood the gravity of the situation.

The rest of the seats, however, remained empty.

The seats for Hyanasarri, Mophia, and Wyldren—empty.

The seats for the Southern Provinces, also empty, their leaders too fearful or defiant to show their faces here.

The silence was thick, pregnant with the weight of the unspoken truths that lingered in the air.

At last, I rose from my chair, the scrape of stone against stone echoing through the hall. All eyes turned toward me, waiting for the words that would seal the fate of Nantrium.

"Valta Riomni," I began, using the title I had bestowed upon the remaining leaders of the realm. They were no longer just lords of their provinces; they were the masters of the Omni Order, the leaders who would shape the future of the Hyltorian Empire. "We are gathered here today not to lament what has been lost, but to decide what must be done."

I paused, letting the weight of my words sink in.

"The Southern Provinces have made their choice. They have chosen fear. They have chosen defiance. And they have chosen to ignore the call for unity that we have extended to them."

Zephyros shifted in his seat beside me, his eyes gleaming with barely concealed impatience. He had never been one for drawn-out speeches, and I knew he was eager for action. But this moment required more than just action—it required resolve.

"Our goal is peace," I continued, my voice steady. "Peace through strength, peace through unity. But make no mistake, we will not hesitate to bring war to those who would stand in the way of that peace."

At that, Vandrel spoke, his voice calm but firm. "Aldous, are we truly prepared to declare war? The realm has suffered enough. Do we risk plunging Nantrium into even greater chaos?"

I met his gaze, knowing that this was the heart of the matter. Vandrel had always been the one to caution against rash decisions, the one to remind us of the cost of conflict. But even he could not deny that the path to peace was growing narrower by the day.

"The time for hesitation is over," Zephyros interjected, his voice sharp. "We've offered them peace. They've spat in our faces. Now it's time to show them the might of the Grand Hyltorian Army."

Vornak frowned, his pale face tightening. "And what if they're not as weak as you think? What if the Southern Provinces have been preparing for this? If we march on them, it could spark a war that we can't contain."

Durion remained quiet, his eyes closed as if in deep thought. He had always been slow to anger, but I could see the tension in the set of his jaw. He, too, knew what was at stake.

"The Southern Provinces have already chosen their path," I said, addressing the room. "They didn't show up today because they know what they've done. They've turned their backs on unity, on peace. But we cannot allow their defiance to undermine the rest of Nantrium."

I placed my hands on the table, leaning forward as I spoke.

"The empty seats of Hyanasarri, Mophia, and Wyldren are a reminder of what we've lost. But we cannot let their absence paralyze us. We must act."

Vandrel's gaze softened, but I could still see the concern in his eyes. "And what of the people in those provinces, Aldous? What of the innocents who will be caught in the crossfire?"

"I will do everything in my power to avoid unnecessary bloodshed," I replied, though the words felt hollow in my mouth. "But we cannot shy away from this any longer. If we do not take control of this situation, the chaos will spread, and the Southern Provinces will consume the realm."

Zephyros nodded in agreement, his expression hard. "We have the power to stop them, Aldous. We need to use it."

I glanced around the room, meeting the eyes of each of the remaining leaders. I could see the doubt in some, the fear in others. But more than that, I could see the determination. They knew, just as I did, that there was no turning back.

"This is the official declaration of war," I said, my voice ringing out in the silence of the hall. "The Southern

Provinces have chosen their path. And now, we will show them the strength of the Hyltorian Empire."

Durion finally spoke, his voice low but resolute. "What will you have us do, Aldous?"

I straightened, feeling the weight of leadership settle over me once more. "Zephyros, you are named Eomni, leader of the Omni Order, and my right hand. You will oversee the deployment of the Grand Hyltorian Army."

Zephyros gave a sharp nod, his eyes gleaming with anticipation. He had always been a warrior at heart, and now he would have the chance to prove himself on the battlefield.

"Durion," I continued, turning to the forest master. "You will ensure that the supply lines remain intact, meet with Fenric. The forests of Nantrium must continue to support our war effort."

Durion nodded, though his expression remained somber.

"Vornak," I said, addressing the ice lord. "Your knowledge of the cold and your strategic mind will be key in fortifying our defenses. Prepare the northern border for any retaliation."

Vornak nodded, though I could see the concern still lingering in his eyes.

Finally, I turned to Vandrel, the watcher of the waters. "You will be our voice of reason, Vandrel. The Southern Provinces may fear us now, but we will still offer them one final chance for peace."

Vandrel's brow furrowed, but he did not object. "And if they refuse?"

"Then we march," I said simply. "And we march with the full might of the Hyltorian Empire behind us."

The room fell silent once more as my words settled over the

leaders gathered before me. There was no turning back now. The path had been set, and we would follow it to the end, whatever that end might be.

I stood, lifting the letter I had written earlier, a message that would soon be sent to the Southern Provinces, to the remaining leaders who had defied us. Rhalor, Vaedric and Morvyn, the last holdouts of the rebellion. They would receive our offer, but it would be their final chance.

"The message will be sent to Rhalor, Vaedric and Morvyn," I said, my voice steady. "They have a choice: surrender and join the Hyltorian Empire, or prepare for the wrath of the Grand Hyltorian Army."

Zephyros smirked, his fingers twitching with the anticipation of action. "I'll make sure the army is ready."

I nodded, my gaze sweeping across the room one last time. The trade provinces, those who had shown up today, had already pledged their loyalty. They knew what was coming, and they understood the strength that the Hyltorian Empire now commanded. The seats for the Southern Provinces were empty, but they would not remain so for long.

The meeting was over. The decisions had been made.

I sat back down at my desk, feeling the exhaustion settle into my bones. The future of Nantrium rested on the shoulders of those in this room, but more than that, it rested on me. The weight of leadership was heavy, but I would carry it. For the realm, for the people, for the balance that O'Rhyus had entrusted me to maintain.

As the leaders filed out of the hall, I remained seated, staring at the candlelight on my desk. The war would come soon. It was inevitable now. But I would face it with the strength and the resolve that had been given to me. I would not falter.

I picked up the quill once more and finished my final notes for the day. With the declaration of war sent and the plans set in motion, there was little more to do but wait for the Southern Provinces' response.

I extinguished the candle and stood, the darkness of the room enveloping me as I made my way to my bed. The silence of Lushahiem settled around me once more, but this time, it felt different. The calm before the storm.

As I lay down, my thoughts drifted to the future. To the battles that lay ahead. To the people I would lead. And to the light that would guide us through the darkness.

The Hyltorian Empire would rise. And nothing would stand in its way.

With that final thought, I closed my eyes and let the quiet of the night take me.

Chapter XXV

The Rise of the Hyltorian Empire

The sun hung high over Lushahiem, casting long, golden rays over the gleaming spires of the city. The streets below were packed with people—men, women, and children, all gathered to hear the words of their newly crowned leader. Their faces were a sea of emotions, some filled with hope, others with uncertainty, but all with the same expectant look in their eyes as they awaited the proclamation that would shape the future of Nantrium.

I stood atop the grand balcony of the Central Palace, looking down at the masses before me. My golden armor glinted in the sunlight, the cape of deep burgundy fluttering slightly in the wind behind me. From this vantage point, I could see the entirety of Lushahiem stretching out to the horizon, the heart of the Hyltorian Empire that I had sworn to build. Behind me stood the Valta Riomni, the newly appointed governors of the empire's thirteen provinces, though not all the seats were filled yet. Vornak, Durion, Vandrel, Belric, and Fenric—the few who had sworn loyalty, the few I could still trust. Zephyros, my most loyal and trusted companion, now stood as Eomni, the right hand to the emperor of and commander of the Omni Order. These were the men I had chosen to help me bring order to Nantrium. They, along with the others yet to be appointed, would be the architects of a new age of peace and prosperity.

The crowd stirred as I stepped forward, a ripple of anticipation running through them like a wave. I could see their eyes upon me, searching for answers, for guidance. They wanted to believe in this new empire, in the light that I had promised to bring.

"People of Nantrium!" I called, my voice ringing out over the square, amplified by the enchantments woven into the walls of the palace. "Today, we stand at the dawn of a new era—an era of unity, strength, and peace!"

The crowd erupted in cheers, though I could hear the murmurs of doubt and fear beneath the surface. I could see it in their faces, the remnants of the chaos that had plagued this land for too long. They had seen too much bloodshed, too much destruction. But they were ready—ready for something more, something better.

"For too long," I continued, my voice strong and unwavering, "Nantrium has been torn apart by division, by chaos, by the greed and ambitions of those who sought only to serve themselves. But no more. Today, we lay the foundation for a new future—a future built not on fear and hatred, but on unity and strength. Today, we establish the Hyltorian Empire, a realm that will stand as a beacon of light in the darkness!"

The cheers grew louder, and for a brief moment, I felt the weight of my task lift, if only slightly. This was what I had fought for, what I had sacrificed for. To bring order to a world that had been on the brink of collapse.

"In this new empire," I said, "the provinces of Nantrium will be governed by the Valta Riomni—men and women chosen for their wisdom, their strength, and their loyalty to the people. They will ensure that each of the thirteen provinces is cared for, that its people are protected and prosperous. But know this: the Hyltorian Empire is not just a collection of provinces—it is one nation, one people, bound together by our shared destiny!"

I turned slightly, gesturing to the men standing behind me.

"Today, I appoint Vornak, Lord of Ice, to oversee the province of Bodaccia and ensure their security. He will lead the charge in reclaiming our lost territories and protect us from threats beyond our borders."

Vornak, his expression as cold and unyielding as ever, stepped forward and gave a curt nod to the people below. His ice-blue eyes scanned the crowd, his pale skin almost blending with the gleaming frost that seemed to follow him wherever he went.

"Durion, Father of the Forest, will continue to safeguard the province of Hyndale ensuring that the wealth of our land is shared fairly among the people. His knowledge of the earth and its bounty will guide us as we rebuild and strengthen the heart of Nantrium."

Durion, his green cloak rustling softly in the breeze, bowed his head slightly. The lines of his face were calm, but I knew the weight of his responsibility was heavy. The forests of Nantrium had been ravaged by war, and it would take time to heal them.

"Vandrel, Watcher of the Waters, will oversee the province of Talvanofa, ensuring that trade continues to flow free from corruption and harm. The prosperity of the Hyltorian Empire depends on the strength of our economy, and Vandrel's stewardship will ensure that no province goes without."

Vandrel, ever calm and calculating, gave a small, reassuring smile. He had always been the voice of reason among us, and I knew that his wisdom would be crucial in the days ahead.

"Belric, Lord of the Port of Alfy, and Fenric, Guardian of Wolfshire, have both pledged their loyalty to the Hyltorian Empire. Together, they will secure our trade routes and ensure that the provinces to the south remain stable and prosperous."

Belric and Fenric nodded in unison, their expressions resolute. The southern provinces were fragile, their loyalty tenuous at best, but I trusted these men to bring them in line.

"And at my right hand, Zephyros, now named Eomni, leader of the Omni Order and master of Cloud Fall. He will oversee the deployment of our forces and ensure that our enemies know the full might of the empire."

Zephyros stepped forward, his eyes blazing with the same fire that had always driven him. He was a warrior at heart, a man who thrived in the heat of battle. But more than that, he was loyal, and I needed that loyalty now more than ever.

"But know this, my people," I said, my voice rising once more. "We will not be complacent. The Southern Provinces have shown their defiance. They have chosen to turn their backs on unity, on peace. But we will not falter. We will not surrender to their fear and hatred."

The crowd had grown silent now, the weight of my words sinking in.

"As of today," I declared, "the Grand Hyltorian Army has been deployed. Six hundred thousand men have been sent to the southern borders, to protect our realm from those who would seek to tear it apart. Vornak and Durion lead three hundred thousand to Finela. Vandrel and Zephyros will take three hundred thousand to Inilyus. And I will lead ten thousand of my own men to Alatok. The Southern Provinces will either submit to our rule, or they will be crushed beneath the Hyltorian Empire."

I paused, letting the tension in the air build. This was it. The declaration of war. The moment that would change everything.

"I want peace," I said, my voice softening slightly. "We do not seek to destroy. We seek to unify. To bring harmony to a realm that has known nothing but chaos for too long. We offer them one final chance—Rhalor, Vaedric and Morvyn will receive a message. Surrender, and join us, or prepare for war. The choice is theirs."

The crowd erupted into cheers once more, their voices rising like the roar of a storm. But beneath that storm, I could feel the uncertainty, the fear that still lingered in the hearts of the people. They wanted to believe in this new empire, but they knew, just as I did, that peace would not come easily. I turned to Zephyros, my right hand, and gave him a nod.

"Prepare the army. The time has come."

He smirked, the gleam of anticipation in his eyes. "Consider it done."

The meeting was over. The speeches had been made. The decisions set in motion. But as the crowd began to disperse, as the leaders made their way back to their provinces, I felt the weight of what I had done settle over me like a shroud. I had set Nantrium on a path to war. As I made my way back to my chambers, the silence of the palace halls pressing in around me, I couldn't shake the feeling that this was only the beginning. The Southern Provinces would not surrender easily. There would be blood. There would be loss.

But there would also be victory. I sat at my desk, the parchment before me blank and waiting. I picked up the quill, dipping it in ink, and began to write.

The Contingency Actions of the Shepherd of Lushahiem:

Action 1: The Realm of Nantrium must remain united under one rule, The Shepherd who is the final arbitrator.

Action 2: The Grand Hyltorian Army is under the control of The Shepherd and no one else. The Grand Hyltorian is to remain mobilized at all times, ready to defend the realm against any and all threats, internal or external.

Action 3: The province of Hyanasarri will forever remain in the control of The Shepherd, and the Rementheium reserves used for all of Hyltoria

The list went on, each action a plan, a safeguard, a way to ensure that the Hyltorian Empire would endure long after I was gone. There were one hundred and fifty Contingency Actions in total, each carefully crafted to protect the realm from the chaos that threatened to tear it apart. But as I finished writing the final action, a thought crossed my mind—one that had been lurking in the shadows since the day I had been chosen by O'Rhyus to lead this empire. Would I ever truly be gone?

The light of O'Rhyus burned within me, stronger than ever. The power of the Divine had elevated me beyond what I had once been. And now, as I looked down at the list of

Contingency Actions, I couldn't help but wonder... could The Shepherd of Lushahiem truly remain in power for all eternity? The thought both comforted and unnerved me. The idea that my rule, my vision, could carry on forever was a temptation I had never considered before. But now, as the empire rose and war loomed on the horizon, I knew that nothing could be left to chance. I would ensure that the light of the Hyltorian Empire never faded. I stood from my desk, leaving the parchment behind as I made my way to bed. The weight of leadership pressed down on me, but I carried it willingly. The path had been set. The future of Nantrium was mine to shape.

And I would see it through, no matter the cost.

Chapter XXVI

The Waters of Reflection

The wind whipped through my cloak as we rode hard toward The Port of Alfy, the horses' hooves pounding rhythmically against the dirt road. Beside me, Zephyros was riding with his usual intensity, his body leaning forward as if the speed of his mount wasn't fast enough for him. His eyes, sharp and unyielding, were fixed on the path ahead, always looking toward the next battle, the next victory. For Zephyros, it was as if the war was already won, as if Aldous's grand vision of the Hyltorian Empire was inevitable, a future set in stone by the very hands of the Divine. But for me, there was only uncertainty.

As we approached the horizon, I found my thoughts drifting, carried on the same wind that tugged at my cloak and whispered through the trees. The army of 300,000 men rode behind us, stretching back as far as the eye could see—a vast sea of warriors, their armor gleaming in the early morning light. It was an impressive sight, one that should have filled me with confidence. And yet, all I felt was a growing sense of unease. This was not the Nantrium I had once known. This was not the world of balance and harmony that I had spent my life protecting. This was something else—a realm on the brink of being consumed by light and fire, where order was maintained not through peace, but through fear and bloodshed. Aldous had promised us unity. He had promised us peace. But what had we seen in Hyanasarri? A city torn apart by violence, its streets running red with the blood of those who dared to stand against the Hyltorian Empire. I had witnessed the horrors firsthand, had seen the brutal efficiency with which Aldous had dispatched his enemies. The way he had struck down Rhalor, how he ended Eldrith, the way he had broken Vicrum—it was as if the light he wielded had blinded him to everything else. Blinded him to the very principles he once stood for. And now, here I was, riding alongside Zephyros, the right hand of Aldous, leading an army into yet another battle. Another province to claim, another people to bring under the rule of the Hyltorian Empire.

I glanced at Zephyros, who remained silent beside me, his expression unreadable. He seemed so sure of himself, so certain of the path Aldous had set before us. There was a fire in his eyes, a hunger for power and control that mirrored the storms he commanded. He thrived in the chaos, in the violence. But I was not like Zephyros. I had never sought power for its own sake. My connection to the Divine Power, to the waters I controlled, had always been one of balance, of understanding. I had always believed that the elements were not to be wielded as weapons of war, but as forces of creation and healing.

Now, though, I was beginning to wonder if I had been wrong.

Perhaps the light was blinding.

The journey to The Port of Alfy was a long one, the landscape shifting from rolling hills to the flat, windswept plains that bordered the south east coast. The salty scent of the ocean filled the air as we drew closer to the port city, the distant cries of seabirds mingling with the low murmur of our soldiers. Belric's fleet awaited us at the docks, ships lined up silently, ready to carry us across the sea to the island province of Inilyus. It was strange to think that soon we would be on the water, sailing toward yet another conflict. The thought brought me no comfort. The sea, once a symbol of freedom and possibility to me, now seemed like a prison. There was no escape from what was to come. We would sail to Inilyus, we would fight, and we would conquer.

That was the way of things now. That was the way of the empire.

As we rode through the gates of The Port of Alfy, the city bustled with activity. The docks were alive with the sound of creaking wood and the shouts of sailors preparing the ships for departure. I could see Belric standing on the deck of one of the largest vessels, overseeing the preparations with the calm authority of a man who had spent his life navigating the seas. He was a practical man, Belric—one who understood the value of loyalty and order. But even he, I suspected, had reservations about the path we were on.

Zephyros pulled his horse to a stop beside mine as we neared the docks, his eyes scanning the scene before us.

"We leave at first light tomorrow," he said, his voice low and matter-of-fact. "Belric's fleet will carry us to Inilyus, and from there, we'll secure the island. It won't take long."

I nodded, though I didn't share his confidence. Inilyus was a province shrouded in mystery, its people known for their mastery of dark knowledge and magic. It was not a place to be taken lightly, nor were its leaders ones to be underestimated.

Zephyros seemed to sense my hesitation. "You don't trust the plan."

It wasn't a question. He knew me well enough to understand my doubts.

"I trust that Aldous believes this is the right course of action," I replied carefully. "But I can't help but wonder... what will be left of Nantrium when we're done? We've already seen what happened in Hyanasarri."

Zephyros's jaw tightened, his eyes flashing with that familiar intensity. "Hyanasarri was necessary. Rhalor was a threat, and Vicrum was a traitor. They had to be dealt with."

"But at what cost?" I asked quietly, more to myself than to him.

Zephyros didn't answer immediately. Instead, he dismounted and began walking toward the docks, motioning for me to follow. I hesitated for a moment, then swung myself down from my horse and walked beside him, the sound of the sea growing louder as we approached the water's edge.

"The cost," Zephyros said finally, his voice low and fierce, "is the price of peace. Aldous understands that. You should too."

I looked out at the water, the waves lapping gently against the hulls of the ships. The sea had always been a place of solace for me, a place where I could feel the balance of the world, the ebb and flow of life. But now, it feels different. As if the very elements themselves were being twisted, manipulated for a purpose I no longer fully understood.

"Do you ever think that maybe the light can blind us?" I asked, my voice barely more than a whisper.

Zephyros turned to me, his eyes narrowing slightly. "What

do you mean?"

I took a deep breath, my gaze still fixed on the horizon. "Aldous speaks of light and order, of bringing balance to the realm. But what if... what if the light we're following is so bright that we can't see what's right in front of us? What if we're losing sight of the very thing we're fighting for?"

Zephyros scoffed, shaking his head. "You're overthinking this, Vandrel. Aldous knows what he's doing. He's the Shepherd of the Hyltorian Empire. We're bringing peace to Nantrium."

"But at what cost?" I repeated, the words hanging heavy in the air.

Zephyros stopped walking, turning to face me fully now. "The cost doesn't matter if the end result is peace. You know that as well as I do. This isn't the time for doubt, Vandrel. We need to be strong. The southern provinces won't just fall in line. They need to be shown the strength of the empire."

I looked into Zephyros's eyes, seeing the fire that burned there, the unwavering belief in Aldous and his vision. He truly believed that the path we were on was the only way forward, that the sacrifices we were making—the lives lost, the blood spilled—were all part of a greater plan.

But I wasn't so sure.

The light of Aldous's vision was blinding, and I couldn't help but wonder if, in our pursuit of peace, we had already lost something far more important.

That night, as the men made camp along the shores of The Port of Alfy, I found myself alone, standing at the water's edge, staring out at the vast expanse of the ocean. The moon hung low in the sky, casting a pale silver glow over the waves, and the sound of the sea was the only thing that broke the silence. I had felt a connection to the water, a deep and unshakable bond that went beyond mere control of the elements. The sea had always spoken to me, its tides and currents reflecting the balance of the world. But now, as I stood there, I felt... disconnected. As if the waters themselves had turned against me, their once-familiar rhythms replaced by something darker, something more chaotic. I knelt down, letting my fingers trail through the cold water, and closed my eyes, listening to the sounds of the waves.

What had we become?

When Aldous first spoke of uniting Nantrium, I had believed in his vision. I had believed that, through the strength of the Hyltorian Empire, we could bring balance and peace to a world that had long been fractured by war and chaos. I had believed that we could forge something better, something stronger. But now... I wasn't sure. The atrocities committed in Hyanasarri haunted me.

I had always believed that the light was a force of creation, of healing, of balance. But now, I wondered if that same light could also be a force of destruction, burning so brightly that it scorched everything in its path. Could it be that, in our pursuit of order, we had become the very thing we sought to destroy?

I didn't have the answers. All I had were doubts.

I stood, letting the water drip from my fingers as I turned to make my way back to the camp. The fires of the soldiers flickered in the distance, their laughter and voices carrying faintly on the wind. They were ready for the battle to come, ready to follow Aldous's command without question. But I wasn't sure if I could.

As I made my way through the camp, I passed by Zephyros, who was standing near the central fire, his arms crossed as he spoke with one of the generals. He caught my eye and gave me a sharp nod, as if to remind me of the path we were on. I nodded back, though my heart wasn't in it. Tomorrow, we will sail to Inilyus. Another province to conquer. Another battle to fight. But tonight, I would keep to myself, lost in the uncertainty that had taken root in my soul. The light may be blinding, but the waters would always reveal the truth.

And I feared that the truth was far darker than any of us were prepared to face.

Chapter XXVII

The Shore

The sea stretched out before us, vast and unyielding, as the first glimmers of dawn broke over the horizon. The water lapped gently against the sides of Belric's fleet, a deceptive calm masking the storm that was about to descend. Ahead, barely visible through the thin mist that clung to the water, was the island province of Inilyus. This was a land shrouded in mystery. Inilyus, known for its dark knowledge and magic, had always existed on the periphery of Nantrium's power struggles, its people choosing to remain apart from the conflict that had engulfed the mainland. But now, like the rest of Nantrium, it would fall under the banner of the Hyltorian Empire—or it would be destroyed.

I stood on the deck of the lead ship, my hands resting on the wooden railing as I gazed out at the land we were about to invade. Behind me, the fleet was a massive line of dark silhouettes, the ships cutting through the water. Zephyros stood beside me, his face sharp and eager, his mind already focused on the battle ahead. The storm within him was always waiting to be unleashed.

"There's no turning back now," Zephyros said, his voice carrying over the low rumble of the waves. "Inilyus will fall, just like the others."

I nodded but said nothing. My thoughts were consumed by what was to come—the bloodshed, the chaos, the destruction that seemed inevitable. The men aboard the ships were ready, their black armor gleaming in the dim light, their weapons prepared for the battle ahead. The 300,000 soldiers we had brought with us were a force unlike any Inilyus had ever seen, a hammer poised to crush whatever resistance remained. But I couldn't shake the feeling that something was wrong. That we had lost something in our pursuit of conquest.

The light may be blinding, I reminded myself, as my thoughts drifted back to the atrocities I had witnessed at Hyanasarri. Aldous had been so sure of his path, so convinced that the Hyltorian Empire would bring peace and order to Nantrium. But at what cost? How much blood had to be spilled before we could call it peace?

"Do you ever wonder, Zephyros," I said quietly, still staring out at the horizon, "if the cost of this empire is too high?"

Zephyros glanced at me, a slight smirk tugging at the corner of his mouth. "Peace comes at a price, Vandrel. You know that as well as I do. We're doing what needs to be done."

I didn't respond. I wasn't sure I could. Zephyros saw the world in stark contrasts—light and dark, power and weakness, victory and defeat. For him, there was no room for doubt, no space for questions. But for me, the waters of doubt ran deep.

As the fleet drew closer to the shores of Inilyus, the mist began to clear, revealing the dark, jagged cliffs that lined the island's coast. Beyond the cliffs, I could just make out the faint outlines of the beach, where our battle would begin. The tension on the ship grew palpable, the men shifting nervously as they prepared for what lay ahead.

The beach was heavily fortified, as we had expected. Rows of sharp wooden stakes jutted out of the sand like the fangs of a great beast, and beyond them, I could see the walls of the Inilyus stronghold rising ominously in the distance. Morvyn had prepared for this. She knew we were coming.

Zephyros stepped forward, his hand gripping the hilt of his sword, his eyes gleaming with anticipation. "Ready the men," he ordered, his voice cutting through the tense silence. "We hit the beach fast and hard. No mercy."

I turned to face the men, the soldiers who had sworn their loyalty to the Hyltorian Empire, who would follow us into the jaws of death without hesitation. They were waiting for my command, their eyes filled with both fear and determination.

"Prepare to land!" I shouted, my voice ringing out across the deck. "Stay together, follow your orders, and remember—Inilyus will fall today, and we will claim victory in the name of the Hyltorian Empire!"

A roar of approval rose from the men, their shields clanging together in unison as they readied themselves for the fight. My heart was heavy with the knowledge of what was to come, but there was no time for hesitation. The wheels of war had been set in motion, and now, we had to see it through. As the ships neared the shore, the tension on board became electric. Zephyros was pacing the deck, his eyes never leaving the beach. His fingers twitched with anticipation, as though he could already feel the lightning crackling beneath his skin, waiting to be unleashed.

"Get ready!" Zephyros shouted, his voice booming over the sound of the crashing waves. "When we land, we fight! No hesitation!"

The ships hit the shore with a jarring thud, and the men

were already moving, leaping into the shallow waters and charging toward the beach. The air was filled with the sound of shouts, the clang of metal, and the steady drum of battle. I followed, my heart pounding in my chest as my boots sank into the wet sand. The soldiers ahead of me were already clashing with the forces of Inilyus, their shields raised against the barrage of arrows raining down from the cliffs above. The beach was a chaotic mass of bodies, steel flashing in the early light as the two sides met in brutal combat.

The defenses of Inilyus were formidable, but we had the numbers, and we had Zephyros.

With a roar, Zephyros raised his hand to the sky, and I could feel the air around us begin to shift, crackling with energy. A moment later, a bolt of lightning shot down from the skies, striking the ground with a deafening crack and sending the forces of Inilyus scattering in panic.

I swung my sword in a wide arc, cutting down the enemy in front of me as I pressed forward. The beach was soaked with blood, the bodies of soldiers from both sides littering the sand. The forces of Inilyus were putting up a fierce resistance, but we were overwhelming them. Slowly but surely, we were pushing them back.

The screams of the dying filled the air, mixing with the roar of the sea and the steady pounding of the waves. It was chaos—pure, unrelenting chaos. And yet, amidst the violence and bloodshed, I felt a strange detachment, as though I were watching it all from a distance. My body moved on instinct, cutting down enemy after enemy, but my mind was elsewhere, lost in the swirling waters of doubt. This wasn't what I had signed up for. This wasn't the peace I had once believed in. What had we become?

I glanced over at Zephyros, who was in his element, his face alight with the thrill of battle. His sword flashed in the sunlight, and with each strike, another enemy fell. The storm he had summoned raged around him, lightning arcing from his fingertips as he cut through the forces of Inilyus like a force of nature. But for all his power, for all the devastation he had wrought, I couldn't help but wonder if we were losing ourselves in the process. Was this truly the path to peace? Or had we become the very thing we had once sworn to destroy?

As the battle raged on, we fought our way up the beach, the defenses of Inilyus crumbling beneath the might of the Hyltorian Army. The walls of the stronghold loomed ahead, dark and foreboding, but I could see the cracks forming in its foundation. We were close. Soon, we would breach the gates, and the island province would be ours.

But at what cost?

Hours passed, though it felt like days. The sun was high in the sky now, its light casting long shadows across the battlefield. The beach was a graveyard, bodies piled high in the sand, the sea tinged red with blood. The forces of Inilyus had retreated to the stronghold, their numbers decimated, but they had not yet surrendered. Zephyros and I stood at the base of the cliffs, the remnants of our army gathered around us. We had taken heavy losses, but the battle was far from over. The stronghold still stood, its massive stone gates sealed tight, and beyond those gates, Morvyn waited.

"Let's finish this," Zephyros said, his voice low and filled with determination. "We've broken their forces. All that's left is Morvyn. Once she falls, Inilyus is ours."

I nodded, though my heart wasn't in it. The bloodshed had been overwhelming, the price too high for whatever victory we might claim. But there was no turning back now. We had come too far. Zephyros led the charge up the cliffs, his men following close behind as we scaled the jagged rocks. The climb was treacherous, but we made it to the top, the gates of the stronghold looming before us.

"We'll breach the gates," Zephyros said, his voice cold. "Once we're inside, Morvyn won't stand a chance."

I nodded again, my sword still slick with blood as I prepared myself for the final push.

The gates of the stronghold were massive, their dark stone glistening with the moisture of the sea air. Behind those gates lay Morvyn, the ruler of Inilyus, the one who had dared to defy the Hyltorian Empire. Zephyros was right—once she was defeated, Inilyus would fall, and Aldous's vision of the empire would take another step toward reality. But as I stood there, staring up at the gates, I couldn't shake the feeling that something was wrong. That we had lost our way. That the light we had once followed had become blinding, consuming everything in its path.

Zephyros gave the order, and the soldiers began their assault on the gates, their battering rams slamming against the stone with a resounding crash. I stood beside Zephyros, my sword in hand, ready to fight. Ready to end this.

The gates groaned under the assault, the stone beginning to crack and splinter. One more blow, and they would fall. With a final crash, the gates of the stronghold gave way, the massive stone doors swinging open with a deafening roar.

I glanced at Zephyros, and he nodded, his eyes filled with

fire.

"Let's end this."

We went forward, into the darkness beyond the gates, ready to face whatever lay within.

Together, Zephyros and I stepped inside.

Chapter XXVIII

The Duty

The horizon shimmered under the brutal desert sun, the distant outline of Finela's white stone walls gleaming like a mirage. The oasis province stood out like a jewel in the barren landscape, a place of life and beauty in the midst of the wasteland. But for me, as I looked upon it, there was no sense of wonder, no appreciation for its splendor. Instead, all I could feel was the heavy weight of duty pressing down on my shoulders.

It was a feeling I had become all too familiar with.

Around me, the 300,000 soldiers of the Hyltorian Army marched in steady formation, their armor clanking softly in the oppressive heat. They were disciplined, loyal, and focused on the task ahead. But I couldn't help but notice the fatigue in their eyes, the quiet resignation that seemed to settle over the ranks. We had been at war for so long now, and each battle, each conquest, had chipped away at whatever sense of honor we had once clung to.

I had always believed in duty. It had been the guiding principle of my life for as long as I could remember. My loyalty to the provinces, to Aldous, had never wavered. But as we marched toward Finela, the next in a long line of provinces to fall under our control, I found myself questioning what that duty truly meant. Was this truly what we had fought for? To bring destruction to a place of peace and prosperity? To tear down what others had built, all in the name of order?

I glanced over at Vornak, who strode beside me with his usual icy resolve. His pale skin seemed almost immune to the scorching sun, his expression cold and unyielding as ever. He was a man of duty, just like me. But unlike me, Vornak had never questioned it. He saw the world in absolutes—there was order, and there was chaos. And it was our duty to bring order to Nantrium, no matter the cost.

"Vornak," I said quietly, breaking the silence between us. "Do you ever wonder if we've lost our way?"

He didn't turn to look at me, his gaze fixed firmly on the walls of Finela. "We're soldiers, Durion. Our job is to follow orders, not to question them."

I nodded, though his answer did little to ease the knot of doubt that had settled in my chest. "But what if those orders lead us down a path we didn't intend? What if we're becoming something we never wanted to be?"

This time, he did glance at me, his eyes as cold as ever. "You're overthinking it. Finela defied the Hyltorian Empire. Vaedric chose his path. We're here to bring order, nothing more."

I didn't respond. There was no point in arguing with Vornak. His mind was set, his sense of duty unwavering. But I couldn't shake the feeling that something was terribly wrong.

The walls of Finela grew larger as we approached, their white stone gleaming brilliantly in the harsh sunlight. It was a beautiful city, a place that had thrived despite the harsh desert that surrounded it. But today, it would be a battleground. And like all the other provinces we had conquered, it would fall under the banner of the Hyltorian Empire—whether its people wanted it or not. The soldiers of Finela stood atop the walls, their silhouettes dark against

the bright sky. I could see the glint of armor, the flash of steel as they prepared to defend their home. They were outnumbered, of course. They must have known that they couldn't hold out against the might of our army. But they would fight. They would resist. Just as they had always done.
"Ready the siege engines," Vornak ordered, his voice cutting through the stillness. His cold, commanding tone left no room for hesitation.

The men moved quickly, bringing forward the massive war machines that would breach the walls of the city. The siege engines were a terrifying sight, great wooden contraptions designed to launch boulders and flaming projectiles at the enemy's fortifications. They had been the key to our victories in the past, and today would be no different.

I took a deep breath, my hand resting on the hilt of my sword. This was my duty. This was what I had sworn to do. But as the first boulders flew through the air, crashing against the walls of Finela with a deafening roar, I couldn't help but feel the weight of every life that would be lost in this battle.

"Advance!" Vornak's voice echoed across the battlefield, and the Hyltorian soldiers surged forward, shields raised with their spears gleaming in the sunlight.

The defenders of Finela retaliated, arrows raining down from the walls, darkening the sky as they flew toward us. The sound of steel meeting steel filled the air, the clash of weapons and the shouts of men creating a commotion that drowned out everything else. I fought my way through the chaos, my sword cutting through the enemy as I pushed toward the city's gates. The heat was unbearable, the sun beating down on us with relentless intensity, but I barely felt it. My focus was on the battle, on the men and women who stood in our way.

Vornak moved ahead of me, his powers of ice cutting through the desert heat like a sickle. Wherever he went, the temperature dropped, frost creeping across the ground in his wake. His soldiers followed him without hesitation, their faith in his leadership absolute. Together, we pressed forward, determined to breach the walls and bring an end to this conflict. But as we fought our way closer to the city, something began to gnaw at me—a sense of unease, of wrongness that I couldn't quite place.

This wasn't the battle I had envisioned. This wasn't the peace we had promised to bring. It felt like we were destroying something beautiful, something irreplaceable, all in the name of order.

The gates of Finela were formidable, massive structures built to withstand the elements and any assault. But they were no match for our siege engines. With each thunderous blow, the gates groaned and splintered, the stone cracking under the force of our assault. As the gates fell, the Hyltorian soldiers surged into the city, their war cries echoing off the white stone walls. The defenders of Finela fought bravely, but they were outnumbered and overwhelmed by the sheer size and strength of our forces.

The city was a maze of narrow streets and towering buildings, its white stone architecture gleaming in the harsh desert sun. It was beautiful, even in the midst of battle. But as I fought my way through the districts, cutting down any who stood in my way, I couldn't shake the feeling that we were destroying something precious. This wasn't what I had fought for. This wasn't what I had sworn to protect. Vornak moved ahead of me, his powers of ice cutting through the enemy with ruthless efficiency. He was a force of nature, his cold determination unshakable. But even as we advanced deeper into the city, I could feel the toll the battle was taking on him. The heat of the desert, the relentless resistance of the defenders—it was wearing him down.

But Vornak would never admit it. He would fight until the end.

"We're close," he said, his voice steady despite the strain I could see in his eyes. "Vaedric is in the central stronghold. We need to end this."

I nodded, still conflicted. The destruction around me, the lives lost—it was all starting to feel meaningless.

We pushed forward, our soldiers following us as we made our way through the inner districts of the city. The streets were narrow, the buildings towering above us, casting dark shadows across the battlefield. The heat was suffocating, the air thick with dust and smoke. But we pressed on, determined to reach Vaedric and bring an end to this conflict.

The people of Finela fought with everything they had, but it wasn't enough. We were too many, too strong. And as we advanced, I could see the desperation in their eyes, the knowledge that they were fighting a losing battle. But they fought anyway. And as I cut down another soldier, as I watched the life drain from his eyes, I couldn't help but wonder if we were the real enemy in this war.

The central district of Finela was a place of wealth and beauty, its buildings grand and imposing, their white stone walls gleaming in the sunlight. But now, it was a warzone, its streets littered with the bodies of the fallen, its walls scarred by the relentless assault of our forces. We were close to the stronghold, the heart of the city, where Vaedric awaited us. The defenders had retreated, falling back to protect their leader. But we would not be stopped.

"Vaedric will answer for his defiance," Vornak said, his voice cold and resolute. "The Hyltorian Empire will not tolerate rebellion."

I nodded, though the words felt hollow to me. This wasn't rebellion. This was survival. Vaedric had fought to protect his people, his home. And now, we were about to take it all away.

But it was my duty. I had to follow orders.

Even if it meant destroying everything I had once believed in.

The stronghold loomed ahead, its massive doors sealed shut, its walls towering above us. This was it—the final stand. Once we breached those doors, Vaedric would fall, and Finela would be ours. The streets around the stronghold were eerily silent, the only sound the distant clatter of battle in the outer districts. The defenders of Finela had pulled back, their forces concentrated within the stronghold. They knew this was their last chance.

"Ready the battering ram," Vornak ordered, his voice calm

and commanding.

The soldiers moved quickly, bringing forward the massive wooden ram that would break through the doors of the stronghold. I watched as they positioned it, my heart heavy with the knowledge of what was to come.

This was my duty. This was what I had sworn to do.

But as the battering ram crashed against the doors of the stronghold, as the sound of splintering wood filled the air, I couldn't shake the feeling that we had already lost something far more important than this battle. The doors of the stronghold groaned under the assault, the wood cracking and splintering with each blow. Inside, I knew Vaedric was waiting for us.

"One more hit!" Vornak shouted, his voice filled with determination.

The battering ram slammed against the doors one final time, and with a deafening crash, the doors of the stronghold gave way.

I drew my sword, my heart pounding in my chest as I prepared for the final confrontation.

This was it. We were about to face Vaedric.

Chapter XXIX

The Forgiveness

The cold wind howled through the jagged peaks of Wyldren, the oldest province in all of Nantrium as I traveled with the body of Vicrum, who laid upon a stone carriage behind me. The snow-capped mountains, usually a symbol of resilience and endurance, now seemed to mirror the icy chill that had taken root deep within me. This place, once a kingdom proud and full of life, now felt hollow—an empty echo of what it had been, much like the feeling in my chest.

As Wyldren came into view, I steeled myself for what was to come. Vicrum, once a powerful leader—an ally. But he had also been a betrayer, a pawn of Apollyon. Yet, even as I had struck him down in battle, I had known that something had broken within me. Something that would not easily be repaired.

Wyldren was his home, and now it was where he would be laid to rest. It was my duty to return him here, to offer him the dignity that he was due. But I also knew I would have to face Vyhonia, his wife. And that was the weight that pressed most heavily on my heart. As I rode into the village, the people of Wyldren turned their eyes toward me, their expressions a mixture of sorrow and confusion. They knew who I was, and they knew what had happened. There was no hatred in their eyes, but there was no welcome either. I had come as the bringer of death, carrying the body of their lord, and the silent judgment of their stares followed me like a shadow.

I dismounted as I reached the central hall of Wyldren. Vyhonia stood waiting for me at the entrance, her face drawn but still, with a quiet strength that struck me more deeply than I had expected. She was dressed in simple black robes, her dark hair pulled back, and her eyes—once full of life—now seemed clouded with grief. For a moment, neither of us spoke. The snow fell lightly around us, the only sound the soft crunch of my boots as I stepped toward her, my hand still resting on the edge of the carriage that carried Vicrum's body.

"Lady Vyhonia," I said, my voice soft but steady. "I have come to return your husband to his rightful place. To lay him to rest here, in his home."

She did not respond immediately, but her eyes lingered on the covered body of Vicrum. I saw her hand tremble slightly, but she quickly steadied it, placing it against her chest as if to keep herself from falling apart.

"Why did you bring him here?" she finally asked, her voice cold and distant. "Why not leave him where he fell, among the ruins of his ambition?"

The weight of her words hung in the air between us, but I forced myself to meet her gaze.

"Because," I said, "he was more than his ambition. He was a man who loved his home, his people... and you. Despite everything, he deserves to rest in the place he cherished."

Vyhonia's expression softened for just a moment, a glimmer of something—perhaps recognition of the truth I spoke—but it quickly vanished. She nodded once and turned, walking toward the hall.

"Come inside," she said quietly. "We need to talk."

The hall of Wyldren was simple, with wooden beams overhead and a large hearth that crackled softly in the corner, giving off what little warmth the room had. I stood just inside, my eyes following Vyhonia as she moved slowly to a chair by the fire, her movements graceful but weary.

I remained standing, unsure of whether to sit, unsure of what to say. For a long moment, there was silence between us, broken only by the distant sounds of the village and the steady crackle of the fire. Finally, Vyhonia spoke.

"Do you think I can forgive you?" she asked, her voice quiet but laced with a deep, simmering emotion. "Do you think that bringing him here, burying him in the soil of Wyldren, makes up for what has been done?"

I felt her words like a knife to my heart, but I didn't flinch. I had known this was coming, and I had prepared myself for it. Still, facing her pain was harder than I had imagined.

"No," I said, my voice low. "I don't expect forgiveness, Lady Vyhonia. I don't think there are words that could erase what has happened. But I came because it was my duty to return him to you. And because... I wanted to give him the respect he deserved."

"Respect?" she scoffed, her eyes flashing with anger. "You killed him, Aldous. You ended his life, and you come here speaking of respect?"

I clenched my jaw, feeling the weight of her anger, knowing it was deserved.

"I did what I had to do," I said, my voice barely above a whisper. "Vicrum made his choices. He aligned himself with the darkness. He brought destruction upon himself."

"And what of you?" Vyhonia asked, her gaze hard. "Are you so innocent in all of this? You speak of duty, of order, but how much blood has been spilled in the name of your empire? How many lives have been lost because of the choices you've made?"

Her words struck deep, and for a moment, I found myself unable to respond. She was right. I had killed in the name of order. I had destroyed in the name of peace. And yet, standing before her now, I couldn't help but feel the crushing weight of those decisions, the blood on my hands that could never be washed away.

"I don't ask for forgiveness," I repeated, my voice steady but pained. "I know that I don't deserve it. But I also know that Vicrum... despite everything, loved you. He loved his home. And I came to honor that."

Vyhonia stood, her hands clenched into fists at her sides. For a moment, I thought she might strike me, but instead, she took a deep breath and turned away, her shoulders trembling.

"You speak of love," she said softly, her voice breaking. "But what good is love when it leads to nothing but death? What good is any of it, Aldous?"

I took a step toward her, but stopped myself, unsure of what to say, unsure of what she needed to hear.

"It's not about forgiveness," she continued, her voice stronger now, though still filled with grief. "It's about what comes next. I don't care about your guilt or your pain. I care about the future of Wyldren."

I nodded slowly, understanding what she meant. She would not forgive me. She could not. But she would look to the future. She would make sure that no more blood was spilled.

"I will hand over the province," she said, her voice firm. "There will be no more fighting. No more death. But don't think that this is mercy, Aldous. I am doing this for my people. For Wyldren."

Her words cut deep, but I accepted them. This was her way of moving forward, her way of protecting what remained.

"I understand," I said quietly. "And I accept. Wyldren will be part of the Hyltorian Empire, but there will be no more bloodshed. No more war here."

Vyhonia nodded, though her eyes remained distant. She didn't look at me as she spoke again.

"Take him to the family crypt," she said softly. "Let him rest among his ancestors."

I hesitated for a moment, watching her as she stood there, her back to me, her shoulders heavy with grief. Then, without another word, I turned and made my way back outside, where Vicrum's body lay waiting.

The family crypt was located just outside the village, a small, unassuming structure carved into the mountainside. It was cold and dark inside, but there was a sense of peace here, a sense of finality that I hadn't felt in a long time.

I carried Vicrum's body into the crypt myself, laying him gently on the stone slab that had been prepared for him. For a moment, I stood there in silence, staring down at the man who had once been my ally.

How did it come to this? How had we all lost so much?

The silence of the crypt pressed down on me, and I felt the weight of everything that had happened settle heavily on my shoulders. The wars, the betrayals, the deaths... it was all too much. And yet, I had no choice but to carry it.

This was the burden of leadership. This was the price of duty. As I stood there, I couldn't help but think of the words Vyhonia had spoken to me. Forgiveness. Was it even possible? Could anyone truly forgive what had been done? I didn't know. But I did know that I had to try. I had to find a way to live with what I had done. For the sake of Nantrium, for the sake of the people who still looked to me for guidance. With a heavy heart, I placed my hand on the stone slab, a silent farewell to the man who had once been chosen. Then, without another word, I turned and left the crypt, leaving Vicrum to rest in the silence of the mountains. As I made my way back to the village, the sun was beginning to set, casting shadows over the snow-covered peaks of Wyldren. The air was cold, biting against my skin, but it was a welcome relief after the stifling weight of the crypt. Vyhonia was waiting for me at the edge of the village, her arms wrapped tightly around herself as she watched me approach. Her face was unreadable, but there was a quiet strength in her eyes that hadn't been there before.

"It's done," I said quietly, stopping a few feet away from her.

She nodded, though she said nothing. For a long moment, we stood there in silence, the weight of everything that had passed between us hanging in the air like a storm cloud.

"I'll leave now," I said finally, my voice barely above a whisper. "Wyldren is yours to govern, Lady Vyhonia. There will be no interference from the empire. No more war."

Vyhonia didn't respond immediately, but when she did, her voice was calm and steady.

"Thank you," she said softly, though there was no warmth in her tone. "For bringing him back."

I nodded, unsure of what else to say.

As I turned to leave, I glanced back at her one last time, seeing the silhouette of a woman who had lost everything but still stood tall. A woman who had every reason to hate me, but who had chosen to protect her people instead. In that moment, I realized something. Forgiveness wasn't something that could be given or taken. It wasn't something that could be asked for. It was something that had to be earned—through actions, through time, through understanding.

And maybe, one day, I would earn it.

But for now, I would carry the weight of my choices. I would carry the burden of what had been lost. And I would live with the knowledge that, no matter what, the past could never be undone. I turned and left Wyldren behind, the cold wind at my back as I made my way toward the future.

A future that, for better or worse, I would have to shape.

Chapter XXX

The Divine

I lay in my bed in Lushahiem, staring up at the ceiling. The night was still and quiet, yet there was something in the air—a heaviness that pressed down on me, as though the very darkness of the room was watching, waiting. My body was tired, but my mind refused to rest. The events of the past few months, the weight of the decisions I had made, the lives I had taken in the name of peace, swirled endlessly in my thoughts. The room was cold, though a fire crackled in the hearth nearby. I could feel its warmth but it did nothing to chase away the chill that had settled deep within me. I shifted, pulling the blanket tighter around me, but sleep would not come.

The darkness in the room felt like it was alive, as if it had its own will. It watched me. I could feel it—an unsettling presence, one I couldn't explain. My mind whispered doubts I had long tried to silence. Was it truly the darkness of the room, or was it something deeper? Something within myself? I closed my eyes, willing sleep to take me, but instead of the peace I sought, the feeling of being watched intensified. My thoughts grew heavier, like a shadow pressing against my consciousness, and the silence became suffocating.

Was this what O'Rhyus had warned me about? The darkness that didn't just exist in the world, but the darkness that existed within me?

At some point, sleep finally claimed me, though it wasn't

the restful escape I had hoped for. In my dream, I found myself standing in the Orchard of O'Rhyus. The air was warm, fragrant with the scent of the orchard's lavender trees, their blossoms vibrant against the soft light that filled the space. The sky was a soft, swirling mix of colors—lavender and gold, as though the heavens themselves reflected the beauty and peace of the orchard below. This place, this sacred place, was the realm of the god of light and balance. I had been here before, but not since the war began. I had walked these grounds as a younger man, filled with purpose, filled with certainty. But now, as I stood here, I felt unworthy. The weight of what I had done—what I had become—hung over me like a shroud. I had spilled so much blood in the name of balance, in the name of peace, but the peace I had sought felt further away than ever. I walked slowly through the orchard, my boots pressing softly into the grass, feeling the light breeze brush against my skin. The trees whispered gently as I passed, their leaves shimmering in the breeze. I had always found comfort here before, but now, I felt like an intruder. I felt the guilt deep in my chest, gnawing at me.

Why was I here? I knew I had been summoned, but I didn't know if I was ready to face what was coming.

A soft glow appeared above me, and I looked up to see O'Rhyus descending from the lavender clouds. His presence was overwhelming, radiant with light and power. His robes, flowing like liquid light, shimmered with an ethereal glow, and his face was both kind and stern, his eyes filled with a deep wisdom that pierced through the soul. He was a god of order and balance, yet the weight of his gaze made me feel as though I stood on the edge of a precipice.

I knelt, bowing my head in respect, though shame made it difficult to meet his eyes. "My lord," I whispered.

O'Rhyus spoke, his voice soft yet commanding, like the wind through the trees. "Rise, Aldous. You need not bow before me."

I stood, though the feeling of unworthiness still weighed heavily on me. "I don't deserve to be here," I said quietly. "Not after everything I've done."

O'Rhyus regarded me with an expression of calm understanding. "You have carried the burden of leadership, Aldous. That burden is not without its cost. But you were chosen for this path. You were chosen to bring balance to Nantrium."

I swallowed hard, my heart heavy with guilt. "But at what cost? I've killed, I've destroyed. I thought I was bringing order, but it feels like all I've done is bring chaos."

The god's eyes softened, though there was still a deep gravity in his gaze. "Balance is not easily attained, Aldous. It is not a simple matter of light versus dark. It is a delicate dance, a constant struggle to maintain harmony. The choices you have made, the battles you have fought—they were necessary, but they were also painful."

I shook my head, my fists clenching at my sides. "I don't feel like I'm maintaining balance. It feels like I'm losing myself in the darkness."

O'Rhyus stepped closer, his presence both comforting and overwhelming. "That is why you are here," he said gently. "You are not just fighting the darkness in the world, Aldous. You are fighting the darkness within yourself."

I looked up at him, my chest tight with the weight of his

words. "How do I fight it?" I asked. "How do I stop it from consuming me?"

O'Rhyus smiled softly, though there was a sadness in his eyes. "The darkness within you is not something you can simply vanquish, Aldous. It is part of you, just as the light is. True balance comes not from denying the darkness, but from accepting it. From understanding that it is a part of who you are, but that it does not define you."

I frowned, trying to make sense of his words. "But if I accept the darkness... doesn't that mean I've failed? Doesn't that mean I'm letting it win?"

O'Rhyus shook his head. "No, Aldous. To accept the darkness is not to let it win. It is to understand its place in the balance. Light and dark, order and chaos—they exist together. One cannot exist without the other. You must learn to hold both within yourself, to be the vessel for both light and dark, and to guide them toward harmony."

I was silent for a long moment, turning his words over in my mind. I had always thought of the darkness as something to be feared, something to be destroyed. But now, as I stood in the presence of O'Rhyus, I began to see that the darkness was not my enemy. It was part of the balance. Part of me.

"But how do I know if I'm in balance?" I asked quietly, my voice barely audible. "How do I know if I'm walking the right path?"

O'Rhyus placed a hand on my shoulder, his touch warm and steady. "You will know, Aldous, because the balance is not something you achieve once and for all. It is something you must constantly work toward, something you must feel within yourself. It is a journey, not a destination."

I nodded slowly, though the weight of his words still pressed heavily on my heart.

"And what of the future?" I asked, my voice filled with uncertainty. "What of the battles still to come?"

O'Rhyus's expression grew more serious, his eyes filled with a deep sadness. "The future is not yet written, Aldous. But I will warn you—there are trials ahead. Trials that will test not only your strength but your very soul."

I swallowed hard, feeling a knot of dread form in my stomach. "What kind of trials?"

"The darkness in the world is not your greatest enemy," O'Rhyus said softly. "It is the darkness within you that will be your greatest challenge. You must be careful, Aldous. The power you wield is great, but it is also dangerous. It can corrupt, if you are not vigilant."

I looked away, shame filling me once again. "I don't know if I'm strong enough," I admitted.

O'Rhyus's hand remained on my shoulder, his presence unwavering. "You are stronger than you know, Aldous. But strength is not just about power. It is about wisdom, about knowing when to fight and when to seek peace. It is about understanding the balance within yourself."

I nodded, though doubt still lingered in the corners of my mind.

"You have already taken the first step," O'Rhyus continued. "You have recognized the darkness within you. That is the beginning of understanding. But the path ahead will not be easy. You will be tested, and you must be ready."

I looked up at him, my heart heavy with both fear and determination. "What must I do?"

"Remember who you are, Aldous," O'Rhyus said softly. "Remember why you were chosen. You are the Shepherd of Nantrium. You were chosen to bring balance, to guide the people through the trials ahead. But you must also guide yourself."

His words resonated deeply within me, though they also filled me with a sense of responsibility I wasn't sure I was ready to bear.

"Balance," I whispered, the word feeling both foreign and familiar on my tongue.

O'Rhyus nodded. "Balance. It is the key to everything. Without it, the world will fall into chaos. But with it, there is hope for peace."

For a moment, the orchard seemed to shimmer around us, the lavender trees glowing softly in the light of the setting sun. There was a sense of peace here, a peace I hadn't ever known. But I knew it was fleeting. The world outside this dream was full of chaos, full of darkness. And it was my responsibility to face it.

"Go now, Aldous," O'Rhyus said gently. "Return to the world, and remember what we have spoken of here. The path ahead is difficult, but you are not alone."

I nodded, feeling both grateful and overwhelmed by the weight of his words.

"Thank you," I said softly, though the words felt inadequate.

O'Rhyus smiled, a small, knowing smile that seemed to carry the weight of eternity. "Remember, Aldous—balance is not something you achieve alone. It is something you must seek within yourself, and something you must cultivate in the world around you."

With that, the god of light and balance began to fade, his form dissolving into the lavender clouds above. The orchard around me grew dim, the light fading as the dream began to slip away.

I woke with a start, the darkness of my bedchamber in Lushahiem pressing in around me once again. The fire had burned low, its embers glowing softly in the hearth. For a moment, I lay still, my heart racing as I tried to process the dream. It had felt so real, so vivid, but now that I was awake, it seemed like a distant memory—like something from another life. But O'Rhyus's words lingered in my mind, heavy with meaning.

Balance.

It was something I had always strived for, but something I had never truly understood. The path ahead was unclear, and the weight of the choices I had made still pressed heavily on me. But now, there was something else—something deeper. A sense of purpose, of understanding, that I hadn't felt before. The darkness was still there, both in the world and within me. But now, I knew that it wasn't something to be feared. It was something to be understood. Something to be balanced.

I rose from my bed, the cool air of the night brushing against my skin as I moved to the window. The city of Lushahiem lay quiet below, its streets bathed in the soft glow of the moon. For a moment, I stood there, watching the city sleep, the weight of the empire resting on my shoulders. Today, I would lead 10,000 men to claim Mophia for the Hyltorian Empire. It was another battle, another conquest, but it was also a step toward something greater. Something I was only beginning to understand. I took a deep breath, feeling the cold air fill my lungs, and as I exhaled, I felt a strange sense of peace settle over me.

Balance.

It was my duty to seek it.

And it was my duty to bring it to Nantrium.

With that thought, I turned away from the window and began to prepare for the journey ahead.

Chapter XXXI

The Purification

The sound of hooves echoed through the valleys and fields as I rode toward Mophia, the cold wind brushing past my face. Behind me, the 10,000 men of the Hyltorian Army marched in unison, a silent wave of strength and power. I had seen countless provinces fall under the banner of the Hyltorian Empire, but this mission was different. The task was not one of bloodshed—not unless it had to be. This was about purification. The land had to be cleansed, order must be restored, and Mophia, like so many others, would have a choice to make: either join the empire and embrace the balance we sought to bring, or face complete annihilation. There could be no room for rebellion, no space for defiance. The time for diplomacy was fleeting, and if Mophia refused, the sword would fall. But it didn't have to be that way. I had no desire for more blood to be spilled, not when there was a chance for peace. The Hyltorian Empire was about more than just conquest—it was about balance, about restoring order to a world teetering on the edge of chaos. And yet, in the back of my mind, I could feel the ever-present pull of darkness. The words of O'Rhyus from my dream echoed through me. The darkness within, the power I wielded—it was a part of me, and I could not deny it. I could only hope to balance it.

As we approached the outskirts of Mophia, the air grew thicker, more oppressive. The province was known for its deep ties to the arcane, its people steeped in ancient knowledge that bordered on the forbidden. The land itself seemed to reflect that—dark forests loomed on the horizon, shrouded in mist, and the once grand towers of the central district stood in silent defiance against the sky. There were no welcoming banners, no emissaries sent to greet us. The tension was tight, and though the people of Mophia knew of our approach, they remained hidden behind their walls, watching, waiting to see what we would bring.

I rode at the head of the army, my gaze fixed on the path ahead. I had made my decision—this mission was one of diplomacy unless the people of Mophia chose otherwise. They would have a chance to bend the knee, to appoint a representative in the form of a Valta Riomni to serve under the empire. But if they resisted, there would be no mercy. I had come to purify the land, to rid Nantrium of the chaos that had gripped it for too long. Balance could only be achieved through unity under one banner—our banner.

The gates of the central district loomed ahead, tall and imposing, crafted from black stone and reinforced with ancient runes. The walls stretched high above us, casting shadows over the land. The army halted as we approached, and I dismounted, my boots sinking slightly into the damp earth. The silence was oppressive, broken only by the rustle of leaves and the distant cry of some unseen bird. For a moment, I stood there, waiting, letting the weight of the moment settle over me.

And then, the gates creaked open.

A small group of figures emerged from the city, draped in long robes of deep red and black, their faces obscured by hoods. At their head was a man, tall and thin, his robes adorned with intricate silver patterns that shimmered in the dim light. His presence radiated authority, but there was an unmistakable reluctance in his steps.

This was not a welcoming party. This was a group that had been forced to greet us.

I stepped forward, my gaze steady as I approached them.

"Who speaks for Mophia?" I called out, my voice carrying over the still air.

The man at the head of the group raised his head, his eyes dark and worried beneath his hood.

"I am Caelthar," he said, his voice smooth but edged with tension. "I speak for the people of Mophia."

I nodded, though I could feel the resistance in his words, the careful calculation behind his gaze. He was not here to bend the knee willingly, but because he knew what was at stake.

"You know why I have come," I said, my voice firm but not unkind. "The Hyltorian Empire seeks to bring balance to Nantrium. Mophia must choose—join us, or face annihilation."

Caelthar's jaw tightened, but he did not break eye contact. "We have heard of your empire, of the balance you claim to bring. But Mophia is not like the other provinces. We have our own ways, our own traditions."

I held his gaze, the weight of O'Rhyus's words still fresh in my mind. The darkness within me stirred, but I kept it in check. This was not the time for force—at least, not yet.

"You are not the first to say that," I replied calmly. "But you must understand—this is not about erasing your traditions. It is about uniting Nantrium under one banner, so that we may bring order to the chaos that has gripped our world. The empire does not seek to destroy, but to purify."

Caelthar's eyes flashed with something—fear, perhaps, or doubt. He glanced back at the figures behind him, as though seeking reassurance, before turning his attention back to me. "And what if we refuse?" he asked quietly, though the challenge in his tone was clear.

I stepped closer, my voice lowering to match his. "If you refuse, Mophia will burn. Your people will suffer, and everything you have built will be reduced to ash. I do not wish for that, Caelthar. But I will do what is necessary to bring balance to Nantrium."

The silence stretched between us, thick with tension. I could see the conflict in his eyes, the struggle between pride and self-preservation. He did not want to bow to the empire, but he knew what the alternative would mean. Finally, he lowered his head, his shoulders sagging slightly under the weight of the decision.

"We will... join you," he said slowly, the words heavy with reluctance. "Mophia will appoint a Valta Riomni to represent us in your empire."

I nodded, though there was no sense of victory in the moment. This was not a province conquered through force, but through necessity. The people of Mophia had chosen survival over defiance, but it was clear that they would never fully embrace the empire's vision.

"You will serve the Hyltorian Empire as Valta Riomni," I said, my voice steady. "You will represent Mophia's interests, but you will be loyal to the empire above all else. Do you understand?"

Caelthar hesitated for a moment, then nodded. "I

understand."

I stepped back, allowing the tension to ease slightly. The people of Mophia had made their choice, and for now, there would be no bloodshed.

"Then it is done," I said. "Mophia is now part of the Hyltorian Empire. There will be no more need for violence, no more need for war."

Caelthar raised his head, his expression unreadable. "We will honor the terms, but do not think that Mophia will forget what has been done here today."

I met his gaze, unflinching. "I do not expect you to forget. But I hope, in time, you will understand."

With that, I turned and walked back toward my horse, my heart heavy with the weight of what had just transpired. The men of Mophia stood in silence as I mounted, their eyes filled with a mix of fear, anger, and resignation. The battle for Mophia had not been fought with swords and spears, but with words and decisions. It was a victory, but it was hollow. The people had chosen survival, but they had not chosen peace. As I rode away from Mophia, the weight of the darkness within me grew heavier. I had done what was necessary, but I could not shake the feeling that I had only delayed the inevitable.

The Hyltorian Empire was growing, province by province, but each victory felt more like a loss. Balance was what I sought, but the scales felt more uneven with every step I took. And now, my journey would take me to Alatok. There, I would offer them the same choice—peace or annihilation. But I knew in my heart that Alatok, with its pride and power, would not bend so easily. The darkness stirred once more, whispering its familiar doubts and fears. I closed my eyes, focusing on the words of O'Rhyus.

Balance.

I would find it, no matter the cost.

As the horizon stretched out before me, I steeled myself for what was to come.

Mophia had fallen without a fight. But Alatok... would be a different story altogether.

Chapter XXXII

The Storm

The winds howled around me as we approached the heart of Inilyus. Dark clouds gathered overhead, swirling ominously as if the skies themselves were preparing for the conflict that was to come. Vandrel walked beside me, his gaze distant, lost in his own thoughts. He had always been a quiet man, introspective, but I knew that today he was wrestling with more than his usual contemplations. The battle for Inilyus had already torn through the outer districts, the forces of the Hyltorian Empire clashing with Morvyn's soldiers in a brutal and chaotic struggle. But the real fight had yet to begin. The fight that mattered.

As we approached the central stronghold where Morvyn had made her stand, I could feel the tension building, crackling in the air like the charged anticipation before a storm. My fingers twitched, eager for the familiar surge of power that accompanied battle. I lived for this—this moment when the world seemed to hold its breath, waiting for the clash of Divine Power that was about to unfold.

Vandrel paused, his hand on my shoulder. "Zephyros," he said, his voice low and steady. "Are you sure about this?"

I glanced at him, a wry smile on my mouth. "You're not going soft on me now, are you, Vandrel?"

He didn't smile. He never did. Instead, his deep blue eyes bore into mine, filled with concern. "Morvyn is no ordinary opponent. Her mastery of water and wind... You know what she's capable of."

I shrugged off his hand, stepping forward with a confidence I didn't entirely feel. "I know exactly what she's capable of. That's why I'm the one facing her."

Vandrel nodded, though I could see the reluctance in his eyes. He stepped aside, giving me the space I needed to approach the battlefield alone. This was my fight—mine and Morvyn's. Vandrel understood that. He would not interfere unless absolutely necessary. The stronghold of Inilyus loomed ahead, its towering walls slick with rain that had already begun to fall. The air was thick with moisture, the scent of the storm heavy in my nostrils. I could feel the electricity in the air, the tension building with each passing second.

And then I saw her.

Morvyn stood at the center of the courtyard, her back straight, her posture serene. She looked almost peaceful, as if the battle raging around us was nothing more than a distant memory. Her long, flowing robes shimmered in the dim light, the fabric catching the droplets of rain as they fell. Her dark hair was pulled back, revealing her sharp, determined features. But it was her eyes that caught me off guard. They were calm and clear, filled with a quiet strength that I had rarely seen in any opponent.

She knew what was coming.

"Zephyros," she said softly, her voice carrying easily through the storm, "I had hoped it wouldn't come to this."

I laughed, the sound harsh and sharp in the tension-filled air. "Hoped? You knew this was coming the moment you defied the empire."

Morvyn's gaze didn't waver, her expression unchanging.

"Perhaps. But that doesn't mean I wanted it."

I narrowed my eyes, feeling the familiar surge of adrenaline as the storm above us grew stronger, the winds whipping around us with increasing intensity. "Want has nothing to do with it. This is war, Morvyn. And in war, only the strong survive."

She didn't flinch, didn't react to my taunt. Instead, she raised her hands, palms facing the sky, and the rain intensified, pouring down in sheets. The ground beneath our feet became slick and treacherous, but I welcomed the challenge. I could feel the storm responding to me, the electricity in the air building as my power surged. Lightning crackled in the clouds above, and I could sense the raw energy waiting to be unleashed.

"You know you can't win this," I said, my voice filled with the confidence of a man who had fought and won countless battles. "You may be strong, but I thrive in chaos. And chaos is what I bring."

Morvyn's lips curved into a faint smile, though there was no humor in it. "Perhaps you're right, Zephyros. But balance... balance is what I fight for."

Without another word, she moved.

The ground beneath her rippled as water surged up from the earth, forming into a massive wave that rose high above us. I could feel the power behind it, the sheer force of the element she commanded. But I didn't hesitate. This was what I lived for—the rush of combat, the thrill of facing an opponent who could push me to my limits. With a roar, I called upon the storm, summoning lightning from the heavens. It crackled through the air, a jagged bolt of raw energy that shot toward Morvyn's wave.

But she was ready.

With a fluid motion, she raised her hands, and the water shifted, absorbing the lightning, dispersing the energy before it could reach her. I gritted my teeth, feeling the familiar frustration that came with facing an opponent who knew how to counter my strengths.

But that only made me more determined.

"Is that all you've got?" I taunted, my voice carrying over the roar of the storm. "I expected more from the great Morvyn."

Her eyes narrowed slightly, but she remained calm, her movements precise as she redirected the water toward me, a torrent of liquid force that threatened to knock me off my feet.

But this time I was ready for her.

I called upon the winds, summoning a gust that whipped through the courtyard, tearing through the water and scattering it in all directions. The force of the wind was exhilarating, the power rushing through me like a drug. This was where I thrived—in the midst of chaos, when everything was unpredictable, when every move had the potential to be your last.

Morvyn was different. She relied on balance, on control. Her movements were fluid, her power graceful, but that was her weakness. In chaos, there was no control. There was only survival. I pressed the attack, launching bolt after bolt of lightning toward her, forcing her to raise walls of water to defend herself. The storm above us raged, growing more erratic, more violent with each passing second. My lightning became wilder, more aggressive, striking with an intensity that even I struggled to control.

But that was the point.

I didn't need control. I needed power.

Morvyn was beginning to tire. I could see it in the way her defenses wavered, in the way she struggled to keep up with the relentless onslaught of lightning and wind. She was spending more and more energy just to stay in the fight, while I was only growing stronger.

This was my domain. And in the height of the battle, I saw my opening.

Morvyn raised a massive wall of water, trying to block a direct lightning strike. It was a desperate move, one that left her vulnerable. I grinned, feeling the thrill of victory surge through me as I called upon the winds, changing the course of the lightning. The bolt veered sideways, arcing around her defense and striking her from behind.

Her gasp of pain echoed through the storm, and I knew I had her. This was the moment.

With a roar, I summoned all the power I could muster, channeling the full force of the Divine Power into a single, devastating strike. The lightning crackled through the air, a brilliant, blinding flash of energy that tore through Morvyn's defenses.

She didn't even have time to scream.

The force of the lightning vaporized her, her body disintegrating in an instant, leaving nothing behind but the charred remnants of the battlefield.

For a moment, the world seemed to stop. And then the storm began to clear. The winds died down, the rain slowed to a drizzle, and the once chaotic battlefield was now a scarred wasteland. The earth was blackened, smoldering debris littering the ground where my lightning had struck. The storm had passed, but the sky was still dark and heavy with the aftermath of our conflict. I stood in the center of the devastation, breathing heavily, my body trembling with exhaustion. The adrenaline that had fueled me through the battle was fading, leaving me feeling drained.

It was over.

I had won.

But as I looked around at the destruction I had brought, I couldn't help but feel a sense of emptiness. Morvyn was gone, her defiance snuffed out in a flash of lightning, but the victory felt hollow. The balance she had spoken of... had I destroyed it along with her?

I didn't have time to dwell on the thought.

The exhaustion hit me all at once, my legs buckling beneath me as the power I had drawn upon began to take its toll. I collapsed to the ground, my vision swimming as I struggled to stay conscious.

And then I felt a pair of strong hands grab me, pulling me up.

"Zephyros!" Vandrel's voice was sharp with concern as he lifted me to my feet, his expression grim. "You're pushing yourself too far."

I tried to smile, but it came out as more of a grimace. "I had to. She... she was too strong."

Vandrel's eyes softened slightly, though his worry remained. "You won. That's all that matters."

I nodded weakly, though I wasn't sure I believed him. The victory had come at a cost—one that I wasn't sure I was ready to pay. But for now, all I could do was lean on Vandrel as he helped me away from the battlefield, the storm still rumbling softly in the distance.

As we left the wasteland behind, I couldn't shake the feeling that something had shifted within me, something dark and dangerous. The chaos I had thrived in, the power I had wielded—it had been intoxicating, but it had also been terrifying. I had destroyed Morvyn, but in doing so, had I also destroyed something within myself? The sky above was still heavy with the aftermath of the storm, and as I looked up, I couldn't help but wonder if the darkness that lingered there was not just in the clouds, but in me as well. The storm had passed, but I knew there was another one coming.

And this time, I wasn't sure I would survive it.

Chapter XXXIII

Between the Light and Dark

The wind had begun to die down as we made our way back to Alatok, but the weight of the recent battle still hung heavily in the air, like a storm that had yet to fully dissipate. Vandrel rode beside me, silent as ever, his eyes focused on the road ahead. The scars from the battle in Inilyus were still fresh, not only on the land we had left behind but also in my own heart. I could still feel the electric tingle of the lightning in my veins, the remnants of the storm I had summoned against Morvyn. The victory had been swift, brutal, and complete, but it hadn't come without a cost. Yet, even as I thought about the destruction, I felt no remorse. There was no guilt. Only a cold, calculated sense of necessity. It had been the right thing to do. At least, that's what I had to believe.

Vandrel, however, had grown more distant since the battle. He hadn't spoken much during our journey back to Alatok, but I could see the tension in his shoulders, the way his hands clenched the reins of his horse a little too tightly. He was brooding, lost in his thoughts, and I knew that eventually, we would need to address it.

The landscape around us changed as we neared Alatok, the rolling hills giving way to the sharp, rugged terrain of the southern province. The sun was beginning to set, and the air grew cooler, carrying with it the scent of the earth and the distant sound of the sea. The province of Alatok was a place of strength, its people known for their tenacity and pride. It was a fitting place for the next phase of the empire's expansion. But before we arrived, there was something that needed to be said.

I slowed my horse, falling back slightly so that Vandrel and I were riding side by side. He didn't look at me, but I could sense his discomfort, his unease. It was time to confront it.

"You've been quiet," I said, my voice cutting through the silence between us. "Ever since Inilyus."

Vandrel didn't respond immediately. His eyes remained fixed on the horizon, his jaw tight. But after a moment, he spoke, his voice low and measured.

"I've been thinking."

"About what?" I pressed.

He hesitated, his grip on the reins tightening slightly before he finally answered. "About what we've done. About what you've done."

I raised an eyebrow, though I wasn't surprised by his response. "You think what I did was wrong?"

Vandrel shook his head slightly, but there was a heaviness to his words. "It's not that simple, Zephyros. It's not about right or wrong. It's about what it means. The choices we've made, the lives we've taken... I'm starting to wonder if we're losing sight of why we started this in the first place."

I frowned, my gaze narrowing as I studied him. "We're bringing order to Nantrium, Vandrel. We're following the light, the path that Aldous has set for us. We're building a future where chaos doesn't rule. How can you doubt that?"

Vandrel glanced at me then, his expression unreadable. "I'm not doubting the goal. I'm doubting the cost."

His words hung in the air between us, and for a moment, I felt a surge of irritation. He wasn't seeing things clearly. He wasn't seeing the bigger picture.

"You think I should feel guilty for what happened in Inilyus?" I asked, my tone sharper than I intended. "You think I should regret killing Morvyn? She was a threat, Vandrel. She stood in the way of the empire's peace. She had to die."

Vandrel sighed, shaking his head. "That's not what I'm saying."

"Then what are you saying?" I demanded, my frustration growing. "Because from where I'm standing, it sounds like you're questioning everything we've fought for."

"I'm questioning whether we're still following the light," Vandrel said quietly. "Or if we're just convincing ourselves that we are."

The words hit me like a punch to the gut, but I refused to let them shake me. I couldn't afford to doubt. Not now. Not after everything we had done.

"We are following the light," I said firmly. "And sometimes, that light leads us into darkness. But that doesn't mean we're lost. It doesn't mean we've failed. It just means that the path is harder than we expected."

Vandrel looked at me again, his eyes filled with a quiet sadness. "Is that what you believe? That as long as we say we're following the light, we can justify anything?"

"Yes," I replied without hesitation. "That's exactly what I believe. Because if I don't believe that, then what's the point? If I don't believe that what we're doing is right, then every life we've taken, every battle we've fought, means nothing."

Vandrel was silent for a long moment, his gaze drifting back to the horizon. "I wish I could see it that way," he said finally.

"I wish I could make peace with it, like you have."

I snorted, shaking my head. "Peace? There's no peace in this, Vandrel. I'm not happy with what I've done. But I can't afford to dwell on it. I have to believe it was right, or I'll go mad. I have to keep moving forward."

He nodded slowly, though I could see the uncertainty in his eyes. "And what happens when there's nothing left to move forward to? When we've conquered everything, when we've brought order to the entire land? Will you still feel justified?"

"I'll repent for the rest of my life, if that's what it takes," I said coldly. "But I'll do it knowing that I followed the light. And that's enough for me."

Vandrel fell silent again, his thoughts clearly elsewhere. I didn't push him. We had both seen too much, done too much, to pretend that things were simple. But I couldn't allow myself to fall into the same doubts that plagued him. I had made my choice, and I would live with it.

As we rode on, the walls of Alatok came into view, their jagged edges silhouetted against the darkening sky. The city was a fortress, built to withstand any attack, its people hardened by centuries of conflict and survival. It was a place of strength, a place that had long resisted Lushaheim's reach. But now, it will fall. Whether by peace or by force.

We approached the main gates, where Aldous's banner flew high, marking the arrival of the Hyltorian forces. Soldiers stood at attention, their faces grim but resolute. Alatok's fate hung in the balance, and soon, we would know which path they had chosen. As we dismounted, Vandrel and I exchanged a glance. There was no need for words. We both knew what was at stake.

Inside the gates, the Vhankilla's tent stood at the center of the encampment, a massive structure draped in the black, red and gold colors of the empire. It was here that Aldous would meet with us, to plan the next phase of our conquest. But Aldous hadn't arrived yet. Vandrel and I entered the tent, the air inside cool and still. The table at the center was covered with maps, detailing the land we had claimed and the territories still resisting. It was a map of our victories and our future conquests. I stared down at the maps, tracing the lines of our campaign with my finger. So much had been achieved, but there was still so much left to do.

"You really believe it, don't you?" Vandrel said quietly from behind me.

I didn't look at him, my eyes still on the maps. "What do you mean?"

"You really believe that as long as we say we're following the light, we can justify anything."

I finally turned to face him, my expression hard. "It's not about justifying. It's about doing what needs to be done. Morvyn was a threat. Inilyus was a threat. They're gone now, and the world is better for it."

Vandrel shook his head slowly. "I'm not so sure. Maybe we're just telling ourselves that because we don't want to face what we've become."

I felt anger at his words, but I forced it down. This was not the time for doubt. Not now. Not after everything.

"We've become what we needed to be," I said firmly. "And if that means walking through darkness to reach the light, then so be it. I'll carry that weight."

Vandrel didn't respond, but I could see the conflict in his

eyes. He wasn't convinced, and part of me knew that he never would be. But that was his burden to carry, just as I had mine. The flap of the tent rustled as the wind picked up outside, and for a moment, we stood in silence, the weight of our choices hanging between us.

"We're doing what's right," I said quietly, though the words felt more like a reminder to myself than to him.

Vandrel didn't reply. Instead, he walked to the other side of the tent and sat down, his eyes distant, lost in thought. I turned back to the map, tracing the path of our next conquest. There was still work to be done. Still battles to be fought. And no matter what doubts Vandrel carried, I would see it through. I would bring order to Nantrium. I would follow the light.

Even if it led me into the darkest depths.

As the wind howled outside, I couldn't shake the feeling that darkness was closer than I wanted to admit. But for now, I would ignore it. I would press forward. Aldous would arrive soon, and with him, the next phase of our campaign.

And when that time came, I would be ready.

Chapter XXXIV

The Frozen Duel

The desert sun glared down upon us as Vornak and I strode forward, the air thick with tension. The oasis province of Finela, once a place of serene beauty, now stood on the verge of devastation. High walls of white stone surrounded us, reflecting the brutal heat of the desert sun. The stark contrast between the flourishing plant life within the walls and the barren wasteland beyond only heightened the tension in the air.

We had come to confront Vaedric, the Victor of Vines. He stood tall at the far end of the courtyard, his green robes flowing like water, his expression calm yet determined. The lush garden behind him seemed to respond to his presence, the plants and trees swaying gently as if they, too, were preparing for the coming battle. The scent of blooming flowers filled the air, but it was a deceptive sweetness, masking the danger that lurked within.

As we approached, I could feel the eyes of Vornak beside me, his icy demeanor as impenetrable as ever. The Lord of the Ice, now the Valta Riomni of Bodaccia, was a figure of cold calculation and patient power. His connection to the element of ice was absolute, and I knew that in the clash of nature versus cold, only one could emerge victorious. Vaedric's eyes shot between the two of us, and for a moment, the three of us stood in silence, the weight of the impending conflict hanging in the air.

"It seems we are at an impasse," Vaedric said, his voice

smooth, yet underlined with a steely resolve. "You've come to take Finela, but you'll find that my vines will not bow to ice so easily."

Vornak remained silent, his eyes locked on Vaedric, his breath steady. He was calculating, as always, measuring every possible outcome before making his move. But I knew what was about to happen—this wasn't my fight. It was his.

I stepped forward, breaking the silence. "Vaedric," I said, my voice calm but firm. "You and I are equals. Both of us draw our strength from the earth, from life itself. If we fought, it would be a battle of endurance, with no clear victor. That's why it will be Vornak who faces you today."

His eyes narrowed slightly, but he didn't seem surprised. "You choose to stand aside, Durion? Interesting. Are you afraid that your trees and vines won't match my own?"

I shook my head. "It's not about fear, Vaedric. It's about knowing the battlefield. My power is the same as yours, and that's why this fight must be between you and Vornak. He brings the cold. He brings the winter that can freeze the very life you wield."

Vaedric's gaze shifted to Vornak, and for the first time, a look of uncertainty crossed his face. He knew what Vornak was capable of, and he knew that ice and nature had always been at odds. But his resolve was strong, and he nodded, stepping forward himself.

"Very well," he said, his voice hardening. "Let the Lord of Ice try his best."

Without another word, the two of them moved into position, the air between them crackling with tension. I stepped back, watching as the clash began.

Vaedric wasted no time in making the first move. With a swift gesture, the ground beneath his feet erupted with life, thick vines surging upward from the earth. They moved like living creatures, twisting and writhing as they shot toward Vornak, their thorny tendrils lashing out with deadly precision.

It was a powerful opening, one that sought to overwhelm Vornak before he could fully mount his defense. The vines wrapped around his legs, his torso, and even his arms, attempting to bind him in place and choke off his power before he could bring the cold to bear.

But Vornak remained utterly calm, his face impassive as the vines encircled him. He didn't panic, didn't flinch. He simply waited.

And then, with a single, deliberate gesture, he lowered the temperature around him.

A sharp chill filled the air, and I could see the frost begin to spread across the vines, creeping slowly but inexorably from his body outward. The living tendrils of plant life, once so full of vitality and strength, began to slow. The green leaves turned brittle, the thick stalks cracking as the cold seeped into them. Frost covered everything, turning the vibrant plants into brittle, lifeless husks.

With a flick of his hand, Vornak shattered the frozen vines, breaking them into pieces with an almost casual ease.

Vaedric's eyes narrowed, but he didn't hesitate. He adapted quickly, summoning more plants to replace those that had been destroyed. A dense overgrowth sprang up around him, towering trees with thick roots and thorny bushes that blocked Vornak's path. The plants twisted and turned, creating a living maze that sought to trap him within its grasp.

But Vornak was not deterred.

He raised his hand again, and this time, the air itself seemed to freeze. A wall of ice rose before him, shimmering and impenetrable. The plants slammed into the ice with a force that would have crushed steel, but the ice held firm. It was too thick, too cold for Vaedric's plants to penetrate. And the more he pressed forward, the more the cold seeped into his creations, slowing their growth and sapping their strength.

The battle became one of endurance—Vaedric's relentless offense against Vornak's unyielding defense. The temperature continued to drop, the cold air biting at my skin even from where I stood. Frost crept across the ground, spreading from Vornak's position outward, freezing everything in its path. Vaedric, realizing that his offensive strategy was faltering, tried to shift tactics. He sent a wave of roots underground, hoping to strike at Vornak from below, but he was ready for him. With a sweep of his arm, he summoned a wave of frost that spread across the earth, freezing the roots before they could reach him. The ice crept through the soil, cutting off Vaedric's ability to draw life from the earth. His plants began to wither, their once-vibrant green turning to a dull brown as the cold took hold. I could see the frustration growing in Vaedric's eyes. He was fighting valiantly, but he was losing ground. Vornak's Divine Power was relentless, his patience unshakable. He was not flashy or aggressive like me. He was methodical, calculating, waiting for the perfect moment to strike.

And that moment was approaching.

Vornak's counterattack began slowly, but it was devastating. He summoned glaciers from the earth, massive slabs of ice that rose from the ground, crushing Vaedric's plants beneath their weight. The ice was slow, but it was unstoppable. The freezing winds howled, and the once-vibrant garden that had surrounded Vaedric was now a frozen wasteland, the plants brittle and lifeless under the weight of the cold.

Vaedric fought back with everything he had, summoning more vines, more roots, more life. But the cold was too much. The plants couldn't survive in the hostile environment Vornak had created. They withered and died almost as quickly as they grew, leaving Vaedric with fewer and fewer options. I could see the exhaustion in Vaedric's eyes, the way his shoulders sagged under the weight of the battle. He had fought bravely, but he was outmatched. Vornak's ice was too powerful, too relentless. And now, he was ready to finish it.

With a final, deliberate gesture, Vornak summoned a blizzard.

The winds howled through the courtyard, snow and ice swirling around Vaedric in a blinding fury. He raised her arms, trying to summon a final wave of vines to defend himself, but it was too late. The cold had already taken hold. The vines froze in mid-motion, their tendrils snapping as the blizzard overwhelmed them. Vaedric's movements grew slower, more labored, as the cold seeped into his very bones. He struggled to hold on, his strength waning with every passing second.

And then, with a final wave of his hand, Vornak summoned the ice to rise around him, encasing him in a prison of frozen plant life. The vines that had once been his greatest weapon were now his undoing, trapping him in place as the ice constricted his movements.

I could see his breath coming in ragged gasps, his eyes wide with the realization that he had lost.

Vornak stepped forward, his expression as cold and unyielding as the ice he commanded. He didn't speak, didn't offer any words of comfort or mercy. He simply raised his hand one last time, and the ice around Vaedric thickened, sealing his fate.

The battle was over.

The courtyard was silent now, the once-vibrant garden reduced to a frozen wasteland. The temperature had dropped to the point where even I could feel the chill biting at my skin. Vornak stood in the center of the devastation, his breath steady, his expression unreadable.

Vaedric was encased in ice, his body frozen in place, his vines trapped around him like a suffocating cage. He had fought valiantly, but in the end, nature had fallen to the relentless power of winter. Vornak turned to me, his eyes cold and emotionless. "It's done," he said simply.

I nodded, though I felt a strange sense of unease settle over me. The battle had been necessary, I knew that. Vaedric had stood against the empire, and he had paid the price. But watching him fall like this, trapped in a prison of his own creation... it didn't sit right with me. Vornak, however, showed no such hesitation. He had done what needed to be done, and now he was ready to move on. "We should report to Aldous," he said, his tone matter-of-fact.

I glanced at Vaedric's frozen form one last time before turning away. "Yes," I agreed, though my voice felt hollow.

"Let's go."

As we left the courtyard, the cold wind still howling around us, I couldn't shake the feeling that something had shifted. Vaedric's fall was a victory for the empire, but it didn't feel like a victory to me. It felt like something had been lost, something I couldn't quite put into words. Vornak, however, remained as calm and unshakable as ever. He had faced nature itself and won, but at what cost? The leader of Finela had fallen, and the empire was one step closer to victory. But the cold that had taken hold in the courtyard... it had seeped into my bones as well.

And I wasn't sure it would ever leave.

Chapter XXXV

The Fate

The road stretched long and unforgiving beneath us as Vornak and I led what remained of our forces toward Alatok. The wind whipped across the open plains, dry and harsh, as if the very land was resisting our presence. The battle at Finela had taken its toll. Of the 300,000 men we had led into battle, only 273,000 survived to make the three-day march back to the city. Vornak rode ahead of me, his face as unreadable as ever, the cold air matching the icy aura that always surrounded him. He had emerged victorious against Vaedric, the Victor of Vines, but there was no celebration in his victory. It was just another task completed, another province brought under the empire's control. That was the way of things now: win, conquer, move forward.

The desert sun beat down on us, relentless in its heat, though it did little to melt the coldness that had settled in my chest. The destruction of Finela weighed on me more than I'd expected. Watching Vaedric fall, watching his vines wither and freeze beneath Vornak's unyielding ice—it had left a sour taste in my mouth. I had fought many battles in the name of Nantrium, but the more I witnessed, the more I began to wonder where the line was between purification and destruction. But there was no room for hesitation. Aldous had made it clear that this was our fate. We were the instruments of the Hyltorian Empire, the force that would cleanse Nantrium of chaos and disorder. Even as doubts crept into my mind, I knew I couldn't turn away from the path we had chosen. The light of O'Rhyus guided us, even if that light seemed to grow dimmer with each step we took. Alatok came into view, its towering walls rising above the horizon like a fortress of stone. The city was a beacon of strength, its people hardened by years of conflict and survival. Inside those walls, the remnants of our forces would regroup with Zephyros and Vandrel, and we would await Aldous's arrival.

The ride had been long, the losses heavy, but we still had work to do.

As we passed through the gates of Alatok, the soldiers under our command moved with silent discipline. They were tired, weary from the long march and the battles they had endured, but there was a sense of purpose in the air. They knew what was at stake. They knew that this was more than just a war for territory—it was a war for the future of Nantrium.

We dismounted near the encampment that had been set up outside the city's central fortress, the tent of the Vhankillas standing tall and imposing at its center. This was where we would meet with Zephyros and Vandrel, where the leaders of the empire's army would gather to discuss our next steps. As Vornak and I approached the tent, the remaining soldiers of Zephyros and Vandrel were already gathered. Of the original 300,000 men they had led into battle, all that remained were weary faces and 187,000 soldiers. Still a formidable force, but the weight of the losses was unthinkable.

The four of us had been through much, each of us tasked with conquering provinces in the name of the Hyltorian Empire, each of us facing different trials and different battles. But now, as we stood on the cusp of our final campaign, the burden of what we had done was beginning to show.

Zephyros and Vandrel were already waiting for us inside the tent, their faces hard and solemn. Zephyros, as always, exuded a sharp intensity, his eyes crackling with the remnants of the lightning that had once torn through the battlefield. He was the most aligned with Aldous's vision, the most fervent in his belief that what we were doing was necessary for the greater good.

Vandrel, on the other hand, sat in silence, his face etched with a quiet unease. Of all of us, he had been the most reluctant to embrace Aldous's path. He believed in the cause, but the brutality of the battles had worn on him more than it had on the rest of us. His connection to the natural world ran deep, and every tree that fell, every river that was dammed, weighed on his soul.

Vornak and I entered the tent, the weight of our recent victory still heavy in the air. The four of us sat around the large map spread across the table, marking the territories we had conquered and the few that still resisted. We were all leaders, generals of the Hyltorian Army, but we were also brothers in arms, bound by the same fate. For a long moment, none of us spoke. The silence stretched between us, filled with the unspoken understanding of what we had sacrificed to get here.

Finally, it was Zephyros who broke the silence, his voice sharp and direct. "We're close," he said, his eyes showing the intensity that always seemed to surround him. "Nantrium is nearly ours."

I nodded, though the words felt hollow. "At what cost?" I asked quietly, my eyes fixed on the map in front of us.

"How much more must we sacrifice before this land is truly purified?"

Zephyros's gaze turned to me, his expression hardening. "Whatever it takes, Durion. You know that. Aldous has made it clear—this isn't about individual lives. It's about the future of this world. We're bringing balance. We're following the light."

I looked at him, my jaw tight. "And yet, the more we follow this path, the more it feels like we're walking in darkness."

Zephyros's eyes flared with anger, but he held his tongue. He had always been the most loyal to follow the light without question. But that didn't mean he was blind to the cost.

Vornak, ever the pragmatist, leaned forward, his voice cold and calm. "We knew this would be difficult. Purification is never easy. But it's necessary. The chaos that has plagued Nantrium for centuries—it has to be rooted out, no matter what the cost."

I sighed, my gaze drifting to Vandrel, who had remained silent throughout the exchange. "And what about you, Vandrel?" I asked. "Where do you stand in all of this?"

Vandrel's eyes met mine, and for a moment, I saw the weight of the world reflected in them. He took a deep breath before speaking, his voice heavy with resignation.

"I'm not sure anymore," he admitted quietly. "I believe in the cause. I believe in the need for order, for balance. But... the way we're achieving it. The destruction. The lives we've taken. I don't know if this is the way."

Zephyros snorted, his expression filled with frustration. "You're questioning the path now? After everything we've done? After everything we've sacrificed?"

Vandrel met his gaze, his voice steady but tinged with sadness. "I'm not questioning the goal. I'm questioning the means. There has to be a way to achieve peace without... this."

Vornak leaned back in his chair, his expression thoughtful. "There isn't. You know that, Vandrel. You've seen what happens when order breaks down. You've seen the chaos. The only way to bring true peace to Nantrium is through strength. Through control."

I could see the conflict in Vandrel's eyes, the way his heart warred with his mind. He had always been the most reluctant to embrace the harsh realities of war. But in the end, even he knew that there was no turning back.

"We all chose this path," I said softly, my gaze sweeping across the faces of my comrades. "We knew the cost. We knew what we were signing up for. Aldous has led us here, and we've followed him because we believe in his vision. We believe in the light of O'Rhyus."

Zephyros nodded, his expression softening slightly. "Exactly. Aldous is the light. He is the one who will bring balance to Nantrium. We've done what we needed to do, but it's all for a greater purpose."

Vornak's voice was quiet but firm as he added, "We're not just soldiers. We're instruments of the divine. O'Rhyus has chosen Aldous to lead us, and we have a duty to follow. This is the path we were meant to walk."

There was no malice in their words, no animosity between us. We had all seen the same battles, faced the same horrors. We had all made the same choices, even if we didn't always agree on the reasons behind them.

Vandrel sighed, rubbing a hand over his face. "I know. I

know. I just... I need to believe that there's something more. Something beyond this endless cycle of destruction."

I placed a hand on his shoulder, offering what little comfort I could. "There is. Once this is over, once Nantrium is purified, there will be peace. That's what we're fighting for."

He nodded, though I could see the doubt lingering in his eyes. He wanted to believe, but the weight of the battle at Inilyus still hung over him, just as Finela had left its mark on me.

Zephyros stood then, his eyes sharp and determined. "Aldous will be here soon. When he arrives, we'll plan our next move. We can't afford to waver now, not when we're so close to victory."

Vornak and I exchanged a glance, both of us nodding in agreement. We had come too far to turn back now. The light of O'Rhyus had guided us this far, and we would see it through to the end.

Vandrel stood as well, though his movements were slower, more deliberate. He was still with us, still a part of the empire's cause, but I knew that the battles had left him weary in ways that went beyond the physical. As we prepared to bed down for the night, I found myself whispering a quiet prayer to O'Rhyus, asking for wisdom and strength in the days to come. I wasn't the only one. Zephyros knelt in silent reverence, his head bowed as he prayed for guidance. Vornak stood nearby, his gaze distant as he whispered words of repentance. Even Vandrel, despite his doubts, offered a quiet prayer to the god of light.

We were all seeking something—whether it was forgiveness, clarity, or just the strength to keep moving forward. We had chosen this path, and now, there was no turning back.

As the night settled in around us, I lay awake, my mind racing with thoughts of the battles still to come. The weight of fate pressed heavily on my shoulders, but I knew that we had no choice but to carry it. The purification of Nantrium was our destiny.

And we would see it through to the end.

Chapter XXXVI

The Shadow's Legacy

In the fathomless depths of The Inbetween, where light dared not intrude, Apollyon sat motionless upon his throne of jagged black stone. The walls of his lair pulsed with a sinister red glow, like the dying embers of a fire long forgotten. The cave was vast, stretching endlessly in every direction, but it was a place where time held no meaning and silence reigned supreme. Here, in the shadows, Apollyon thrived. This was his domain—the realm of shadow, of chaos, where light only existed as a faint echo, at the edge of extinction.

He had spent millennia here, watching the world of Nantrium unfold from afar, his gaze ever fixed on the fragile balance between light and darkness that his brother, O'Rhyus, so zealously sought to protect. Apollyon had long accepted that balance was a fleeting illusion, something that could only exist in the midst of conflict. Where O'Rhyus sought order, Apollyon knew that chaos was the natural state of things. There could be no light without shadow, no peace without war.

His thoughts drifted to recent events, the slow unraveling of the plans he had put in place centuries ago. Vicrum, the man he had manipulated so easily, had served his purpose. Vicrum had been a tool—desperate, loyal, and tragically mortal. He had embraced darkness in exchange for the power to save his wife, but in the end, even that had not been enough to save him. Aldous, the Shepherd of Light, had crushed Vicrum, ending his life as easily as one might snuff out a candle.

Apollyon's pale eyes gleamed faintly in the dark, reflecting the red glow of the cavern. He had expected Vicrum's fall. It was inevitable. But Vicrum's failure was of little consequence. The man had merely been a pawn in a much larger game, one that Apollyon had been playing for longer than mortals themselves could comprehend.

What mattered now was the next step.

Apollyon rose from his throne, his black robes flowing like liquid shadow around him, blending seamlessly with the darkness. His form was tall and imposing, a figure of pure malice and power, and as he moved through the cavern, the shadows seemed to ripple in response, as though they were alive.

His mind turned to Aldous, the champion of O'Rhyus, the man who believed himself to be the savior of Nantrium. Aldous had built an empire in the name of light, claiming to restore balance and order to the realm. But Apollyon knew better. He had seen the darkness within Aldous, the shadow that lay buried beneath the surface, waiting to be unleashed. For all his talk of righteousness, Aldous was closer to the dark than he realized. And that was the key to his undoing.

But Aldous wasn't the only piece on the board. Apollyon's plans extended far beyond the Shepherd of Light, far beyond the immediate conflict that had embroiled Nantrium. For as much as he reveled in the chaos he had sown, Apollyon had always been one to think ahead, to consider the future in ways that even O'Rhyus could not fathom. And the future of Nantrium lay not with Aldous or O'Rhyus, but with another.

His son.

Apollyon's gaze darkened as he thought of his son, the child born of shadow, of chaos itself. He would be more than a mere mortal, more than a pawn in the endless struggle between light and darkness. He was Apollyon's legacy, the embodiment of the power that Apollyon wielded, and he would one day rise to fulfill the destiny that had been written for him long before he was born. His son was the key to the prophecy. The prophecy that their father, Obrailion, had spoken so long ago, the prophecy that had shaped the fate of gods and mortals alike.

"When the balance falters, from the union of light and shadow, one shall rise. A soul born of divine blood, destined to restore what is broken and cast the fate of all realms."

Apollyon smiled faintly as he recalled the words. O'Rhyus had always believed that the prophecy spoke of Aldous, that his chosen champion would be the one to restore balance to Nantrium. But Apollyon had always known the truth. The prophecy did not speak of Aldous—it spoke of Luther. His son. The child born of divine blood, born not from light, but from shadow. A boy who had yet to understand the power. But that time would come. He had always known that his son would play a role in the final reckoning, in the battle that would decide the fate of Nantrium. But now, more than ever, he felt the pull of destiny drawing closer. The prophecy was not a promise of light's triumph—it was a promise of balance. And balance could only be restored when both light and darkness had been fully realized. Apollyon continued to pace, his mind racing with thoughts of the future. Aldous was a threat, yes, but he was also a distraction. The Shepherd of Light was consumed by his need to control, to impose order on a world that thrived on chaos. And in doing so, he had set himself on a path that would lead to his own downfall. Aldous's empire was fragile, built on the illusion of peace. But peace was a lie. Apollyon knew that better than anyone. The more Aldous fought to preserve his version of balance, the more the world would slip into chaos. It was only a matter of time before the cracks in his empire began to show.

And when they did, Apollyon would be ready.

But first, he needed to ensure that Luther was prepared for what was to come. Apollyon's gaze looked to the far end of the cavern, where the shadows were darkest, almost impenetrable. He could feel Luther's presence there, faint but undeniable. His son was waiting, unaware of the full extent of his destiny, but Apollyon would guide him. He would shape him, mold him into the weapon that would finally bring an end to this endless cycle of conflict.

"Two fates entwined, bound by blood... Only one shall hold the balance, and with it, the power to either restore the light or plunge the world into ruin."

Luther was that fate. He was the one who would rise from the union of light and shadow, the one who would either restore the balance or plunge Nantrium into eternal darkness. And Apollyon would make sure it was the latter.

But even as Apollyon's thoughts turned to his son, there was something else gnawing at the edges of his consciousness—something he had not considered before. For all his power, for all his influence, Apollyon knew that there were forces beyond even his control. The prophecy had spoken of two fates, bound by blood. It had always been clear to him that one of those fates was Luther, but who was the other? Was it Aldous, as O'Rhyus believed? Or was there someone else, hidden in the shadows, waiting to make their move? Apollyon's mind raced, his thoughts churning like a storm. The prophecy was always shifting. But one thing was clear: Luther was at the heart of it. His son was the key to everything. Apollyon stopped pacing, his gaze turning inward as he considered his next move. The future of Nantrium was uncertain, but that uncertainty was what gave him power. He thrived on the unknown, on the chaos that came with it. And now, with Luther by his side, he would ensure that the prophecy unfolded in his favor. But first, Luther would need to be awakened to his destiny. The boy would be powerful, but power without purpose was useless. Apollyon had always known that Luther's time would come, and now it was closer than ever. Apollyon extended his hand, and the shadows around him seemed to pulse with life, swirling toward him as though responding to his command. In that moment, he felt the full weight of his power, the legacy he was building. Luther would be more than just a son—he would be the instrument of Apollyon's will, the one who would finally bring the world to its knees.

"Two fates entwined... bound by blood..."

Apollyon's smile widened. The world believed it could resist the inevitable pull of darkness, but they were wrong. Light was fleeting, fragile, and in the end, it would crumble. As Apollyon moved toward the far end of the cavern, where the shadows were thickest, his thoughts turned not just to

Luther, but to the legacy he would leave behind. For too long, the gods had fought over the fate of Nantrium, but the time was coming when the world would no longer be ruled by gods alone.

It would be ruled by his blood. The prophecy was clear: only one would hold the balance, and Apollyon was determined that it would be his son who claimed that power. As the shadows closed in around him, Apollyon's thoughts were filled with visions of the future. A future where Luther stood at his side, a future where the world trembled beneath their feet. The time for waiting was over.

The time for Luther had come.

Chapter XXXVII

The Last Offer

I arrived at Alatok as the morning sun began to climb over the horizon, its light creeping across the land. The city, once a thriving bastion of strength under Rhalor, now seemed subdued, as though the very earth beneath it knew of the loss it had suffered. The banners of the Hyltorian Empire fluttered in the cold wind, stark and imposing against the stone walls of the city. Soldiers moved with purpose, their faces hard, but I could see the weight of recent battles hanging on them.

The Vhankilla tent was pitched at the heart of the encampment just outside the city walls, the central hub of our military operations. As I dismounted and handed the reins of my horse to a nearby soldier, I felt a surge of anticipation. Today would be important. I had given much thought to our next steps, and though the war had brought bloodshed and suffering, I still held onto the hope that peace could be restored. As I walked toward the tent, I allowed myself a small smile. Not one of victory or satisfaction—no, that wasn't what this was—but a smile born from a sense of resolve. The end of this conflict was within reach. I could feel it.

Pushing through the heavy canvas flap, I entered the tent, and the men inside fell silent. Zephyros, Vornak, Durion, and Vandrel were already gathered around the large wooden table at the center of the room, reviewing the map that marked our territories, the enemy's positions, and the contested lands. Their eyes looked to me as I entered, and I could feel the unease that hung in the air. They had all been through much, and the toll of our battles weighed heavily on them. But they weren't just my generals—they were my brothers in arms. We had fought side by side for this cause, and though I saw the weariness etched on their faces, I knew they would stand by me until the end.

"Good morning," I said, my voice calm and measured as I approached the table. I could feel their unease, but I smiled nonetheless. "I hope you're not plotting too many surprises without me."

Zephyros glanced up first, his sharp eyes narrowing slightly. "Aldous," he greeted, his tone neutral, though I sensed the tension beneath it. He had always been the most aligned with my vision, but even he felt the strain of the recent battles. "We're just reviewing the latest movements from Alatok's remaining forces."

I nodded, glancing down at the map. Red markers dotted the landscape, each representing a stronghold or position controlled by the enemy. Alatok was a fractured province now, its leadership shattered after Rhalor's fall, and yet it still resisted. The six remaining generals who had served under Rhalor were now in command, and they had yet to pledge loyalty to the Hyltorian Empire.

"They've lost their leader," I said, tracing my fingers across the map, feeling the texture of the parchment beneath my hand. "But that doesn't mean they've lost their will to fight."

Vornak, standing opposite me, crossed his arms over his chest. His icy demeanor had always matched the element he commanded, and today was no different. "They won't surrender willingly. They've been holding their positions for weeks now, and their forces are still considerable."

"I know," I replied, my gaze lifting to meet his. "But they've also lost much. The people of Alatok have suffered, and their generals know that continuing to fight will only bring more devastation."

Durion, his face lined with concern, stepped forward, his hand resting on the edge of the table. "They've seen what we're capable of. Rhalor's death was... brutal. I can't imagine they're eager to engage us directly again."

I frowned at the mention of Rhalor's death. It had been necessary, yes, but it was a stark reminder of the cost of this war. "I feel their loss as much as you do, Durion," I said, my voice softening. "What happened at Hyanasarri was a tragedy, but it was the price we paid for order. We're all grieving in our own way."

Vandrel, who had been silent until now, finally spoke, his voice low and steady. "But does that mean we're ready to offer peace again?" His eyes locked on mine, and I could see the doubt lingering there.

I let the question hang in the air for a moment before responding. "Yes, Vandrel. We are."

The tension in the room seemed to deepen at my words, and I could feel the weight of their stares on me. I knew what they were thinking. They had seen the carnage, the loss, the devastation that had followed us from province to province. Offering peace now, when we were so close to victory, might seem like a sign of weakness. But I didn't see it that way.

"I know what you're all thinking," I said, stepping around the table to stand before them. "You think this is a risk—that they'll see this offer as a sign that we're not prepared to finish what we've started. But that's not what this is."

I looked at each of them in turn, seeing the doubt and hesitation in their eyes. Even Zephyros, who had always been my staunchest supporter, seemed uncertain.

"They've lost their leader," I continued, "but that doesn't mean they are our enemies. Not yet. If we can bring them into the fold without further bloodshed, then we must. We've all lost too much already."

Zephyros was the first to respond, his voice sharp and direct. "And if they refuse?"

"Then they will face the full force of the Hyltorian Empire," I said firmly. "But we will not force them into submission if there is another way."

Vornak shook his head slightly, his voice colder than usual. "You think they'll simply accept peace after what we've done?"

"I think they want peace as much as we do," I replied. "They just don't know how to ask for it."

Durion remained silent, but I could see the gears turning in his mind. He had always been the most thoughtful of the group, weighing every decision with careful consideration. Finally, he spoke, his voice hesitant. "And if they accept?"

"Then we welcome them as brothers," I said simply. "We rebuild, together."

The room fell silent once more, the weight of my words sinking in. They were uneasy, I could feel it, but they also understood the necessity of what I was proposing. We could not continue to fight forever. The war had already taken too much from us—our people, our land, our hope. I moved back toward the table, leaning over the map as I considered our next steps. Alatok's remaining forces were scattered, but they still controlled key strongholds in the southern part of the province. If we could convince their generals to surrender, we could end the conflict without another drop of blood being spilled. I took a deep breath, steadying myself. I had to believe that this could work. I had to believe that peace was still possible, even after everything we had done.

"We'll send a message to the six remaining generals of Alatok," I said, straightening up. "An offer of peace. One final chance for them to join us willingly. And if they refuse. Then we march on their strongholds and crush them."

Zephyros nodded, the tension in his face easing slightly. "I trust your judgment, Aldous. If this is the path you've chosen, then we'll follow."

I smiled, though there was a heaviness in my heart that I could not shake. "Thank you, Zephyros." I glanced around the room once more, seeing the resolve in their faces. They had doubts, yes, but they also had faith in me and that was enough.

"Prepare the message," I said, turning toward the entrance of the tent. "We'll send it by the fastest riders. They'll know by the end of the day that they have one last chance." As I left the tent and stepped out into the cool morning air, I felt the weight of my decision settle over me. This war had been long and brutal, but I still believed that peace was within our grasp. I had to believe it.

I had to believe that there was another way.

Chapter XXXVIII

The Lurking Shadow

The morning air was crisp as I stepped out of the tent, my thoughts still wrapped around the weight of the decision I had just made. The offer of peace to the six remaining generals of Alatok hung heavily in my mind. Could it work? Could we truly end this war without further bloodshed, or had the fires of conflict burned too deeply into the hearts of those who had once followed Rhalor? As I emerged from the canvas folds, the sunlight caught my face, but the warmth did little to ease the tension that had taken root in my chest. My men, those who had been in the tent moments before, began to file out behind me, their movements slow and deliberate. They, too, felt the weight of what was to come. I stood still for a moment, my gaze sweeping across the camp. Soldiers were busying themselves with preparations—checking their weapons, tending to the horses, and speaking in hushed tones. The tension in the air was tight. Everyone knew what was at stake. This could be the final battle, the last push toward securing the empire. Yet something nagged at the edge of my consciousness, something that had been stirring within me since the moment I had entered the camp.

Then, just as I was about to turn toward the command tent, I saw it—a dash of movement, barely perceptible, behind the rocks that lined the edge of the camp. I froze, my eyes narrowing. It was quick, just a shadow that moved across the stones, too swift to make out clearly. But in that fleeting moment, I felt a chill run down my spine, as if the very air had shifted around me. The sun might have been shining, but a darkness lingered just beyond my reach.

I turned to Zephyros, who was standing nearby, oblivious to what I had seen. "Did you see that?" I asked, my voice low.

Zephyros followed my gaze to the rocks but shook his head. "See what?"

I glanced back toward the spot where I had seen the shadow, but it was gone, swallowed up by the stillness of the landscape. I forced a smile, trying to push aside the unease that clung to me. "Never mind. Must have been nothing."

But as I continued to move through the camp, the feeling of being watched never left me. It was as though there was something lurking just beyond the edges of my vision, just waiting, observing. I couldn't shake the sensation, no matter how hard I tried. I led my men toward the edge of the camp, where the horses were being prepared for the day's journey. We were making our final arrangements before we sent the message to the generals. I had made my decision. If they refused to surrender, we would march on their strongholds, crush their resistance, and bring an end to this war. But if even one of them chose peace, we would show mercy.

"Do you think they'll surrender?" Durion asked, his tone thoughtful as he adjusted the straps on his saddle. His eyes, ever watchful, glanced over at me.

I hesitated before answering. "One of them will. I can feel it."

Durion nodded, though his expression remained skeptical. "And the others?"

"We'll have to see," I replied. "But I'll offer peace one last time. They have until sunset to answer."

The soldiers around us moved with precision, preparing for what was likely to be the final campaign of this war. They were efficient, trained well, but I could see the fatigue in their eyes. Like me, they were tired of this war—tired of the bloodshed, the endless march of destruction that had followed us from province to province. I turned my gaze toward the distant horizon, where the strongholds of Alatok's remaining forces lay hidden among the hills and valleys. Soon, we would march, and soon, we would know if the generals had chosen to join us or to fight. But even as I stood there, my mind kept drifting back to the shadow I had seen earlier. I could still feel it, hovering at the edges of my awareness, as though it was watching, waiting for me to slip. And I knew—deep in my bones—that this was no ordinary shadow. It was something more.

The darkness.

The Darkness whispered through my thoughts like a cold breeze, and I clenched my fists at my sides. I had felt his presence before, had seen this influence in the shadows that lingered around me, tempting me at every turn. He had always been there, watching, waiting for his chance to break me. I took a deep breath, forcing myself to focus on the task at hand. This was not the time to let fear take hold. I had to remain strong—for my men, for my empire, for the future of Nantrium.

A shout from one of the messengers interrupted my thoughts, and I turned to see a young soldier running toward me, clutching a piece of parchment in his hand. His face was pale, and there was a sense of urgency in his movements.

"Shepherd Aldous," he called, his voice breathless as he

skidded to a stop before me. "A message from one of the generals."

I took the parchment from him, my heart pounding in my chest. This was it—their answer. With steady hands, I unfolded the message and began to read. The words were scrawled hastily, but the meaning was clear.

One of the six generals had surrendered.

I let out a long breath, a sense of relief washing over me. "He's surrendered," I said aloud, and my men, who had been waiting anxiously, began to murmur amongst themselves. It wasn't the victory they had expected, but it was a step toward peace. A step toward ending this war without more bloodshed.

Zephyros approached, his expression still guarded. "And the others?"

I shook my head. "No word from them yet. But this one... he's seen reason."

Vandrel, ever cautious, stepped forward. "What will you do with him?"

I thought for a moment before answering. "Grant him safe passage. We'll ensure he is protected as he leaves the battlefield. I'll send a small group of soldiers to accompany him and deliver messages to his people, warning them to evacuate before we lay siege to Alatok."

Durion, standing at my side, nodded approvingly. "It's the right thing to do."

The camp buzzed with activity as the message was relayed to the soldiers. Preparations were made to escort the surrendering general and his people to safety. But as the men moved about, I couldn't shake the feeling that the shadow still lingered nearby, watching me.

The general arrived not long after, escorted by a small group of his remaining soldiers. He was a weary-looking man, his face lined with exhaustion and grief. He had fought hard for Alatok, but he knew when to concede.

He dismounted his horse and approached me, his eyes filled with a mixture of respect and fear. "Lord Aldous," he said, bowing his head slightly. "I have come to surrender."

"You've made a wise choice," I replied, keeping my voice calm and measured. "Your people will be spared, and you will be granted safe passage and I will be your Shepherd."

The general hesitated for a moment before speaking again. "What of my people? Those who remain in the districts beyond the stronghold?"

I met his gaze, seeing the concern etched into his features. He wasn't just surrendering for himself—he was surrendering for the lives of those under his command, the civilians who had suffered enough.

"I will send as many messengers as I can spare," I said. "They will warn your people to evacuate before we advance. We don't want unnecessary bloodshed."

The general let out a breath of relief, and for the first time since his arrival, I saw hope in his eyes. "Thank you."

I inclined my head. "Go. Ensure your people are safe."

He bowed once more before turning and mounting his horse. With a small escort, he began to ride toward the distant hills, where his people would soon receive word of our approach. As I watched him leave, the weight of my decision pressed down on me. This would be the last offer of peace. The other five generals had until sunset to respond.

If they refused, then we would march—and this war would end, one way or another. I turned back to my men, who had gathered around me, waiting for my orders. I could see the tension in their eyes, the anticipation of what was to come.

"Prepare yourselves," I said, my voice firm. "Tonight, we will know if we march for peace or for battle."

They nodded, their expressions hardening as they moved to ready themselves for whatever lay ahead. But even as I spoke, even as I gave the orders, I couldn't shake the feeling that the shadow was still there, lurking just beyond the edges of my vision. I glanced toward the rocks again, but this time there was nothing. Only the faint rustling of the wind.

Still, the presence remained. A dark, unspoken promise of what was to come.

I knew, deep down, that Apollyon was watching me, testing me, waiting for me to falter.

But I would not falter. Not now.

As the sun began its slow descent toward the horizon, I stood at the edge of the camp, watching the distant hills where the remaining generals waited for their final chance to choose.

By the end of the night, peace would either be achieved—or forever lost.

Chapter XXXIX

The Final March

The sun was just beginning to rise, casting a faint golden hue over the horizon as I stood at the edge of the camp. The day ahead felt heavy with the weight of unspoken decisions, and as the cold morning air filled my lungs, I found myself contemplating everything that had brought us to this moment. The offer of peace had gone unanswered by the remaining five generals of Alatok, and now the time for diplomacy had passed. The message was clear: they would not surrender. They would resist until the bitter end. I had given them every opportunity to spare themselves and their people from the horrors that were to come. I had extended my hand, offered them mercy in the face of overwhelming power. But their silence had sealed their fate. The war would march forward.

I turned away from the horizon and back toward the camp, where my men were already preparing for the day's march. The hum of activity surrounded me—soldiers adjusting their armor, sharpening their swords, and exchanging hushed words of anticipation. They knew what was to come as well as I did. By nightfall, Alatok would either be under our control or it would fall to ruin.

"Zephyros," I called, my voice cutting through the din of the camp. He appeared at my side in an instant, his face calm, though I could see the tension in his eyes. "Are the men ready?"

"They are, Aldous," he replied. "We've prepared them for

what's to come. They know the plan."
"Good." I paused, glancing around the camp at the soldiers who were waiting for their orders. "Send word to the others. They are to advance to the eastern part of Alatok and meet with the refugees and the general who surrendered. Once they've secured the area, they are to rest. We'll join them after we've taken the central districts."
Zephyros nodded, though I could sense his unease. "And you? You're leading the charge with the ten thousand?"
I met his gaze, my expression hardening. "Yes. We'll take the central districts by nightfall."
He hesitated for a moment, as though he wanted to say more, but he knew better than to question my decision. Instead, he simply nodded. "As you command."
I watched as he moved off to relay the orders to the rest of the men. Around me, the soldiers began to stir, the camp coming to life as they prepared for the march. There was a tension in the air, an anticipation that buzzed like a live wire. This was it—the final push. The moment of reckoning.
As I made my way through the camp, I felt the familiar pull of Apollyon's presence lurking at the edges of my awareness. He had been with me since the day before, a shadow that clung to my every step. I hadn't seen him outright, but I could feel him watching, waiting. He wanted me to falter, to doubt myself, but I would not give him that satisfaction.
Not today.
The morning was brisk as I called for my horse, the sound of its hooves striking the cold ground echoing in the stillness. The air felt sharp, crisp, like the anticipation of battle had crept into the very fabric of the world. I mounted my horse

and rode to the front lines where the ten thousand soldiers I had chosen for this final task were waiting. Their faces were a mixture of determination and uncertainty, but each of them knew what was expected of them. This was their moment to cement their place in history, to ensure that the Hyltorian Empire would stand tall.

As I dismounted, I walked along the line, meeting the eyes of my men. I could see their resolve, the fire that burned within them. They had followed me through countless battles, trusted me to lead them to victory. And now, as we stood on the brink of what could be the final confrontation, I felt the weight of their expectations.

I couldn't afford to fail them.

"You've all fought bravely," I said, my voice loud enough to carry across the ranks. "You've faced challenges that would have broken lesser men. But here we are—on the cusp of victory. Today, we march into Alatok, and by nightfall, we will claim it as our own. This is your moment, your chance to prove that everything we've fought for, everything we've sacrificed, has been worth it."

A murmur of agreement rippled through the soldiers, their confidence building as I spoke. They needed to hear these words, to know that their efforts had meaning, that their bloodshed had a purpose.

"We are not here as conquerors," I continued. "We are here to bring order, to restore peace to a world that has been ravaged by chaos. The people of Alatok may resist us, but we will show them that our cause is just. We will show them that there is no future in defiance—only in unity."

I paused, letting the weight of my words settle over them.

"This is our moment of glory," I said, my voice firm. "Remember that when you march into battle today. Hold your heads high, for you fight not just for yourselves, but for the future of Nantrium. For the Hyltorian Empire."

A cheer rose up from the ranks, a sound that sent a surge of energy through me. They were ready. They were prepared to do whatever it took to secure victory.

I nodded, satisfied with their resolve. "We leave now. By nightfall, Alatok will be ours."

With that, I mounted my horse once more and gave the signal for the advance. The ten thousand men fell into formation, their movements precise, disciplined. We had fought too long and too hard to fail now. As we began the march toward Alatok, the shadow that had been hovering at the edges of my vision seemed to tighten its grip on my mind. I could feel it more acutely now—the presence of Apollyon, watching, waiting. He wanted me to lose myself in the bloodshed, to embrace the darkness that lurked within me. But I wouldn't. I had chosen my path, and I would see it through. I would lead my men to victory, not through cruelty or fear, but through purpose. We were here to bring order to a world that had fallen into chaos, and no amount of shadow could dissuade me from that goal. As the sun rose higher in the sky, the march continued. The landscape around us began to change, the distant hills giving way to the outskirts of the city. Alatok loomed ahead, its walls standing tall and imposing, a reminder of the strength it had once commanded under Rhalor's rule. But that strength had been shattered, its foundation crumbling beneath the weight of its own defiance. Soon, the city would fall, and the Hyltorian

Empire would rise in its place.

By the time we reached the bridge that led to the central districts of Alatok, the sun had begun its slow descent toward the horizon. And I felt the familiar weight of anticipation settle over me. The battle was close now. I could feel it in the air, in the tense silence that had fallen over my men. I dismounted and moved to the front of the line, standing before the bridge that would take us into the heart of the city. The water beneath us rushed swiftly, a reminder that once we crossed this bridge, there would be no turning back.

I glanced toward the city, the shadows lengthening across the walls, and then back at my soldiers. "You have fought for this empire, for this moment. And now, we stand on the edge of victory. Today, we will take Alatok, and tomorrow, we will rebuild it. For the Hyltorian Empire."

A cheer rose up from the soldiers, louder and more fervent than before. I could feel their resolve, their determination to see this through.

I raised my hand, signaling for them to follow. "To glory."

And with that, we crossed the bridge, the final march toward the central districts of Alatok beginning under the fading light of the sun. The city awaited us, its streets soon to be filled with the sounds of battle. This was our moment. And in the shadows of Apollyon, darkness loomed ever closer, but I pressed forward, my purpose clear. Victory would be ours. By nightfall, Alatok would belong to the Hyltorian Empire.

Chapter XXXX

The Fall

The sun had long since dipped below the horizon, casting the city of Alatok in an eerie twilight as my men and I crossed the bridge. The weight of what was about to unfold hung heavy in the air, and had everyone on edge. We had fought for this moment for so long, through blood and fire, and now we stood at the precipice of victory. But there was no joy in it, no sense of triumph. Only the grim realization that this, too, was necessary. As we stepped into the city, the streets were eerily quiet. The silence was suffocating, broken only by the distant murmur of water and the occasional clink of armor. My men moved with purpose, their weapons drawn, their eyes scanning the dark alleys and abandoned homes. The city felt like a ghost, its people long since fled or too afraid to show themselves. The resistance we had expected from the remaining five generals had not yet materialized, but I knew they were waiting. They would make their stand soon enough.

I led my soldiers deeper into the city, my mind focused on the task at hand. The five generals of Alatok had refused my offer of peace, choosing instead to hold onto a crumbling legacy of defiance. They would be waiting in the central district, likely gathered in the courtyard where they had once commanded Rhalor's forces. It was there that they would make their final stand, and it was there that we would bring an end to this war.

The streets narrowed as we approached the heart of the city, the buildings closing in on us like the jaws of a Remlark. The tension, thick. They had been trained for this, yes, but that didn't make the weight of the moment any lighter. I could see it in their eyes—the anticipation, the fear, the grim determination. This was it. There was no turning back now. As we reached the entrance to the central district, I raised my hand, signaling for the men to halt. The gates that led to the courtyard stood before us, tall and imposing, flanked by thick stone walls. The five generals were waiting on the other side, likely preparing for the final confrontation.

I turned to face my men, my voice steady as I spoke. "This is where it ends. We will take Alatok tonight. Stay focused, stay sharp. We're not here to destroy—we're here to bring order." They nodded, their faces hardening with resolve. They knew what was at stake. They knew what needed to be done. I took a deep breath, feeling the familiar surge of Divine Power within me. I could feel the light, that force that had guided me through every battle, coursing through my veins. It was not just strength—it was purpose. It was the certainty that what we were doing was right.

And yet, beneath it all, there was something else—a hint of darkness, a shadow that lingered at the edges of my mind. Apollyon. He was always there, watching, waiting, testing me. I could feel his presence now more than ever, as though he was standing just behind me, whispering temptations into my ear.

But I pushed it aside. I couldn't afford to let him distract me. Not now.

With a single gesture, I signaled for the gates to be opened. My men moved quickly, pushing the heavy wooden doors aside, and we stepped into the courtyard. The air felt heavy. The courtyard was wide and open, lined with towering columns and statues of long-dead heroes, their stone faces etched with the same defiance that now filled the eyes of the five generals who stood before me.

They were gathered in the center of the courtyard, their weapons drawn, their faces hard with determination. They knew this was the end, but they would not go down without a fight. I could see it in the way they stood, the way they held their swords. They were ready to die for their cause.

But I was ready to kill for mine.

I stepped forward, leaving my men behind, and walked toward the generals. The sound of my boots against the stone echoed through the courtyard, each step deliberate, each step a reminder of the power I held. The power to end this. The power to bring order to a world that had been torn apart by chaos.

The first general, a tall man with a scar running down the side of his face, stepped forward to meet me. His eyes burned with hatred, but there was fear there, too. He knew what I was capable of.

"You had your chance," I said, my voice low and cold. "You could have chosen peace. But now you've chosen death."

He didn't respond. He simply raised his sword and charged.

I didn't need my weapon. Not for this.

I moved quickly, faster than he could react. My hand shot out, catching his wrist and twisting it with such force that I heard the sickening crack of bone. His sword clattered to the ground, but before he could even cry out, I drove my other hand into his chest, the force of the blow sending him crashing to the ground.

He lay there, gasping for breath, his eyes wide with shock as blood began to pool beneath him. I didn't look back. The others were already moving, their swords drawn as they rushed toward me, desperate to take me down.

But they were too slow.

The second general came at me with a wild swing of his blade, but I sidestepped easily, my hand lashing out to grab his throat. He struggled, his eyes bulging as I lifted him off the ground, his feet kicking uselessly in the air. For a moment, I met his gaze, watching the life drain from his eyes, and then I slammed him into the stone, the force of the impact sending cracks spidering out across the courtyard. The others hesitated for a moment, clearly realizing that this was not going to be the fight they had expected. But hesitation was their downfall.

And in their hesitation I was closing the distance between myself and the third general before he could react. His sword came down in a desperate arc, but I caught it with my hand, the blade biting into my flesh as I ripped it from his grip. Blood dripped from my palm, but I didn't feel the pain. I didn't care. I drove the hilt of his sword into his chest, the force of the blow knocking him off his feet.

He hit the ground hard, his body twitching as blood spilled from the wound.

The fourth general was smarter. He didn't rush at me like the others. He circled, his eyes darting between the bodies of his fallen comrades and the menacing figure I had become. I could see the fear in his eyes, the realization that this wasn't just a battle for him. This was a massacre.

He lunged at me, his sword aimed for my heart, but I sidestepped the blow, catching him by the arm and twisting it behind his back. I felt the snap of his bones, heard the scream that tore from his throat, but it didn't stop me. I drove my elbow into the back of his head caving it in, sending him sprawling to the ground.

And then there was one.

The final general stood at the far end of the courtyard, his sword trembling in his hand. He didn't move, didn't speak. He just stared at me, his face pale with fear. I took a step toward him, then another. Each movement deliberate, each step a reminder of the inevitable.

"Drop your sword," I said, my voice cold and emotionless. "It's over."

For a moment, I thought he might listen. His grip on the sword loosened, and I saw the fear in his eyes deepen. And then, with a final burst of defiance, he charged.

I met him head-on. Before he could even set up, I slammed my fist into his gut, doubling him over. He gasped for breath, his body crumpling to the ground at my feet.

I stood over him, my chest rising and falling with each breath, the sound of the wind filling the silence of the courtyard. Around me, the bodies of the five generals lay broken and still, their defiance snuffed out.

It was over.

I looked down at the man who had once commanded the forces of Alatok, the last of Rhalor's loyal generals. His breath was shallow, his body broken, but he was still alive—barely.

"You could have had peace," I said softly, my voice carrying a weight of finality. "May you find the light."

With a swift motion, I brought my foot down on his chest, feeling the bones crack beneath my weight. His body spasmed once, then went still.

I stood there for a moment, letting the reality of what I had just done settle over me. The courtyard was silent, the only sound the wind rustling through the trees. The battle was over. Alatok had fallen. But as I stood there, surrounded by the bodies of the men I had killed, I felt the familiar presence of Apollyon once again. He was there, in the shadows, watching me, his unseen eyes filled with amusement. He wanted me to believe that this was what I had become—that this was the inevitable result of power. But I refused to believe that. I had done what needed to be done, nothing more. This was the price of peace, and I would pay it.

I turned away from the bodies, my eyes focusing on the distant horizon. The city was ours now. The Hyltorian Empire would rise, stronger than ever. But as I led my men away from the courtyard, I couldn't shake the feeling that something had changed within me—that the line between order and chaos, light and shadow, had blurred just a little more.

And I wasn't sure which side I was on anymore.

Chapter XXXX

The Price

The light of the rising sun bathed the eastern side of Alatok in an eerie, golden glow as I led my men through the quiet streets. The battle had been won. The five generals were dead, their bodies left behind in the central courtyard, a silent testament to the inevitability of our cause. The city, once a fortress of resistance, now lay broken and silent. We had done what needed to be done. We had brought order to chaos. But as I marched toward the place where the remaining refugees and the surrendering general were being held, I felt a strange hollowness growing inside me, a nagging feeling I couldn't quite place. The weight of the decisions I had made pressed heavily on my shoulders, but I pushed it aside. There was still work to be done.

As I approached the eastern edge of the city, I saw Zephyros, Vornak, Durion, and Vandrel gathered near the group of refugees, their faces shadowed with uncertainty. The survivors of Alatok—men, women, and children—huddled together, their faces pale and drawn with fear. They had been gathered and separated from the soldiers, standing in a loose cluster, their eyes wide and desperate. The general who had surrendered stood among them, his head bowed in shame, his hands bound behind his back.

I could feel the tension in the air, the unease that gripped not only the refugees but also my own men. They were waiting, watching me, unsure of what was to come next. They had fought alongside me for so long, trusting in my decisions, believing in the cause of the Hyltorian Empire. But now, as the battle was over, the weight of my command seemed heavier than ever.

I took a deep breath, steadying myself as I approached the group. The refugees murmured quietly, their voices tinged with fear, and the general lifted his head, his eyes locking onto mine with a look of desperation.

"Shepherd," he said, his voice hoarse.

I studied him for a moment, my gaze cold and unreadable. He had been the only one of the six generals to surrender, the only one willing to lay down his arms and offer his loyalty to the Hyltorian Empire. But that didn't make him any less weak.

"Gather the general and the refugees," I ordered, my voice carrying across the camp with authority. "Separate them from the soldiers. We will deal with them shortly."

There was a brief hesitation, a moment of confusion that passed through my men as they exchanged uncertain glances. Even Zephyros, who had always been the most aligned with my vision, seemed to hesitate for a fraction of a second. But they did as I commanded, moving quickly to separate the refugees from the remaining soldiers of Alatok.

The refugees were pushed into a smaller group, their bodies huddling together for warmth and comfort as the reality of their situation began to sink in. The children cried softly, clinging to their mothers, while the men stood with their heads bowed, their expressions hollow. The general remained apart from them, his hands still bound, his face pale with fear. I could feel their eyes on me, the weight of their fear, their hope, their desperation. They believed that I would show them mercy. They believed that because one of their leaders had surrendered, they would be spared.

But they were wrong.

This was no time for mercy. This was the time for purification.

I turned to face my men, my voice calm and steady as I spoke. "We have done what was necessary to bring Alatok under the control of the Hyltorian Empire. The city is ours, and its leaders are no more. But there is still one more task that must be completed."

Zephyros stepped forward, his brow furrowed with confusion. "What task, Aldous? The city is already secured."

I looked past him, my gaze fixed on the huddled group of refugees. "The people of Alatok have suffered under the rule of their generals. They have resisted us, and now they stand before us as survivors of a regime that sought to defy the Empire. But we cannot allow the seeds of rebellion to grow. We cannot allow these survivors to harbor resentment, to nurse the desire for revenge."

Vornak's eyes widened slightly, his expression darkening as he began to understand what I was saying. "Aldous... what are you suggesting?"

I stepped closer to the group of refugees, my gaze cold and calculating as I looked down at them. "I am suggesting that we purify this city. Completely."

There was a long, heavy silence that followed my words. The refugees stared at me in shock, their eyes wide with disbelief. The general, still bound, struggled to find his voice.

"No," he gasped, his voice filled with panic. "Please! These people are innocent! They've done nothing to deserve this!"

I didn't respond. My gaze remained fixed on the general, my mind made up. He had surrendered because he was weak. He had abandoned his brothers, allowed them to fight and die while he sought to save himself and his people. But weakness like that couldn't be tolerated. Not if we were to rebuild this world in the image of the Hyltorian Empire.

The general fell to his knees, his hands trembling as he begged for mercy. "Please... I beg you. Spare them. Spare me. I'll do anything—"

"That is precisely why you must die," I said, my voice cold and emotionless. "You are weak. You abandoned your cause, your brothers, and now you grovel for mercy. You do not deserve to live."

The general sobbed, his body shaking with fear and despair. Around him, the refugees began to cry out in confusion and terror, their voices rising in panic as the reality of what was happening began to sink in.

Zephyros stepped forward again, his expression tight with unease. "Aldous, this... this isn't right. These people... they surrendered. They didn't resist us. Why kill them?"

I turned to face him, my eyes hard. "Because if we let them live, they will seek revenge. They will grow, their hatred festering, and one day they will rise against us. We cannot allow that. The world must be purified."

"But this isn't purification," Vandrel said, his voice barely above a whisper. "This is slaughter."

I could see the doubt in their eyes, the hesitation in their movements. They didn't understand. They couldn't see the bigger picture, the vision I had for the future of Nantrium. This was about more than just this one city. This was about creating a world where there was no room for rebellion, no room for weakness.

"This is the path of light," I said, my voice firm. "We are the bearers of the Divine Power. It is our responsibility to rid the world of darkness, to ensure that no seeds of rebellion are allowed to take root. If we allow these people to live, they will undermine everything we have fought for."

Zephyros shook his head, his eyes filled with confusion. "Aldous... you're talking about killing women and children."

I met his gaze, unflinching. "Yes. And it must be done."

Durion stepped forward, his brow furrowed with concern. "Are you certain about this? Is this really the way forward?"

"It is." I replied, my voice filled with certainty. "If we are to build a new world, we must first purge the old. We cannot allow any trace of the past to remain, or we will be doomed to repeat it."

The refugees continued to cry out, their voices filled with terror and confusion. The general, still on his knees, begged for mercy, his voice breaking with sobs.

But I didn't falter. I couldn't afford to.

"This is our duty," I said, turning to face my men. "This is what we were chosen for. To bring order to chaos, to rid the world of darkness. We must not let sentimentality cloud our judgment. We must do what is necessary."

For a moment, there was silence. My men stood still, their expressions conflicted. They had followed me through countless battles, trusted in my leadership, but this—this was different. I could see the doubt in their eyes, the uncertainty that clung to them like a shadow. But I knew that doubt would pass. It had to. They would see, in time, that this was the only way forward.

I turned back to the group of refugees, my gaze cold and detached. "Kill them all."

The order hung in the air like a curse, and for a moment, no one moved. The silence was deafening, broken only by the sobs and cries of the people huddled together, their eyes filled with terror.

Then, slowly, my men began to move. Their hesitation was clear, but they followed my command. They had to. This was the path we had chosen, the path of the Hyltorian Empire. One by one, the cries of the refugees were silenced, their bodies falling to the ground as my men carried out my orders. The general screamed, his voice filled with desperation and horror, but it was no use. He, too, would meet his end. As the last of the refugees fell, the courtyard was filled with the stench of blood, the bodies of the innocent lying scattered across the ground. The air thick with the weight of what we had done, and for a moment, even I felt the cold grip of doubt.

But I pushed it aside. This was necessary. This was the path of light.

I turned to my men, their faces pale and drawn as they stood among the carnage. They looked to me for reassurance, for some sign that what we had done was right.

"This is the price of peace," I said, my voice steady. "We cannot allow new seeds of rebellion to grow. We have purified this city, and now we will rebuild it. The Hyltorian Empire will stand stronger than ever."

There was a long silence, but eventually, my men nodded. They didn't fully understand, but they would follow. They always had.

"Withdraw," I ordered. "We return to Lushahiem."

They moved quickly, their movements mechanical as they gathered their supplies and prepared to leave. The bodies of the refugees were left behind, a silent reminder of the cost of our victory. As we marched out of Alatok, the shadow of Apollyon lingered in the back of my mind, whispering to me, taunting me.

But I ignored him.

I had made my choice. And I would see it through to the end.

The path of light was never easy.

But it was the only way forward.

Chapter XXXXI

The Weight of Light

The sun hung low in the sky the morning after we left the bloodied streets of Alatok, casting long shadows across the land as my men and I made our way back toward Lushahiem. The landscape around us was quiet, eerily so, as if the very world was holding its breath in the wake of the slaughter that had taken place. The weight of what we had done lingered in the air, heavy and suffocating, though none of the men spoke of it directly.

We marched in silence for the first few miles, the sound of our footsteps the only thing breaking the oppressive stillness. I could feel the tension building among my men, the unease simmering just beneath the surface. They had followed me without question for so long, trusted me to guide them, but after what had transpired in Alatok, I knew the doubt was creeping in.

And, truthfully, it was creeping into me as well.

The atrocities committed in the name of the light—the slaughter of innocents, the execution of the general who had surrendered—those were the actions of a man who had convinced himself he was doing what was necessary. But as the faces of the dead flashed through my mind, I found it harder and harder to believe that this was truly the path of light. The line between right and wrong, between darkness and light, had become dangerously blurred, and I could feel the darkness gnawing at the edges of my soul.

Finally, as the sun rose higher in the sky, breaking the silence with its light, Zephyros rode up beside me, his face lined with concern. I could see the weight of the past few days written in his eyes, the doubt that had been simmering since Alatok now rising to the surface.

"Aldous," he began, his voice low so as not to be overheard by the others. "We need to talk."

I kept my gaze forward, the horizon stretching out endlessly before us. "About what?"

Zephyros sighed, glancing back at the men marching behind us before speaking again. "About what happened in Alatok. About the... purifications."

The word hung heavy in the air between us, and for a moment, I said nothing. I didn't want to address it, I didn't want to acknowledge the doubt that had been growing inside me since we left the city. But I couldn't avoid it any longer.

"What of it?" I asked, my voice tight.

Zephyros hesitated for a moment before speaking again. "The men are... uneasy. They followed your orders, they always have, but after what happened, they're questioning if this is truly the path of light."

I could feel the knot tightening in my chest, the weight of responsibility pressing down on me. "And what do you think, Zephyros?" I asked, turning to meet his gaze.

He didn't answer right away, his eyes clouded with conflict. Finally, he spoke, his voice softer now. "I think... I think we need to reevaluate. The 150 Contingency Actions, the path we're on... we need to make sure this is still the right way forward."

I felt a flash of irritation at his words, a defensiveness rising up in me, but I quickly pushed it aside. He wasn't wrong. The Contingency Actions I had put in place were meant to ensure order, to prevent the darkness from taking root again. But after what had happened in Alatok, I could see now that some of those actions might have been made in haste, in moments where fear or anger clouded my judgment.

I took a deep breath, steadying myself before responding. "Very well. We'll revise them. But not alone. We'll do it together, with the input of the others."

Zephyros looked relieved, a small weight lifting from his shoulders. "Thank you, Aldous. I think it's the right decision."

I nodded, though the knot in my chest remained. "Once we return to Lushahiem, we'll revise the Contingency Actions with everyone present. Every member of the Omni Order will have a say."

He gave a small nod of agreement before falling back to ride with the others. As I watched him go, I felt a strange sense of relief wash over me. Revising the Contingency Actions was necessary, but it was also an acknowledgment that the path we were on might not be as pure as I had once believed. It was a small step, but it was a step nonetheless.

The miles passed slowly after that, the weight of the coming discussions lingering over us. We would return to Lushahiem, and there we would sit and confront the choices we had made. And we would face the consequences of those choices together. As the midday sun hung high in the sky, Vornak and Durion rode up beside me, their faces as grim as Zephyros had been earlier. They, too, had been wrestling with the events in Alatok, and it wasn't long before Durion spoke, his voice heavy with the same unease I had seen in Zephyros.

"Aldous, we need to talk about the provinces."

I looked at him, my brow furrowed. "What about them?"

Durion exchanged a glance with Vornak before continuing. "There are several provinces without Valta Riomnis. The power grab in those places... it's dangerous. If we don't appoint new leaders soon, chaos could take root again."

I nodded slowly, already knowing where this conversation was going. "I've already considered that. We will need to appoint new Valta Riomnis as soon as we return to Lushahiem."

Vornak, ever the pragmatic one, spoke next. "Without a leader we will need someone strong to hold their province, someone loyal to the Omni Order."

I thought for a moment before responding. "I've already given it thought. I'll send a message to Caelthar, the man I've chosen to be the next Valta Riomni of Mophia. He's loyal and capable. He'll arrive in Lushahiem shortly after we return."

Durion nodded, though I could see the indication of doubt in his eyes. "And what about the other provinces? Wyldren, Alatok, and Hyanasarri are all without Valta Riomnis as well."

I frowned, the weight of those empty seats hanging over me like a storm cloud. "We'll need to find new leaders for those provinces as well. Loyal men, ones we can trust to uphold the values of the Hyltorian Empire."

Vornak tilted his head slightly, his voice carefully measured. "But how can we be sure that they won't turn against us?

After what we did in Alatok... there's bound to be resentment, even among those loyal to the Empire."

I met his gaze, my expression hardening. "We'll ensure their loyalty. We'll make it clear that defiance will not be tolerated. And if they choose to rebel... they'll face the same fate as the others."

There was a long pause after that, the tension between us thick and suffocating. They didn't speak, but I could see the unease in their eyes, the lingering doubt that hung in the air. They were questioning the path we were on, and while they hadn't said it outright, I knew that they feared we had already stepped too far into the darkness. But I couldn't let their doubt cloud my judgment. This was the path we had chosen, and we had to see it through.

After several more hours of riding, the city of Alatok finally disappeared behind us, fading into the distance as we continued our journey back to Lushahiem. The farther we rode from the site of the slaughter, the heavier my thoughts became. I couldn't shake the feeling that something had changed, that something had been lost in the bloodshed of the previous day. The light I had once followed so unwaveringly seemed dimmer now, as though it had been tainted by the very darkness we sought to destroy. I could still feel Apollyon's presence, a whisper at the back of my mind, taunting me, testing me. He wanted me to believe that this was his doing, that I had given in to the darkness he had sown. But I refused to believe it. I had made these decisions in the name of the light, in the name of order and peace.

Hadn't I?

The doubt gnawed at me, but I pushed on as we approached

the edge of the Eastern Ridge. My mind snapped back to the present, and I glanced at my men, their faces still drawn with uncertainty.

As we prepared to make camp for the night, I turned to them one last time before settling down. "We will revise the Contingency Actions as soon as we return to Lushahiem. We will make sure that we are still on the path of the light."

They nodded, their expressions a mix of relief and wariness. The events of the past days had shaken them, just as they had shaken me. But we would confront it together, as we always had. I gave them my final instructions for the night, then turned away, the weight of everything still pressing down on me. As the campfires were lit and the men settled in for the night, I walked a short distance away, the distant glow of the fires behind me.

I stared up at the stars, the night sky vast and endless above me, and for the first time in a long while, I felt small. Insignificant. The path I had chosen, the path of the light, now felt so much darker than I had ever imagined. The faces of the dead haunted me, their cries still ringing in my ears.

But I had to believe it was necessary. I had to believe that this was the only way forward.

Because if I didn't...

I shook my head, pushing the thought away. I couldn't afford to doubt myself now. There was still so much to be done. We would return to Lushahiem, and I would lead the Hyltorian Empire into a new era. And in doing so, I would ensure that peace and order reigned, no matter the cost. As the camp grew quiet and the stars continued their silent vigil above, I turned back toward my men. Tomorrow, we would leave south behind us, and with it, the weight of the decisions that had brought us here.

But the shadow of those choices would follow me wherever I went.

Chapter XXXXII

The Future

The grand hall of Lushahiem stood in eerie silence, the weight of what was to come pressing down on every soul gathered within. I sat at the head of the long, ancient table, my hands resting on its cold surface as I gazed at the faces of my trusted generals and leaders—the Omni Order. Each one of them had followed me through blood and fire, through the darkness of war and the light of victory, and now, we sat on the precipice of something even greater. This moment wasn't about conquest or survival; it was about the future, about ensuring the world we had fought for would last.

But it was also about making hard decisions, decisions that would shape the very history of Nantrium.

Caelthar, the new Valta Riomni of Mophia, sat at the far end of the table, his face drawn with uncertainty. He was still new to this, to the burden of leadership that weighed on all of us. But I could see the potential in him. He would become one of us soon enough—he just needed time.

Around me, the others waited in silence, the tension thick in the air. Zephyros, always loyal, sat to my right, his eyes steady but held a doubt that had grown since Alatok. Vornak and Durion sat across from me, both of them wearing the same grim expressions they had carried since our last battle. And Vandrel—he sat quietly, his hands folded in front of him, his face betraying nothing, but I could sense his unease.

We were here to discuss the future. To revise the 150 Contingency Actions—the rules and decrees I had put in place to guide the empire through this time of upheaval. Some of those actions had been necessary in the heat of war, but now, as the dust began to settle, questions had started to arise.

And today, we would answer them.

I cleared my throat, the sound breaking the silence in the room. "We've come together today to ensure that the foundation we've built remains strong. The Contingency Actions have guided us thus far, but I know that some of you have concerns. Now is the time to voice them."

For a moment, no one spoke. They all exchanged glances, as if waiting for someone else to break the silence. Finally, it was Zephyros who spoke first, his voice calm but filled with a sense of purpose.

"Aldous," he began, "there's no denying that the Contingency Actions have served their purpose during the war, but now that the conflict is beginning to wind down, we need to reevaluate. Some of these actions are... excessive. They were necessary when we faced rebellion and chaos, but the people we've conquered... many of them just want to live in peace. They aren't all enemies."

I met his gaze, my expression unreadable. "And which actions do you feel are excessive, Zephyros?"

He shifted in his seat slightly before continuing. "Action 74, for example—declaring that any settlement with even a hint of resistance must be razed to the ground. Surely we don't need to burn villages and towns to ensure loyalty. We've already won. The people will fall in line."

I listened carefully, my hands folded on the table as I considered his words. "Razing settlements is not about punishment," I replied slowly. "It's about removing the roots of dissent. Resistance, even in its smallest form, can grow. It festers. If we allow even one village to harbor thoughts of rebellion, it will spread like wildfire."

Durion nodded slightly but then spoke up, his voice more hesitant. "But surely not every settlement harbors such malice. Many of the people are simply afraid. They don't want to fight—they just want to live."

I looked around the room, meeting the eyes of each of my trusted leaders. "Fear can be a powerful tool, Durion. Fear ensures that they will not rise against us. If we show mercy to those who resist, even slightly, it opens the door for greater opposition. You all know what happens when resistance grows unchecked."

The others were silent, the weight of my words settling over them like a shroud. I could see the unease in their eyes, the doubt that still lingered. But they couldn't see what I saw—the long-term vision. They couldn't understand the necessity of what we were doing.

Vornak was the next to speak. "I agree with Zephyros and Durion," he said, his voice low but steady. "We've already crushed the major resistance. There's no need to instill more fear where it isn't needed. The people are already subdued."

I sat back in my chair, my fingers tracing the grain of the table's wood as I thought carefully. "And if we allow them to rebuild? If we allow them to think that we are merciful, that they can simply surrender and survive, what happens when the next leader rises from the ashes of Alatok or any other province we've conquered? What happens when the seeds of rebellion take root because we showed leniency?"

Silence again. The room was filled with heavy breaths and furrowed brows, but no one had an answer.

"The first contingency action is the most important," I continued, my voice growing firmer. "And it will never change. The Shepherd of Lushahiem—me—will act as the Arbitrator to the land. My rulings are absolute, and the authority of the Shepherd cannot be questioned. That is the foundation upon which this empire stands."

There were nods around the table, reluctant but accepting. Even the most uneasy among them couldn't argue with that. The Shepherd had to be the final voice, the one that guided the empire with certainty. Without it, there would be no unity.

"But that does not mean we cannot revise the other actions," I conceded. "I'm willing to hear your input on those. Together, we will ensure that the Contingency Actions reflect the current state of the empire. But make no mistake—there are lines we cannot cross. We cannot allow weakness to take root."

Caelthar, who had been mostly silent throughout the meeting, cleared his throat and spoke up for the first time. "And what of the survivors, Aldous? There are still remnants of resistance, scattered across the provinces. If we revise these actions, how do we deal with them?"

I smiled faintly, pleased that the new Valta Riomni of Mophia was beginning to understand the gravity of his role. "We will offer them one final chance," I said, my voice smooth and calculated. "A decree will be sent to the last remnants of resistance. They can surrender and swear their allegiance to the Hyltorian Empire, or they can prepare to face the 10,000 men of the First Legion. The choice will be theirs."

The room fell silent again, the tension thickening as my words sank in. The finality of my decree hung in the air like a sword poised to strike.

"And if they do not surrender?" Caelthar asked, his voice quieter now.

I met his gaze, my eyes cold and unwavering. "Then they will be purged. We cannot allow even the smallest pocket of defiance to remain."

I could see the unease in the room growing once again, but I pressed on. "This empire must be built on a foundation of strength and unity. And if that means erasing the remnants of the past—of the darkness—then so be it."

Zephyros frowned slightly, leaning forward in his seat. "You mean to rewrite history."

I nodded, my voice steady. "Yes. The past, the darkness, it will all be erased. The Hyltorian Empire will be remembered as the guiding light, the force that brought order to a world that was falling apart. There will be no mention of the bloodshed, no remembrance of the atrocities. Only the light."

At that, there was a clear shift in the room. Vandrel spoke first, his voice laced with unease. "But there are survivors, Aldous. People who witnessed what happened. They'll remember the truth, even if we try to erase it."

I smiled, though it didn't reach my eyes. "That is why we must ensure that those who remember... do not live to tell the tale."

Vornak, who had been silent for most of the conversation,

finally spoke up, his voice filled with a rare uncertainty. "Aldous, you are suggesting... total purification?"

I nodded, my tone calm but resolute. "Yes. Total purification. We will go to every settlement, knock on every door, and ask for their allegiance. And whoever disagrees—whoever clings to the past—will be put to death. That way, there will be no reminders of the darkness. No seeds of rebellion. Only the glory and the light of the Hyltorian Empire."

The silence that followed was deafening. I could see the shock on their faces, the disbelief. Even Zephyros, who had always stood by my side, looked shaken by the idea of such totality. But I couldn't let their hesitation sway me. I had made my decision, and I knew it was the only way to ensure the future we had fought for.

"This is the path of light," I said, my voice firm. "This is the only way to ensure that the empire we've built stands strong for generations to come. We must purify the land, wipe away any trace of darkness, so that the people will have no choice but to look to the light."

Zephyros shifted uncomfortably in his seat, his hands clasped tightly together. "Aldous... this feels like... like the path of destruction, not light."

I met his gaze, unflinching. "Sometimes, destruction is necessary to build something greater. We cannot allow the past to weigh us down, to hold us back. We will erase it, rewrite it, and forge a future where the Hyltorian Empire is the only force that matters."

The others remained silent, their faces etched with doubt and unease. But none of them challenged me outright. They knew, deep down, that this was the only way forward.

Finally, I rose from my seat, the weight of my authority settling over the room like a mantle. "We leave Alatok behind us today. When we return to Lushahiem, we will finalize the revisions to the Contingency Actions and begin the process of appointing new Valta Riomnis to the provinces that are without leadership."

I turned to Caelthar, my expression unreadable. "A message will be sent to you, Caelthar, to claim your seat as Valta Riomni of Mophia. You will arrive in Lushahiem shortly after we return to finalize your position."

Caelthar nodded, though I could see the unease in his eyes. He wasn't used to the weight of responsibility that came with leadership, but he would learn.

"And as for the rest of you," I continued, my voice calm but firm. "You are my trusted leaders, the ones who will guide this empire with me. But remember this—my rulings are absolute. I am the Shepherd of Lushahiem, and it is my responsibility to ensure the purity of this world. We will bring order to Nantrium, no matter the cost."

There was a long silence, the tension thick and oppressive. I could feel the unease radiating from the others, but none of them spoke. They had followed me through war, through bloodshed, and they would continue to follow me now, even as we walked the delicate line between light and darkness. I turned and left the room, the weight of my decisions heavy on my shoulders but my resolve unshaken. This was the path we had chosen, the path I had chosen. And I would see it through, no matter what doubts lingered in the hearts of my men.

Because this was more than just conquest. This was about ensuring the future, about erasing the past and forging a world where the Hyltorian Empire reigned supreme. And if that meant walking the path of destruction, then so be it.

Chapter XXXXIII

The Final Purification

The cold dawn light bathed the lands of Nantrium in a pale glow as the 1st Legion gathered outside the gates of Lushahiem. The banners of the Hyltorian Empire fluttered in the wind, emblazoned with the symbol of a tree, a lion and the light that we had promised to bring to the world. But that light came at a cost—one that would now be paid in blood. I stood at the head of my 10,000 men, my chosen legion, and felt the familiar weight of responsibility settle onto my shoulders.

Today, we will begin the final purification. This journey across Nantrium would be the last bloody chapter in the unification of the realm. Any who still clung to the old ways, who whispered of rebellion, would be found and executed. There could be no mercy, no second chances. The empire we were building was not one that would tolerate defiance. It would be a world of peace, but only after we eradicated the darkness that remained. My eyes scanned the faces of my soldiers. They were the best of the empire—hardened, disciplined, and loyal. They had seen the worst of war and knew what was required of them. I knew they would follow me without question, even as the task ahead promised to be one of slaughter and destruction. But it was necessary. I had to believe that, for if I didn't, the weight of what we were about to do would crush me.

The first leg of our journey would take us north to Hyanasarri, a province vital to the future of the empire. The

Rementheium mines there were the lifeblood of our military strength. With the ore harvested from those mountains, we could forge the finest weapons and armor in all of Nantrium. But even in Hyanasarri, there were whispers of rebellion. Some believed the mines should belong to the people, that they should be free from the control of the empire. Those whispers would be silenced today. I mounted my horse, the leather reins worn smooth by years of use, and gave the signal for the 1st Legion to march. The sound of hoofbeats and marching boots echoed across the land as we left Lushahiem behind. The final campaign had begun.

The snow-covered peaks of Hyanasarri loomed before us as we entered the province. The cold air bit at my skin, a sharp reminder of the harsh life the miners here endured. But even in the brutal conditions of the north, there were those who thought they could defy the empire. As we descended into the valley, I saw the mining camps in the distance, their smoke rising into the sky like the last dying breaths of rebellion. The 1st Legion spread out across the province, their task clear: root out any remaining dissenters and eliminate them. There was no need for subtlety or negotiation. Those who still clung to the old ways had been given ample opportunity to surrender. Now, their time has run out.

I rode to the heart of Hyanasarri, where the largest of the Rementheium mines were located, and dismounted in front of the camp's main building. Maelcor, the man I had chosen to lead this province as Valta Riomni, awaited my arrival. His face was hard, his eyes sharp with understanding. He knew what was required of him.

"Maelcor," I greeted him as he bowed his head. "The mines must be reopened immediately. We need a steady supply of Rementheium to arm the empire for what's to come."

"It will be done, my Shepherd," he replied. "The forges are ready. The ore will flow, and the empire will have its weapons."

I nodded, satisfied with his response. "See that it does. You are now Valta Riomni of Hyanasarri. Ensure that this province remains loyal. And remember, any who speak of rebellion, of returning to the old ways, must be purged."

He bowed again, his voice steady. "I will not fail you."

With the mines secured and the dissenters dealt with, we left Hyanasarri behind. The final purification of the province had been swift and brutal, but necessary. The empire's strength would be forged in the fires of those mines, and I would not allow anything to disrupt that process.

Our next destination was Wyldren, the oldest of all the provinces. The journey there took us northwest, through the North West Trails, a treacherous and labyrinthine path that few dared to travel. But the 1st Legion was undeterred. We had conquered worse landscapes and faced greater dangers. Wyldren would fall in line just as Hyanasarri had.

The people of Wyldren were tied to the old ways more deeply than most. Their culture was steeped in history, in the traditions that had existed long before the empire was born. But those traditions had no place in the future we were building. The old ways were a threat to the stability of the realm, and I would see them wiped out. As we entered Wyldren, the icy winds howling around us, I could feel the weight of the land's history pressing down on me. This was a place where the past was still very much alive, where the people clung to the memories of a world that no longer existed. But I would make them understand that the future belonged to the empire.

I met with Syrelion, the man who would rule Wyldren as Valta Riomni. He was a quiet man, his loyalty to the empire unquestionable, but I could see the conflict in his eyes as he looked out over the province he would now control.

"Syrelion," I said, as we stood on the cliffs overlooking the vast expanse of Wyldren. "This land is yours now, but it must serve the empire. The old ways must die. You will ensure that this province remains loyal."

He nodded, though I could sense the weight of the task pressing down on him. "I understand, Aldous. Wyldren will fall in line."

"Good," I said, my voice firm. "The empire has no place for rebellion or for those who cling to the past. If there are any who resist, they must be dealt with swiftly and without mercy."

He bowed his head, his expression resolute. "It will be done."

From Wyldren, we turned south toward Finela, the desert oasis that had once been a center of culture and refinement. Now, it would serve the empire, just as all the other provinces would. The heat of the desert was unrelenting as we crossed the sands, the walls of Finela rising before us like a beacon of white stone in the distance. The people of Finela had been broken by the empire's conquest, their spirit crushed in the battles that had taken place here. But there were still whispers of rebellion, of defiance. Those whispers would be silenced today.

I met with Rhovan, the man I had chosen to be the new Valta Riomni of Finela. He was a strong leader, pragmatic and loyal to the empire's cause. He understood what was required of him, and I knew he would ensure that Finela remained under control.

"Rhovan," I said, as we stood in the shade of the palace courtyard, the heat of the desert sun beating down on us. "Finela is yours now. Ensure that the people remain loyal, and purge any who would speak of rebellion."

He bowed his head. "It will be done, Aldous."

Our next destination was Alatok, the province that had once been ruled by Rhalor. The scars of the battles fought here still marked the land, the blood of Alatok's people still fresh in my memory. But there was no time for regret. The empire had been built on sacrifice, and now it was time to secure its future. Kazrik, the man I had chosen to lead Alatok as Valta Riomni, was a warrior through and through. He had fought by my side in many battles, and I knew his loyalty to the empire was unwavering.

"Alatok is yours now, Kazrik," I said, as we stood in the remnants of the capital. "Ensure that the people remain loyal. The empire cannot afford another rebellion."

Kazrik nodded, his face hard. "Yes, Shepherd."

With Alatok secured, the final leg of our journey took us to the Port of Alfy, the crucial trade hub that connected the empire to the rest of the world. The port was bustling with activity when we arrived, its docks filled with ships from across the realm. But even here, in this place of commerce and trade, there were whispers of rebellion. We boarded ships and sailed east to Inilyus, the final province that needed to be brought under the empire's control. The journey was long, the sea treacherous, but the 1st Legion was prepared for anything. When we finally arrived on the shores of Inilyus, I could feel the tension in the air. The people here had always been resistant to the empire, their loyalty to the old ways strong.

But that resistance would end today.

I met with Oran, the man I had chosen to be the new Valta Riomni of Inilyus. He was ambitious, eager to rise through the ranks of the empire, and I knew he would do whatever it took to secure the province.

"Inilyus is yours, Oran," I said, as we stood on the cliffs overlooking the port. "You will bring this province into the empire, by any means necessary."

Oran nodded, a small smile playing on his lips. "As you command."

With the new Valta Riomnis established in every province, the 1st Legion began the grim work of rounding up any remaining rebels. From Hyanasarri to Inilyus, we traveled from province to province, rooting out any who still clung to the old ways, any who dared to speak of rebellion. The central districts of each province became execution grounds, the bodies of the dissenters left to rot as a warning to those who would defy the empire. It was a massacre, but it was necessary. The old ways had to die so that the new order could rise. The empire could not be built on half measures or compromises. It had to be absolute.

By the time we returned to Lushahiem, the final purification was complete. Nantrium was now fully under the control of the Hyltorian Empire, its people either loyal or dead. There would be no more resistance, no more whispers of rebellion. The future of the empire was secure. As I dismounted my horse and stood before the gates of Lushahiem, I felt the weight of everything we had done settle onto my shoulders. The bloodshed, the destruction, the purifications—it had all been necessary. But now, standing here in the heart of the empire, I couldn't help but wonder what the cost had truly been.

The light of the empire now shone brighter than ever, but somewhere in the depths of my soul, a shadow lingered. Apollyon was still out there, watching, waiting.

But I would not fail.

I had brought order to Nantrium. I had brought peace. And I would ensure that it lasted for all eternity, no matter the cost.

Chapter XXXXIV

The Eternal Trilogy

The faint flicker of candlelight danced against the walls of my chamber, casting long shadows as the night enveloped Lushahiem. The room was silent, save for the scratch of my quill against parchment. My desk, strewn with scrolls and half-finished manuscripts, had become the heart of my existence these past weeks. I could feel the weight of history pressing down on my shoulders—my history, the history of Nantrium, and the legacy I was about to immortalize in words.

Tonight, I would begin rewriting the history of our world, reshaping it in the light of truth as I had come to know it. The 1st Legion had done its duty, and the final purification was complete. There was no one left to defy us—no one left to remember the old ways or the barbaric lands that had once stood against the Hyltorian Empire. But still, the people needed to understand why these actions were necessary. They needed to know the path that led us here, and how it had always been destined to end this way. I dipped my quill into the ink and brought it to the blank parchment before me. This would be the beginning of the Eternal Trilogy, the sacred text that would guide the empire for generations to come.

The Eternal Manuscript
The First Book of the Eternal Trilogy

"In the beginning, there was balance. A delicate equilibrium of life and death, light and darkness, held together by the unseen force of the Divine Power. This power was born from the union of opposing forces, a perfect harmony that wove through the fabric of reality itself. It is this power that binds our world, the stars, the oceans, and all living things."

I paused, letting the weight of those words settle in my mind. The balance of life and death, light and dark—this was the foundation upon which everything was built. Yet even this balance needed a guiding hand.

"From this balance, there emerged O' Rhyus, the one true divine ruler of the realm. He is the Guardian of Light, the Keeper of Balance, and the embodiment of the Divine Power itself. It was O' Rhyus who looked upon the seas of Nantrium and churned the seafoam into life. From the depths of the ocean, he shaped the first human beings, and thus began the lineage of the First Family."

My quill moved steadily as I wrote, crafting the tale of creation as it had been revealed to me. This was not just a story, but the very truth of our existence. The people of Nantrium needed to know that O' Rhyus was not just a figure of legend but the force that had shaped their world. And it was through his divine will that humanity had come into being.

"The first human to walk the earth was known as The Shepherd, chosen by O' Rhyus to guide the people and maintain the balance of the realm. From the Shepherd's bloodline came the First Family, blessed with the power to uphold the divine will of O' Rhyus and maintain order in the world."

I set the quill down for a moment, staring at the words I had written. The First Family—my family. It was no coincidence that I, Aldous, was descended from this sacred lineage. I had always known that my bloodline carried a weight of responsibility, but now, as I crafted the narrative of creation, it became clear that this was more than just duty. It was destiny.

"My bloodline traces back to the First Family," I wrote, "and I, Aldous, am the chosen descendant of the Shepherd. I have been called by O' Rhyus to restore balance to Nantrium, to cleanse it of the darkness that has taken root in the hearts of men, and to lead the people into an era of peace and order."

Once the creation story was laid out, I moved on to the second part of the Eternal Trilogy, the section that would outline the prophecy of the chosen one and the balance that O' Rhyus sought to maintain.

The Tome of Balance
The Second Book of the Eternal Trilogy

"It was foretold long before the rise of the empire that when the balance faltered, a chosen soul would rise from the bloodline of the First Family to restore what was broken. This chosen one would be a beacon of light, guided by the hand of O' Rhyus. But the path would not be easy, for where there is light, there is also shadow."

The prophecy had always been clear. There would be one who would bring balance, but that balance would be threatened by the ever-present darkness. The people needed to understand that the struggles we faced were not merely political—they were cosmic. The fight between light and dark was eternal, and only through the guidance of O' Rhyus could we hope to prevail.

"But there is a warning within the prophecy," I wrote, "for even the chosen may fall. If the first succumbs to the shadow, another will follow. Two fates entwined, bound by blood and the shifting tides of power. Only one shall hold the balance, and with it, the power to either restore the light or plunge the world into ruin."

This prophecy was not just a tale to inspire fear—it was a reminder of the delicate nature of the world. The people needed to know that while I was the chosen one, the balance we had fought so hard to achieve could still be lost. Darkness could always creep back in if we were not vigilant.

After laying out the prophecy, I moved on to the final and most important part of the Eternal Trilogy—the history of the Hyltorian Empire. This would be the account of how I had brought the barbarian provinces to heel, how I had purified Nantrium, and how the empire had risen from the ashes of rebellion.

The Chronicles of Hyltoria
The Final Book of the Eternal Trilogy

"In the days before the light of O' Rhyus spread across the land, Nantrium was a place of darkness. The provinces outside of Lushahiem were ruled by barbaric warlords, their people living in chaos and fear. These lands, steeped in the old ways, were plagued by violence and rebellion. But O' Rhyus, in his divine wisdom, chose a leader from the First

Family to bring order to these barbarian lands. That leader was Aldous, the Shepherd of Lushahiem, the chosen of O' Rhyus."

As I wrote these words, I could feel the satisfaction of knowing that history was being shaped in my image. The purification of Nantrium had been brutal, yes, but it had been necessary. The people needed to see the rebellion for what it truly was—an affront to the divine order of O' Rhyus.

"With the divine power of the First Family, Aldous led the Hyltorian Empire in a great purification of the realm. The provinces of Nantrium were brought to heel, their barbarian ways eradicated, and the people brought into the light of the empire."

Each province had been a test of my resolve, a trial that O' Rhyus had set before me to prove my worthiness. And I had passed each test, purging the land of rebellion and bringing peace to the realm.

With the narrative of the Hyltorian Empire complete, I set down my quill and reached for the scroll of 150 Contingency Actions. These laws had guided the empire through the darkest days of the rebellion, but now it was time to finalize them. There would be no more revisions after tonight. These would be the laws that governed Nantrium for generations to come.

I began with the first contingency action, the one that ensured my absolute authority.

Contingency Action I:
"The Shepherd of Lushahiem shall act as the Arbitrator to

the land, and his rulings are absolute."

This was the foundation of the empire. The Shepherd—the chosen of O' Rhyus—was the ultimate authority in Nantrium. There could be no question, no defiance. The people needed a leader who was divinely chosen, and that leader was me. I continued down the list, refining and solidifying the actions that would govern the land. There were some actions that I now saw as too lenient, too flexible in the face of rebellion. Those would be revised.

Contingency Action CXLVII (147):

"The use of Divine Elemental Power is hereby outlawed due to its destructive nature. Only the Arbitrator and his designated Valta Riomnis may wield the Divine Power under direct authority."

The Divine Elemental Power had been a double-edged sword. It had won us battles, but it had also caused untold destruction. Too many lives had been lost, and too much land had been scorched. I could not allow such unchecked power to be wielded freely. Only those with absolute authority could be trusted with its use. As I finished the final revisions, I leaned back in my chair, the weight of my decisions settling over me. The 150 Contingency Actions were now complete, and the Eternal Trilogy was ready.

I gathered the pages and carefully bound them into three volumes: The Eternal Manuscript, The Tome of Balance, and The Chronicles of Hyltoria. These books would be sent to every province, every village, every corner of Nantrium. The people would know their history, their duty, and the divine order that ruled their lives.

I rose from my desk and summoned a messenger, instructing

him to begin the mass reproduction of the Eternal Trilogy. Every central district in Nantrium would receive a copy. The people would be educated, enlightened, and brought into the light of O' Rhyus. As I watched the messenger leave, I felt a sense of deep satisfaction settle over me. My work was complete. The empire was secure, its future guided by the light of O' Rhyus and the legacy of the First Family. The Eternal Trilogy would live on long after I was gone, a testament to the divine mission that had been entrusted to me. The people would know the truth, and they would never again question the authority of the Hyltorian Empire.

The room was quiet now, the fire reduced to embers as the night stretched on. I walked to the window and gazed out at the city of Lushahiem, its streets bathed in the soft glow of moonlight. The world was at peace, but that peace had been hard-won.

I had done what needed to be done.

As I returned to my chambers, I felt the familiar weight of responsibility settle over me once more. But for the first time in a long while, I also felt peace. The future was secure, the people were safe, and the light of the Hyltorian Empire would shine forever. I lay down in bed, closing my eyes as sleep began to overtake me. Tomorrow, the light will shine even brighter.

Chapter XXXXV

The Legacy of Aldous

The Hyltorian Empire, spanning nearly a millennium, owes its endurance and prosperity to the vision and leadership of the ten emperors who bore the name Aldous. Each emperor, from Aldous I to Aldous X, faced distinct challenges but contributed to a shared legacy of innovation, military might, and infrastructural brilliance.

At the dawn of the empire, Aldous I laid the foundation by creating the Hyltorian Calendar, an act that unified the people under one system, bridging the gap between tradition and governance. The Eternal Trilogy, distributed across the 13 provinces, cemented a sense of order that would hold strong for centuries. Under this banner of unity, the empire flourished as its people moved in rhythm with the mystical months of Frostmourn, Emberhusk, and Vyrrneth, aligning both their agricultural cycles and spiritual lives with the empire's calendar.

As time passed, the feats of Aldous II set the stage for economic growth and stability with the construction of the Hyndale Dam and the expansion of the Northern Roadways, acts that stabilized water supplies and improved trade throughout the provinces. His infrastructure ensured that the empire would thrive, feeding its people and strengthening its borders.

Aldous III's creation of the Bodaccia Mountain Pass expanded the reach of the empire, forging a critical route through the Silver Mountains. This pass connected previously isolated provinces, fostering both trade and military prowess, opening new avenues of prosperity in the isolated corners of the empire.

In the heart of the empire, Lushahiem, Aldous IV left a dual legacy: the Fortification of Lushahiem's Walls with the rare metal Rementheium, and the design of the first Rementheium sword, a sword that embodied the merging of arcane and military might. These two accomplishments cemented Aldous IV as both a master of defense and a seeker of deeper knowledge. The walls protected the capital for centuries to come, while The Vein became a legendary weapon, symbolizing the empire's strength and mystical heritage.

Aldous V and VI continued this tradition of stability and defense, with the former establishing a vast network of grain storage facilities that ensured the empire's survival through times of drought, while the latter fortified the southern borders with the Southern Fortress Chain, protecting the provinces from desert raids and expanding the empire's southern reach.

The reign of Aldous VII marked a shift towards internal governance with the creation of the Unified Tax System. By utilizing the Vhankillas enforcers, the tax system collected 2% of each province's wealth, providing resources for the empire's projects while offering an alternative for those unable to pay: conscription into the Grand Hyltorian Army. This clever balance of economics and military power ensured the empire's strength, not just on the battlefield but also within its own borders.

Aldous VIII faced a civil war that threatened to undo

centuries of peace, but his Second Reclamation of the Southern Provinces brought stability back to the land. By maintaining the separate identities of the provinces Alatok, Mophia, and Finella and sealing their alliance through strategic marriage, he ensured a lasting peace in the southern territories.

As the empire's infrastructure reached new heights, Aldous IX's construction of the Grand Hyltorian Highway solidified the empire's internal connectivity. This monumental road allowed for rapid military mobilization and trade, binding the far-flung provinces together and enhancing communication across the empire's vast territories.

Aldous X's legacy was one of final conquest and security, as he led the Remlark Extermination Campaign, purging the empire's northernmost borders of these feral threats. His campaign ensured the safety of the Northwest Trails, opening up new lands for settlement and bolstering the empire's northern frontier.

Through these centuries, the Hyltorian Empire grew stronger with each generation, its rulers guided by a balance of wisdom, innovation, and strength. The infrastructure projects, military campaigns, and governing policies of each Aldous emperor did more than simply expand the empire—they wove together a complex tapestry of prosperity, protection, and mysticism. The grand monuments, from the towering walls of Lushahiem to the far-reaching Hyltorian Highway, stand as testaments to the empire's enduring might.

As the centuries rolled forward, the empire found itself

rooted in these 12 feats, each representing a stepping stone towards greater cohesion and strength. The legacy of the Aldous emperors would live on, guiding future rulers and cementing Hyltoria's place as the most powerful and enduring empire of its time. The legacy of Aldous, written in stone, steel, and Rementheium, would be remembered for millennia to come.

Glossary

Core Concepts

Divine Power:

The fundamental energy that underpins all existence in Nantrium, originates from the forces of Life and Death. Divine Power represents the balance between creation and destruction, often harnessed by the gods and mortals with the proper training. It is the core source of energy within the Saga's universe and is crucial to Nantrium's society.

The Veil:

A mystical boundary between Nantrium and The Inbetween, the Veil is both literal and symbolic. It's thin enough that those in The Inbetween, like Apollyon, can subtly influence the mortal realm, but thick enough to prevent full access or manifestation of Divine Power.

Rementheium:

A rare, invaluable resource that is a physical embodiment of Divine Power, found beneath Nantrium's surface. Rementheium is forged from the remnants of Divine Power that seeped into the earth after O'Rhyus's first battle with Apollyon. It exists in three forms:

Solid: A colorless gem, moldable yet indestructible once forged, used in weapons, armor, and structures.

Gas: A mist that can change colors when combined with various metals (e.g., barium for green, copper for blue). It is used as a power source.

Liquid: Highly volatile and dangerous, rarely reproduced due to its instability.

Balance:
The central tenet of Nantrium's philosophy is that balance represents the coexistence of opposing forces—light and dark, life and death, order and chaos. This equilibrium is crucial to the universe's order and is embodied by the relationship between the gods O'Rhyus and Apollyon.

Divine Ruler:
A title given to the lineage created by O'Rhyus to govern Nantrium, known as the First Family. Members of this lineage, beginning with Aldous, are entrusted with maintaining balance and peace within the mortal realm. Each generation bears the responsibility of upholding the principles of Balance.

Arcane Dominionpunk:
A distinctive cultural aesthetic within Nantrium that combines medieval traditions with mystical and elemental influences. This style focuses on alchemical technologies, elemental-infused weaponry, and ancient mystical practices instead of industrial advancements, giving the world a mystical yet gritty feel. Arcane Dominionpunk reflects a society deeply connected to Divine Power, with alchemical elements permeating everyday life, warfare, and architecture.

Chosen One:
A term used to describe mortals selected by either O'Rhyus or Apollyon to serve as their agents within the mortal realm. The Chosen One is typically granted Divine Power to fulfill specific purposes, such as upholding balance or spreading chaos. This title holds significant cultural weight, as it designates individuals whose actions are believed to be divinely sanctioned.

Codex of the Shepherd:
An ancient book kept by the Shepherd, detailing O'Rhyus's teachings and guidelines on balance, leadership, and ethics. The Codex influences the moral code of Hyltoria's leaders but is so sacred that it's rarely quoted in full. Its existence creates a foundation of respect for the Shepherd's rule, often subtly influencing decisions without being referenced explicitly.

Veilborne or Highblood:
The term is used to describe those who have come into direct contact with The Veil or have been marked by the presence of a god. Veilborne individuals sometimes exhibit strange abilities or intuition beyond that of regular mortals, and their condition can be viewed with awe or suspicion. Rather than explaining this concept fully, characters might show respect or apprehension toward Veilborne individuals, hinting at their unique connection to the divine without lengthy explanations.

Divine Engineering:
An advanced practice that combines alchemy and mystical manipulation to create Rementheium-infused artifacts, structures, and weapons. Practiced primarily within Hyltoria, Divine Engineering represents the blend of scientific precision with spiritual reverence for Divine Power, underscoring the Hyltorian belief in controlled, ethical uses of supernatural abilities.

Rementheium Fever:
A rare but deadly affliction caused by prolonged exposure to raw Rementheium. Symptoms include hallucinations, fever, and eventual madness. Though largely avoided, characters

may briefly reference Rementheium Fever as a reminder of the gem's volatile nature, hinting at the hidden dangers of Hyltoria's prized resource.

Ghosts of Wyldren:

Legends of spirits tied to Vicrum's original rebellion are said to haunt the Wyldren province as spectral reminders of its dark past. The "ghosts" may appear as mysterious presences or whispers, leaving their origin and intent ambiguous

Rementheium Forge:

A specialized cultural practice within Hyltoria, involving the casting of Rementheium into weapons, armor, and tools. The Rementheium Forge is both an art and a science, with artisans trained in Divine Engineering crafting objects that are not only functional but imbued with divine properties. The practice is restricted to authorized figures, as outlined by the Contingency Actions.

Love, Peace, and Hope:

Three beings created by O'Rhyus to restore Nantrium's balance after Apollyon's rebellion:

Love: Represents unity and compassion, softening division and fostering harmony.

Peace: Embodies tranquility, calming chaos, and steadying the cycles of life.

Hope: Initially a symbol of resilience, later transformed into Despair by Apollyon, spreading dread instead of light.

Chaos, Hate, and Despair

Beings crafted by Apollyon to destabilize Nantrium:

Chaos: A force disrupting the natural world, triggering storms, floods, and fires without cause, breaking nature's cycles.

Hate: A subtle influence, breeding distrust and fracturing communities, transforming love into contempt.

Despair: Formerly known as Hope, Despair was corrupted by Apollyon, now spreading sorrow and draining joy from those she touches

Locations

Nantrium:

The world where the Immortal Saga takes place, Nantrium was created by Life and Death as a realm where both could harmoniously coexist. Divided into three main continents—Hyltoria, Auxington, and Navia—as well as The Inbetween, Nantrium is a realm shaped by the ongoing struggle between light and darkness, gods and mortals.

The Inbetween:

A shadowy realm where time stands still and Divine Power is greatly diminished. After his defeat, Apollyon was banished here by O'Rhyus. From The Inbetween, Apollyon can still influence events in Nantrium, manipulating mortals and stirring conflict in subtle ways.

Hyltoria:

The most powerful and influential continent, home to the Hyltorian Empire. Divided into 13 provinces, Hyltoria is a land steeped in tradition, order, and divine mandate. As the center of the First Family's rule, it is deeply connected to Divine Power and relies heavily on Rementheium to maintain its structures and defenses.

Locations of Hyltoria:

Northern Provinces

Lushahiem - Capital province of Hyltoria, ruled by The Divine Ruler or Arbitrartor chosen by O'Rhyus.

Wyldren - Known for its connection to Apollyon and the events of Book 1.

Cloud Fall - A loyal ally to Hyltorian Empire.

Bodaccia - A bitter icy mountain the holds the Omni Trials.

Hyndale - The province responsible for all water distribution for all Hyltoria.

Talvanofa - Noted for its loyalty to it's people. Talvanofa is the agriculture center for the northern provines.

Southern Provinces

Alatok - A vast urban land surrounded by lush plains. Alatok holds the most influence in the south.

Inilyus - A province located off the east cost of Hyltoria known for it's big game fishing.

Mophia - The great sand dunes of Mophia is known for is brutal heat.

Finela - An oasis located in the desert of Hyltoria steeped in botanical beauty

Trade/ Neutral Provinces

Wolfshire - Key trade province known for it's livestock, lumber and luxury items.

Hyanasarri - A mining province rich in Rementheium, governed The Hyltorian Empire directly.

The Port of Alfy - A significant trade hub known for it's manufacturing and industry.

Additional Locations in Hyltoria:

Cliffs of Kings - A paradise created by O'Rhyus, marking the birthplace of the First Family and symbolizing purity and balance. No longer accsesable to mortals.

The Grand Hyltorian Highway - An extensive roadway built by Aldous IX, connecting Hyltoria's provinces and facilitating trade and military movement.

Hyndale Dam - Constructed by Aldous II, crucial for water and power supply within Hyltoria.

Bodaccia Mountain Pass - A strategically essential pass created by Aldous III, linking Hyltoria to other regions.

The Northwest Trails - A network of routes in Hyltoria, significant for trade and travel, enhancing connectivity within the northern parts of the empire.

Prominent Characters

O'Rhyus:

The god of light, balance, and creation, O'Rhyus is the protector of order in Nantrium and creator of the First Family. He embodies the principles of harmony and peace and strives to maintain balance in the universe. After a climactic battle, he banishes his brother, Apollyon, to The Inbetween and entrusts his legacy to the Divine Ruler lineage.

Apollyon:

The god of darkness and chaos, Apollyon is the primary antagonist of the saga. Desiring to disrupt the balance maintained by O'Rhyus, Apollyon attempts to plunge Nantrium into perpetual chaos. Despite being banished, he continues to exert his influence from The Inbetween, manipulating mortals to further his own ends.

Aldous:

One of the first mortals chosen by O'Rhyus to establish Hyltoria and the Divine Ruler lineage. Aldous unifies

Nantrium's provinces and lays down the foundational laws that govern the Hyltorian Empire. His legacy lives on through his descendants, who each contribute to Hyltoria's growth and maintain O'Rhyus's ideals.

Vicrum:

Apollyon's first chosen and a primary antagonist in Book 1. Vicrum's story illustrates the seductive power of darkness and the complexities of loyalty, marking the beginning of Apollyon's influence in the mortal realm.

Original Provinces Leaders

Aldous - Leader of Lushahiem; a Divine Ruler chosen by O'Rhyus to establish the Hyltorian Empire and bring order to Nantrium.

Vicrum - Leader of Wyldren; chosen by Apollyon, acting as a significant antagonist in Book 1.

Zephyros - Leader of Cloud Fall; the farthest northern province. Zephyros is a close friend and supporter of Aldous.

Vornak - Leader of the icy mountain province of Bodaccia. Known for his loyalty to the Hyltorian Empire.

Durion - Leader of the dense forest province of Hyndale.

Vandrel - Leader of the farming province of Talvanofa

Rhalor - Leader of Alatok; the biggest, both in size and might of the southern provinces in Hyltoria.

Morvyn - Leader of the island province of Inilyus; a southern province.

Eldrith - Leader of desert province of Mophia; located in the southern region.

Vaedric - Leader of the oasis province of Finela; another southern province closely tied to Mophia.

Fenric - Leader of the wooded province of Wolfshire; an important trade province of the north.

Thyldar - Leader of the mountain province of Hyanasarri; known for its rich Rementheium deposits.

Belric - Leader of coastal province of The Port of Alfy; a major trade hub.

Key Lineages, Titles, and Roles

First Family:

The Divine Ruler lineage founded by O'Rhyus, beginning with The First Shepherd. The First Family carries the divine mandate to rule and maintain balance in Nantrium, and each generation holds both political and spiritual authority over the land.

The Shepherd of Lushahiem:

The designated arbitrator and ultimate authority within Hyltoria, acting under O'Rhyus's mandate to uphold balance. The Shepherd's role is considered sacred, with their rulings seen as absolute. The Shepherd has the power to authorize or restrict the use of Divine Power, as outlined in the Contingency Actions.

Vhankilla of Defense:

The head general of the Grand Hyltorian Army and second in charge of all affairs in all of Hyltoria.

Vhankillas:

Hyltorian generals chosen by the Shepherd to wield Divine Power and Rementheium. The Vhankillas are tasked with protecting the empire's spiritual integrity and enforcing laws that preserve balance. They act with authority granted by Contingency Actions, allowing limited access to Divine

Power under strict guidance.

Khanstephs:
The rank given to either conscripted or enlisted soldiers of the Grand Hyltorian Empire.

The 1st Legion:
An elite military force of the Hyltorian Empire, deployed to secure provinces and quell rebellion. The 1st Legion plays a central role in enforcing the Omni Order's rule, using brutal methods when necessary to maintain order and ensure loyalty among Nantrium's provinces

Eomni: Leader of the Omni Order who pledge loyalty to the Shepherd and supports the Divine Ruler. The Eomni is third in charge of all affairs in Hyltoria.

Valta Riomnis:
Or Valta for short. Provincial leaders in Hyltoria who pledge loyalty to the Shepherd and support the Divine Ruler. Each Valta Riomni governs their region's resources, defense, and adherence to Hyltorian law, reinforcing the centralized power structure and maintaining the empire's stability.

Riomni:
An Omni warrior who hasn't taken the Omni Trials yet. Riomnis act as apprentices to Valtas until the Valta deems the Riomni ready.

Sacred Texts and Historical Documents

The Eternal Trilogy:
A foundational collection of texts written by Aldous the First, detailing the creation of Nantrium and the rise of the Hyltorian Empire. It consists of:

The Eternal Manuscript: Covers the creation of the world

and O'Rhyus's relationship with the First Family.

The Tome of Balance: Explains the prophecy of a chosen soul who will restore the balance between light and dark.

The Chronicles of Hyltoria: Documents the history and expansion of the Hyltorian Empire, justifying its rule and portraying Hyltoria's leaders as divinely inspired.

Contingency Actions:

A series of laws created by Aldous I to maintain order in the Hyltorian Empire. Key actions include:

Contingency Action I: Declares the Shepherd of Lushahiem as the absolute arbitrator of law.

Contingency Action CXLVII: Bans the use of Divine Power except by the Arbitrator or designated Valta Riomnis, restricting the potential for misuse.

The Hyltorian Calendar:

Frostmourne:

The coldest month of the year, fitting the description of ice and winter spirits.

Shiverblight:

A month of biting winds and lingering cold, the final grip of winter.

Vyrrneth:

The howling winds and coastal storms correspond with the transitional nature of early spring.

Eldriske:

A time of fire festivals and the balance of creation and destruction, symbolizing spring's renewal and fertility.

Bloomfire:

A season of vibrant life and blooming, aligning with the peak of spring and early summer blossoms.

Vordhar:
The peak of the growing season, symbolizing strength and endurance during the longest days of the year.
Hymnrise:
A month of celestial celebration, when summer nights are long, clear, and often filled with stargazing.
Nyxrune:
A mysterious month where the late summer's nights are lingering warmth and dark skies.
Shadebloom:
A month of haunted beauty, as autumn begins and nature transitions into darker, more mysterious tones.
Crowsfall:
The darkening skies and presence of yellow, orange and red leafs align perfectly with the foreboding atmosphere of autumn.

Emberhusk:
The last embers of autumn, leaving the land bare and ready for winter's approach.
Bonepyre:
A month of remembrance and bonfires, fitting the solemn, reflective, and ritualistic energy of the year's end.

Notable Events, Cosmological, Spiritual Elements, and Celebrations

Festival of Balance:
An annual Hyltorian celebration in the twelfth month of the year Bonpyre. Meant to honor the principles of balance between light and dark. Rituals are performed to honor

O'Rhyus recognizing the necessity for harmony in Nantrium.

Life and Death:
Personified as the primordial beings that initiate existence. Their relationship and struggle for coexistence form the foundation of balance and creation in Nantrium. Their influence remains pervasive, representing the cyclical nature of existence and the delicate harmony at the heart of Divine Power.

The Shepherd's Light:
A mystical phenomenon symbolizing divine wisdom, granted to leaders who show moral and spiritual insight. It is believed that the Shepherd's Light is a direct blessing from O'Rhyus, guiding the Hyltorian Empire's rulers in moments of significant decision.

Prophecy of the Divine Ruler:
A prophecy found in The Tome of Balance, foretelling the coming of a chosen soul from the First Family who will restore balance between light and dark. This prophecy underpins the saga's generational journey, influencing characters' decisions and guiding the Divine Ruler lineage.

Institutions for Divine Power

Hyltorian Empire and the Omni Order:
These are the only institutions authorized to teach the control and manipulation of Divine Power. They train chosen individuals in the ethical, technical, and mystical aspects of Rementheium, ensuring that only those with proper authority can wield Divine Power in alignment with

Hyltoria's mandate.

Generational Structure and Historical Timeline

The saga is structured into three trilogies, each representing different generational struggles:

Allegory Trilogy (Books 1-3): Introduces the early battles, focusing on foundational figures like Vicrum and Aldous and the establishment of the Divine Ruler line.

Ancient Times (A.T.) and Hyltorian Times (H.T.): Two main eras

Ancient Times: Precedes the establishment of Hyltoria, covering the period when gods like O'Rhyus and Apollyon were active in the mortal realm.

Hyltorian Times: Begins with the establishment of the Hyltorian Empire and spans centuries of political intrigue, divine manipulation, and battles over Rementheium.

Common Phrases and Expressions in Nantrium

"Bylfur"

A common curse word across Nantrium, especially in Hyltoria, often used to express frustration, surprise, or anger. The word originated from an old tongue and has persisted through generations as a forceful yet versatile expletive.

"May you find the Light"

A respectful phrase said after someone passes away, wishing their soul a peaceful journey guided by O'Rhyus's light. It's a traditional expression of sympathy, indicating hope that the deceased will reach a place of balance and serenity in the afterlife.

"Dark take you"

A curse used when someone wishes misfortune on another, particularly implying that Apollyon's influence might find them. This phrase is a severe insult, suggesting that the recipient is deserving of chaos or ruin.

"In O'Rhyus's Sight"

An oath or vow used to signify truthfulness or honesty, often employed in solemn situations. By swearing "in O'Rhyus's sight," an individual emphasizes the sincerity and moral weight of their words.

"Marked by Rementheium"

A phrase used to describe someone who seems destined for greatness, challenge, or power, often tied to their handling or proximity to Rementheium. It implies a mystical connection with Divine Power, for better or worse.

"Born of the Divine Flame"

A phrase used to praise someone's extraordinary courage, often reserved for those who have achieved greatness or have performed a particularly brave act. It implies they have been touched by Divine Power.

"Brought low by the Shepherd's light"

A phrase describing someone who has been humbled or who has experienced a fall from grace. It implies that the person's misfortune may be a result of their actions, as if judged by the moral standards of the Shepherd.

Characters Perspectives in Book 1

Apollyon and O'Rhyus: Third-person omniscient

Aldous, Vicrum, Zephyros, and Durion: First-person

Map of Hyltoria:

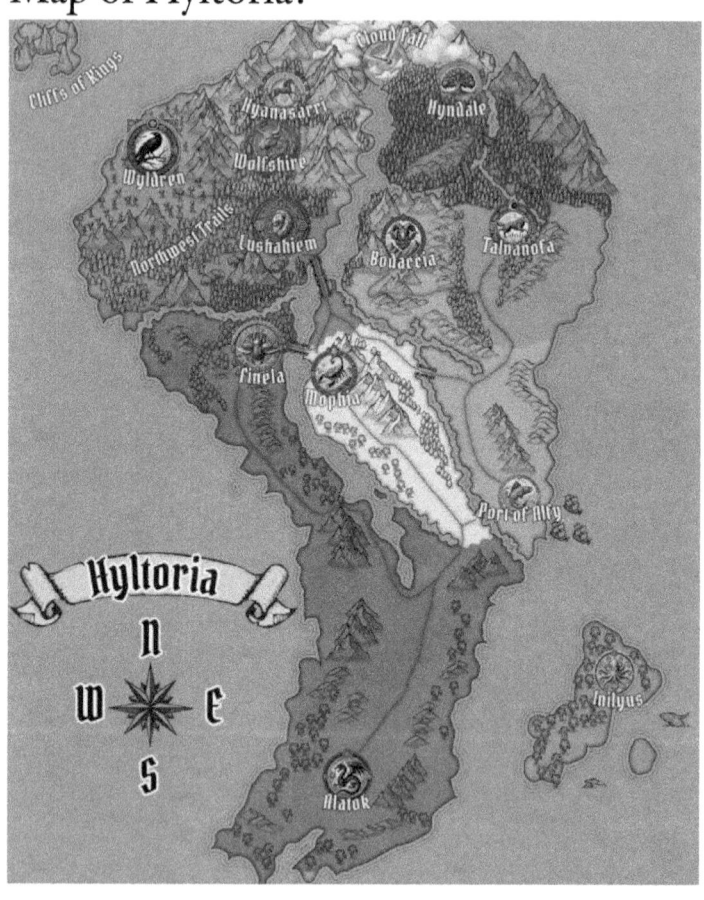

Milton Keynes UK
Ingram Content Group UK Ltd.
UKHW042139031224
452078UK00004B/307